Wilhelm Ritter v. Wymetal

Joseph Smith

The prophet, His Family and His Friends

Wilhelm Ritter v. Wymetal

Joseph Smith
The prophet, His Family and His Friends

ISBN/EAN: 9783337127572

Printed in Europe, USA, Canada, Australia, Japan

Cover: Foto ©Andreas Hilbeck / pixelio.de

More available books at **www.hansebooks.com**

"Post Tenebras Lux"

Mormon

Portraits

OR

THE TRUTH

ABOUT THE

MORMON LEADERS

FROM 1830 TO 1886

———

Story of the Danite's Wife; Mountain Meadows Massacre Re-
examined; A Thousand Fresh Facts and Documents
Gathered Personally in Utah from
Living Witnesses

BY

Dr. W. Wyl

A GERMAN AUTHOR

———

SALT LAKE CITY
Tribune Printing and Publishing Company
———
1886

Joseph Smith

THE PROPHET

His Family and His Friends

A Study Based on Facts and Documents

With Fourteen Illustrations

SALT LAKE CITY

TRIBUNE PRINTING AND PUBLISHING COMPANY

1886

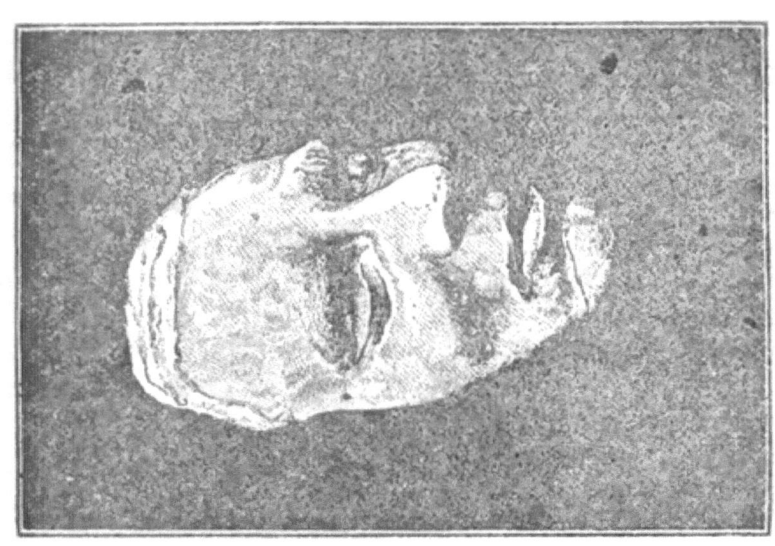

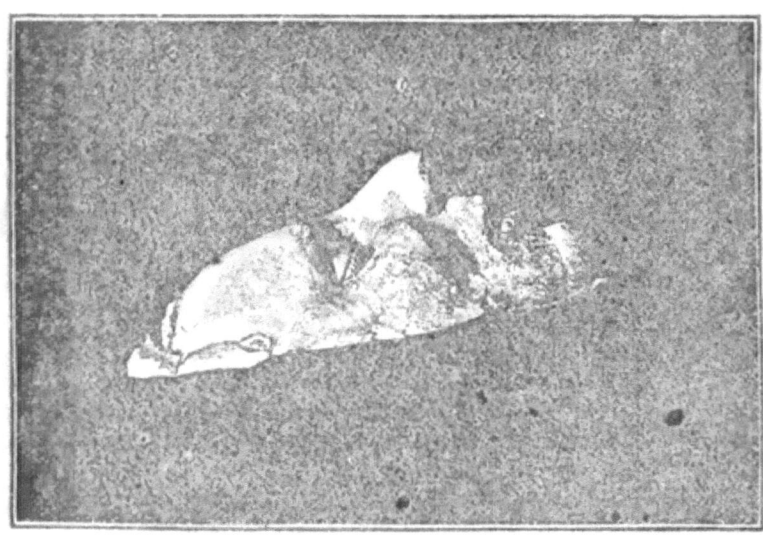

DEATH MASK OF JOSEPH SMITH.
From a Cast in the Possession of Brigham Young.

JOSEPH SMITH:

" Nobody knows what the other world will be."

" I have got the damned fools fixed and will carry out the fun."

" The world owes me a good living and if I cannot get it without, I'll steal it—and catch me at it if you can."

" We will all go to hell together and convert it into a heaven by casting the Devil out; hell is by no means the place this world of fools supposes it to be, but on the contrary, it is quite an agreeable place."

BRIGHAM YOUNG:

" There is not a bishop in this whole Territory who is not a damned thief."

" We have the meanest devils on the earth in our midst and we intend to keep them, for we have use for them."

" I have many a time dared the world to produce as mean devils as we can; we can beat them at anything. We have the greatest and smoothest liars in the world, the cunningest and most adroit thieves and any other shade of character that you can mention. We can pick out elders in Israel right here who can beat the world at gambling; who can handle the cards; who can cut and shuffle them with the smartest rogue on the face of God's foot-stool. I can produce elders here who can shave their smartest shavers and take their money from them. We can beat the world at any game. We can beat them because we have men here that live in the light of the Lord; that have the holy priest-hood and hold the keys of the Kingdom of God."

NOTICE.

Volume Second of MORMON PORTRAITS, which I have entitled *Brigham Young and His People*, will appear in a few months.

I respectfully solicit information, either in personal interviews or by post, from all trustworthy sources and shall be much obliged for the same; as well as for the pointing out of any errors of statement, however slight, that may by accident have crept into this volume. My address is

DR. W. WYL,
SALT LAKE CITY, UTAH.

JULY 17, 1886.

The family is the unit of the modern State. Woman is the heart and crown of the modern family. In Mormonism womanhood has been outraged and crucified from Emma Smith to the last polygamous victim and martyr.

Looking around me and afar, and seeing no brighter or braver spirit opposing this monstrous evil, I take the liberty to inscribe this little volume on Mormonism to one who seems to be equally at home on either side of the Atlantic,

MISS KATE FIELD.

TESTIMONIALS.

Territory of Utah, Executive Office,
Salt Lake City, May 2, 1885.

To whom this may come :

Dr. W. Wyl, a representative of the *Berliner Tage-blatt*, and who is commended to me from a high personal and official source as a " highly cultivated and thoroughly reliable gentleman," has for four months assiduously labored in the investigation of the questions involved in Mormonism. I am satisfied that he has given the subject careful study, and is therefore qualified to write advisedly of the situation, past and present.

Respectfully,

Eli H. Murray,
Governor.

We, the undersigned, hereby certify that we know that Dr. W. Wyl, a German author and correspondent, has worked very earnestly for months to collect facts from a number of witnesses living in Salt Lake City, relating to the history of Mormonism. We believe that Dr. Wyl has done his work in a thoroughly honest and truth-loving spirit, and that his Book will be a valuable addition to the material collected by other reliable writers.

W. S. Godbe,
H. W. Lawrence,
E. L. T. Harrison.

Salt Lake City, Utah Ter., April 28, 1886.

6

Dr. W. Wyl:

MY DEAR DOCTOR:—I have been doing myself the honor to keep a pretty close watch of you in this city for several months. I believe I never saw a more earnest, conscientious or persistent searcher after facts. I believe you know as much about Mormonism as any man who never spent more than twice the time you have in investigating it.

I believe you will be of good service to man and to free government by presenting the array of facts which you have accumulated either in book or lecture form. I believe the conclusions you have drawn from the facts are sound, and now, Dear Sir, "Hail and Farewell."

Most sincerely yours,

C. C. GOODWIN.

SALT LAKE, UTAH, May 7, 1885.

To Dr. W. Wyl:

DEAR SIR:—I think, from the manner in which your inquiries have been conducted, that you have obtained a more thorough knowledge of the past history and present aspect of Mormonism than any one who has ever visited our Territory with this object in view. You have gathered materials for a book which ought to be of absorbing interest, and your ability as a writer (if you will allow me to be the judge) insures the presentation of the facts in hand in such a manner that the reader who once opens your book will not be able to lay it aside until it is finished.

With the hope that your book may have the success that it is sure to deserve, I remain very sincerely yours,

CORNELIA PADDOCK.

To whom this may come:

I have been thoroughly acquainted with the Mormon Church *for over fifty years.* I attended grammar school

with Joseph Smith in Kirtland, Ohio, in the winter of
1834 and 1835, and assisted in teaching Joseph Smith, the
prophet, English grammar. I witnessed the history of the
Church in Kirtland, Ohio, in Caldwell and Davies counties, Mo., in Nauvoo, Ill., and in Salt Lake City. I was
intimately acquainted with Joseph Smith and his family
for *eleven years*; also with all the leading men of the
Church down to the present time. I have been thoroughly
acquainted with the system and all the important facts of
the history of the Mormon Church. In many interviews
during March, April and May, 1885, I have given all the
facts within my knowledge to Dr. W. Wyl, who wrote
them down in shorthand. I think Dr. Wyl has enjoyed
the best facilities for obtaining a thorough knowledge of
Mormon History, and I look forward to his intended publication with great interest.

C. G. WEBB.

SALT LAKE CITY, May 14, 1885.

To whom it may concern:

I was baptized into the Mormon Church forty-five years
ago, in the river Mersey at Liverpool, by Elder John
Taylor, now President of the Mormon Church. I have
lived for twenty-five years in Southern Utah, city of Paro-
wan, and have known personally nearly all those who were
implicated in the "Mountain Meadows Massacre." I
was cut off from the Church because I could not convince
myself that murder and stealing were agreeable to God.
I came very near being killed as an apostate by the
"Danites" or "Destroying Angels" of the Church. I
think there are few persons living in Utah who have a
more complete knowledge of the history of Mormonism
in Southern Utah, especially during the terrible time of
the so-called "Reformation," when the spirit of murder
was supreme in the Church. I have told in many interviews all the important facts stored up in my memory to
Dr. W. Wyl, and he has taken them down in shorthand.
I feel satisfied that he has collected a great number of

facts which have never been published, and that he has acquired a very good inside view of the History and spirit of the Mormon Church.

JAMES McGUFFIE,
N. 425 E. Third South Street.
SALT LAKE CITY, May 14, 1885.

To whom it may concern :

This is to certify that the writer has been associated with the Mormons for a period of over thirty years, and for the past seventeen years principally in Salt Lake City. I am personally and thoroughly acquainted with the *political* and religious institutions of the Mormons; also with their history as a people, as well as with their public character as a community residing in the Territory of Utah.

I have known the bearer, Dr. W. Wyl, author and correspondent of Berlin, Germany, for the past few months since he has resided in this city. He has been engaged in collecting data from which to write and publish a book on Mormonism. From the well-known characters and abilities of his "witnesses," I feel safe in saying that he has obtained a fund of the most trustworthy information possible, and such as no preceding writer has ever been able to disclose. Dr. Wyl, through his evident impartiality and the entire absence of personal prejudice, has made a host of substantial friends in this city, from whom he has obtained a clear and vivid insight into the inner life of this "peculiar people," as well as the most comprehensive conception of their objects, aims and purposes. From the pen of such an author the public may reasonably expect a thorough and complete elucidation of the subject to be treated, and learn—probably for the first time—that the Mormons are *politically* an aggressive people, and that Mormonism, as regards the secret aims and teachings of the leaders, is nothing less than organized TREASON.

Yours truly,

JOSEPH SALISBURY.

SALT LAKE CITY, April 27, 1885.

To whom it may concern:

My friend, Dr. W. Wyl, has spent nearly five months in Salt Lake City, in the spring of 1885, and in April and May, 1886, and has made a special and exhaustive study of the history of the Mormon Church, from its inception to date. Having carefully digested most of the publications *pro* and *contra* on this subject, and having worked day after day with living witnesses, the very best to be had in the Territory, taking down their depositions in shorthand, Dr. Wyl has succeeded in collecting a mass of material which, in my opinion, will enable him to produce a book full of new facts relating to Mormon history. Such a book is much desired by all good citizens, and will do a great deal of good, especially in the present crisis of Utah affairs. Dr. Wyl's clear and full insight into Utah matters, past and present, his zeal and fidelity in collecting and sifting data, justify the earnest hope that he will ere long present to the reading public of this country, Great Britain and Germany, a really standard book on the characters and history of the most noted among the Mormon leaders. DAVID F. WALKER.

SALT LAKE CITY, May 9, 1886.

LETTER TO THE PUBLIC.

I do not wish to insult anybody in this book, or to hurt anybody's feelings. I desire to do my simple duty as a writer. That is all; to do it as a critic and observer, having the courage of my opinions, and being happily free from "all entangling alliances."

I came first to this fine Territory in December, 1884; stayed a few weeks and received my first general impressions about the state of Utah affairs; took my first dip into Mormon history and into the "Problem." I was received in the kindest manner by Governor Murray, Mr. David F. Walker, Judge C. C. Goodwin, Col. W. Nelson, Col. O. J. Hollister; by Wm. S. Godbe, H. W. Lawrence and E. L. T. Harrison, the well-known Mormon Apostates and Reformers and their friends; by the venerable and clear-headed widow of the "Paul of Mormonism," Mrs. Sarah M. Pratt, herself an exhaustless mine of curious information; by the eminent authoress, Mrs. Cornelia Paddock; also by a number of Apostles, Priests and Presidents in the Mormon Church. My interest got awakened. I returned to Utah early in February, '85, remaining till the latter part of May. This second sojourn was devoted exclusively to the taking of depositions from the mouths of living witnesses: I have examined some eighty, all men and women of recognized probity, and most of them of superior intelligence. For months have I worked with them from eight to ten hours a day, repeating my interviews until I had all the information they had to give. I am still working daily in this way.

I have made studies in Rome, Naples and Sicily, in France and England; have published some books about Italy, and about the Passion Play in Oberammergau, but never have I felt so interested, in all my life, as now in the history and workings of Mormonism. What is the secret charm of this study? I don't know. It may be the fact, that the study of a strikingly peculiar religious sect affords more insight into human nature than any other investigation; it may be, that the analysis of a modern theocracy calls back so vividly the forms, workings and general history, more or less dark, of older theocracies, as that of the Jews, the Mohammedans and the Jesuits; it may be that a book like the "Confession" of John D. Lee shows not only in vivid and startling colors the organism of one bloody fanatic and his murderous mates, but that it explains at the same time, by analogy, monsters like the Duke of Alva; shows that religious fanaticism has taught at all times that crimes committed in the name of God are meritorious, and shows, again, that such teachings find many believers, who, having devoted themselves to the service of some fancied "Lord," can lie and perjure themselves, rob and butcher, believing that they do the bidding of that God whom Jesus of Nazareth taught to be a loving father to all.

The *witnesses* whose depositions are contained in my book have been, for the most part, victims of a great delusion. The Mormon missionaries told them in Europe that the Gospel of Christ had been restored ; that miracles of all kinds, including the gift of the Holy Ghost, daily revelations of the Almighty, and scores of other blessings would be given to the faithful followers of Joseph Smith, the great Seer and Prophet ; that here in Utah was the "home of the pure;" a paradise of innocence and goodness ; nothing but brotherly love, peace and fidelity ; that this was the new "Zion." But when they came here, they saw a different picture. They saw that Brigham Young was just as Joseph Smith had been, the great shark and that the faithful were the carp. They did not hear any more of the Bible, as they had heard in the old country ; in "Zion" the Gospel was : Pay your tithing, obey the priesthood in all things ; ask never any question, but do as you are told ; take more wives, and if you have only a little one-roomed log cabin, never mind, take wives and build up the Kingdom. so that Brigham Young might soon be king of an independent State of the Union ; pay your tithing and pay besides to swell all kinds of donations; give away your money; ask never for an account, but be happy in your poverty, while the High Priesthood are living upon the fat of the land. Be spied upon every day in your actions by the "teachers," and even in your thoughts, and be a spy yourself on your neighbor; see whether he is strong in the faith, and if he is not, kill him—"cut his throat to save his soul; that is the way to love your neighbor." * Hate your enemies—"Pray for them," as Kimball said publicly; "yes, that God may damn and destroy them"—and hate all that are not of your clan. Hate all that is American, and swear terrible oaths, in the Endowment House, that you will avenge the blood of the Prophet on this nation. To make it short: "You may do anything, you may be the most brutal wretch, you may marry twenty wives and neglect one after the other, you may rob and even kill your fellow-citizens (non-Mormons) —if you *pay* and *obey* you are all right ; so long as you do this you are a faithful and worthy brother, and sure of your kingdom and eternal glory in the other world." Such were the public teachings in the earlier times of the Utah theocracy. Since 1870 the talk and practice have become milder, *but the principles are still the same.*

How could this tale, told to me a hundred times over, fail to convince me that this whole "religion" was a speculation to enrich a few, give them gold, power and all the brute pleasure hidden in the Greek word "polygamy?" It has convinced me, sure enough ; because this tale came from the mouths of good, honest, sincere people, who had "gathered to Zion" full of religious zeal, who were terribly disappointed, and finally, when they showed a change in their opinions, ostracized, robbed and threatened with violence and even death. Do you suppose, reader, that all these people lie, or is the lie, perhaps, on the other side? Is not all the interest in keeping up the original fraud and the highly profitable system *on this other side ?* I should think so.

---

* Literally quoted from the speeches of Brigham Young, the great philanthropist.

Mormonism has too long fooled the world, the new and the old. It has too long claimed immunity as a "religion," as an honest religious faith, with the known and long-established facts attending its original fabrication and its appalling development. Is it not indeed puerile for the great Government of the United States to still continue tampering and temporizing with the outrageous fraud as it has hitherto done? You prattle of "polygamy" and refuse to see the constant rebellion and treason ; you see a tree and are blind to the forest. You like to joke about the "old monarchical countries" and about ironclad Prince Bismarck. But I tell you, that he would solve the "Mormon Problem" in a week, while you are puzzled by it since fifty years. He would not, like you, stand a helpless babe before the high-schools of treason and licentiousness, called "Mormon Temples." He would bid them go, those builders of the Kingdom, and build elsewhere. Little Italy broke down the Pope's theocracy and great America stands a giant gagged and pinioned with red tape and circumlocution, helpless before that of King John Taylor!

But enough of this. I simply transcribe in my book what my witnesses have told me, respectable and respected people, who have been connected with Mormonism for fifty, forty and thirty years. I have not doctored one fact set forth in "Mormon Portraits." Let the Mormon leaders try to prove that I have lied or exaggerated, but do it in a decent manner, gentlemen, if you please. Don't get angry when a man expresses his honestly acquired conviction. In March, 1885, I wrote a dozen of letters to the great Berlin paper, the *Tageblatt*, published by my excellent friend, Rudolf Mosse. It seems that those letters were extensively circulated and much read. At least a Mormon missionary, a hopeful son of High Priest A. M. Musser, wrote from Mannheim to his "very dear" father : "In my last letter I enclosed some clippings written by a man named *Wyl*. The papers continue to publish like articles from him, strongly impregnated with the hatred and gall which Satan alone can furnish."—(*Deseret News, the official Church organ, May 11, 1885.*)

Now, this isn't fair. I have never been, to my best knowledge, in any literary connection with "Satan," and I have never had any other than superficial knowledge of him, till I got acquainted more intimately with some of his choice doings, for example the Yates and Aikins murders and the Mountain Meadows Massacre. Why abuse a man instead of fighting him with facts and argument? Let us come to an understanding. I am no enemy of the Mormon *people*. On the contrary, I sympathize with them. Leading merchants, bankers, etc., in this city, assure me that this people are good-hearted, industrious and honest, and I believe it readily. But the Mormon leaders are enemies of the Mormon people, enemies of the United States, enemies of the law, simply because they do not want to be disturbed in the piling up of great fortunes, exercising absolute power and lordship, and enjoying the embraces of as many "childbearing" (*id est* young and tender) concubines as they have a mind to. I admire this Territory. I never saw a finer climate, never finer scenery. I find here the breezes of Naples and Palermo and all the grand sights of Switzerland. This should be a country full of independent men and happy women, teeming with freely developed talent and individual enterprise. The inhabitants of this paradise should learn to think and act for themselves, the women should learn to be men's equals and companions instead of their "handmaids." It is the duty of the Government of this great Republic to raise both men and women of Utah to the dignity of citizens truly free, and the duty of every honest writer to help on so noble a cause by *telling the truth*.

This is the purpose, the only purpose of "*Mormon Portraits.*" I tell the truth so far as I have succeeded in finding it by diligent and honest search.

W. WYL.

SALT LAKE CITY, May, 1886.

PART I.

JOSEPH SMITH,

HIS FAMILY AND HIS FRIENDS.

———

I had read of the several movings and strange migrations of the Mormons; of their troubles and turmoils with their always-persecuting neighbors; with state and national authorities. It was hard for me to believe that in free America any religious sect could be persecuted merely because it was too pure and good. Still, might not Mormonism be just the one *exception* proving the *rule* of perfect religious toleration in this most tolerant and easy-going Republic? I resolved to examine the matter and see for myself on which side was the burden of wrong-doing, and what of truth there might be in this strange and continual charge from the Mormon side of "persecution." It has been my way to study eccentric and exceptional movements, political and religious, in the personal characters of the leading spirits of such movements.

Having applied my usual method in the case of Joseph Smith and his associates, I find that the world at large and especially the thousands of Mormons in Utah know but little of the true life, character and actions of Joseph Smith and the ringleaders of the so-called Mormon Church and Kingdom. In my investigations I learned to my surprise that Mormons by the thousand have left their leaders in the early times of the Church and neither came to Utah nor rejoined their ranks. The vast majority of the poor dupes in Utah and surrounding Territories, never having passed through such experiences as drove Mormons by the wholesale into rebellion and indignant apostacy, and drove those who continued steadfast in their infatuation from their places of settlement and sojourn in Ohio, Missouri and Illinois, are utterly incredulous, even refusing to believe the facts when recited and fully sustained, and thus remain in profound and blissful ignorance of much they ought to know, and which, if known, would undoubtedly influence them to repudiate any institution making it possible to have committed such acts in the name of God and religion.

Stories and reports of the criminal conduct of Joseph Smith, Brigham Young and their henchmen, did not rise from nothing, but are found to have had their origin in *facts*, which can be fully established and proven under the rules of historical investigation and criticism. Let me first introduce those of my witnesses who knew Joseph Smith's parents. It must be interesting to the reader to know the tree from which fell this prodigious apple.

THE PROPHET'S PARENTS.

The Old Patriarch and Blesser, Joseph Smith, Sr.—A Mother of Lies—A Pair of Splendid Gypsies—The Father of the Prophet Lectures on Money-Digging and Geology.

Mrs. P. states: "Joseph's father, the first Patriarch (if not President) of the Mormon 'Church,' was very tall; his crooked nose was very prominent; he was a real peasant, without any education. Joseph looked very much like him. Old Smith sold the blessings, which he used to pronounce on the heads of the faithful, at $3 apiece, and sold a good many of them for years."

Mr. W. states: "I knew old father Smith when he was about eighty years old; he was a great fanatic, and believed that Joseph was inspired from his boyhood on."

Mrs. P. states: "Joseph's mother was a little woman; she looked very vulgar. She was full of low cunning; no trick was too mean for her to make a little money. You could not believe a word of what she said. She used to talk a great deal about Mormonism. Everybody's opinion of her was, that she was a thorough liar. Her daughter wrote that book about Joseph for her. She and her husband looked like a pair of *splendid gypsies*. They looked wild and ignorant. Seeing them, nobody could doubt the stories about their money-digging, fortune-telling, etc."

Now, this is rather hard on the old couple. I know that the excellent lady who gave me these details spoke the absolute truth, but I cannot enjoy it. I rather like old "Mr. Smith" and Mrs. Lucy Smith, *nee* Mack. Why admire Mr. and Mrs. Micawber and be hard on Mr. and Mrs. Smith? They are splendid people in their way. Lying was as natural to them as drinking water, and they do it in a delightful way; it's prestidigitation with the truth, you see; artistic skill, acquired by a life's practice. Just read old Lucy's book on Joseph the prophet, for instance where she tells that Mrs. Harris wanted to force money on her, and that she refused it scornfully; read her description of the "breast-plate," which she valued at five hundred dollars, and that other of the "Urim and Thummim," which consisted of "three-cornered diamonds set in glass." And Joseph wore them always on his person. . . . . It is not vulgar lying, it is the talent of Sheherezade, without the bloody Sultan, and without — alas! — the dreamy atmosphere of the Orient.

Old "Mr. Smith" is the Micawber of the family. His imagination is an Ophir of delightful absurdities, hatched in an atmosphere filled with the sound of the urgent but never-heeded claims of his countless creditors. I will give you one example of his, a little lecture on money-digging, with a smack of geological discoveries of his own, showing a real but neglected talent for this branch of science.   Peter Ingersoll, an old acquaintance of his, puts it in this shape :*

"I was once ploughing near the house of old Joseph Smith. When about noon, he requested me to walk with him a short distance from his house, for the purpose of seeing whether a mineral rod would work in my hand, saying at the same time he was confident it would. When we arrived near the place at which he thought there was money, he cut a small witch-hazel bush and gave me direction how to hold it.   He then went off some rods, and told me to say to the rod, '*Work to the money*,' which I did in an audible voice.   He rebuked me severely for speaking it loud, and said it must be said in a whisper.   While the old man was standing off some rods, throwing himself into various shapes, I told him the rod did not work.   He seemed much surprised at this, and said he thought he saw it move in my hand. . . . Another time he told me the best time for digging money was in the heat of summer, when the heat of the sun caused the *chests of money* to rise near the top of the ground.   'You notice,' said he, 'the large stones on the top of the ground — we call them rocks, and they truly appear so, but they are, in fact, most of them, chests of money raised by the heat of the sun.''

Now, let us compare a little tale of Mother Lucy's with one of Abigail Harris :

LUCY SMITH.	ABIGAIL HARRIS.
"Joseph Smith the Prophet," page 110.	*Affidavit dated Palmyra, Nov. 28, 1833.*
"She (Mrs. Harris) commenced urging upon me a considerable sum of money, I think some seventy-five dollars, to assist in getting the plates translated. I told her that I came on no such business; that I did not want her money. . . . Yet she was determined to assist in the business, for she said she knew that we should want money, and she could spare two hundred dollars as well as not."	"Old Lucy Smith took me into another room, and after closing the door, said : ' Have you four or five dollars that you can lend until our (Gold Bible) business is brought to a close? The Spirit has said that you shall receive fourfold.' I asked her what her particular want of money was, to which she replied : ' Joseph wants to take the stage and come home from Pennsylvania to see what we are all about.' To which I replied, he might look in his stone, and save his time and money. The old lady seemed confused, and left the room."

---

*Affidavit dated Palmyra, Dec. 2, 1833.

This surely shows talent, or I don't understand anything about such things. But let us leave the humble parents, and turn to the great son. irreverently called by the wicked. " Joe Smith."

VIEWS OF JOSEPH SMITH.

The Prophet Believes in Astrology—Laughs Heartily About Mormonism—Does not know what the other World will be—Elder Rockwell's Curiosity.

There are two things you would naturally expect from a prophet. First, a belief in some sort of a religion, and then a belief in his own particular shop. Now, Joseph Smith didn't believe in any religion, he had no hopes of a future life, and as to Mormonism, he laughed about it just as you would expect from an impostor who had, as he said himself, "fixed the damned fools," and "wanted to carry out the fun." The only thing the Prophet believed in was astrology. This is a fact generally known to old "Nauvoo Mormons." Wm. Clayton. his chief clerk, used to cast figures and make calculations for him. Brigham Young copied Joseph in this as in many other things.

John C. Bennett says in his book : "I will mention a short conversasion that passed between Joseph and myself, as we were one day riding together up the banks of the Mississippi. After a short interval of silence, Smith suddenly said to me, in a peculiarly inquiring manner: 'General Harris says you have no faith. and that you do not believe we shall ever obtain our inheritances in Jackson County, Missouri.' Though somewhat perplexed by the Prophet's remark, and still more by his manner, I coldly replied : 'What does Harris know about my belief or the real state of my mind? I like to tease him now and then about it, as he is so firm in the faith and takes it all in such good part.' 'Well,' said Joe, laughing heartily,

'I guess you have got about as much faith as I have. Ha! Ha! Ha!' 'I should judge about as much,' was my reply.'' (This anecdote, told by Bennett, pp. 175 and 176 of his book, was fully confirmed to me by *Mrs. Sarah Pratt*, to whom it was told by Bennett shortly after the dialogue occurred.)

Mr. Johnson told me in the presence of Lawyer Jonasson, now deceased, thi following story: '' *Port Rockwell*, who used to be Joseph's coachman and factotum in Nauvoo, once asked the Prophet the following question: 'Brother Joseph, how is it in in the other world?' Joseph said in answer: 'Don't you bother, Brother Rockwell, about the other world; try to be as comfortable as possible in this and make the most of it; *nobody knows what the other world will be.*'' Mr. Johnson was a guard at the Penitentiary, and having heard that Rockwell had made such a statement, he went to him and asked him, whether the Prophet had really expressed himself in such a manner. Rockwell confirmed fully what he had told to others, and repeated Joseph's answer word for word.''

JOSEPH SMITH AND HIS PLATES.

The Prophet's Curious Proposition to His Bosom Friend, Bennett—The Same Fully Confirmed by Mrs. Pratt.

The truth about the golden plates, from which Joseph pretended to '' translate '' the Book of Mormon, has been established since 1834, by E. D. Howe. I give the substance of the very curious affidavits, obtained by him from Smith's neighbors, in the Appendix to Part I. of this book. There were never any plates of any kind. The book, a stupid historical novel, was written by Solomon Spaulding, stolen and '' religiously '' remodeled by Sidney Rigdon and published through Joseph Smith, whose widespread fame as '' Peeper '' and '' Treasure-finder '' enabled him admirably to assume the role of discoverer of golden plates. Sidney Rigdon was a man of taste in the matter of choosing the right kind of a rascal to do his dirty jobs. But he failed in one respect; he thought he found a tool and he really found a master in Peeping Joe.

Now it will surely be interesting to the reader, that I can not only convict Joseph Smith out of his own mouth, giving his full confession of the original fraud, but I am also able to show that he contemplated an additional fraud with the "plates," and that, as usual, he thought to make a pile of money out of the second fraud, too. The witness in the case is Joseph's Nauvoo accomplice, Dr. John C. Bennett. Those who would refuse his testimony, will not be able to contradict that of Mrs. Sarah Pratt.

Bennett says: "Shortly after I located in Nauvoo, Joe proposed to me to go to New York and get some plates engraved and bring them to him, so that he could exhibit them as the genuine plates of the Book of Mormon, which he pretended had been taken from him, and 'hid up' by an angel, and which he would profess to have recovered. He calculated to make considerable money by this trick, as there would of course be a great anxiety to see the plates, which he intended to exhibit at twenty-five cents a sight. I mentioned this proposition to Mrs. Sarah M. Pratt, on the day the Prophet made it, and requested her to keep it in memory, as it might be of much importance." When asked by me in the spring of 1885 about this statement of John C. Bennett, *Mrs. Pratt confirmed it fully* and stated also that Bennett had reported to her this conversation with Joseph on *the very day* when it happened.

JOSEPH LIKES HIS GLASS.

The Prophet Gets Drunk Now and Then—His Sprees and Adventures—"Awfully Funny."

Let Bacchus to Venus libations pour forth and *vive la compagnie!* Let the sober historian of Joseph paint him

as he was. Who could be vindictive or malicious with
such an eccentric as Joe? The prophet with all his vices
and wickednesses was yet neither malicious nor vindictive.
He had a very strong, healthy stomach, excellent digestion. He was almost the very antipode of dyspeptic,
reticent Brother Brigham. Joseph dearly loved the social
glass. Brigham much preferred a flowing bowl of—oat-
meal porridge. The great prophet of this dispensation
of the fullness of time was a real Bacchant. Perhaps he
thought with his long-time bosom-crony, the famous O.
Porter Rockwell, Esq., that he should "lose the spirit and
testimony of Mormonism," if not "steamed up." The
intelligent reader of this book will not fail to see that the
inspiring deities of Joseph were rather Venus, Bacchus
and Pluto, than the pretended Scriptural Trinity of
Father, Son and Holy Spirit.

Mrs. P.: "A good deal of whisky was consumed in
Nauvoo. Joe himself was often drunk. I have seen him
in this state at different times. One evening one of the
brethren brought Joseph to my home. He could not walk
and had to be led by a helpful brother. The prophet asked
me to make some strong coffee, which I did. He drank
five cups, and when he felt that he could walk a little
better, he went home. He dared not come before Emma
in this state. Joseph was no habitual drunkard, but he
used to get on sprees. When drunk he used to be 'awfully
funny.' He sometimes went to bed with his boots on."

Mr. W.: "Whisky, good whisky, was then 25 cents
a gallon. No wonder that Joseph sometimes went to bed
with his boots on, or that he slept, as he sometimes did, in
a ditch. He was a right jolly prophet. No sanctimonious
humbug about him."

Mrs. J.: "Joseph used to preach: 'Brethren and
sisters, I got drunk last week and fell in the ditch. I suppose you have heard of it. I am awfully sorry, but I felt
very good.' He used to get drunk on military occasions,
after the parades of the Nauvoo Legion."

JOSEPH THE WRESTLER.

---

*Joseph and the Tax Collector—Passion for Fine Horses—
Foot-Races—The U. S. A. Major—Two Reverends
Who do not Want to Wrestle.*

No, there was no holy humbug about Joseph. He
made no "long face," he gave himself as the jolly brigand
he was, and that is what made him loved and admired by
the motley crowd of impecunious vagabonds and adventurers that surrounded him. Brigham was, though always obeyed, feared and hated by his "friends;" they
knew that he would sacrifice anything and anyone to his
passion for gold; but Joseph was a good comrade in the
midst of brigands of a lower order; they admired his physical strength and agility and loved his jolly, cordial ways.
He had physical courage, he even died game, while Brigham was the greatest coward of his time, the greatest
among a whole set of cowards like Geo. A. Smith and the
rest of them. There was something of Macbeth in that
fellow Joseph and he died like Mac. But hear our witnesses:

Mr. K.: "A tax collector once asked a certain amount
from Joseph; he stopped the prophet, who was riding in
his carriage. Joseph said that he had paid him and owed
him nothing. The collector said: "If you say this, you
are a liar." Joseph jumped out of his carriage and struck
the collector such a blow that he went flying a distance
of three or four yards. Joseph took his seat in the carriage and drove away."

Mrs. P.: "Joseph had a passion for fine horses. He
had a fine carriage. He used to drive the buggy himself,
but the carriage was generally driven by a coachman."

Mr. K.: "Charlie" was the favorite family horse;
Emma used to drive him. Emma often rode on horseback
in company with Joseph, especially on military parades.
Joseph was always ready to show his force and cleverness

in some sport. He liked foot races and would have his boots off in a moment, to the great grief of old bigots. I remember the visit of a U. S. A. major, who came as a guest to the Nauvoo House. The major was of higher build than Joseph, but not so strong as the prophet. Joseph wanted to wrestle with him. He threw off his coat and cried : 'I bet you five dollars that I will throw you, come on !' The major declined. Joseph laughed and said : 'Now you see the benefit of one's being a prophet : I knew you wouldn't wrestle.' One of the Saints felt so scandalized by this joke of the prophet that he left the Church.''

"Two reverends came one day to Nauvoo. They wanted to see the Prophet and to hear the principles he was teaching. Joseph took them to his study, and talked to them about repentance, baptism, remission of sins, etc. The two reverends interrupted Joseph frequently. After half-an-hour or so, getting impatient the Prophet said to the two holy men, while he stood up in his full hight : 'Gentlemen, I am not much of a theologian. but I bet you five dollars, that I will throw you one after the other.' The reverends ran away and Joseph laughed himself nearly to death.''

JOSEPH AS A STUDENT.

A Poor Writer and Reader — Little Tricks Played by Him and the Elders—Study of Hebrew — Kimball's Desperate Fight With Grammar.

When, surely to his own surprise, arrived at the hight of his ambition, Joseph, who was naturally " smart,'' felt keenly the want of some ornamental learning. As usual he decided to make the world believe that he had what, in fact, he had not. He did in this respect just the same thing which he had done in regard to plates, apparitions of angels, etc. Let the witnesses talk :

Mrs. P.: " Joseph was a very poor writer and reader. He readily confessed this: it was a fulfillment of Scripture."

Mr. W.: " Joseph was the calf that sucked three cows. He acquired knowledge very rapidly, and learned with special facility all the tricks of the scoundrels who worked in his company. He soon outgrew his teachers. He studied Hebrew. he wanted to be fit for his place and enjoy the profits and power alone. He learned by heart a number of Latin, Greek and French common-place phrases, to use them in his speeches and sermons. For instance: *Vox populi, vox diaboli :* or *Laus Deus (sic)* or *amor vincet omnium (sic)*, as quoted in the Nauvoo ' Wasp.' Joseph kept a learned Jew in his house for a long time for the purpose of studying Hebrew with him; the Jew used to teach his language in a room of the ' Temple " to Joseph and a number of the elders." It was probably his rapidly augmenting knowledge of the sciences, that made him say, a few months before his death: ' *I know more than the whole world.*' " I taught him the first rules of English Grammar in Kirtland in 1834. He learned rapidly. while Heber C. Kimball never came to understand the difference between noun and verb."

JOSEPH'S HABITS, APPEARANCE. ETC.

The Prophet at Table—Uses Tobacco—Is Well Dressed —The Prophet's Jewelry—The Prophet on Horseback —His Laughter—His Conversation.

Mrs. P.: " Joseph was no *gourmand* at all. He ate heartily. but was not particular about the kind of food. I believe that he used tobacco in some form. He was always well dressed, generally in black with a white necktie. He looked like a Reverend. On the little finger of his left hand he wore a heavy gold ring ; he wore a gold watch and chain ; people used to make him presents of such things. When I saw him for the first time he rode on a splendid black horse that had been given to him by some admirer. He was a very good horseman. He was, when walking, very lank and loose in his appearance and movements."

Mr. K.: " People coming to Nauvoo expected to find a kind of John the Baptist, but they found a very jolly prophet. He used to laugh from the crown of his head to the soles of his feet, it shook every bit of flesh in him."

Mrs P.: " Joseph did not talk much in society, his talk was not very fluent. He used to make a remark now and then, letting the others talk. Whenever he spoke of Church affairs, his talk grew intelligent. He had no great choice of words, and generally expressed his ideas in a very humble, common-place way. At all events, he was by no means interesting in company. It looked as if he wanted to keep those who surrounded him in respect by talking little."

JOSEPH AS A PREACHER.

Strong Voice, no Oratorical Art, but much Magnetism —Gets very Pale—Joseph and Brigham Young Compared.

There was an old Dane in a Mormon settlement. He had half a dozen buxom daughters ; one of them had been sealed to the bishop. Whenever the bishop was absent from his flock, the old Dane used to preach in his stead in the Sunday meeting. Once—the bishop was in Salt Lake —our old Dane goes on the " stand " with a letter in his hand. " The Bishop writes from Salt Lake," says he, " that Brother Brigham does not want any round dancing any more. The bishop writes that this command must be obeyed. The bishop is the representative of God and I am his father-in-law. Amen." This may be taken as no unfair example of "preaching" as introduced by the founder of this motley "creed." Joseph used to say whatever came on his tongue, and so do all who are Joseph's. Jokes and curses, meekness and bravado, temporal and spiritual, the Holy Ghost and stock-raising, irrigation and baptism for the dead—all is " preaching."

Mr. K.: "Joseph's voice was very strong and could easily fill the remotest corner of a big hall."

Mrs. P.: " Joseph was no orator. He said what he wanted to say in a very blundering sort of way. John Taylor is the best speaker the Church ever had. Joseph had great magnetic influence over his audience, more than Brigham ever had. He had uncommon gifts in this line; he was what spiritualists call a strong medium. His eyes had nothing particular. When excited in speaking, he used to get very pale. The Saints thought that this change of colour came through the influence of the Holy Ghost. Whenever he had been ·tight,' he used to confess it in next Sunday's meeting. In the same way he confessed often that he had been wrong in some act. Brigham never did such a thing. But Joseph lied at the same time, stating that he had done so *to try the faith of the Saints.* The Lord would have a tried people."

JOSEPH AS A GENERAL.

Lots of Generals—Colonel Orson Pratt—The Modern Mahomet—A Terrible General Order—"Blood must be Shed"—Fine Uniforms—A Jolly General.

Yes, he was even a general at Nauvoo, not only a "prophet, seer and revelator." There were innumerable colonels in the Nauvoo Legion ; even dreamy Orson Pratt bore that warlike title. · But Joseph and his next friends

were generals, of course.   And he looked fine in his military rig-out, to be sure.

I quote from a letter in the New York *Herald*, dated
Nauvoo, May 8, 1842:

"Yesterday was a great day among the Mormons.   Their Legion,
to the number of two thousand men, was paraded by Generals Smith,
Bennett and others, and certainly made a noble and imposing appearance.   There are no troops in the States like them in point of enthusiasm and warlike aspect, yea, warlike character. .... Joseph, the chief,
is a noble-looking fellow, a Mahomet every inch of him."

It was in perfect keeping with this style, when Hugh
McFall, Adjutant General, gave the following "General
Order" at "Head-Quarters, Nauvoo Legion," "by order
of Lieut.-General Joseph Smith:"

"The requisition from the Executive of Missouri, on the Executive of Illinois, for the person of the Lieutenant-General for the
attempted assassination of ex-Governor Boggs, makes it necessary that
the most able and experienced officers should be in the field, for if the
demand should be persisted in, BLOOD MUST BE SHED."

Hear now a living witness:

Mrs. P.: "There was a great deal of gold on his
uniform.   Bennett was the man who introduced this grand
style. he always wanted everything of the finest ; they both
rigged themselves out wonderfully.   The Nauvoo Legion
looked very well.   Bennett understood parading thoroughly.   Bennett did not look well on a horse, but Joseph
looked splendid, and so did 'General' Hyrum.   Notwithstanding all this style. Joseph was very cordial with
everybody, shook hands with all the world, and was always
addressed 'Brother Joseph.'   The people fairly adored
him."

Joseph got crazy about his greatness in Nauvoo. His general's uniform, the Urim and Thummim, the Plates, the Breastplate, Laban's sword — all went to his head at once and made a fool of him. In this state of vertigo he conceived the glorious idea to be a candidate for the Presidency of the United States. It is a very curious sight, that announcement* in the *Times and Seasons:*

FOR PRESIDENT,

GENERAL JOSEPH SMITH.

FOR VICE-PRESIDENT,

SIDNEY RIGDON, Esq.

The greatest impostors and swindlers of the time, as bidders for the highest gifts of the Nation ! And, looking over the yellowish leaves of the same Church organ, to see only a few numbers later the sacred columns in mourning, announcing the tragic death of the great candidate !

Well, he has paid for his crimes and his follies ! Let us honor death, even in the corpse of an impostor. At that moment, when he cried out of the window of Carthage jail: "Is there no help for the *widow's son?*" hoping to find mercy from the hands of some brother Mason, he felt the bitterness of death as keenly as it can be felt. In this terrible moment he must have become

---

*And this announcement was a lie. Joseph presents himself "of Illinois," but Sidney Rigdon, who had resided with Joseph all the time in Nauvoo, hails "of Pennsylvania." This was done to satisfy the well-known necessity of naming two different States. "They can't do a thing without lying!" as an old apostate said to me the other day, with flaming eyes and clenched fist.

aware that the hour of his own "blood atonement" had
come, the hour of payment of his tremendous debt to
outraged, swindled, robbed and murdered humanity.

Joseph sent 337 elders to canvass for him all over the
country. *John D. Lee* was one of them, and though an
admirer of the Prophet, he says in his book, pp. 148–149:
"I left Nauvoo on the fourth of May, 1844, with greater
reluctance than I had on any previous mission. It was
hard enough to preach the gospel without purse or scrip,
but it was nothing compared to offering a man with the
reputation that Joseph Smith had, to the people as a candidate for the highest gift of the Nation. I would a
thousand times rather have been shut up in jail than to
have taken the trip, but I dared not refuse."

Mrs. P.: "The Mormons found it very natural that
Joseph Smith wanted to be President of the United States,
and Sidney Rigdon Vice-President. They thought the
time was sure to come soon when he would be at the head
of the Nation. This belief was part of their fanaticism.
Joseph and Sidney spoke in public about their candi-
dacies, and gave instructions to the elders whom they
sent abroad. They said they would soon get the whole
United States, and then they would make laws to suit
themselves; and the people believed what they said."

JOSEPH AND NERO BOGGS.

*"The Land of Your Enemies"— The House of Israel
Claiming the State of Missouri — A Noble Deed —
"Lend Me Your Husband's Rifle"—Elder Rockwell's
Reward.*

Missouri was to be the Canaan of the Saints. "My
servants Sidney and Joseph" had promised it to them a
thousand times, just as Don Quixote promised to Sancho
Panza the idol of his wishes, the island. Look at the
"revelation" of June, 1831, where the Lord speaks to
the elders assembled in Kirtland :

" And thus, even as I have said, if ye are faithful, ye shall assemble yourselves together to rejoice upon the land of Missouri, which is now THE LAND OF YOUR ENEMIES."

And the same Lord, who is evidently a first-class Mormon himself, says to the same elders in February, 1831 :

" For it shall come to pass, that which I spake by the mouth of my prophet, shall be fulfilled ; for I will consecrate the riches of the Gentiles unto my people which are of the House of Israel."

Now let any person possessed of common sense read these two communications of the Mormon Lord, and he will need no other explanation of the " Mormon war " in Missouri and of the tribulations and turmoils of the Saints in general. Everywhere they go, there is " Zion "; what is not theirs, is their " enemies' " and what is their " enemies' " must become theirs. It did not take the Missourians long to find out the kind intentions of the " House of Israel " towards them, and a civil war with its attending horrors ensued. Boggs, a faithful officer of the metal of our Murray, found out soon that quick amputation was the only method of healing this case of blood poisoning. He gave his celebrated order to drive the Mormons away or, " if it should become necessary for the public peace," to exterminate them. Would not any energetic patriot have acted just the same in such a case? Look at the evidence given in the trial of Joseph Smith and others, quoted in our Appendix to Part I., and then call Boggs the " Nero of Missouri," as the Mormon leaders did then and do to-day.*

---

*Here is an example of a modern Mormon Sunday school teaching as to Governor Boggs. This is one instance out of hundreds showing how the minds of the young in Utah get filled with lies and hatred of the American name :

Q. " Who acted as the chief persecutor of the Saints ?

A. " The *infamous* Lilburn W. Boggs, Governor of the State of Missouri.

Q. " Whom did Governor Boggs unjustly charge with this attempt to murder him ? "

A. " *Brother* O. P. Rockwell, and that Joseph Smith prompted him to do it, or was accessory before the fact."

(Deseret Sunday School Catechism No. 1. Questions and answers on the life and mission of the Prophet Joseph Smith. 1882.)

Boggs was the embodiment of the lawful wrath of the Missourians, kindled by the arrogance and the crimes of the band of fanaticized adventurers called "Mormons." Boggs was, even in Nauvoo times, Macbeth-Smith's *Banquo;* while he lived there was no rest for the King of Nauvoo.   He was hated for what he had done and feared for what he could do.   While he lived Joseph's extradition at the call of the Missouri authorities was only a question of time.   He must die, like Banquo, and then, what a fine effect on the "Mormon people," themselves, was to be expected from a sudden violent death of Nero! Was there not an admirable opportunity to show that Joseph, having predicted it, was the greatest of all prophets?   The Lord was always on hand to smite his enemies with a timely stroke of lightning, and would not the death of Boggs, the "persecutor," deter other would-be Boggses from interfering with the Lord's chosen people and frighten the enemies of Zion in general?

Let us first glance at Bennett's book again.   He says: "Joseph Smith in a public congregation in the city of Nauvoo, in 1841, *prophesied* that Lilburn W. Boggs, Ex-Governor of Missouri, should die by *violent hands* within a year.   Smith was speaking of the Missouri difficulties at the time, and said that the exterminator should be exterminated, and that the *Destroying Angel should do it by the right hand of his power.* ' I say it,' said he, ' in the name of the Lord God !'   In the spring of the year 1842 Smith offered a reward of five hundred dollars to any man who would secretly assassinate Gov. Boggs.   I heard the offer made at a meeting of the Danites in the Nauvoo lodge room . . . *O. P. Rockwell* left Nauvoo from one to two months prior to the attempted assassination of Governor Boggs, and returned the day before the report reached there.   The Nauvoo *Wasp,* of May 28, A. D. 1842, a paper edited by William Smith, one of the twelve Mormon apostles, and brother of the Prophet, declared: "Who did *the noble deed* remains to

be found out."* Some weeks after Rockwell left Nauvoo
I asked Smith where he had gone. 'Gone?' said he;
"gone to fulfill prophecy,' with a significant nod, giving
me to understand that he had gone to fulfill his prediction
in relation to the violent death of Governor Boggs.   Soon
after Rockwell's return, Smith said to me, speaking of
Governor Boggs: "The destroying angel has done the
work, as predicted, but Rockwell was not the man who
shot; *the angel did it."* †

No impartial writer about Mormon history has ever
doubted Joseph's connection with this attempted assassination,‡ but nobody has yet given direct proof. I am
able to lay it before the reader, introducing the testimony of

Mrs. Sarah Pratt: "One evening Dr. Bennett called
at my house and asked me to lend him my husband's rifle.
This was an excellent arm, brought from England by
Orson Pratt; it was known to be the best rifle in that part
of the country. I asked him what he wanted the rifle for,
and he said: "Don't be so loud; Rockwell is outside —
Joseph wants it; I shall tell you later." . . . I suspected
some foul play, and refused to give him the rifle, stating
that I dared not dispose of it in the absence of my husband.   Bennett went away, and when the news came that
Gov. Boggs had been shot at and all but killed, Bennett
came and told me that he had wanted the rifle of my hus-

---

*This is correct. The author saw the *Wasp* in the Historian's
office at Salt Lake. And, *en passant*, I observe that President John
Taylor in his celebrated discussion in France, in the year 1850, is
strangely oblivious of this noble deed, dismissing with a virtuous
flourish the charge as a weak invention of the enemy; in effect
denying (as he also at the same time and place denied polygamy,
etc.,) that Boggs' life had ever been sought by Mormon thugs:
"Governor Boggs is residing at the present time in the State of
California."

†Bennett, pp. 281-2.

‡May 6th 1842, Boggs was shot at Independence, Mo., while
reading a newspaper. The pistol was loaded with buckshot and
three balls took effect in his head, one penetrating his brain. His
life was despaired of for several days, but he recovered. See *Wasp*
of May 28.

band for "that job," and that Joseph had sent him to get it. I have not the slightest doubt that Joseph had planned and ordered the assassination of Gov. Boggs."

So far Mrs. Pratt, whose testimony, as all decent people in Salt Lake City well know, is absolutely reliable. It shows that our aspiring friend, Bennett, was an accomplice in the murderous plot, as he was in the other rascally schemes of his friend, the prophet; he was, indeed, in this college of crime, more teacher than disciple; and, not unlikely, the first suggestion of murdering Boggs came from Bennett himself. But, as to his own guilt, his book is like that of John D. Lee, telling any amount of truth concerning others, while lying about and screening himself.

Rockwell, it seems, got a good reward from the prophet for his zeal in fulfilling prophecy; Joseph was much more liberal in this respect than Brigham, who wanted his assassins to work for the Lord at their own expense, to murder "without purse or scrip."

John C. Bennett: "I would further say that Rockwell was abjectly poor before he left Nauvoo, but since his return he has an elegant carriage and horses at his disposal, and his pockets filled with gold. These horses and carriage belonged to Smith, and the gold was furnished by him."

C. G. Webb: "I saw the fine carriage, horses and harness which Rockwell got from Joseph after the attempt on the life of Gov. Boggs."

THE LORD'S BANKERS IN KIRTLAND.

My Friend Webb, the aged Father of Wife Number Nineteen—Interviews with Webb, James McGuffie and his Wife—Joseph as Land Speculator, Banker and Auctioneer of Town-lots—Those Window-glass Boxes and fine Bank Notes.

Do you remember, my excellent friend *Webb*, that balmy Sunday afternoon, in April. 1885, when you told me about that famous bank whose President and Cashier were the two chosen servants of the Lord, Sidney Rigdon and Joseph Smith? It was one of our many interviews in that cosy house of stalwart, sterling old James McGuffie and his good, honest soul of a wife. We sat, as usually, in the kitchen, not far from McGuffie's pride, that stove with "Zion" in shining nickel-letters on it. I put question after question, with note-book and pencil in hand, and you and James McGuffie were busy answering. I have studied a great many old paintings in many cities of the old world, in Rome, Florence and Venice, in Vienna, Berlin and Paris, in Amsterdam, Brussels and London. But, I assure you, I have never seen better heads in any picture than yours and McGuffie and wife's; I never saw more sound sense, solidity and crystallized honesty in old heads, and good, well-meaning eyes besides, shining with all that makes eyes dearest to us—love of truth and interest in humanity's progress and welfare. I wish those over-cultivated people in the East could have some interviews with you three "vile apostates." They would soon see what Mormonism really is, and not talk any more nonsense about it. But I want to dish before the reader what you said about that famous bank, friend Webb. So let me introduce you in your own words, dear old Liveoak:

"I personally lost $2,500 in that famous bank, of which Sidney Rigdon was President and Joseph Smith Cashier. I got for my money the blessing of the Lord. and the

assurance that bye and bye the notes of that bank would
be the best money in the country ! The bank was founded
in 1836. Its origin dates from Joseph's idea to secure to
all the Saints 'inheritances,' which they should possess in
this life and in the other. Consequently, many elders
were sent east with the instruction to get as much money
as possible. The elders returned with money, and Smith
now bought a tract of land called the 'Smith farm.'
The temple was built and the city lots surveyed. But
instead of receiving their 'inheritances,' the Saints had to
buy them, and at good round prices, too. Joseph played
auctioneer, and a very good auctioneer he was. The
Saints were full of enthusiasm and lots went up from a
hundred dollars to three and four thousand. This transaction brought some money into Joseph's capacious pockets
and he now began to think of starting a bank in Kirtland.
It was to be secured by real estate; but this was never
done. They went to New York and had notes engraved,
beautiful notes, the finest I had ever seen. In the bank
they kept eight or nine window-glass boxes, which *seemed*
to be full of silver; but the initiated knew very well that
they were *full of sand, only the top being covered with 50-
cent pieces.* The effect of those *boxes* was like magic;
they created general confidence in the *solidity* of the bank,
and that beautiful paper money went like hot cakes. For
about a month it was the best money in the country. But
the crash came soon, as everybody knows."

Yes, the crash came and the two bankers of the Lord
had to leave Kirtland " between two days." But not because of their bank-swindle; the above-quoted " Sunday-
School Catechism No. 1" tells us that they left "to escape
mob-violence." The swindled *mob* behaved shamefully
indeed towards the man who had been appointed " Commander-in-chief of the Armies of Israel," and to whom
Moses, " the great law-giver to ancient Israel," had given
personally " the keys of the gathering of Israel." All
that is in this useful little Catechism of 1882.

COUNTERFEITING APOSTLES.

Brigham Young's Official Money a Counterfeit — A Jewel of a Confession, Contributed by Brigham's Brother — Nine Apostles as Criminals — Brigand William Smith.

I am glad to be able to give some positive and partly very picturesque proof for this department of Mormon elders' iniquity. Should you come to Utah, reader, some old Mormon or apostate will show you the gold coins of Zion, coined by Brigham Young. Even this official money of the Kingdom, now out of course, is counterfeit; it bears on its face "*Five Dollars,*" and is in reality only worth about $4.30. For proof of my assertions as to the earlier times of the "Church," the times in Missouri and Illinois, I rely principally on the confession of that daisy, *Phineas Young,* brother of Brigham, which, in my opinion, is worth fifty volumes on Mormon history. I give it in the very words of my informant, who is one of the most cultivated and reliable men of Salt Lake City:

"Phineas Young, a near relative of mine, said to me in 1875: 'We have been driven (from Missouri and Illinois) *because our people stole too much.* They stole horses, cattle and beehives, robbed smokehouses, and anything you may imagine, and then scores of us *passed counterfeit money on the Gentiles.*'"

Gov. Thomas Ford: "During the winter of 1845-6 the Mormons made the most prodigious preparations for removal (from Nauvoo). The twelve apostles went first, with about two thousand of their followers. *Indictments had been found against nine of them in the Circuit Court of the United States,* for the District of Illinois, at its December term, 1845, *for counterfeiting the current coin of the United States.*"*

In the beginning of May, 1885, while stopping at the Metropolitan Hotel, in Salt Lake City, I met a lady of

---

*History of Illinois, pp. 412-413.

the name of Mrs. E ——, who had lived in Nauvoo as a child. She told me the following story: "My parents lived for a time at what was called 'Joseph Smith's Tavern,' in Plymouth, thirty-three miles from Nauvoo, and fifteen miles from Carthage. We children played hide and seek, one day, as we often did. We came, by chance, to an upper room, which Apostle Bill Smith, Joseph's brother, used as a bedroom when he was at the 'tavern.' While running about and trying to hide, we suddenly came upon a long, heavy sack, which we opened and found full of coined money—silver and gold. At least, it looked so. We were very happy to become so rich. We little girls put lots of money in our small aprons, called together the children of the neighbors, and gave them some of the money. Our parents were not at home, but when they came we ran up to them: 'Oh, pa! oh, ma! we have a whole bread-pan full of money for you!' Father gave us a severe rebuke, and ordered us to get all the money together, and to get back from our little friends all that we had given to them. We obeyed, with our eyes swimming in tears, and laid all the money before our father, who put it back in the sack and buried the sack. He said he would wait till Bill Smith and his comrades would ask him for the money. A few days after, Apostle Bill came to the 'tavern,' and with him came Zinc Salisbury and Luke Clayborn, both brothers-in-law of Bill. They searched for the money, and, not finding it, invited my father to go coon-hunting with them. My father divined that they wanted to punish him for the disappearance of the money, so he said to them: 'Why don't you tell me, honestly, that you wanted your money?' And so saying he showed them where he had buried the treasure. They took it, and threatened my father that they would kill him if he talked to anybody about it. There was great excitement in the country about this bogus money, and it finally became so intense that the authorities had to interfere. The officers found the machinery, with which the money was made, in Plymouth. Whenever Joseph Smith owed money he paid with this kind of coin."

JOSEPH IN MONEY MATTERS.

The Lazy Prophet and His Secretary—A Hotel for the New Abraham and His Posterity—The Prophet Robs and Defrauds Poor and Rich Alike.

Lying and laziness—there is an alliteration for you—were the two great characteristics of Joseph in early youth. There are extenuating circumstances in the case, however; he inherited both qualities from the "splendid gypsies," his parents, so that telling the truth and working hard would really and literally have been against his nature. His innate hatred of all serious work made him a money-digger and a fortune-teller, and finally a prophet. As such he had in his employ a factotum and secretary, who wrote down all that Joseph needed for the execution of his plans, which always tended to his power, profit or lust. This secretary, or chum of his, he used to call the "Lord," and what he had dictated to him, "revelations." Brigand Joseph and his next friends knew this funny circumstance perfectly well, but thousands of dupes swallowed the celebrated formula "*Thus saith the Lord*" notwithstanding.

Let us hear some of those funny "revelations," dictated by Joseph to his "Lord" and then published in the latter's name :"

"If thou lovest me thou shalt keep my commandments and thou shalt consecrate *all* of thy properties unto me, with a covenant and *deed* which cannot be broken."

"Deed" shows the smart Yankee in dictating Joseph. He is not content with a religious "covenant," he wants a good, solid, ironclad deed. I proceed to quote from the official church books :

"Who receiveth you receiveth me and the same will feed you and clothe you and give you *money*—and he who does not these things is not my disciple."

That secretary of the prophet is a thoroughly good fellow, it seems. But he can do better :

"And let all the moneys which can be spared, it mattereth not unto me whether it be little or much (!), be sent up unto the land of Zion, unto those I have appointed to receive it."

Now, getting all the spare money people have is surely very nice, but Joseph had to show to the people still more clearly what he could do with his above mentioned "pard." So he made him write :

"It is meet that my servant Joseph should have a *house* built in which to live and translate. And, again, it is meet that my servant Sidney Rigdon should live as seemeth him good, inasmuch as he keepeth my commandments. Provide for him (Joseph) food and raiment, and *whatsoever* he needeth—and in temporal labor thou (Joseph) shalt have no strength, for this is not thy calling."

This is one of those great contradictions in nature to puzzle even a Darwin. Joseph, the wrestler, 6 feet high, and weighing 212 pounds, is too feeble to work. But the chum can do better. Joseph has a house and *whatsoever he needeth*, but he wants the comfort of a hotel, you see, with bar and all other appurtenances. Such a concern is just the thing for the necessities of a daily increasing polygamous or celestial household. So the chum sits down and writes :

"And now, I say unto you, as pertaining to *my boarding house*, which I commanded you to build for the boarding of strangers, let it be built unto my name and let my name be named upon it, and let my servant Joseph and his house have places therein *from generation to generation*. For this anointing have I put upon his head that this blessing shall also be put upon the heads of his prosterity after him, and as I said unto Abraham even so I say unto my servant Joseph, in thee and in thy seed shall the kindreds of the earth be blessed. Therefore, let my servant Joseph and his seed after him have place in that house from generation to generation forever and ever, *saith the Lord*, and let the name of that house be called the "Nauvoo House." (January, 1841.)

Now this is perfectly delightsome. It is *religion*, you know. Don't you see the smart Yankee-eyes through the *peep*-holes of the prophetic mask, and don't you hear him laugh behind that mask at the d—d fools he has got fixed? Let us give Joseph his due. The Prophet declared he was going to carry out the fun, and he did carry it out to the bitter end.

But I have to hasten to my notes and introduce my witnesses after this reproduction of old, well-known "revelations," without which, however, no biography of the imposter would be complete. Let us hear first

Mrs. P.: "Whenever a man of means came into the Church Joseph was sure to get a revelation that the money of the new comer must be "consecrated." He had no rest till he got hold of it. Examples are, Hunter, Shurtliff, Bosley and others. Joseph had not so much opportunity to make money, as Brigham, but both acted just alike. Joseph had great talents in the art of making himself agreeable to those whom he wanted to plunder. He borrowed money wherever he could and never returned a cent of it. If you wanted your money back he laughed in your face. He grew rapidly worse under the influence of John C. Bennett in this and every other respect. To rob people was called "consecrate to the Lord."

Mrs. Sw.: "Two good, honest people, Mr. and Mrs. Farrar, came to Nauvoo from England. They had been in the service of Sir Robert Peel and had amassed a little competence, about eight hundred pounds of English money, each. Joseph got the money from them. He told them that he would build up the kingdom with it, and, said he, emphatically: 'I shall die for you, if necessary!' When Joseph was shot, Mr. Farrar became crazy; Mrs. Farrar died long afterwards, a pauper in Salt Lake."

Mr. W.: "Joseph was in money matters just like Brigham and Taylor. Whoever had money had to consecrate it to the Lord. When people were stripped of every dollar they had, they got sometimes a little pittance from the tithing office; that was all. I am convinced that Joseph never entertained the least idea of returning any money he had borrowed. He became rich through the sale of town lots."

Mrs. P.: "When people asked for their money, Joseph sometimes made dreadful scenes. How could they dare to ask for money from the Lord's priesthood, which has the right to use everybody's money for the upbuilding of the kingdom? In this regard, indeed,

Joseph's mantle fell on the shoulders of Brigham Young."

Mr. S. : " Whenever Joseph sold a lot to somebody, he gave a church deed. Soon afterward the buyer got "counsel" to join the order of Enoch, and in this way Joseph got the lot back and kept the money. *He sold as Mayor and took back as Enoch.* For either emergency he had another name."

Mr. K. : " Money was like sand in Joseph's hands ; it ran through his fingers. Bishop Hunter gave Joseph eleven thousand dollars in gold." [In Kirtland money *was* sand, as we have seen.]

Mr. R. : " Solomon Wixom was a poor but hardworking farmer in Nauvoo. Out of his scant earnings he managed to save about one hundred and twenty dollars, and laid it by in the Fall to buy a yoke of cattle in the Spring, to enable him to work a piece of land. Joseph Smith got wind of the little treasure by a ' revelation ' —an unsuspecting brother, to whom Wixom told his plans, chanced to speak of it in the presence of a confidant of Joseph. The prophet went to see Wixom, and after a few commonplace remarks which rather flattered the latter, said : ' Brother W., I am hard up for some money, I need it badly ; do you know of anyone that could lend me a little ? ' ' Well, Brother Joseph, really I don't know. I have a little laid by, but I cannot spare it, for I want it to buy a yoke of cattle in the Spring.' ' Oh,' was Joseph's reply, ' let me have it, Brother Wixom, and I can easily pay it back before you want it, and God will bless you.' ' Well, well, if you can, Brother Joseph, I'll lend it you.' He went and put the amount in Joseph's hand. When the prophet counted the money, he turned to Wixom and said : ' It's all right, I need not give you a note, Brother Sol., I suppose.' ' Oh no, no, Brother Joseph, your word is good enough to me for that.' Spring came, and advancing toward the middle, but Joe never advanced toward Wixom. The poor man becoming uneasy went to his prophet-debtor : ' The Spring is come, Brother Joseph, and I come to ask you to be kind enough to give me that money I lent you.' ' Money, what money, Brother Sol. ? ' ' Why, don't you recollect the money I lent you last Fall which you promised to pay me in the Spring to buy my oxen?' After a moment's pause, apparently to jog his memory, the prophet replied: 'No, Brother Sol., I never got any money from you that I know of. Have you got a note?' 'No, I haven't; you said there would be no need to give a note, for you would be sure and pay it, as it obliged you so much.' 'I don't remember any such transaction, and will not pay it,' said the man of God. The poor man never received his money, and when asked what he thought of the dishonest trick, he said that Joseph must have done it *to try his faith.*"

This incident comes from a near relative of Wixom who is now a faithful polygamous Saint in Utah.

The following is a most characteristic story: Among the proselytes who came to Kirtland to enjoy the blessings of the new gospel, was a good honest spinster by the name of Vienna J—, who herself related the occurrence. She came from away down East, where she had accumulated by hard work, dime by dime, some fourteen or fifteen hundred dollars. Joseph hearing of it immediately got a revelation concerning this money. He told Vienna, that the Lord wanted her to return East, gather up her substance and bring it on to Kirtland. Vienna obeyed and brought the money. When she arrived, Joseph was away from Kirtland. Some of the Elders, who were in the secret, itched to get hold of the money; one of them succeeded in getting a loan of fifty dollars from Vienna, one of those loans that are like Shakespeare's immortal traveler that never returns. Vienna followed the prophet to the place where he had gone. She had made up her mind, good soul, to give the prophet a big present in money—a hundred dollars! She thought that was much, and, considering her circumstances and the way she had saved her dimes, it was much, sure enough. Well, she finds Joseph, and full of pious zeal, eager to surprise the prophet of the Lord, she hastens to lay before him the hundred dollars, well counted. But Joseph's countenance darkened and fell; he assumed a searching, severe look and cried: "*Where is the rest of it? What have you done with the* *money, sister!*" The poor thing "shelled out" very soon ; her whole earnings and savings went to Joe. Being asked what was done with it? "Oh," said she, "Joseph bought a gold watch, and Hyrum got a gold watch, and so did some others." Asked further: "And this did not shake your faith in the prophet?" "Oh no," said the good soul. "The Lord said I should have an inheritance in Zion. *But I was to be industrious.* You can see the revelation in the Doctrine and Covenants. I saw it in manuscript before it was printed, only they changed it a little in the print. In the revelation it first read *her* money, they made it say *the* money. But it was all right. Well, I never was lazy in my life, but I suppose the Lord saw I might get lazy." Well, that poor, old creature died "fixed" in the faith, over ninety years old, and the story shows what hold such a "religion" can have on simple, confiding, devout souls.*

SECRET MURDERS IN NAUVOO.

Fine Nauvoo Tales by Brother Lee—Thrown in the Lime Kiln, Body, Clothes and All—The Drowning of the Good Old Woman, Described by R. Rushton—Some Graceful Lies by John Taylor.

They are "secret" no more since Lee's book, and they will be less so after this little book of mine shall have seen the light. Murder is the most natural thing in the world with despotism; look for instance at Venice, Spain, etc. It is no wonder, therefore, that the Mormon form of theocracy, the most searching, brutal and absolute form of all tyrannies ever known in history, should resort to murder for the purpose of protecting itself from enemies— Boggs, for example—and screening its criminal and treasonable *secrets*, which form such an important part of

---

* Told to the author by a witness, who heard it more than once recited by the old aunt, now in heaven.

this " religion." We are, therefore, not surprised in the least to find, that from the infancy of this " Church " up to our days, *murder* has always been the preferred instrument for fighting the enemies of the " Kingdom." Only a few weeks ago U. S. Attorney Dickson was attacked by a number of Mormon hoodlums, bearing the name of Cannon, a name synonymous with the most impudent kind of lying and misrepresentation. And why was Dickson attacked? Because he is the most able, energetic and incorruptible of all public accusers Utah ever had. Deputy Marshal Collin escaped barely with his life, a few months ago, while attacked by three or four " Danites " in a dark alley. The reason? He is a faithful officer.

Let me first introduce the testimony of John D. Lee, who, while in Nauvoo, (like Abraham O. Smoot and Hosea Stout), was only a modest Danite and policeman, but later became the most celebrated of assassins in the service of Brigham Young, outshining even stars like Porter Rockwell and Bill Hickman. What he says cannot but be true; there is too much proof for it.

"I knew of *many* men being killed in Nauvoo by the Danites. It was then the rule that all the enemies of Joseph Smith should be killed, and I knew of *many a man* who was quietly put out of the way *by the orders of Joseph and his apostles* while the church was there. It has always been a well-understood doctrine of the church that it was right and praiseworthy to kill every person who spoke evil of the prophet. This doctrine has been strictly lived up to in Utah, until the Gentiles arrived in such great numbers that it became unsafe to follow the practice; but the doctrine is still believed, and no year passes without one or more of those who have spoken evil of Brigham Young being killed in a secret manner. In Springville it was *certain death* to say a word against the authorities, high or low. In Utah it has been the custom with the priesthood to make *eunuchs* of such men as were obnoxious to the leaders. This was done for a double purpose; first, it gave a perfect revenge, and next, it left the poor victim a living example to others of the dangers of disobeying counsel, and not living as ordered by the priesthood. In

Nauvoo it was the orders from *Joseph Smith and his apostles* to beat, wound and castrate all Gentiles that the police could take in the act of entering or leaving a Mormon household under circumstances that led to the belief that they had been there for immoral purposes. *I knew of several such outrages while there.*"

The official murderers in the service of the Mormon priesthood were always called "City Police," and are so called to-day.

Lee, one of the high priests who officiated at the great religious sacrifice, called "Mountain Meadows Massacre" by wicked Gentiles and apostates, says (Confession, p. 287): "Soon after I got to Nauvoo I was appointed seventh policeman. I had superiors in office, and was sworn to secrecy and to obey the orders of my superiors, and not let my left hand know what my right hand did. It was my duty to do as I was ordered, and not to ask questions. I was instructed in the *secrets* of the priesthood to a great extent, and taught to believe, as I then did believe, that it was my duty, and the duty of all men, to obey the leaders of the church, and that no man could commit sin so long as he acted in the way that he was directed by his church superiors. I was one of the lifeguard of the prophet Joseph."

I now introduce living witnesses.

Mrs. Pa.: "It was not rare for people who owned fine pieces of property in Nauvoo to disappear all of a sudden. An English family sold all the property they had in England, and then went to "Zion." The husband and father arrived first in Nauvoo, and soon wrote home to England that he owned a fine house and garden. The wife came later, but could not find her husband or his property. He had simply *disappeared.* She was told that he had died suddenly, but they could not show his grave. The woman had sold her property in England after her husband had left, but she was smart enough not to say a word about it in Nauvoo, that she had the money in her pockets. She told the prophet that she had tried to sell her property, but had not succeeded, and that she left it in trust. She managed to get out of Nauvoo."

Mrs. J.: "While I was in Nauvoo, the following was very common talk there: 'What is it?' 'Oh, nothing, only a dead man has been picked up.' I had been very strong in the faith, but such things opened my eyes."

A man by the name of *Thompson* is authority for the following statement. He was for years an employee of the Tithing office in Salt Lake; he had been a long time in Nauvoo and apostatized in 1860. He told one of my chief witnesses, who thinks him a perfectly reliable man, the following: "All those that were inimical to the Kingdom of God in Nauvoo, were put away. I knew a man who was looked upon as an enemy to the church. They threw him, body, clothes and all, in the lime kiln and burned him up. But I believed then [just like John D. Lee] that it was all right; it had been commanded by Joseph the Prophet and was done for the safety of the Kingdom."

"*Dead men tell no tales*" was a favorite word of Joseph Smith, and Brigham Young adopted and used it very frequently. One might say that it was the motto of the two prophets as to the treatment of their enemies. But sometimes the motto was changed a little and then it had to read: "Dead *women* tell no tales." This is proved by a terrible tale related by old Richard Rushton, the faithful steward of the "Nauvoo Mansion," where Joseph lived as hotel-keeper.

"Old Sister ———, —well-known in early times in Nauvoo—was a good, generous woman, a faithful Saint, and tried to be worthy the name by being kind and truthful. Having some means she could spare, she helped the 'prophet' and gave amply to the 'church.' She attended to the sick—and there were many there—alleviating their distresses and speaking words of cheer to the disconsolate. She was respected by many as a 'mother in Israel.' But she was outspoken, and seeing so much that appeared to her corrupt, she would sometimes 'blab' about the brethren's doings. Her reproofs showed that she knew too much, and she might become dangerous to them. Though she knew but little, comparatively, of what was going on, the priesthood became alarmed, and as it was easier to get

rid of an old woman that to reform their lives, it was considered necessary to 'attend to her case.'   A council was
held in Joseph's room, at which were Joseph Smith, O. P.
Rockwell and a few others.   After Rockwell had accused
her, the subject was broached of drowning her, the council concluding that for the safety of some of the brethren,
and especially Joseph, although she was a 'purty good
'oman,' *she must be silenced at all hazards*.   The plan
devised then and there, was that, as she was 'kind o' kind
to the church,' the church would make her a present of a
piece of land and a house on it which they owned 'over
the river.'   The next night they would take her 'over the
river' and land her safely 'on the other side.'   All present consented, and the evening being dark and propitious
to carry out the plan, a few of those consenting met at the
boat at the river-side to execute 'the will of the Lord
concerning her.''

"It was a dark night.   Darkness on the city and on the
great stream, rolling peacefully but a few rods distant.
Profound silence in the low part of the city.   But hark!
a wild shriek is heard by a trembling listener in the little
office of the 'Mansion,' coming as from a throat gurg-
ling with water; it was only a moment, and again—
silence; but hark! another shriek from the same quarter,
from the same voice, a piercing shriek as from some one
struggling for dear life; and again silence.   Then a final
shriek, much fainter, telling .the breathless listener that
the end had come.   All is now hushed as death.   The
cry is heard no more, the old soul is silenced now, the
baptism is complete without the usual religious formula,
and the lifeless body floats in the broad arms of the
Father of the Waters, no more to vex the souls of these
pitiless conspirators, until the great day of account, when
'the sea shall give up its dead.' ''

"In less than five minutes after the ceasing of the
screams from the drowning victim, the prophet, O. P.
Rockwell and two others rushed wildly into the hotel.
The prophet was dripping wet.   He was loudly expostu-
lating with 'Port' and the others: 'You should not have
drowned her; she couldn't have done us much harm.'

' We had to do it,' was the response, 'for your safety and our own, as well as for the good of the church. She can't harm us now.' 'I am very sorry ;' said the prophet, 'if I had thought of it a few minutes sooner, you wouldn't have drowned Sister ———.' It appears that although the prophet consented the night previous to her murder, under the impulse of the misrepresentation and fears of her accusers, he relented on reflection and expected to appear with the murderers at the river's edge in time to prevent them from putting their purpose into effect. He was too late, and in his effort to save her then he was wet through and through, being baffled by the combined strength of his followers. The prophet was impulsive and fitful, and in his better moments, no doubt, thought the poor old soul should not be ' blood-atoned,' and really tried to save her. But what a state of society, that made it possible to drown an innocent, defenceless, confiding old woman!'' (Richard Rushton heard the shrieks of the victim while sitting in the office of the " Mansion.'')

There must have been strong rumors current about the secret crimes committed in Nauvoo at that time, since the church organ called *Times and Seasons*, while advocating Joseph Smith's election as President of the United States, found it necessary to issue the following characteristic denial to those floating rumors :

"Gentlemen, we are not going either to murder ex-Governor Boggs, nor a ' Mormon in this State ' for not giving us his money ;' nor are we going to ' walk on the water,' * nor ' drown a woman,' nor defraud the poor of their property,' nor ' marry spiritual wives,' etc.

Now I assert that the Mormon leaders *did* commit the crimes and abominations charged to them by public rumor in 1844 and denied impudently in the church organ. I have proved the attempted assassination of Governor

---

*I am informed that Mr. Deming, of Painesville, Ohio, is prepared to prove in his book that old story of Joseph's having " walked on the water" in Kirtland to imitate one of the best known miracles of the Savior. There were, it seems, planks put some inches below the surface of the water, and Smith walked (in perfect security) over the deep ! But a wag having contrived to remove one of the planks, the modern miracle-worker took a dip that nearly cost him his interesting life.

Boggs and the drowning of the old woman; the truth of the remaining charges admits of no doubt in the light of proofs furnished on all sides for similar and worse offenses. Was not *polygamy* confessed officially in 1852, after having been denied most solemnly by the church organ and leaders up to that time, and by John Taylor in a public discussion in 1850, in Boulogne, France? "We are not going to marry spiritual wives." How does this read, I ask thee, O righteously indignant Mormon doubter, in the glaring light of historic truth emblazoning polygamy since the time that Lieutenant General Joseph Smith was posing as presidential candidate?

STEALING IN NAUVOO.

Ridiculous "Gentile" Notions—John Taylor very Solemn—Abel, the Colored Priest—Stealing Cattle and Healing the Sick.

To understand this chapter fully, you have to get rid of your Gentile notions and prejudices first, gentle reader. To kill a fellow in some canyon, because he is an apostate, is not *murder* in Mormonism, but saving the poor fellow's soul. Taking from the Gentiles is not *stealing*, but *consecrating to the Lord* what rightfully belongs to him. This is a "higher law," too. For is not "*the earth the Lord's and the fullness thereof, and the cattle on a thousand hills?*" Now just stick to this, reader, and don't forget that it is more than an official test of Mormon faith; it is a part of the life blood of the elders of the school of Joseph and Brigham. Nobody ever expressed this axiom better than John Taylor did once in New York. A Mormon lady told him that her servant girl used to bring home bits of silverware and like articles whenever she had been visiting Gentile friends. "What shall I do, Brother Taylor?" said the lady. "Dear Sister H——," said the man of God, with that ghostly unction of his, "*you* CANNOT *steal from Gentiles !*"

No, you cannot. Taylor is right, and his answer was a masterpiece of strict logic. Can it be stealing, if you take from your *enemies*, whom God will destroy very soon for not accepting the gospel of Joseph Smith? What the wicked Gentiles possess is *stolen* from the Lord ; so bring it back, brethren, to the Lord, that obliging " pard " of Joseph's, who hands the trash over to Joseph, of course.

But hear another of the Lord's choice "revelations" and you will understand fully that the " founder " of Mormonism authorized his followers *directly* to appropriate " whatsoever HE needeth : "

> " Behold, it is said in my laws, or forbidden to get in debt to thine enemies (the Gentiles); but, behold, it is not said, at any time, that the Lord should not *take when he please* and *pay as seemeth him good*; wherefore, *as ye are agents*, and ye are on the Lord's errand, and whatsoever ye do according to the will of the Lord *is the Lord's business*, and he has sent you *to provide for his Saints . . .* "

Here's richness. This is from the " Book of Doctrine and Covenants," a book, remember, as sacred in the eyes of a fanatic Mormon as the New Testament is to any zealous Christian. Hear now our brave old witnesses:

Mr. W: " Abel was the name of a colored man in Nauvoo who had received the Priesthood from Joseph. This was an exception to the rule, colored people not being entitled to the blessings of Mormon priesthood (but Joseph and Co. fixed it). Abel, the black priest, at Joseph's command, stole a quantity of lumber, which was needed for coffins, at one time there being great mortality in Nauvoo on account of malaria. A little later Joseph ordered Abel to steal a whole raft of lumber. Abel had scruples about this second order. The first one he had considered all right, since the lumber served to bury the dead. But he was a good Saint, the black priest, and stole the raft all the same. He told me the story himself.

" One day I was ordered to go and lay hands on the sick, in a place up the river some miles from Nauvoo. Elder M. R., now a bishop in Salt Lake, went with me,

We laid our hands on the sick and it seemed to have good effect : they felt better. Not long ago I met Bishop M. R. in the street. Says he, ' Do you remember how we cured the sick near Nauvoo? I cannot understand how we could succeed, since I had been the very same day driving in forty-five head of cattle which the brethren had stolen on the plains.' W. answered :   'Well, *I had not been stealing*, and that, perhaps, explains our success."

Mrs. Pa. : " Vilate Kimball, the apostle's first wife, an honest woman, told many things to her intimate friends. She used to say that her house in Nauvoo was a regular deposit of the 'spoils of the Gentiles.' It was a favorite sport with the Mormons to rob the stores of their enemies, and to 'consecrate' all the goods to the Lord. Mrs. Kimball had in her house innumerable pieces of calico, muslin, etc., generally of the length of fifty yards. ' I know it to be a fact that our people used to go out nights for the purpose of stealing the wash from the lines of the Gentiles in a circuit of twenty miles around Nauvoo,' sister Vilate used to say."

W. W. Phelps, a prominent saint in olden times, " Joseph's Speckled Bird," and for many years " Devil " in the Endowment House, said to an old friend of his in Salt Lake : *"If the Mormons had behaved like other people, they would never have been driven from Illinois and Missouri ; but they stole, robbed and plundered from all their neighbors, and all the time."* (The daughter of Phelps' friend told this little confession to the author.)

Mr. Sh. : " When I came to the church at Nauvoo my first experience was this : The priesthood wanted me to be captain of a band whose task it was to stampede the cattle of the apostates, and to kill them if they offered any resistance. I had given the church all I had — $23,000 — and I declined the honor of being captain of such a band."

Mr. W. : " Bogus Brigham, *alias* Bishop Miller (of Provo), was a big, fleshy, stupid fellow. He had a flat-boat on the Mississippi. He went down the river and stole from a mill a whole boat-full of flour. He has told me this himself."

THE DON JUAN OF NAUVOO.

———

*Don Juan in Seville and in Nauvoo — A Well-Counted
  Hecatomb of Victims — Celestial Assignation Houses —
  The Little Oil Bottle — The Innocent Girl at the Keyhole — Eliza R.; first Spy and then Mistress — Orgies
  in Nauvoo — Abortion and Infanticide.*

———

Yes, "Don Juan"; that's a good name. I remember
to have heard that glorious opera of Mozart at least thirty
times. I remember how I used to be overcome with two
powerful sensations whenever I left the Vienna Opera-
house : one was a strong emotion in my breast, such as
a decent fellow must always feel after having witnessed
the punishment of an unscrupulous libertine ; and second,
any amount of smell of burnt gunpowder in my nostrils,
proceeding from the fireworks which represented pretty
well a middle-sized, old-fashioned, fire-and-brimstone hell
to burn the great sinner in.

Now, Joseph's career and fearful end are, to my heart
and nose, exactly the same over again ; same emotion,
same smell, coming now from the smoking rifles of those
treacherous "Carthage Grays." So let us say "Don
Juan," and introduce Joseph's amorous history as such.

It is now a well established historical fact that the
origin of Mormon polygamy, or "celestial marriage,"
was nothing but the unbounded and ungoverned passion
of the prophet for the other sex. "*Joseph and John D.
Lee were the most libidinous men I ever knew,*" says my
friend Webb, who knew the prophet for eleven years.
"*Joseph was the most licentious and Brigham Young the
most bloodthirsty of men,*" says Mrs. Sarah Pratt, who has
known all these Mormon leaders during almost their
whole career in the church.

In one of my many interviews with the aged, life-long
martyr of polygamy, I said once to her: "I have seen

a statement in a book that Joseph had eighty wives at the time of his death. Is that true?" Mrs. Pratt smiled and said: "He had many more, my dear sir; at least he had seduced many more, and those with whom he had lived without their being sealed to him, were sealed to him after his death, to be among the number of his "queens" in the other world. All those women were divided among his friends after his tragic death, so that they might be "proxy-husbands" to them on earth; while in the celestial kingdom they would, with their offspring, belong to Brother Joseph, the Christ of this dispensation."

Notwithstanding that I had lost, while pursuing my study of Mormon history, a good deal of my original faculty of becoming surprised, it astonished me a little to hear of five scores of ladies entitled to the high distinction of being called "wife of the prophet." But, comparing notes, which I have collected from many witnesses, I cannot but come to the conclusion that Mrs. Pratt has not exaggerated: that Brother Joseph, as a wholesale sealer "for time and all eternity," was the greatest Don Juan of this or any other dispensation.

Mrs. P.: "Everybody knew in Nauvoo that the Partridge girls lived with Joseph a long time before he got his celebrated revelation about celestial marriage, dated July 12, 1843. The Partridge girls were very good-natured. After Joseph's death one was sealed to Brigham and the other to Apostle Amasa Lyman. Joseph's taste was of very large dimensions, he loved them old and young, pretty and homely. He sometimes seduced mothers to keep them quiet about his connection with their daughters. There was an old woman called Durfee. She knew a good deal about the prophet's amorous adventures and, to keep her quiet, he admitted her to the secret blessings of celestial bliss. I don't think that she was ever sealed to him, though it may have been the case after Joseph's death, when the temple was finished. At all events, she boasted here in Salt Lake of having been one of Joseph's wives. Heber C. Kimball and Brigham Young took the lion's share at the division of Joseph's wives after his death. Joseph had a number of lady friends, sealed or not sealed, who permitted him to use their houses as a kind of assignation houses for rendezvous with other women."

Mr. Jo.: " You remember that passage in the Revelations about celestial marriage, where ' the Lord ' says to Joseph : ' and if she be with another man, and I have not appointed unto her *by the holy anointing,* she hath committed adultery.' Well, an old Mormon, who had been very intimate with Joseph in Nauvoo, assured me that the prophet always carried a small bottle with *holy oil* about his person, so that he might ' anoint ' at a moment's notice any woman to be a queen in Heaven. A curious little anecdote was told me by a gentleman who had it direct from that pure man of God, Heber C. Kimball. Brigham's *alter ego* said as follows : ' I sat once with Joseph in his office in the Mansion House. He looked out of the window and saw weeding in a garden a young married woman whom we both knew. He told me to go to her and request her to come to him, and he would have her sealed to himself *this very moment.* I went and told the woman to come to Brother Joseph. She ran to the house to comb her hair and ' fix up ' generally, and then followed me to the prophet. I performed the sealing ceremony, and retired.' "

Mr. J. W. C.: " Joseph knew himself well. He said to one of his intimate friends, ' If the Lord had not taken me in hand, I would have become the greatest w——— of the world.' And to another friend he said : ' Whenever I see a pretty woman, I have to pray for grace.'

Mrs. P.: " Joseph did not content himself with his *spiritual* brides, who surrendered themselves to him 'for Christ's sake.' There lived on the Mississippi, near the steamboat landing, a certain young woman, a Mrs. White, very pretty and always very fashionably dressed. She was in the habit of being very hospitable to the captains of the steamboats . . . Joseph was one of her customers and used to contribute to the expenses of her establishment."

Mr. Wa.: "I used to employ a poor Mormon woman for domestic sewing. She had been a fanatic Mormon in

her time, but had cooled down considerably in consequence
of her experience in the direction of celestial marriage.
Her husband had taken 'another woman' and entirely
neglected her, and that is what made her shaky in the
faith. She once felt very dull, and in this mood she told
me the following little story. 'When in Nauvoo, I was a
very young girl, and there I happened to be witness of an
event that gave me the first doubt about Joseph the prophet. I was servant in the house of a Mr. Ford, a merchant who had a store in Nauvoo. He was wont to go by
steamer to St. Louis, to make purchases. Whenever Mr.
Ford was absent from his house, the prophet used to call
on Mrs. Ford. He would come, chat with her awhile, and
then they would retire to the lady's chamber. For a while
I saw nothing in this, being a very young, innocent girl,
and very strong in the faith. But some way or other suspicion arose in my mind. So when Joseph called again
—Mr. Ford had gone to St. Louis the day before—I could
not master my curiosity any more. I followed the pair
stealthily, and putting my eye to the keyhole I saw ————
————.' Here the poor woman gave me a description of
a scene which was surely calculated to shake even the most
fanatic faith. But this is not all. She said: 'Whenever Mr. Ford came home from St. Louis, he used to com-
plain about business: 'I cannot understand it,' he used
to say, 'when I am here money comes in all the time, and
when I am away not a red cent gets into the house.'
Now the explanation is very simple. Whenever Joseph
had *prayed* with Mrs. Ford, she used to give him all the
money in the till, to the last cent. Since that time I do
ask myself sometimes, whether Joseph was really the right
kind of a prophet.''*

The women in Nauvoo considered it a high honor to
receive their celestial blessings from Joseph himself. He
was prophet, seer and revelator, lieutenant general, mayor;
he was not only the Lord's mouthpiece, but *might be*
President of the United States. At any rate, he was,

---

*This story has been told the author by a perfectly reliable gentle-
man, a business man of high and long standing in Salt Lake.

without having the title, the autocrat, the emperor of the rapidly growing Mormon empire. Is it any wonder that those poor souls should feel greatly elated whenever the anointed of the Lord deigned to accept their all?

Mr. W. : "Joseph's dissolute life began already in the first times of the church, in Kirtland. He was sealed there secretly to Fanny Alger. Emma was furious, and drove the girl, who was unable to conceal the consequences of her celestial relation with the prophet, out of her house."

Mrs. D. : "A Mrs. Granger proved a very reliable and useful friend to the prophet. He was once at her house, in bed, and not alone. The bed had old-fashioned curtains. All at once Sister Emma, the prophet's wife, came in, and said excitedly to Mrs. Granger: 'Is Brother Joseph here?' 'No,' said Mrs. Granger, 'he has just been in, but went out again,' getting Sister Emma out of the house as hurriedly as possible. Joseph used to tell his intimate friends how dreadfully he had felt in that bed, expecting every moment that his wife might look behind the curtains."

Mrs. J.: "Eliza Partridge, one of the many girls sealed to the prophet, used to sew in Emma's room. Once, while Joseph was absent, Emma got to fighting with Eliza and threw her down the stairs. 'That finished my sewing there,' Eliza used to say."

"In Kirtland, Joseph was once caught in a —— house with one of the sisters. This —— house might be called the humble birthplace of the revelation on celestial marriage."

Mr. IV.: "Joseph kept eight girls in his house, calling them his 'daughters.' Emma threatened that she would leave the house, and Joseph told her, 'All right, you can go.' She went, but when Joseph reflected that such a scandal would hurt his prophetic dignity, he followed his wife and brought her back. But the eight 'daughters' had to leave the house."

"Miss" Eliza R. Snow, one of the most curious figures in the history of Mormondom, played an important part in the events relating to celestial hymenology. She is the great poetess (and such a poetess!), and is a

sort of high priestess generally of Mormonism. She
used to anoint the sisters in the Endowment house and to
play the part of Eve in the celestial drama enacted there.
She is now over eighty years old, yet doing the same
thing in the Logan temple in Utah. Sister Eliza became
the church's "elect lady" when "the Lord" became
thoroughly incensed with Sister Emma for her con-
tumacy. She is the very prototype of what is called
"female roosters" in Zion, always ready to enslave and
drag men and women into polygamy. She was one of
the first (willing) victims of Joseph in Nauvoo. She
used to be much at the prophet's house and "Sister
Emma" treated her as a confidential friend. Very much
interested about Joseph's errands, Emma used to send
Eliza after him as a spy. Joseph found it out and, to
win over the gifted (!) young poetess, he made her one of
his celestial brides. There is scarcely a Mormon unac-
quainted with the fact that Sister Emma, on the other
side, soon found out the little compromise arranged
between Joseph and Eliza. Feeling outraged as a wife
and betrayed as a friend, Emma is currently reported as
having had recourse to a vulgar broomstick as an instrument of revenge : and the harsh treatment received at
Emma's hands is said to have destroyed Eliza's hopes of
becoming the mother of a prophet's son. So far one of
my best informed witnesses. Her story becomes corroborated by another reliable source. Elder Bullock, who
was church historian at that time, used to tell the following little tale : " Joseph said on the morning of the first
parade of the Nauvoo Legion ·This is the proudest day
of my life.' Many people believed that this outburst
of pride was entirely of a military character. But I and
some other intimate friends of the prophet knew very well
that he was proud of another thing, not of a parade, but
of a conquest, the conquest of Eliza."

Mr. W. : "There were many small rooms, with
beds, in the temple in Nauvoo. They turned the house
of the Lord into a house of prostitution. The wife of
Amasa Lyman, apostle and apostate, used to say that they
had many little bedrooms in the temple, and that the

newly-sealed couples used to retire to those rooms with provisions for two or three days.''

Mr. S.: ''Amasa Lyman, the apostle, who later became a 'vile apostate,' told me that Joseph, Brigham Young, and other apostles used to dance in the Endowment house with the Lord's 'hand-maids,' their spiritual wives. Those dances were performed in Adamic costume; and a fiddler was 'ordained and set apart' for the purpose. I know this to be an absolute fact; it has been confirmed to me by other well-informed persons. That fiddler went with a party of Mormons to California, San Bernardino County, and remained there.''

It seems that the ''souvenir'' of the orgies in Nauvoo was kept alive by some of the men who had been initiated into the jolly secrets of the innermost ring of the prophet's friends, of both sexes. Elder Thomas Margetts, while in England, established, in Southampton, a ''mock endowment house,'' whose walls were ornamented by the most obscene of pictures, and where orgies were performed at least the equals in brutality to those celebrated in Nauvoo. I know this to be a *positive fact.* It was attested to me by two former elders of the church who held positions of influence in the ''conferences.'' One of them was present at the church trial of the offenders. Margetts was later killed on the plains by Elder Porter Rockwell, whose sacramental duty consisted in blowing out the brains of all suspected or guilty persons.

Mrs. P.: ''You hear often that Joseph had no polygamous offspring. The reason of this is very simple. *Abortion was practiced on a large scale in Nauvoo.* Dr. John C. Bennett, the evil genius of Joseph, brought this abomination into a scientific system. He showed to my husband and me the instruments with which he used to '*operate for Joseph.*' There was a house in Nauvoo, 'right across the flat,' about a mile and a-half from the town, a kind of hospital. They sent the women there, when they showed signs of celestial consequences. Abortion was practiced regularly in this house.''

Mrs. H.: ''Many little bodies of new-born children floated down the Mississippi.''

May 21, 1886, I had a fresh interview with Mrs. Sarah M. Pratt, who had the kindness to give me the following testimony additional to the information given by her in our interviews in the spring of 1885. "I want you to have all my statements correct in your book," said the noble lady, "and put my name to them; I want the truth, the full truth, to be known, and to bear the responsibility of it.

"I have told you that the prophet Joseph used to frequent houses of ill-fame. Mrs. White, a very pretty and attractive woman, once confessed to me that she made a business of it to be hospitable to the captains of the Mississippi steamboats. She told me that Joseph had made her acquaintance very soon after his arrival in Nauvoo, and that he had visited her dozens of times. My husband (Orson Pratt) could not be induced to believe such things of his prophet. Seeing his obstinate incredulity, Mrs. White proposed to Mr. Pratt and myself to put us in a position where we could observe what was going on between herself and Joseph the prophet. We, however, declined this proposition. You have made a mistake in the table of contents of your book in calling this woman ' Mrs. Harris.' Mrs. Harris was a married lady, a very great friend of mine. When Joseph had made his dastardly attempt on me, I went to Mrs. Harris to unbosom my grief to her. To my utter astonishment, she said, laughing heartily: ' How foolish you are! I don't see anything so horrible in it. Why, I AM HIS MISTRESS SINCE FOUR YEARS!'

"Next door to my house was a house of bad reputation. One single woman lived there, not very attractive. She used to be visited by people from Carthage whenever they came to Nauvoo. Joseph used to come on horseback, ride up to the house and tie his horse to a tree, many of which stood before the house. Then he would enter the house of the woman from the back. I have seen him do this repeatedly.

"Joseph Smith, the son of the prophet, and president of the re-organized Mormon church, paid me a visit, and I had a long talk with him. I saw that he was not inclined to believe the truth about his father, so I said to him: 'You pretend to have revelations from the Lord. Why don't you ask the Lord to tell you *what kind of a man your father really was?*' He answered: 'If my father had so many connections with women, where is the progeny?' I said to him: 'Your father had mostly intercourse with married women, and as to single ones, Dr. Bennett was always on hand, when anything happened.'

"It was in this way that I became acquainted with Dr. John C. Bennett. When my husband went to England as a missionary, he got the promise from Joseph that I should receive provisions from the tithing-house. Shortly afterward Joseph made his propositions to me and they enraged me so that I refused to accept any help from the tithing house or from the bishop. Having been always very clever and very busy with my needle, I began to take in sewing for the support of myself and children, and succeeded soon in making myself independent. When Bennett came to Nauvoo Joseph brought him to my house, stating that Bennett wanted some sewing done, and that I should do it for the doctor. I assented and Bennett gave me a great deal of work to do. He knew that Joseph had his plans set on me; Joseph made no secret of them before Bennett, and went so far in his impudence as to make propositions to me in the presence of Bennett, his bosom friend. Bennett, who was of a sarcastic turn of mind, used to come and tell me about Joseph to tease and irritate me. One day they came both, Joseph and Bennett, on horseback to my house. Bennett dismounted, Joseph remained outside. Bennett wanted me to return to him a book I had borrowed from him. It was a so-called doctor-book. I had a rapidly growing little family and wanted to inform myself about certain matters in regard to babies, etc.,—this explains my having borrowed that book. While giving Bennett his book, I observed that he held something in the left sleeve of his coat. Bennett smiled and said: "*Oh, a little job for Joseph, one of his women is in trouble.*" Saying this, he took the thing out of his left sleeve. It was a pretty long instrument of a kind I had never seen before. It seemed to be of steel and was crooked at one end. I heard afterwards that the operation had been performed; that the *woman* was very sick, and that Joseph was very much afraid that she might die, but she recovered.

" Bennett was the most intimate friend of Joseph for a time. He boarded with the prophet. He told me once that Joseph had been talking with him about his troubles with Emma, his wife. ' He asked me,' said Bennett, smilingly, ' what he should do to get out of the trouble ? ' I said, ' this is very simple. GET A REVELATION that polygamy is right, and all your troubles will be at an end.'

" The only ' wives ' of Joseph that lived in the Mansion House were the Partridge girls. This is explained by the fact that they were the servants in the hotel kept by the prophet. But when Emma found out that Joseph went to their room, they had to leave the house.

" I remember Emma's trip to St Louis. I begged her to buy for me a piece of black silk there.

" You should bear in mind that Joseph did not think of a marriage or sealing ceremony for many years. He used to state to his intended victims, as he did to me: ' *God does not care if we have a good time, if only other people do not know it.*' He only introduced a marriage ceremony when he had found out that he could not get certain women without it. I think Louisa Beeman was the first case of this kind. If any woman, like me, opposed his wishes, he used to say : ' Be silent, or I shall ruin your character. My character must be sustained in the interest of the church.' When he had assailed me and saw that he could not seal my lips, he sent word to me that he would *work my salvation*, if I kept silent. I sent back that I would talk as much as I pleased and as much as I knew to be the truth, and as to my salvation, I would try and take care of that myself.

" In his endeavors to ruin my character Joseph went so far as to publish an extra-sheet containing affidavits against my reputation. When this sheet was brought to me I discovered to my astonishment the names of two people on it, man and wife, with whom I had boarded for a certain time. I never thought much of the man, but the woman was an honest person and I knew that she must have been *forced* to do such a thing against me. So I went to their house; the man left the house hurriedly when he saw me coming. I found the wife and said to her rather excitedly: 'What does it all mean?' She began to sob. 'It is not my fault,' said she. 'Hyrum Smith came to our house, with the affidavits all written out, and forced us to sign them. '*Joseph and the church must be saved*,' said he. We saw that resistance was useless, they would have ruined us; so we signed the papers.' "

Let us introduce now a statement as to the reliability of Mrs. Pratt. She is well known in Salt Lake City and all over Utah as possessing all the virtues of an excellent wife and mother; but outsiders may wish to know of Mrs. Pratt's standing in this community, and I take pleasure in giving a testimonial:

SALT LAKE CITY, May 1886.

We, the undersigned, cordially bear witness to the excellent reputation of Mrs. Sarah M. Pratt. We feel well assured that Mrs. Pratt is a lady whose statements are absolutely to be depended upon. Entire frankness and a high sense of honor and truth are regarded in this community, where she has dwelt since 1847, as her ruling characteristics.

CHARLES S. ZANE,
Chief Justice Utah Territory.

ARTHUR L. THOMAS,
Secretary Utah Territory.

REV. J. W. JACKSON,
U. S. A. Chaplain, Fort Douglas.

I could very readily augment this testimonial with many others were it deemed worth while.

THE NAUVOO PANDEMONIUM.

*Don Juan at the Hight of His Wickedness — Poor
Emma ! — Rushton Describes a Family Scene with
Blows and Sobs—Ben Winchester's Tale—Swapping
Wives — A Wife for Cat-fish — The Wives of the
Twelve.*

The way of the transgressor is, as a rule, not only
hard, but pretty rapid, too. Look at the celebrated
ancestors of our prophet, the emperors Caligula and
Nero; look at his very prototype, John of Leyden, and
other crowned debauchees, rushing from passion to
frenzy, from frenzy to raving madness. The gods blind
whom they want to destroy. As to King Joseph and his
capital, Nauvoo, it may be truly said that there never was,
and—let us trust—never will be in any community of this
"sweet home" loving, pure-principled republic another
edition of such a whirlpool of secret vice,* of such a demo-
niac bacchanal, including as dancers all the prominent men
and even many "ladies" of a city. Let it be remembered forever that the men who know all the facts
published by me, and more, deny them daily as "infamous
slanders," and that these same men are the leaders of
this abomination called a "church" by its illiterate
dupes only and by the over-cultivated ladies and gentlemen of the East.

Joseph Smith was shrewd enough to have a few *honest*
men around him whom he placed in responsible positions,
who filled them with fidelity and self-sacrifice, being at
the same time in a great measure ignorant of the duplicity
and wickedness of the impostor. None were more

---

* "What would it have done for us if they had known that *many*
of us had more than one wife when we lived in Illinois? They
would have broken us up, doubtless, worse than they did....but we
shall come to a point where we shall have all the wives and they will
have none."—Orson Hyde's sermon in 1854, *Journal of Discourses*,
Vol. II., p. 83.

faithful or truthful than Elder Richard Rushton, the
trusty steward employed by Joseph in the Mansion
House in Nauvoo. Rushton was a good, honest man
of fine instincts, and had served faithfully for some
years, holding that position when the bodies of Joseph
and Hyrum were brought to Nauvoo, and he received
them. It was his duty to lock up, every night, most
of the rooms, especially the pantry, storeroom, larder,
etc., and then to give the keys to "Sister Emma." She
would, on retiring, place the bunch of keys in a large
pocket that was nailed on the wall at the head of her
bed. About 4 o'clock every morning Brother Rushton
would tap at the bedroom door in order to receive the
keys and open the hotel. Emma on hearing the raps
would say, " Come in, Brother Rushton," and would hand
him the keys from the pocket, and give such orders as
were needed.

It so " came to pass " once upon a time, that the
groceries and other provisions necessary for the use of the
hotel were nearly exhausted, and a famine seemed pending
in the larder. Fortunately, however, Joseph sold a fine,
black horse which had been presented to him, for three
hundred and fifty dollars or so, and also a city lot or two,
for about four hundred dollars. With the sales of the
horse and land, and a little cash on hand, he mustered
up about nine hundred dollars, which he cheerfully
placed in Emma's hands, saying: "We are out of provisions; take this and go down to St. Louis, and buy
what is needed. Capt. Dan Jones will fire up the 'Maid
of Iowa' (a little steamboat always ready for church use)
and take you down." Emma started for St. Louis. The
going, purchasing and return occupied about a week.
At night, after the departure of the "elect lady," the
steward gave the keys to the prophet, and in the morning
he as usual stepped lightly and rapped at the door of the
bed-room. A voice, strange to his ear, yet of feminine
softness, rather startled him in response with the words
"Come in." He entered timidly, when lo and behold ! there lay in Emma's bed and stead the beautiful
and attractive young wife of Elder Edward Blossom, a

high councilor of Zion, (afterwards exalted to the apostle-ship by Brigham Young). With a pair of laughing, glistening eyes and with a smile of happy sweetness, she spoke in soft and pleading accents : "*I suppose, Brother Rushton, I shall have to be Sister Emma to you this morning,*" as she gracefully handed the keys to him. Astonished and blushing, the faithful steward left the room to resume his duties, leaving the adulterous prophet and his charmer to themselves. The same thing was repeated each morning during the week Emma was away purchasing supplies for the prophet's hotel.

In relating this occurrence to another of my most precise and valuable witnesses, Brother Rushton, though no seeker after effect, added the following picturesque details : "Emma used to keep the keys of the hotel in a richly ornamented wallet given to her by some well-to-do English friends. When Joseph saw how dumbfounded I was he sat up in his red flannel night robe and said in a hasty, commanding tone : '*That's all right, Brother Rushton,*' making a movement with his outstretched right hand towards me. The prophet's gesture and tone gave me to understand that I was to go and keep my mouth shut.'"

"One afternoon," said Mr. Rushton, the steward, "after the hurry of the dinner work was over, I was sitting in my little office, when looking through my window, I saw the Prophet Joseph, followed by the two Partridge girls, coming from the back part of the lot and enter, all three, the little log cabin which had been the first home, in Nauvoo, of the prophet before the " Mansion " was built. A minute or so afterwards Sister Emma came to my office door and asked me : ' Did you see Brother Joseph and the two Partridge girls go into the cabin?' Mr. Rushton didn't like to split on the prophet, and yet didn't like to tell a lie ; and at last he replied hesitatingly : "Well—I think — perhaps — well—I may have seen them." "I'll just put on my sun-bonnet and go and see what they are about," replied she, and stepped over. A very short time after her entry she appeared at the door of the cabin, being pushed out rudely, and came to the office door crying bitterly. "Oh Brother Rushton," she said in broken sobs, "I went into the cabin, I found those two girls with my husband, and Joseph jumped up in a rage when he saw that I had surprised them and struck me a horrid blow;" at the same time she showed me the mark of the blow on her cheek. She then dropped fainting on a chair, weeping and uttering words of despair. A few minutes afterward Joseph entered and going up to Emma, said in a meek, repentant manner, "Oh, my dear Emma, I am so sorry I struck you. I did it in a passion; you must forgive me. I did it without a thought, or I wouldn't have done it. Forgive me. But you shouldn't be running after me, watching me, and prying at my actions." He apologized, and kissed Emma, and apologized again, and then finally she arose and they went into the parlor together apparently reconciled."

Another characteristic anecdote connected yet with the Kirtland times of the "church," was related to me by an ex-elder of perfect reliability. I insert it here, because it shows what kind of a woman-eater this prophet had been in early days already. A large, influential "branch of the church" existed in Philadelphia, over which Ben Winchester successfully presided. Joe visited that church occasionally and enjoyed the associations much. On one occasion, it having been announced that the prophet was to preach, he sat on the platform by the side of his faithful presiding elder while awaiting the time to open services. Now and then as some handsome young woman came up the aisle and took a seat, Joe would turn to Elder Winchester and ask, "Who is that beautiful lady?" or, "Who is that fine, lovely creature?" On being told, "that is Miss So-and-so," or, "Mrs. So-and-so," or, "Sister So-and-so," he did not at all disguise his wishes; he made no "bones" of it; but would say in reply, "I'd just like talk to her alone for a while," or, "I would like her for a companion for a night," and other expressions too plain and vulgar for me to write. [I can give names if needed.]

After the polygamy doctrine was secretly whispered

about among the chosen few in Nauvoo, there were great
surmisings on the part of those who desired to know the
"mysteries of the kingdom." Many imperfect theories
were ventilated, and false conclusions arrived at. Joe had
formulated no plan, and did not, as yet, have any rules
whereby to direct his intimate friends, much less the common saints who were not in the ring. Hence, having no
"law," every man and woman was a law to himself or
herself, and they went on their own course. In a small
house in Nauvoo, consisting only of two rooms, dwelt two
men and their wives. Each man and wife occupied one
room. These couples having got some inkling of the new
order of things, came to the conclusion that they might as
well live up to their privileges. They accordingly exchanged partners, and lived in this condition for several
weeks, when former relations were resumed. Such incidents, with variations, were by no means uncommon.
(My friend Webb says there was a great deal of swapping
and exchanging done in Nauvoo as to wives. Old Cooks
sold his wife for a load of catfish, and from that time on
he was always called "Catfish Cooks.") Another party
was anxious for a similar exchange, and the little story
proves that the sisters were sometimes as desirous for it as
the brethren. Brother Rushton and his wife were at last
reluctantly compelled to know what was going on among
the saints in Nauvoo, but they repelled all attempts of
either male or female to draw them into the new practices.
Brother Blossom, a high priest and member of the high
council of that stake of Zion, had his eyes upon and
coveted Mrs. Rushton, his neighbor's wife; the high
priest's wife had her own upon Brother Rushton, and this
nice pair sought an exchange with Rushton and wife.
Sister Blossom approached Brother R. with her sweetest
smiles, telling him that B. had sent her to arrange with
him that he (R.) should have her as a wife, and B. should
have Sister R. for his wife, and that mutual arrangement
could and should be made to that effect; she and B.
were perfectly willing to thus exchange, if R. and wife
were, and that it was according to the "law and will of
the Lord." Knowing the antipathy of Mrs. R. to such

proposals, R. told Mrs. B. *to ask his wife about it*, and whatever she agreed to, he would do. The mission was in vain; the good lady refused to accede to their vile proposal. On a future occasion the high priest sent his wife to Mrs. R. with a basket of fresh sweet potatoes as a present, and renewed the request for an exchange of partners. The good lady became indignant at the persistency of the pair, and ordered her to take the basket out of her sight. " Does he think," she said, " he can bribe me with a basket of potatoes ?"

At another time, a rather interesting old maid, sister of one of the dignitaries of the church, came a distance of some sixty miles to see Brother R., and begged him piteously to take her as a plural wife —she had a revelation that he was to be her husband "right now." On his positive refusal, she left him in tears, prostrate with disappointment.

There were in Nauvoo, when Joseph was in his glory as "the greatest prophet that ever lived," a young merchant and his wife whom he dearly loved. She bore to him several children, but became fascinated with Joe and with his claims to "exalt " any woman who would yield to his wishes and become his "wife." The husband was sent on a mission, and during his absence Joseph "gathered" the wife to his embraces, and she was " sealed " one of his harem. After Joe's "martyrdom," she became the wife of Brigham, as a *proxy wife* for Joe, that any posterity which might ensue should be *Joe's in heaven.* One child, a daughter, was the result of this relation, but the young lady was always known by the name of Young, never by name of Smith, robbing Brother Joseph of his earthly glory, at least. This same wife of three men is often sent as a representative of the women of Utah to the women's conventions abroad in America, and to the lobbies of Congress. If she truly represents Utah women, the reader may guess the character of those represented ; and if these are not such as she represents, then Utah women are not represented — yet she is their choice. (Lee says, in his " Confession," of this lady : " H. B. Jacobs accompanied me as a fellow companion.

Jacobs was bragging about his wife and two children — what a true, virtuous, lovely woman she was. He almost worshiped her; but little did he think that in his absence she was sealed to the prophet Joseph, and was his wife." p. 132.)

Joseph Smith finally demanded the wives of *all* the twelve apostles that were at home then in Nauvoo. And why not? Were the "apostles" not his slaves, his property, including all they had? Woman in Mormondom has been, from the beginning a chattel, and man, a slave. That Joseph *did* demand and obtain the wives of the twelve, is proved beyond doubt by irrefutable testimony. But there is further proof from a very high authority. Jedediah Grant, Brigham's counselor, and soul of the horrible "Reformation" which culminated in the Mountain Meadows Massacre, said in one of his harangues which were as bloody as they were filthy: *"Do you think that the prophet Joseph wanted the wives of the Twelve that he asked for, merely to gratify himself? No; he did it to try the brethren. But if President Young wants my wives, or any of them, he can have them,"* etc. (He didn't consult his "wives"—oh, no; they are only like cattle, to be given away if desired. Is the Mormon woman equal to the man, according to that?) That was said publicly before thousands of hearers, men and women. Mormonism has produced the most abject slavery ever witnessed in the history of the world. Hear "Jeddy" Grant again:

"What would a man of God say, who felt right, when Joseph asked him for his money?' He would say: 'Yes; and I wish I had more to build up the kingdom of God.' Or if he came and said: 'I want your wife!' 'Oh, yes,' he would say; '*there she is.* There are plenty more.' " *

And Orson Pratt, another man of God, follows in the same strain:

"Consecrate everything to the Lord that you have — flocks and herds, gold and silver, wearing apparel, watches, jewelry, your wives and children — of course. The wives have given themselves to their

---

* Journal of Discourses, the official collection of Mormon sermons, vol. i., p. 14.

husband, and he has to consecrate them. They are the Lord's [*id est*, His chosen prophet's.—*IV.*] He has only *lent* them to us." *

Mrs. Leonora Taylor, first and legal wife of the present head of the church, and aunt of George Q. Cannon, told ladies who still reside in this city, that *all* the wives of the twelve were, in fact, consecrated to the Lord, that is, to his servant, Joseph; and that Joseph's demands, and her husband's soft compliance so exasperated her as to cause her 'the loss of a finger and of a baby.' The latter she lost by a premature delivery, being at the time in a delicate condition, and in her fury for help, having thrust her clenched fist through a window-pane, lost one of her fingers. Her honor was saved from the attack of Don Juan. Mrs. Taylor was mistaken, however, in her general statement, which is just a little too sweeping. She, no doubt, was lied to by John Taylor himself, or by some one else 'in authority,' for the purpose of overcoming her wifely scruples. Besides herself, there were two others, who were exceptions in this atrocious case. Vilate Kimball, the first wife of Heber C. Kimball, later the righthand-man and clown of King Brigham, and one of the most disgusting types of Mormon history—Vilate was a good, pure woman, she was better than her 'religion,' though a slave to it in a manner. She loved her husband, and he, not yet developed as the brute he later became, loved her, hence a reluctance to comply with the Lord's demand that Vilate should be consecrated like the moveable property of the other 'Apostles.' Still, Joseph was to them a prophet, and therefore the act might be right in him, though simply damnable in any other man. They thought the command of the Lord must be obeyed in some way, and a 'proxy' way suggested itself to their minds. They had a young daughter only getting out of girlhood, and the father apologizing to the prophet for his wife's reluctance to comply with his desires, stating, however, that the act must be right or it would not be counselled—the abject slave of a father asked Joe *if his daughter wouldn't do as well as his wife.* Joe replied that she would do just as

---

* Journal of Discourses, vol. i., p. 98.

well, and *the Lord would accept her instead.* The half-ripe bud of womanhood was delivered over to the prophet. Helen Mar Whitney—this is her name now—still lives and belongs to that undefinable class of wrinkled old women, only to be found in Mormonism, who pride themselves in their shame, in speeches and in print.   She writes pamphlets on the divinity of polygamy!   Other 'plurals' do the same.   It is the saddest, the most disheartening kind of literature I have ever seen in any country.   It makes me do desperate things.   It makes me prefer the worst of mother-in-laws to such 'ladies,' and gives me a wonderfully favorable idea of the odalisques of those old bearded Turks—they are pretty and they don't write, you see.

The other intended victim, who escaped the prophet's clutches was high-spirited Mrs. Sarah M. Pratt.   She stoutly repelled his repeated approaches, though she had to pay the penalty for refusing to 'consecrate' her honor. She has been ever since hated and slandered by the Mormon leaders.   Joe threatened her, if she divulged to her husband or anyone else what he had proposed; adding "if you do, I will ruin your character.   I will deny everything, and the Church will believe me and not you.   My standing in the Church must be upheld at any cost and sacrifice."   He kept his word.   He tried to starve her and her children; he used all his influence against her; even leading mob demonstrations for that purpose, and abusing her from the pulpit.   He caused evil reports to be circulated about her and tried to make her an object of detestation as an apostate   Brigham Young took up Joseph's course in this, as he did in everything else, and tried to rob her of her modest property in Salt Lake City, the support of herself and a family of small children, mostly sons, whom she has reared to man's estate and who would do honor to any community.   Her husband, Orson Pratt, who became, under the influence of polygamy, as coarsely selfish as any other "polyg," went so far in his abject slavery, as to join Prophet Brigham in his attempt to defraud the victim, his own wife and the mother of his children.   It was my earliest interview with Mrs. Pratt, in January, 1885, which gave me the first insight into the pernicious working of a system invented by impostors and carried out by outlaws all the way through.

———— • • ————

EMMA, THE PROPHET'S WIFE.

Old Hickory Hale—Emma Loves the "Peeper"—King and Pope—Wretched but Proud—"All Guesswork"— Emma Wants to Expose the Humbug—A Crushing Doc- ument—"Peeper" Joseph—The White Dog Sacrificed— Joseph a Crocodile—That old White Hat—The Bleeding Ghost—The Prophet of the Lord Becomes a Methodist —Emma Finds out What "Spiritual" Means.

Yes, don't doubt it a moment; I *have* looked out for a bright point in Joseph's life and would have been very happy in finding it. I am naturally given to admiration of all that is good and noble in human nature. I have learnt, besides—I am on the wrong side of forty—that man is a curious composite of good and bad, and that a little good goes far in making up for a great amount of bad. Thackeray is right. Each of us has his "skeleton in the closet." Why should I rattle with the bones in my neighbor's cellar, lest somebody might come and open the door of my own well-guarded closet?

But the case of our prophet is different. There is nothing *but* skeletons. His house is full of them, and so is his city. Rattling becomes a public duty. The pro- prietor of this vast anatomical museum claims to be the founder of a new religion, the best religion of all, the restorer of truth and moral purity all over the wide world. Don't you think I am justified in rattling?

No, I could not find a bright point, an extenuating cir- cumstance, in the whole life of the great impostor. It is lie and crime all through. Just think of the multitude of excellent people, virtuous, devout women and good men,

who have staked their all in this life upon the prophetship
of " Joseph Smith, Junior"!   Why, Joe would have been
the captain of a pirate-ship or a slave-dealer as soon as a
prophet.   There is not even a beam of light in those days
that are such happy ones for purer minds—the days of
wooing and early wedlock. He likes old Hale's daughter,
but the first thing he does is to pervert the moral sense of
the honest farmer's darling and make her an accomplice
of his fraud.   The proud, intelligent young wife becomes
likewise an impostor; he crushes her conscience, and it
appears a crushed one even on her death bed, when she
declared that Joseph had never been in polygamy.   She
had learned from him to lie to further her ends. But what
he could not crush in her were the wife and mother.   He
tried hard to make an Eliza R. Snow of her, a harem-
queen.   He did not succeed.   He had to cow before this
firm wife and proud mother.   In this she remained old
Hale's child, even when threatened with destruction by
that climax of silly impudence and impious balderdash,
the " revelation on celestial marriage."   You might even
construe that death-bed lie of hers as the outcome of her
pride, her firmness and her love for her family, which she
wanted to appear pure and decent before the world.
Though tainted with her husband's fraud, the prophet's
wife shines out from Mormon History as a great, sympa-
thetic figure.

Emma was the bright, handsome, black-eyed daughter
of a sturdy, honest, humbug-hating Pennsylvania farmer,
Isaac Hale.   His character may be fairly judged by a letter which he wrote in 1834 about his son-in-law and the
Gold Bible; the reader finds this remarkable document,
among others, at the end of Part I., of this volume.

When Emma fell in love with young Joe, he was a
shiftless vagabond, swindling money-digger and fortune-
teller, who got his living, as he called it himself, by " glass-
looking."   This was not the kind of son-in-law fancied
by old Hickory Hale.   Oh, no!   He would have liked
a steady-going, hardworking farmer, with 320 or at least
100 acres of good land, fine horses, cows, good house,
barn and stables, a family Bible and good fences.   Seven

years after Smith's elopement with the old man's darling,
Emma, the wound was yet smarting; you feel it in every
line of that letter of 1834. But Emma fell in love with
the money-digger all the same. How do you explain it?
Why, Emma was a country girl after all. Joe must have
had a certain mysterious charm for her, with his secret
" looking " powers, his wonderful stone and that *old white
hat* filled with dark secrets. She didn't believe in it altogether, but still there was something out-of-the-way in it,
it was more interesting than that absurd talk about cows
and bulls, corn and barley, oxen and sheep. Father
wouldn't hear of her taking " that slouching, shiftless fel-
ler from York State," so she ran away with him. A near
relative of hers, a Mr. Hiel Lewis, says about that elopement and its effect in old Isaac Hale's house: " The Hale
family was greatly exasperated, and perhaps it would not
have been safe for Smith to have shown himself at his
father-in-law's house. Emma was or had been the idol or
favorite of the family, and they all still felt a strong
attachment for her, and the permission to return and reconciliation was effected and accomplished by her and perhaps her sister, Mrs. Wasson, who lived near Bainbridge,
N. Y. The permission for Smith to return all came from
the other side, not from Mr. Isaac Hale or his family in
Harmony, Pa." *

Later on in married life Emma found out fully, no
doubt, that Joseph was a wretched impostor. But what
could she do, even if the blood of honest old Hale did
rebel in her veins against the continual negation of all
honor and truth in her husband's life and actions? Was
she not his wife, the mother of his children? And then,
(" don't you forget it ") there was a good deal of
womanly satisfaction in this part, too. Joseph was a
daring brigand, and woman has always admired and
loved and will always admire and love a daring brigand.
I have seen that in Sicily, where beautiful girls told me

*I quote from a letter of this old gentleman, most kindly furnished
to me by my learned friend, James T. Cobb, Esq., who has very great
merits in investigating the earliest history of Mormonism. The letter
is dated Amboy, Lee Co., Ill., Sept. 11, 1879.

with flaming eyes of the heroic deeds of the "*Mafiosi.*"
Smith became the Lord's friend and mouthpiece, a
prophet, soon after his marriage ; in time the founder of
cities and temples, a general and mayor, a leader of the
people, a ruler of thousands of votes, flattered and
cajoled by demagogues of all parties ; his role was important
tant and to a certain degree picturesque, imposing and
brilliant. All that other men have to toil for was showered
upon him, fat living, landed property, money, jewelry,
good houses, fine horses, titles, honors, the admiration
and submission of thousands. Yes, he was a king, that
blue-eyed, wandering "peeper" and money-digger of
yore, the only king in America, forsooth ! A king and a
pope in one !

Was it not nice to ride out with him, the prophet and
general, in a fine carriage, or dash with him on horseback
over the prairie, or shine on a charger at the parade of
the *Nauvoo Legion ?* Was it not fine to be the focus of
general admiration, to be the first lady of the kingdom,
yea, the queen, to have everybody greet and bow to the
"elect lady" of the church?

And Emma played her part well. Let our witnesses
take the stand : "She was tall, dark, dignified and very
ladylike," says one of them who knew her intimately;
"she was rather above the average for talent and would
have passed for a lady anywhere. Her education had
not been a careful one ; she had attended very indifferent
schools, but she had any amount of good, sound sense,
and knew how to use everything to the best advantage.
She loved Joseph very much, and felt most wretched over
his oft-recurring *trespasses* (see revelation of July 12,
1843 and others), but she was too proud to talk about her
grief."

"Emma was very proud," says Mrs. P.; "pride was
one of her chief characteristics. She gave me to understand
stand that she would like to know whether Joseph had
any relations with other women, and I saw how unhappy
she felt through her well-founded jealousy ; but she
struggled hard to conceal the real state of her feelings,
and never showed it to her children.

"She was very much attached to her family; this was her chief thought and care. She was capable of talking about everything, but in those times all the talk turned about Mormonism," says another cotemporary of the "elect lady." The same witness affirms that Emma was squint-eyed. But this last I prefer not to believe. Such things are never true. "Her figure was very stately and after Joseph's violent death, when she had overcome the first shock, she looked rather fresher and stouter than before. She had been too much worried by Joseph's conduct with the sisters." So says another informant, an old lady yet living in Salt Lake, to whom Emma once said in 1846 while talking about his revelations, "It was *all guesswork.*" Pretty good for the wife of the greatest prophet that had ever lived, and herself aiding and abetting her son Joseph in still riveting the fraud—minus polygamy!

It was not long after the martyrdom of her liege lord that the elect lady and Attorney Woods (the last legal counselor of the Lord's anointed prophet) laid their heads together to *reveal the exact truth* about the Mormon leaders and the Mormon humbug in general. For some reason this most laudable design was never executed. Probably because Sister Emma saw that she could not possibly make such a crushing disclosure without seriously incriminating herself. At any rate, I am positively informed that old lawyer Woods still holds in his possession the material then compiled for their joint exposure of Mormonism. The *Times and Seasons*, the church organ, denied at the time that any such design existed, but denials of this kind have about the same value as those of my lamented friend Napoleon III., that is, they prove the exact contrary of what they assert.

I am now going to introduce a document of the very greatest importance, which will enable the reader to see Joseph, Emma and the Gold Bible humbug in a kind of family picture, not brilliantly drawn, but full of the color of life. It is a letter from the brothers Hiel and Joseph Lewis, sons of the Rev. Nathaniel Lewis, of old Harmony, Pennsylvania, and all of them near relations of Emma

Hale. It is dated Amboy, Lee County, Ill., April 23, 1879. The original belongs to Mr. James T. Cobb, the above-named pathfinder in early Mormon history. The document concerns what the two gentlemen "saw and heard of the sayings and doings of the Prophet Joseph Smith while he was engaged in peeping for money and hidden treasures and translating his Gold Bible in our neighborhood, township of Harmony, Susquehannah County, Pa., our home and residence being within one mile of where he lived and transacted his business." The most prominent citizens of the little town of Amboy, the mayor, aldermen, attorneys, editors, merchants, bankers, justices of the peace, etc., testify that the witnesses are "truthful, honorable, Christian gentlemen," and that "their statements are entitled to the fullest credence." Here is the document :

"Some time previous to 1825,* a man by the name of Wm. Hale, a distant relative of uncle Isaac Hale, came to Isaac Hale and said that he had been informed by a woman by the name of Odle, who claimed to possess the power of seeing under ground (such persons were then commonly called *peepers*), that there were great treasures concealed in the hill northeast from Isaac Hale's house, and by her directions Wm. Hale commenced digging. But, being too lazy to work and too poor to hire, he obtained a partner by the name of Oliver Harper, of York State, who had the means to hire help. But after a short time operations were suspended, for a time, during which Wm. Hale heard of PEEPER Joseph Smith, jr., and wrote to him and soon visited him, and found Smith's representations were so flattering that Smith was either hired or became a partner with Wm. Hale, Oliver Harper and a man by the name of Stowell,† *who had some property.*

---

* This would be, according to Mormon annals, after the time when "the Father and the Son" appeared to the prophet Joseph and held a conference with him.

† Lucy Smith, the mother of the prophet, and Munchhausen of the family, lets a good-sized cat out of her big bag in her biography of Joe. She confesses in it, unwittingly, to all the money-digging part of the prophet, and this was one of the reasons that made Brigham put her gossipy little book on the Mormon Index librorum prohibitorum. Munchhausen-Lucy says (pp. 91-92): "A man by the name of Josiah Stoal came from Chenango County, N. Y., with the view of getting Joseph to assist in digging for a silver mine. He came for Joseph on account of having heard that he possessed *certain keys* by which he could discern things invisible to the natural eye.

They hired men and dug in several places. The account given in the history of Susquehanna County, p. 580, of a *pure white dog* to be used as a *sacrifice to restrain the enchantment*, and of *the anger of the Almighty* at the attempt to *palm off on Him a white sheep for a white dog*, is a fair sample of Smith's revelations, and of the God that inspired him. Their digging in several places was in compliance with 'Peeper' Smith's revelations, who would attend *with his peep-stone in his hat, and his hat drawn over his face*, and tell them how deep they would have to go; and when they found no trace of the chest of money, he would *peep* again and *weep like a child*, and tell them that the enchantment had removed it on account of some sin, or thoughtless word, and finally the enchantment became so strong that he could not see, and the business was finally abandoned. *Smith could weep and shed tears at any time if he chose to.**

"But while he was engaged in looking through his peep-stone and *old white hat*, directing the digging for money, and boarding at uncle Isaac Hale's, he formed an intimacy with Mr. Hale's daughter, and after the abandonment of the money-digging speculation, he consummated the elopement and marriage to the said Emma Hale, and she became his accomplice in his humbug *Golden Bible* and Mormon religion.

"The statement that the prophet Joseph Smith made in our hearing at the commencement of his translating his book in Harmony, as to the *manner of his finding the plates*, was as follows: He said that by a DREAM he was informed that at such a place in a certain hill, in an *iron* box, were some gold plates with curious engravings, which he must get and translate, and *write a book;* that the plates were to be kept concealed from every human being for a certain time, some two or three years; that he went to the place and dug till he came to the stone that covered the box, when he was knocked down; that he again attempted to remove the stone, and was again knocked down. This attempt was made the third time, and the third time he was knocked down. Then he exclaimed: 'Why can't I *git* it?' or words to that effect, and then he saw a man standing over the spot, who, to

---

Joseph endeavored to divert him from his vain pursuit, but he was inflexible in his purpose, and offered high wages to those who would dig for him in search of said mine, and still insisted upon having Joseph to work for him. Accordingly, Joseph and several others returned with him and commenced digging. After laboring for the old gentleman about a month, without success, Joseph prevailed upon him to cease his operations, and it was from this circumstance of having worked by the month at digging for a silver mine, that the *very prevalent* story arose of Joseph having been a money-digger." [The italics are mine.]

* Let any half-witted person compare this testimony with those of Ingersoll, Chase and others, in our Appendix of Part I., and deny that Joseph was the champion humbug of our time!

him, appeared *like a Spaniard* [Oh, you great son of Lucy!], having
a long beard down over his breast to about here (*Smith putting his
hand to the pit of his stomach*), WITH HIS (the ghost's) THROAT CUT
FROM EAR TO EAR, AND THE BLOOD STREAMING DOWN, who told
him that he could not get it alone; that another person whom he
(Smith) would know at first sight must come with him, and then he
would get it; and when he saw Miss Emma Hale he knew that she
was the person, and that after they were married she went with him to
near the place and stood with her back towards him while he dug
after the box, which he rolled up in his frock, and she helped carry
it home; that in the same box with the plates were spectacles; * the
bows were of gold and the eyes were stone, and by looking through
these spectacles all the characters on the plates were translated into
English.

"*In all this narrative there was not one word about visions of God
or of angels or heavenly revelations; all his information was by that*
DREAM *and that* BLEEDING GHOST. The heavenly visions and mes-
sages of angels, etc., contained in Mormon books, were *afterthoughts,
revised to order.* While Smith was in Harmony he made the above
statements, in our presence, to Rev. N. Lewis. It was here, also, that
he *joined the Methodist Episcopal Church.* He presented himself in
a very serious and humble manner, and the minister, not suspecting
evil, put his name on the class-book in the absence of some of the
official members, among whom was the undersigned, Joseph Lewis,
who, when he learned what was done, took with him Joshua McKune
and had a talk with Smith. We told him plainly that such a character
as he was *a disgrace to the church;* that he could not be a member of
it unless he broke off his sins by repentance, made public confession,
renounced his fraudulent and hypocritical practices, and gave some
evidence that he intended to reform and conduct himself somewhat
nearer like a Christian than he had done. We gave him his choice,
to go before the class and publicly ask to have his name stricken from
the class-book, or stand a disciplinary investigation; he chose the
former, and immediately withdrew his name. So his name as a
member of the class was on the book *only three days.* It was the
general opinion that his only object in joining the church was to
bolster up his reputation and gain the sympathy and help of Christians;
that is, putting on the cloak of religion to serve the Devil in."

When interrogated as to the time of Joe's joining the
Methodist Church, Mr. Hiel Lewis wrote back that it was
in June, 1828.

---

*The celebrated "Urim and Thummim" of Mormon history.
One can "catch on" nicely here: Spaniards having buried treasures,
whether of *gold* or *golden* plates, the *ghost* of a Spaniard would
naturally have to stand guard over them, whatever the state of his
windpipe.

This disclosure will prove vastly edifying to the world in general, and to Mormons in particular. Joseph, with the sacred plates in his possession and while he is "translating" them, BECOMES A METHODIST !! And this, too, after the Lord's (both the Father and the Son) telling him that all existing religions are false and corrupt and on no account to join any of them, he being the favored instrument elected by Them in *founding the true one !!* I think tke great jury, called public opinion, Mormons included, might give their verdict in the impostor's case without leaving their seats.

Our letter goes on :

"We will add one more sample of his prophetic power and practice. One of the neighbors, whom Smith was owing, had a piece of corn on a rather wet and backward piece of ground, and as Smith was owing him, he wanted Smith to help hoe corn. Smith came on, but to get clear of the work and debt, said : ' If I kneel down and *pray in your corn*, it will grow just as well as if hoed.' So he prayed in the corn and insured its maturity without cultivation, and that the frost would not hurt it. But the corn was a failure in growth and killed by the frost. This sample of prophetic power was related to us by those present, and no one questioned its truth." *

The "revelation on celestial marriage" is a much more candid document than could be supposed. It permits us to "peep" into the peeper's household. We see how he tries to overcome the desperate resistance of the strong wife against—let me use the exactly significant term—religious whoredom. What scenes must there have been enacted in that prophetic household ! He begs and flatters, thunders and threatens—all in vain. Finally, he

---

* This startling document, which I have copied from the original most carefully, is attested in the following manner :

STATE OF ILLINOIS, } ss.
Lee County. }

I, Everett E. Chase, a Justice of the Peace in and for the County of Lee, State aforesaid, do hereby certify that the above named Joseph Lewis and Hiel Lewis, personally known to me to be respectable, truthful and honorable men, came before me and in my presence signed the above statement, and each of them before me made affidavit to each and all of the allegations therein set forth according to their best memory. EVERETT E. CHASE,

J. P.

changes tactics.   He tells Emma, it is "all spiritual, my
dear."   "Let us show the people"—he may have said—
"that you *do* look at celestial marriage in the right light,
by being present at such a ceremony. It means marriage for
the other world, and it is necessary that you should dis-
pel, through a fearless act of yours, the ugly rumors spread
everywhere.   I may have sinned now and then, dearest,
but from now on—you will see—everything will be strictly
spiritual."

Emma, perplexed and exhausted, consents.   The Partridge girls are to be sealed to her husband in her presence.
"It is only a formality, deary, and will strengthen my
position very much," says the prophet.   It was in May or
June, 1843, before the revelation was dictated to the
"pard."   An elder was selected, whose talents and profession promised something extraordinary in the way of
impressive solemnity. His name was George J. Adams,
and he was a strolling player and great libertine besides.
He performed the sealing ceremony and all went well for—
two or three hours. Emma found out what the word "spiritual" really meant with that chaste husband of hers. She
demanded imperiously the immediate annulment of the
ceremony.   Joseph hesitated, but the blood of old Isaac
Hale was up in the veins of the prophet's wife.   She
threatened to arouse the city with a terrible display of
matrimonial fireworks.   The Prophet had to give in.
Emma went on suffering what she could not prevent, but
her official honor as a wife was safe.   She remained the
queen of her household instead of stooping to the role of
concubine.   She did not go to Washington to use her
shame as an argument in debate.   She did not write pamphlets about it, either.

THE REVELATION ON POLYGAMY.

For What Purpose it was "Received"—Emma Burns It— They "Had been Given" to Joseph—The Author Visits the Utah Penitentiary for Enlightenment—The Caged Apostle—Three Pilates—He "Made a Business of it"— The Scene on the Log—Sketch of the History of Mormon Polygamy—Lots of Pure, Holy Lies—Special Instructions —The Clerk's Affidavit—The Celebrated Revelation in Extenso.

The celebrated revelation on celestial marriage, dated July 12, 1843, was "received" like all other "revelations" for the selfish purposes of the prophet. He had, as we have seen, revelations that the Saints had to feed and clothe him and build him a big hotel in Nauvoo, for him and his offspring for all time. Now the revelation on polygamy was, as it confesses stupidly itself, nothing but an *"escape"* out of a terrible difficulty. Emma, the proud mother and wife, was worried beyond measure by Joseph's conduct with the "sisters," and the prophet needed a religious mantle to cover his sins and quiet Emma. The revelation says:

"Behold, I have seen your sacrifices and will forgive all your sins . . . . Go, therefore, and I make a way for your *escape* . . . ."

But "the Lord" was not very successful in making the "escape" for "Mine Anointed." Emma declared the revelation to be the work of the devil, and *burned* the original which had been shown to her. Happily for the salvation of this sinful world, two copies had been preserved. The Lord said to Emma in his polite way, always used by him while speaking to ladies:

"Let mine handmaid Emma Smith receive all those that *have been* given to my servant Joseph, and who are virtuous and pure before me . . . ."

Now that is clear enough, especially when the aforesaid Lord says to the same handmaid :

"And again, verily I say, let mine handmaid forgive my servant Joseph his *trespasses* . . . ."

But it's useless even for the Mormon Lord to talk reason to an insulted wife and mother. Emma persisted in her opposition to the blessings of Abraham and Jacob and finally, after having left the church, declared that Joseph had never lived in Polygamy. She wanted to purge the memory of her martyred husband, whose wrongs she had forgiven the dead while she had been unable to forgive them the living sinner; and she wanted to protect the good name of her sons. Can you blame her for it? I can't.

But to the revelation. It is clear that Joseph confesses in it that a certain number of "virgins" *had been* given to him before July 12. 1843, the date of the revelation. I now want to introduce a witness, whose testimony will not be impeached. You may doubt an *apostle* of the church while behind a bottle of good wine or while on the stand in the tabernacle, but you cannot doubt him while he is in the hands of his enemies, in vile prison, the victim of the most shameful religious persecution ever enacted. Oh, Zane and Dickson, remember Pilate and his present state of terrible roasting !

It was on the most beautiful first of May I ever saw in my life, that I went to the Salt Lake Penitentiary. We had a fine horse and buggy, I and my excellent friend, Henry Weinheimer. of Highland, Ill. Marshal Ireland — there is another Pilate for you — had given me a special permit, empowering me to talk with some of the prisoners, and I hereby beg to thank Mr. Ireland for his kindness, declaring that I rarely met a more frank and genial man than this fanatic enemy of the kingdom. We saw that "penitentiary" which, in fact, is nothing but a disgusting corral. It is well known that Brigham Young put the appropriation granted by the Government into his pockets, and got his slaves to build this monument of shame and adobe bricks. The Warden called out the apostle, Lorenzo Snow, at our request.   He came——

An interesting old man, the apostle, of about seventy years; narrow, rather distinguished head, lively gray eyes, but face much wrinkled and of a yellowish color; manners very agreeable, talk fluent and intelligent, expression that of a clever Jesuit.   He had been a good saint since his youth.   He had not intended to marry, but to devote himself entirely to missionary work; but the prophet explained the new law to him, and, being convinced that Joseph *was* a prophet, he went at it like a man, and, using his own expression, "*made a business of it*," though he contented himself with only nine wives; two of them he took in one day, and four or five in three or four months.

We had a very pleasant chat.   The apostle has been in Switzerland, England and Italy, even in Jerusalem.   I asked him how it was with that revelation — when was it that it was made known to the saints?   The apostle said: "I had been away on a mission; I returned to Nauvoo in April, 1843.   A friend of mine, called Sherwood, told me very soon after my arrival that Joseph had married my sister, Eliza R. Snow, for time and eternity, some three months before [at least six months before July 12, 1843]. Joseph sent for me: he wanted a private interview with me.   I went to him.   I did not tell him that I knew of his marriage with my sister; I waited till he would tell me.   He went with me to the shore of the Mississippi, about fifty rods from his house.   There we sat down on a log, and there he explained to me the law on celestial marriage, and told me that he had married my sister for time and eternity about three months ago.   I was not at all surprised; I *knew* that this thing was coming."

"Why did Emma Smith burn the revelation, Mr. Snow?"

"Allow me to answer your question with another question.   Why did Lucifer rebel against God?   Emma apostatized; she left the path of truth and light, and went to darkness and perdition!"

I tried to look suitably disgusted with so much wickedness on the part of a wife; and we chatted of many

other things.   Apostle Snow hopes that the saints will
soon be "on top again," and expressed a mysterious
expectation that "a change of government would soon
enable the saints to *practice their religion.*"

Now, who is right, the imprisoned apostle who talks
so kindly to a "gentile dog" like me, or the Josephites,
who go on stating that Joseph never was in polygamy?
Snow tells you the thing was *coming* — he knew that such
a revelation was on the way, and, by Jove, a blind man
must have seen it !

This chapter would be incomplete without a bit of
elaborate historical analysis.   If Mormon history in
general, as represented by Mormon sermons, books and
newspapers, has been one continual chain of misrepresentation, from 1830 to this day, the *history of polygamy* has
been a solid little group of lies apart, like a cluster of
islands in an ocean of falsehood.

Up to 1852 there was no official "celestial marriage."
It had been denied and denied till further denial became
impossible.   Remember that the "revelation" was given
on July 12, 1843, and that Joseph and Hyrum and many
of their intimate friends had taken degrees in the new
celestial order.   The highly dramatic affidavit of Martha
Brotherton (see Appendix to Part I.) alone proves this,
and our very unctuous friend, Apostle Lorenzo Snow,
confirmed it in his cage.   Some of the elders felt an
urgent necessity to unfold the glorious new gospel to the
world; but that wouldn't do.   The Lord wanted his
special friends to enjoy the thrice-bolted blessings of
Abraham, but not the abominably rude fare of an Illinois
State Prison.   In February, 1844, seven months after the
revelation, the official church organ, *Times and Seasons*,
contained the following :

NOTICE.

As we have been credibly informed that an elder of the Church of
Jesus Christ of Latter-day Saints, by the name of Hyrum Brown, has
been preaching polygamy and other false and corrupt doctrines in the
County of Lapeer and State of Michigan, this is to notify him and
the church in general, that he has been cut off from the church for his

iniquity, and he is further notified to appear at the special conference, on the 6th of April next, to make answer to those charges.

JOSEPH SMITH,
HYRUM SMITH,
Presidents of the Church.

This was seven months after the revelation. Now hear what the present Mormon church organ has to say about this official lie :

Until the open enunciation of the doctrine of celestial marriage by the publication of the revelation on the subject in 1852, no elder was authorized tŏ announce it to the world. The Almighty has revealed things on many occations which were for His servants and not for the world. *Jesus* enjoined His disciples on several occasions to keep to themselves principles that he made known to them. And his injunction, "Cast not your *pearls* before swine, lest they trample them under their feet and turn again and rend you," has become as familiar as a common proverb. In the rise of the church the Lord had occasion to admonish His servants in regard to revelations that were afterwards permitted to be published :

"I say unto you, hold your peace until I shall see fit to make all things known unto the world concerning this matter."

"And now I say unto you, keep these things from going abroad into the world until it is expedient in me."

"But a commandment I give unto them that they shall not boast themselves of these things, neither speak of them before the world, for these things are given unto you for your profit and your salvation."— (Doc. & Cov.)

Under these instructions elders had no right to promulgate anything but that which they were authorized to teach. And when assailed by enemies and accused of practicing things which were really not countenanced in the church, they were justified in denying those imputations and at the same time avoiding the avowal of such doctrines as were not yet intended for the world. This course which they have taken when necessary, by commandment, is all the ground which their accusers have for charging them them with falsehood.—(*Deseret News*, May 20, 1886.)

But there had been other official denials of polygamy earlier than this. Our wide-awake friend, Bennett, had published his book in the fall of 1842 and given away as much as he could without hurting his own "dignity." The "great stink"—to talk with Brother Brigham— caused by Bennett's book was to be counteracted by the perfume of innocence exhaled from this declaration in the Nauvoo *Times and Seasons* (October 1, 1842) :

We, the undersigned, members of the Church of Jesus Christ of Latter-day Saints and residents of the City of Nauvoo, persons of family, do hereby certify and declare that we do know of *no other rule or system of marriage* than the one published from the Book of Doctrine and Covenants, and we give this certificate to show that Dr. J. C. Bennett's "secret wife system" is a creature of his own make, as we know of no such society in this place nor ever did.

S. BENNETT,	N. K. WHITNEY,
GEO. MILLER,	ALBERT PETTY,
ALPHEUS CUTLER,	ELIAS HIGBEE,
REYNOLDS CAHOON,	JOHN TAYLOR,
W. WOODRUFF,	E. ROBINSON.
AARON JOHNSON.	

We, the undersigned, members of the Ladies' Relief Society and *married* females, do certify and declare that we know of no other system of marriage being practiced in the Church of Jesus Christ of Latter-day Saints save the one contained in the Book of Doctrine and Covenants, and we give this certificate to show that J. C. Bennett's "secret wife system" is a disclosure of his own make.

EMMA SMITH,
President.
ELIZABETH ANN WHITNEY,
Counselor.
SARAH M. CLEVELAND,
Counselor.
ELIZA R. SNOW,
Secretary.

MARY C. MILLER,	CATHERINA PETTY,
LOIS CUTLER,	SARAH HIGBEE,
THIRZA CAHOON,	PHEBE WOODRUFF,
ANN HUNTER,	LEONORA TAYLOR,
JANE LAW,	SARAH HILLMAN,
SOPHIA R. MARKS,	ROSANNAH MARKS,
POLLY Z. JOHNSON,	ANGELINE ROBINSON.
ABIGAIL WORKS.	

Very well, now let us see what the New Testament of the Mormon Bible, the "Book of Doctrine and Covenants," says about marriage. Let me illustrate this holy command by a practical example of the way in which Brigham Young and his long-time bosom friend, Danite John D. Lee, "lived their religion:"

BOOK OF DOCTRINE AND COVENANTS.	CONFESSION OF JOHN D. LEE.
" You mutually agree to be each other's companion, husband and wife, observing the legal rights belonging to this condition; that is, *keeping yourselves wholly for each other and from all others during your lives* . . . And inasmuch as this Church of Christ has been reproached with the crime of fornication and polygamy; we declare that we believe that one man should have one wife and one woman but one husband, except in case of death, when either is at liberty to marry again."	" In 1847, while at Council Bluffs, Brigham Young sealed me to *three women in one night,* viz.: my eleventh, Nancy Armstrong; she was what we called a *widow.* She left her first husband in Tennessee in order to be with the Mormon people; my twelfth, Polly W. Young; my thirteenth, Louisa Young: these were two sisters . . . Brigham said that Isaac C. Haight and I needed some young women *to renew our vitality,* so he gave us both a 'dashing young bride'" [one year after the Mountain Meadows Massacre.]

You see, gentle reader, the kind of *pearls* that were too precious to cast before the Gentile swine. Three women in one night, and two of them sisters. Fine pearls. They remind me forcibly of the spirited word said by a young Mormon lady: "Polygamy is all right when properly *carried out*—on a shovel.". The young lady was a daughter of "Jeddy" Grant.

But let us return to our *ladies.* "Ladies' relief society"—that sounds respectable, surely. They were all true ladies, in the American sense of the word, these female believers and relievers: you would suppose it, since they call themselves *ladies.* But how is it that Sister Eliza R. Snow calls herself a "married woman" on October 1, 1842? Apostle Lorenzo Snow, her brother, my crucified friend, tells me that she had been married—for time and eternity, of course—in the beginning of 1843. And how can I believe *this* apostle capable of lying when speaking from his cross at the penitentiary? We must suppose that there was *real* marriage between sweet Eliza and Joseph *before* 1843—without any more impressive ceremony than that little extempore blessing by Emma's broomstick. But how about the other "ladies?" Hear Mrs. Sarah M. Pratt:

" Emma Smith, whom Joseph made lead a life of misery through his infidelities, had founded the relief society for the purpose of spying her husband. At least Joseph often said so. Elizabeth Ann Whitney, the second 'lady,' had been seduced by Joseph; he seduced her daughter, too. Sarah M. Cleveland, the third 'lady,' was the same who, as I have told you, kept a kind of assignation house for the prophet and Eliza R. Snow—you know *her.*" As to the rest of the ladies, fifteen in number, Mrs. Pratt states that the prophet had seduced most of them before the date of the declaration, October 1, 1842. " He had a terrible influence over women," says Mrs. Pratt. " Many pure and good women, who never would have fallen, became his victims *through his prophetic pretensions,* and I myself [with a slight shudder at the remembrance] was perhaps only saved from his clutches through my devoted love for my husband who at that time was my all, and I his."

But leaving aside the private character of our *ladies,* what does the passage referred to by them in the " Doctrine and Covenants" mean but the strictest injunction of *monogamy?* " Keep yourselves wholly for each other and from all others during your lives." Is this not most pointed and exact? And the scathing denunciation of all such as shall teach that it is *right for any man to have more than one wife living at the same time,*—comparing such a preacher to Cain, the first murderer,*—what, I repeat it, does it all mean? Is not the very citing of such an article of marital faith and practice,—" Keeping yourself wholly for each other and from all other during your lives,"—to brand with infamy ANY other rule or system of marriage?

---

* *Times and Seasons,* p. 715 (November, 1844): The law of the land and the rules of the church do not allow one man to have MORE THAN ONE WIFE ALIVE AT ONCE, but if any man's wife die he has a right to marry another and to be sealed to both for eternity, to the living and the dead. This is ALL THE SPIRITUAL WIFE SYSTEM THAT EVER WAS TOLERATED IN THE CHURCH. And *Times and Seasons,* p. 888 (May 1, 1845): For once let us say that CAIN who went to Nod and taught the DOCTRINE OF A PLURALITY OF WIVES and the giants who practised the same INIQUITY.

But no, the "ladies" did *not* lie. Hear the church organ of May 20, 1886:

> "So with that spiritual wife doctrine which lustful men attempted to promulgate at that period. Joseph the prophet was just as much opposed to that false doctrine as any one could be. It was a counterfeit. The true and divine order is another thing. The errors which those *ladies* who signed the affidavits declared were not known to them as doctrines of the church, were not, are not, and never will be part of the creed of the Church of Jesus Christ of Latter-day Saints. They were *conscientious* in their statements. Joseph and Hyrum were consistent in their action against the false doctrines of polygamy and spiritual wifeism, instigated by the devil and advocated by men who did not comprehend sound doctrine nor the purity of the celestial marriage which God revealed for the holiest of purposes."

You see how it was. The "ladies'" denial went against the counterfeit of the real pearls, of which Brother Brigham gave three big specimens to Brother Lee in one night "for the holiest of purposes." Lee was then thirty-five, and did not need yet the holiest of all holy purposes, the renewal of his vitality. That came later, when Brigham wanted to reward his fellow hyena for the "holy and pure" job done at the Mountain Meadows.*

Let us see another link in the chain of denials furnished by the happy proprietors of whole strings of gospel pearls. No pearls for the swine in 1842 and 1843. In July, 1845, another denial. Apostle Parley P. Pratt, who had several wives at that time, denounced polygamy in a public card as a "doctrine of devils and seducing spirits, but another name for whoredom, wicked and unlawful connection, confusion and abomination." Very good, Brother Parley. That's what polygamy really is. But marrying three women in one night and occupying with mother and daughter the same bed, that belongs to

---

* Historian Stenhouse touchingly refers in his "Rocky Mountain Saints" to the "vast energy and benevolence" of the prophet Joseph. Of his benevolence, especially towards his "sisters" and "daughters," there remains no doubt, but his energy, vast as that must have been, seems less than that of John D. Lee, though we have no precise data from the prophet Joseph's pen, as we have from Lee's, in his little Harem-Almanac, page 289 of his priceless and dreadful book.

the "pearl" department of sound doctrine and the
purity of celestial marriage, revealed by the "pard"
for the "holiest of purposes." Of a truth there is
nothing ASIATIC in it. Any savage Asiatic would blush
at such "purity!" Why do I speak of *Asiatic?* Let
the *News* answer :

> "Polygamy, in the ordinary and ASIATIC sense of the term, never
> was and is not now a tenet of the Latter-day Saints. That which
> Joseph and Hyrum denounced, and for preaching which without
> authority an elder was cut off the church in Nauvoo, was altogether
> different to the order of *celestial marriage* including a plurality of
> wives, which forms the subject of the revelation."

But we have yet another apostolic denial furnished by
John Taylor, at a public discussion with some Eng-
lish Reverends in Boulogne, France, July, 1850. Says
Apostle Taylor :

> "We are accused here of polygamy and actions the most indelicate,
> obscene and disgusting, such as none but a corrupt heart could have
> contrived. These things are too outrageous to admit of belief. There-
> fore I shall content myself by reading *our views of chastity and
> marriage* from a work published by *us*, containing some articles of
> *our* faith."

Taylor then read the very article of the *Doctrine and
Covenants* quoted by the eighteen *ladies* eight years before
1850. And how deep did he stick himself in "celestial"
mud at this very moment? Let me quote the statement of
a Mormon Elder, who is privy to many of the secrets of
this "Church." He says :

> "At the very time that Taylor denied the facts in France by read-
> ing from the *Doctrine and Covenants*, he had TEN women as wives—
> he took the tenth *woman* in 1847 or 1848, and she was actually his
> thirteenth *woman*. Three had left him. In order that your readers
> may know that I only write the truth in this respect, I will name those
> whom I recollect and have seen, as follows : Leonora (Cannon)
> Taylor, his first wife; Elizabeth Kaighn, her cousin; Mary Rams-
> bottom, called Moss; Miss Ballintyne, Annie Ballintyne, Miss Oakley,
> Harriet Whitaker, Sophia Whitaker, and two others whose names I
> forget—one, I think was a Mrs. Gillam, whom I have seen. Thus,
> from 1843, when the pseudo revelation was given, to 1847—four years
> —he had thirteen *women* sealed to him, and ten whom he still owned
> when he told the huge lie in France. John Pack and Curtis E. Bolton,
> who were his companion elders in the discussion, heard the denial and

sanctioned this utterance and course—they were polygamists then also."

And let me add one well-known fact : While John Taylor, the husband of ten wives, was denying polygamy, he was even then courting a young English woman, no doubt for the holiest of purposes, and tried to rob a friend of his, an Elder, of his promised wife. Isn't it a whole bushel of pearls? But everything must have an end, even the endless lying of the Mormon leaders. It was in the fall of 1852 when Brigham Young decided to let the celestial " cat out of the bag," as he said. His clown, Heber C. Kimball, announced the same event to his friends by saying that " the cat would have kittens." I have this from people who heard it themselves. And, sure enough, cat and kittens play now right lustily in the open sunlight in the columns of the church organ. The " Church " now concedes that Joseph knew the Abra-hamic scheme of his " pard " already in 1831 or 1832. Hear the *News* again :

The revelation on celestial marriage, published [NOW] in the *Doc-trine and Covenants*, was given July 12, 1843. The principles it contains, with further intelligence on the same subject, were revealed to the Prophet *many years before*, but not formulated in writing for the church. Acting under instructions from the Lord, the prophet had several wives sealed to him before the date of that revelation. There are other matters spoken of in the revelation that pertained to the time when it was written, showing that the statement in the heading, as it appears in the book, is correct; namely, that the revelation was given on that date, although the doctrines it contains were known and had been acted upon *under special instructions* previous to that date.

Apostle Orson Pratt, the great champion of polygamy —he married nearly all his servant girls for the holiest of purposes and made a martyr of one of the brightest and best wives and mothers—Apostle Pratt said in 1878, in a public sermon, that Joseph had received "revelations" upon that *principle* as early as 1831 and had wives sealed to him as early as April 1841.* That pearl business began early, you see. I think myself that the *principle* was made known to this anointed oil-bottle-prophet at

---

*Deseret News, November 23, 1878.

the age of puberty, if not earlier! What do you see here, people of the Great Republic, but organized secret crime and most infamous lying? Didn't I say from the outset that the Mormon leaders were enemies of the Mormon people? Am I right or wrong? I said it because everywhere I have found the masses of people honest, nor shall I make an exception of *Mormon* masses. I am not prepared to believe, I do not believe, that these Mormon masses sustain their leaders in deliberate lying. Simply they are ignorant—must be ignorant—of the true character of their leaders, past and present. But if they only knew how terribly funny they are, those priestly chaps! Whenever Joseph seduced a servant girl of his, or an adopted daughter, whenever he stole away from Emma's, the peacefully slumbering mother's side, to enjoy an adventure worthy of the pen of Boccaccio or Bandello, he always acted under "*special instructions*" of the Lord. It was under those special instructions that he made a pitiable wreck of Emma's wedded life. It was the same kind Lord, I suppose, who sent Dr. Bennett to Nauvoo with that instrument, which the handy doctor could clap into his coat sleeve, when any of Joseph's women "were in trouble!" Oh, most ingenious and generous of all "pards!" Oh, most anointed and anointing of all prophets! Oh, most credulous and docible of all peoples! Has there ever been such a sinister farce in *all* history?

Let me present now an affidavit of Wm. Clayton, who was the confidential clerk of Joseph in Nauvoo. Mrs. Pratt says that he was a brute and a drunkard, and that may readily explain his elevation to such an important position. The affidavit appeared for the first time in that very same memorable number of the *Deseret News*, May 20, 1886. The reader will see that it confirms all my statements. Cat and kittens are all on my side. Clayton's affidavit is dated February 16, 1874. Clayton himself is dead since four or five years.

WILLIAM CLAYTON'S TALE.

"Inasmuch as it may be interesting to future generations of the members of the Church of Jesus Christ of

Latter-day Saints to learn something of the first teachings of the principle of plural marriage by President Joseph Smith, the prophet, seer, revelator and translator of said church, I will give a short relation of facts which occurred within my personal knowledge, and also matters related to me by President Joseph Smith.

"I was employed as a clerk in President Joseph Smith's office, under Elder Willard Richards, and commenced to labor in the office on the 10th day of February, 1842. I continued to labor with Elder Richards until he went East to fetch his wife to Nauvoo.

" After Elder Richards started East, I was necessarily thrown constantly into the company of President Smith, having to attend to his public and private business, receiving and recording tithings and donations, attending to land and other matters of business. During this period I necessarily became well acquainted with Emma Smith, the wife of the prophet Joseph, and also with the children —Julia M. (an adopted daughter), Joseph, Frederick and Alexander — very much of the business being transacted at the residence of the prophet.

"On the 7th of October, 1842, in the presence of Bishop Newel K. Whitney and his wife, Elizabeth Ann, President Joseph Smith appointed me temple recorder, and also his private clerk, placing all records, books, papers, etc., in my care, and requiring me to take charge of and preserve them, his closing words being, 'When I have any revelations to write, you are the one to write them.'

"During this period the prophet Joseph frequently visited my house in my company, and became well acquainted with my wife, Ruth, to whom I had been married five years. One day in the month of February, 1843, date not remembered, the prophet invited me to walk with him. During our walk he said he had learned that there was a sister back in England to whom I was very much attached. I replied there was, but nothing further than an attachment such as a brother and sister in the church might rightfully entertain for each other. He then said: 'Why don't you send for her?' I replied:

'In the first place, I have no authority to send for her, and if I had, I have not the means to pay expenses.' To this he answered : 'I give you authority to send for her, and I will furnish you the means,' which he did. This was the first time the prophet Joseph talked with me on the subject of plural marriage. He informed me that the doctrine and principle was right in the sight of our heavenly Father, and that it was a doctrine which pertained to celestial order and glory. After giving me lengthy instructions and information concerning the doctrine of celestial or plural marriage, he concluded his remarks by the words, 'It is your privilege to have all the wives you want.' After this introduction our conversations on the subject of plural marriage were very frequent, and he appeared to take particular pains to inform and instruct me in respect to the principle. He also informed me that he had other wives *living* besides his first wife Emma, and in particular gave me to understand that Eliza R. Snow, Louisa Beaman, Desdemona C. Fullmer and others, were his lawful wives in the sight of Heaven.

"On the 27th of April, 1843, the Prophet Joseph Smith married to me Margaret Moon, for time and eternity, at the residence of Elder Heber C. Kimball, and on the 22d of July, 1843, he married to me, according to the order of the church, my first wife Ruth.

"On the 1st day of May, 1843, I officiated in the office of an elder by marrying Lucy Walker to the Prophet Joseph Smith, at his own residence.

"During this period the Prophet Joseph took several other wives. Amongst the number I well remember Eliza Partridge, Emily Partridge, Sarah Ann Whitney, Helen Kimball and Flora Woodworth. These all, he acknowledged to me, were his lawful, wedded wives, according to the celestial order. His wife Emma was cognizant of the fact of some, if not all of these being his wives, and she generally treated them very kindly.

"On the morning of the 12th of July, 1843, Joseph and Hyrum Smith came into the office in the upper story of the ' brick store,' on the bank of the Mississippi river. They were talking on the subject of plural marriage. Hyrum said to Joseph, 'If you will write the revelation on Celestial Marriage, I will take and read it to Emma, and I believe I can convince her of its truth, and you will hereafter have peace.' Joseph smiled and remarked, 'You do not know Emma as well as I do.' Hyrum remarked, 'The doctrine is so plain, I can convince any reasonable man or woman of its truth, purity and heavenly origin,' or words to their effect. Joseph then said, 'Well, I will write the revelation and we will see.' He then requested me to get paper and prepare to write. Hyrum very urgently requested Joseph to write the revelation by means of the Urim and Thummim, but Joseph in reply said he did not need to, for he knew the revelation perfectly from beginning to end.

" Joseph and Hyrum then sat down and Joseph commenced to dictate the revelation on Celestial Marriage, and I wrote it, sentence by sentence, as he dictated. After the whole was written, Joseph asked me to read it through, slowly and carefully, which I did, and he pronounced it correct. He then remarked that there was much more that he could write, on the same subject, but what was written was sufficient for the present.

" Hyrum then took the revelation to read to Emma. Joseph remained with me in the office until Hyrum returned. When he came back Joseph asked him how he had succeeded. Hyrum replied that he had never received a more severe talking to in his life, that Emma was very bitter and full of resentment and anger.

" Joseph quietly remarked, 'I told you you did not know Emma as well as I did.' Joseph then put the revelation in his pocket, and they both left the office.

" The revelation was read to several of the authorities during the day. Towards evening Bishop Newell K. Whitney asked Joseph if he had any objections to his taking a copy of the revelation ; Joseph replied that he had not, and handed it to him. It was carefully copied the following day by Joseph C. Kingsbury. Two or three days after the revelation was written Joseph related to me and several others that Emma had so teased and urgently entreated him for the privilege of destroying it, that he became so weary of her teasing, and to get rid of her annoyance, he told her she might destroy it and she had done so, but he had consented to her wish in this matter to pacify her, realizing that he knew the revelation perfectly, and could rewrite it at any time if necessary.

"The copy made by Joseph C. Kingsbury is a true and correct copy of the original in every respect. The copy was carefully preserved by Bishop Whitney, and but few knew of its existence until the temporary location of the Camp of Israel at Winter Quarters, on the Missouri River, in 1846.

"After the revelation on celestial marriage was written Joseph continued his instructions, privately, on the doctrine, to myself and others, and during the last year of his life we were scarcely ever together, alone, but he was talking on the subject, and explaining that doctrine and principles connected with it. He appeared to enjoy great liberty and freedom in his teachings, and also to find great relief in having a few to whom he could unbosom his feelings on that great and glorious subject.

"From him I learned that the doctrine of plural and celestial marriage is the most holy and important doctrine ever revealed to man on the earth, and that without obedience to that principle no person can ever attain to the fulness of exaltation in celestial glory.

[Signed]   WILLIAM CLAYTON.

"SALT LAKE CITY, February 16th, 1874."

Lots of *pearls* in that oily document. The prophet invites his clerk to a walk. Who knows whether they didn't sit down on the identical log on which he sat with Brother Lorenzo? That log was there for the holiest of purposes, no doubt. And now look how the prophet "tackles" his disciple. It reads like the talk of the serpent to mother Eve. There is a sister "back in England," whom Clayton, the married man, doth covet, but only for the holiest of purposes, to be sure. Joseph gives him "authority" to send for the girl. This he does as the Lord's anointed prophet. He then agrees to pay the expenses of the girl's trip ; and this, of course, he would do as trustee-in-trust of the church funds. Finally, as the very "buckler of Jehovah," as he used to vaunt himself, he explodes a whole bombshell of patriarchal blessings in the ear of his staggering scribe: "*It is your privilege to have all the wives you want.*" Ah, glorious! Under the sky of hospitable Illinois, in the face of modern civilization, in the teeth of the salutary moral laws of a noble commonwealth, the conspirator recruits accomplices of his secret infamies by appealing to the basest passions of his associates.

The woman "back in England" comes to Nauvoo and Joseph seals her to Clayton. Then—perhaps after a little broomstick-episode—Ruth, the lawful wife of the clerk, gets sealed to him. We are soon in a very platoon-fire of sealing: I seal you, you seal me, we seal each other. The revelation says that Joseph alone has the sealing power—but that's nothing; the "pard" doesn't mind such petty details where the holiest of purposes are on stake.

But now, how is this? Emma knew that other women were married to her husband and treated them "very kindly." You must be joking, Brother Clayton. Emma has no appreciation of your pearls and holy purposes. Would she have given Hyrum such a terrible raking down, would she have burned the revelation if she cared the snap of her haughty finger for them? You are decidedly mistaken, Brother Clayton. Sister Emma stands to the "law of Sarah (!)," firm as a rock, on the *broomstick* standpoint. If she ever changed in this respect, it was from broomstick to poker and tongs, but to nothing else. "If any of the elders preaches polygamy to you, get hold of a poker or a pair of tongs, sisters, and drive the fellow away—." That was a plain little speech of the Elect Lady in one of the meetings of the "Ladies' Relief Society." The fact is simply this, Brother Clayton: Your statement was concocted to show to the world in general, and to refractory Mormon wives in particular, that the first of all "first wives," the Eve of celestial marriage, liked the harem business awfully well after all. But your lie is clumsy, Elder Clayton, and you contradict it yourself.

Clayton's statement proves the truth of what the *enemies* of the Church have always affirmed. This silly humbug of a revelation was gotten up to pacify and if need be, terrify Emma into submission. Hyrum is the official busybody and go-between in this attempt at celestial reconciliation. "You will hereafter have peace," says that excellent brother and brother-in-law. But he insists on getting for the Prophet the old white hat and the peepstone for this holiest of purposes. Clayton puts it finer; he speaks solemnly of the "Urim and Thummim," — Lucy - Munchhausen's "two smooth three-cornered diamonds set in glass, and the glasses set in silver bows which were connected with each other in much the same way as old-fashioned spectacles." * Emma Smith says, on her death bed, that he dictated "sitting with his face buried in his hat, with *the* stone in it." † 'Twas just the old peepstone and nothing else.

But poor Hyrum! He put his brotherly hand in a wasp-nest when he read that stuff to Emma. Good heavens, she didn't treat *him* "very kindly!" And those curtain-lectures to the anointed of the Lord! My servant Joseph was in an awful fix. The "pard" must have been dreadfully angry at that woman, much more wrathy than he was over the white dog affair; but there was no convincing "mine handmaid" of the genuine value of the *pearls.* So the new Abraham had to eat crow. The rest was silence as to celestial law in Emma's house; "my house is a house of order," she says to Joseph, and "the ruler over many things" has to stop "the works of Abraham" in *her* house. But there was, for the holiest of purposes, that blessed log by the river, a furlong away from the "brick store" and from the ears of mine elect handmaid, Mrs. Emma Caudle. There, seated on the log (and just as easy as rolling off it), could they receive and impart revelations. There could these godly brigands talk unmolested about their boundless "privileges;" about "all the women they wanted," and they wanted ALL the women!

---

* "Joseph the Prophet," p. 107.
† Tullidge, "Life of Joseph," p. 793.

Let me finish this chapter with a reproduction of the revelation on the " most holy and important doctrine ever revealed to man."

I may hope that with the aid of notes and comments this tedious document may prove intelligible if not amusing :

CELESTIAL MARRIAGE.

A Revelation on the Patriarchal Order of Matrimony, or Plurality of Wives, Given to Joseph Smith, the Seer, in Nauvoo, July 12, 1843.

1. Verily, thus saith the Lord unto you, my servant Joseph, that inasmuch as you have inquired of my hand, to know and understand wherein I, the Lord, justified my servants Abraham, Isaac* and Jacob, as also Moses (?), David and Solomon, my servants, as touching the principle and doctrine of their having many wives and concubines: Behold ! and lo, I am the Lord thy God, and will answer thee as touching this matter : Therefore, prepare thy heart to receive and obey the instructions which I am about to give unto you; for all those who have this law revealed unto them must obey the same ; for behold ! I reveal unto you a new and an everlasting covenant, and if ye abide not that covenant, then are ye damned ; for no one can reject this covenant and be permitted to enter into my glory ; for all who will have a blessing at my hands shall abide the law which was appointed for that blessing, and the conditions thereof, as was instituted from before the foundation of the world ; and as pertaining to the new and everlasting covenant, it was instituted for the fulness of my glory; and he that receiveth a fulness thereof, must and shall abide the law, or he shall be damned, saith the Lord God.

2. And, verily, I say unto you, that the conditions of

---

*Isaac was the model for all polygamists, he had only one wife.

this law are these: All covenants, contracts, bonds, obligations, oaths, vows, performances, connections, associations or expectations, that are not made and entered into and sealed by the Holy Spirit of promise, of him who is *anointed*, both as well for time and for all eternity, *and that too most holy*, by revelation and commandment, through the medium of mine *anointed*, whom I have appointed on the earth to hold this power (and I have appointed unto my servant Joseph to hold this power in the last days, and *there is never but one on the earth at a time* on whom this power and the keys of this priesthood are conferred), are of no efficacy, virtue or force * in and after the resurrection from the dead; for all contracts that are not made unto this end, have an end when men are dead.

3. Behold! mine house is a house of order, saith the Lord God, and not a house of confusion. Will I accept of an offering, saith the Lord, that is not made in my name! Or, will I receive at your hands that which I have not appointed! And will I appoint unto you, saith the Lord, except it be by law, even as I and my Father ordained unto you before the world was! I am the Lord thy God, and I give unto you this commandment, that no man shall come unto the Father but by me. or by my word, which is my law, saith the Lord; and everything that is in the world, whether it be ordained of men, by thrones, or principalities, or powers, or things of name, whatsoever they may be, that are not by me, or by my word, saith the Lord, shall be thrown down. and shall not remain after men are dead, neither in nor after the resurrection, saith the Lord your God; for whatsoever things *remaineth* are by me, and whatsoever things are not by me shall be shaken and destroyed.

4. Therefore, if a man marry him a wife in the world, and he marry her not by me, nor by my word, and he covenant with her so long as he is in the world, and she with him, their covenant and marriage is not of force

---

* What does this make of all earth's marriages? No wonder so many Mormon elders have robbed Gentiles of their " time " wives — " for all eternity! "

when they are dead, and when they are out of the world;
therefore, they are not bound by any law when they are
out of the world; therefore, when they are out of the
world they neither marry nor are given in marriage, but
are appointed angels in heaven; which angels are ministering servants, to minister for those who are worthy of a
far more, and an exceeding, and an eternal weight of
glory; for these angels did not abide my law, therefore
they cannot be enlarged, but remain separately and
singly, without exaltation, in their saved condition, to all
eternity, and from henceforth are not Gods, but are angels
of God for ever and ever.

5. And again, verily I say unto you if a man marry a
wife, and make a covenant with her for time and for all
eternity, if that covenant is not by me or by my word,
which is my law, and is not sealed by the Holy Spirit of
promise, through him whom I have *anointed* and appointed
unto this power, then it is not valid, neither of force
when they are out of the world, because they are not
joined by me, saith the Lord God, neither by my word;
when they are out of the world, it cannot be received
there, because the angels and the Gods are appointed
there, by whom they cannot pass; they cannot, therefore,
inherit my glory, for my house is a house of order, saith
the Lord God.

6. And again, verily I say unto you, if a man marry a
wife by my word, which is my law, and by the new and
everlasting covenant, and it is sealed unto them by the
Holy Spirit of promise, by him who is *anointed*, unto
whom I have appointed this power, and the *keys* of this
priesthood, and it shall be said unto them, ye shall come
forth in the first resurrection, and if it be after the first
resurrection, in the next resurrection, and shall inherit
thrones, kingdoms, principalities, and powers of domin-
ions, all heights, and depths — then shall it be written in
the Lamb's Book of Life, that he shall commit no murder
whereby to shed innocent blood; and if *ye* abide in my
covenant, and commit no murder, whereby to shed innocent blood, it shall be done unto *them* in all things
whatsoever my servant hath put upon them, in time and

through all eternity, and shall be of full force when they
are out of the world; and they shall pass by the angels,
and the Gods, which are set there, to their exaltation
and glory in all things, as hath been sealed upon their
heads, which glory shall be a fulness and a continuation
of the seeds for ever and ever.

7. Then shall they be Gods, because they have no end;
therefore shall they be from everlasting to everlasting,
because they continue; then shall they be above all,
because all things are subject unto them. Then shall
they be Gods, because they have all power, and the
angels are subject unto them.

8. Verily, verily I say unto you, except ye abide my
law, ye cannot attain to this glory; for strait is the gate,
and narrow the way that leadeth unto the exaltation and
continuation of the lives, and few there be that find it,
because ye receive me not in the world, neither do ye
know me. But if ye receive me in the world, then shall
ye know me, and shall receive your exaltation, that where
I am, ye shall be also. This is eternal LIVES, to know the
only wise and true God, and Jesus Christ whom he hath
sent. I am He. Receive ye, therefore, my law.* Broad
is the gate and wide the way that leadeth to death; and
many there are that go in thereat, because they receive
me not, neither do they abide in my law.

9. Verily, verily I say unto you, if a man marry a
wife according to my word, and they are sealed by the
Holy Spirit of promise, according to mine appointment,
and he or she shall commit any sin or transgression of the
new and everlasting covenant whatever, and all manner of
blasphemies, and if they commit no murder, wherein they
shed inncent blood, yet they shall come forth in the first
resurrection, and enter into their exaltation; but they
shall be destroyed in the flesh, and shall be delivered unto
the buffetings of Satan unto the day of redemption,
saith the Lord God.

10. The blasphemy against the Holy Ghost, which
shall not be forgiven in the world, nor out of the world,

---

* "I AM HE! RECEIVE YE THEREFORE MY LAW." This is the
vertical point of Mormon blasphemy.

is in that ye commit murder, wherein ye shed innocent blood, and assent unto my death, after ye have received my new and everlasting covenant, saith the Lord God, and he that abideth not this law can in in no wise enter into my glory, but shall be damned, saith the Lord.

11. I am the Lord thy God, and will give unto thee the law of my Holy Priesthood, as was ordained by me and my father, before the world was. Abraham received all things, whatsoever he received, by revelation and commandment, by my word, saith the Lord, and hath entered into his exaltation, and sitteth upon his throne.

12. Abraham received promises concerning his seed, and of the fruit of his loins—*from whose loins ye* are, namely, my servant Joseph*—which were to continue so long as they were in the world ; and as touching Abraham and his seed, out of the world, they shall continue ; both in the world and out of the world should they continue as innumerable as the stars ; or if ye were to count the sand upon ths sea-shore, ye could not number them.´ This promise is yours also, because *ye are of Abraham*, and the promise was made unto Abraham ; and by this law are the continuation of the works of my Father, wherein He glorifieth himself. Go ye, therefore, and do the works of Abraham ; enter ye into my law, and ye shall be saved. But if ye enter not into my law, ye cannot receive the promises of my Father, which He made unto Abraham.

13. God commanded Abraham, and Sarah gave Hagar to Abraham to wife.† And why did she do it ? Because this was the law, and from Hagar sprang many people. This, therefore, was fulfilling, among other things, the promises. Was Abraham, therefore, under condemnation ? Verily, I say unto you, Nay ; for I, the Lord, commanded

---

* *Ye* is Joseph.

† Joe's inspired translation and correction of the Holy Scriptures, Genesis, 16th chapter, runs, " *God does not acknowledge Hagar as Abram's wife.*" Joe's inspired Bible correction "was begun in June, 1830, and finished July 2, 1833." It was Rigdon's work. The Lord (we are told) revealed polygamy to Joe as early as 1831. At that time He does not acknowledge Hagar as Abram's wife. He does, though, on the 12th July, 1843—"for I the Lord commanded" that Sarah give Hagar to Abraham to wife. Who forgets? Does Joe, or his " pard ? "

it. Abraham was commanded to offer his son Isaac; nevertheless, it was written, Thou shalt not kill. Abraham, however, did not refuse, and it was accounted unto him for righteousness.

14. Abraham received concubines, and they bare him children, and it was accounted unto him for righteousness, because they were given unto him, and he abode in my law; as Isaac also, and Jacob did none other things than that which they were commanded; and because they did none other things than that which they were commanded, they have entered into their exaltation, according to the promises, and sit upon thrones, and are not angels, but are Gods. David also received many wives and concubines, as also Solomon, and Moses my servant, as also many others of my servants, from the beginning of creation until this time; and in nothing did they sin, save in those things which they received not of me.

15. David's wives and concubines were given unto him, of me, by the hand of Nathan, my servant, and others of the prophets who had the *keys* of this power; and in none of these things did he sin against me, save in the case of Uriah and his wife; and therefore he hath fallen from his exaltation and received his portion, and he shall not inherit them out of the world, for I gave them unto another, saith the Lord.

16. I am the Lord thy God. and I gave unto thee my servant Joseph, an appointment, and restore all things; ask what ye will, and it shall be given unto you, according to my word: and as ye have asked concerning adultery * — verily, verily I say unto you, if a man receiveth a wife in the new and everlasting covenant, and if she be with another man, *and I have not appointed unto her by the holy anointing,* † she hath committed adultery, and shall be destroyed. If she be not in the new and everlasting covenant, and she be with another man, she has committed adultery; and if her husband be with another woman, and he was under a vow, he hath broken his vow,

---

* And well you might, Joseph!

† Here's where my servant's little oil-bottle comes in; a few drops make adultery all right.

and hath committed adultery; and if she hath not committed adultery, but is innocent, and hath not broken her vow, and she knoweth it, and I reveal it unto you, my servant Joseph, then shall you have power, by the power of my Holy Priesthood, to take her, and give her unto him that hath not committed adultery, but hath been faithful, for he shall be made ruler over many; for I have conferred upon you the *keys* and power of the priesthood, wherein I restore all things, and make known unto you all things in due time.*

17. And verily, verily I say unto you, that whatsoever you seal on earth shall be sealed in heaven, and whatsoever you bind on earth, in my name, and by my word, saith the Lord, it shall be eternally bound in the heavens; and whosoever sins you remit on earth shall be remitted eternally in the heavens; and whosoever sins you retain on earth shall be retained in heaven.

18. And again, verily I say, whomsoever you bless I will bless; and whomsoever you curse I will curse, saith the Lord, for I, the Lord, am thy God.

19. And again, verily I say unto you, my servant Joseph, that whatsoever you give on earth, and to whomsoever you give anyone on earth, by my word, and according to my law, it shall be visited with blessings and not cursings, and with my power, saith the Lord, and shall be without condemnation on earth, and in heaven; for I am the Lord thy God, and will be with thee even unto the end of the world, and through all eternity; for verily I *seal* upon you your exaltation, and prepare a throne for you in the kingdom of my Father, with Abraham, your father. Behold, I have seen your sacrifices,† and will forgive all your sins; I have seen your sacrifices in obedience to that which I have told you: Go, therefore, and I make A WAY FOR YOUR ESCAPE, as I accepted the offering of Abraham, of his son Isaac.

20. Verily I say unto you, a commandment I give unto *mine handmaid, Emma Smith,* your wife, whom I have

---

* What devilish trickery and doings of the Lord's Anointed servants and handmaids are here hinted at! Lust *in labyrintho.*

† But be sure to take a white *dog,* and not a white sheep!

given unto you, that she stay herself, *and partake not of that which I commanded you to offer unto her,** for I did it, saith the Lord, *to prove you all*, as I did Abraham ; and that I might require an offering at your hand, by covenant and sacrifice : and let mine handmaid Emma Smith receive all those that HAVE BEEN GIVEN unto my servant Joseph, and who are virtuous and pure before me ; and those who are not pure and have said they were pure, shall be destroyed saith the Lord God, for I am the Lord thy God, and ye shall obey my voice ; and I give unto my servant Joseph, that he shall be made ruler over many things, for he hath been faithful over a few things, and from henceforth I will strengthen him.†

21. And I command mine handmaid, Emma Smith, to abide and cleave unto my servant Joseph, and to none else.   But if she will not abide this commandment, she shall be destroyed, saith the Lord, for I am the Lord thy God, and *will destroy her* if she abide not in my law ; but if she will not abide this commandment, then shall my servant Joseph do all things for her, even as he hath said,‡ and I will bless him and multiply him, and give to him a hundred-fold in this world, of fathers and mothers,§ brothers and sisters, houses and lands, wives and children, and crowns of eternal lives in the eternal worlds.   And again, verily I say, let mine handmaid forgive my servant Joseph HIS TRESPASSES, and then shall she be forgiven her trespasses, wherein she has trespassed against me, and I, the Lord thy God, will bless her and multiply her and make her heart to rejoice.

22.   And again, I say, let not my servant Joseph put

---

* I will explain this.   Conspicuous among "all the women," Joe "wanted," was pretty Jane Law ; and in " General" William Law's house Emma had once sought refuge after a pitched battle with Mine Anointed.   A transfer of marital partners was at one time on the tapis, but Emma would not be induced to " partake."   This I have from one who personally knew of the proposed swap.   Oh, those " special instructions!"

† That will not be amiss under the circumstances !

‡ That means, I suppose, put her away and provide for her.

§ -in-law ?

his property out of his hands,* lest an enemy come and destroy him, for Satan seeketh to destroy : for I am the Lord thy God, and he is my servant, and behold ! and lo, I am with *him*, as I was with Abraham, *thy* father, even unto his exaltation and glory.

23. Now, as touching the law of the priesthood, there are many things pertaining thereunto. Verily, if a man be called of my Father, as was Aaron, by mine own voice, and by the voice of him that sent me, and I have endowed him with the *keys* of the power of the priesthood, if he do anything in my name and according to my law, and by my word, he will not commit sin, and I will justify him. Let no one therefore *set on my servant Joseph*,† for I will justify him, for he shall do the sacrifice which I require at his hands for *his transgressions*, saith the Lord your God.

24. And again, as pertaining to the law of the priesthood : If a man espouse a virgin, and desire to espouse another, and the first give her consent ; and if he espouse the second and they are virgins, and have vowed to no other man, then is he justified ; he cannot commit adultery, for they are given unto him ; for he cannot commit adultery with that that belongeth unto him, and to none else ; and if he have TEN ‡ virgins given unto him by this law, he cannot commit adultery, for they belong to him, and they are given unto him — therefore is he justified. But if one or either of the ten virgins, after she is espoused, shall be with another man, she has committed adultery, and shall be destroyed ; for they are given unto him to multiply and replenish the earth, according to my commandment, and to fulfil the promise which was given by my Father before the foundation of the world ; and for their exaltation in the eternal worlds, that they may

---

* Had mine Handmaid Emma insisted upon a division of the property ?

† Joe here hurls his *pard* in the teeth of those of his friends who, like William Law, opposed strongly his "new and everlasting covenant " of celestial whoredom.

‡ John Taylor had fulfilled the *law* to the letter, when he denied polygamy.

bear the souls of men; for herein is the work of my
Father continued, that He may be glorified.

25. And again, verily, verily I say unto you, if any
man have a wife, who holds the *keys* of this power, and he
teaches unto her the law of my priesthood, as pertaining
to these things, then *shall she believe,** and administer
unto him, or she shall be *destroyed*, saith the Lord your
God, for I will destroy her; for I will magnify my name
upon all those who receive and abide in my law. Therefore it shall be lawful in me, if she receive not this law,
for him to receive all things† whatsoever I, the Lord *his*
God, will give unto him because she did not believe and
administer unto him according to my word; and she then
becomes the transgressor, and he is exempt from THE LAW
OF SARAH, who administered unto Abraham according to
the law when I commanded Abraham to take Hagar to
wife. And now as pertaining to this law, verily, verily
I say unto you I will reveal more unto you hereafter,
therefore, let this suffice for the present. Behold, I am
Alpha and Omega, Amen.

---

* That is the *free consent* of Mormon women; they *shall* believe,
or be destroyed.

† So Mormon women are *things*, are they? and the Mormon
priest may have "all the women he wants," his first *thing* of a wife
consenting or not.

THE PROPHET'S BROTHERS.

———

Hyrum Smith—Easily Celestialized—John D. Lee, the Pious and Cautious Danite—Night Scenes in Nauvoo—Nine Fresh Wives in One Year — Brigham Young as " Polyg" in Nauvoo — Character of Hyrum—William Smith, the Apostolic Brute, Criminal, and Pious Writer.

———

Hyrum Smith, born February 11, 1800, was a little better than Prophet Joe, and William, born March 13, 1811, was worse than the prophet. Like Joe, they had never been engaged in any honest profession or work, but were money-diggers and vagabonds, and joined heart and hand in the great imposture of the prophet.

Hyrum was one of the first to go into polygamy, after Joseph had received the " revelation " from his accommodating *Lord*. John D. Lee tells us in his " Confession " how he was initiated by the Patriarch Hyrum into the " new law : "

"One day the chief of police came to me and said that I must take two more policemen that he named and watch the house of a widow named Clawson. I was informed that a man went there nearly every night about ten o'clock and left about daylight. I was also ordered to station myself and my men near the house, and when the man came out we were to knock him down and castrate him, and not to be careful how hard we hit, for it would not be inquired into if we killed him. I felt a timidity about carrying out these orders. It was my duty to report all *unusual* orders that I received from my superiors on the police force, to the Prophet Joseph Smith, or in his absence to Hyrum, next in authority. I went to the house of the prophet, but he was not at home. I then called for Hyrum and he gave me an interview. I told him the orders that I had received from the chief and asked him if I should obey or not. He said to me: 'Brother Lee, you have acted wisely in listening to the voice of the spirit. It was the influence of God's spirit that sent you here. You would have been guilty of a great crime if you had obeyed your chief's orders.' Hyrum then told me that the man that I was ordered to attack was Howard Egan, and that he had been sealed to Mrs. Clawson, and that their marriage was a most holy one; that it was in accordance to a *revelation* that the prophet had recently received direct from God. He then explained to me fully the doctrine of polygamy, and wherein it was permitted, and why it was right. I was greatly interested in the doctrine. It accorded exactly with my views of the Scripture, and I at once accepted and believed in the doctrine as taught by the revelations received by the prophet. As a matter of course, I did not carry out the orders of the chief. I had him instructed in his duty, and so Egan was never bothered by the police. A few months after that I was sealed to my second wife. I was sealed to her by Brigham Young, then one of the twelve. *In less than one year after I first learned the will of God concerning the marriage of the Saints I was the husband of nine wives.*" — [Lee, p. 288.]

In course of time, Lee, the worthy disciple of Joe, Hyrum and Brigham, had nineteen wives and sixty-four children; which constitutes, in the Mormon idea, a good, middle-sized "kingdom." It must have been an interesting life in Nauvoo; it might look very "celestial" to the Mormon leaders, but it looks like a beastly pandemonium to a stupid Gentile. Policeman Lee takes nine wives in a twelvemonth! "Joseph never had any other wife except me," says Sister Emma on her death-bed! "The Prophet Joseph had eighty, a hundred, or more, wives sealed to him," says one of our witnesses! "Polygamy— touch it, and you trample upon our religious rights guaranteed to us by the Constitution," shout Mormon men and women, in grand chorus!

Lee says (p. 167): "Plural marriages were not made public. They had to be kept still. *A young man did not know when he was talking to a single woman.* As far as Brigham Young was concerned, he had no wives at his house, except his first wife, or the one that he said was his first wife. Many a night have I gone with him, arm in arm, and guarded him while he spent an hour or two with his young brides, then guarded him home and guarded his house until one o'clock, when I was relieved."

But to return to Hyrum Smith. Mrs. Sarah Pratt says of him : " He was smarter than Joseph, always inclined to mercy, no drinker, and a tolerable speaker. He liked good horses and was a good rider." Another witness says : " Hyrum was rather reticent and dignified, entirely different from Joseph in his disposition. Joseph and Hyrum loved each other very much and had great confidence in each other." A third witness states : " Hyrum was gentlemanlike in appearance and manners : he was a great fanatic in Mormonism, but had more general knowledge than Joseph."

The following letter, dated February 15, 1844—a year after Wm. Clayton's walk with the prophet—shows clearly that Hyrum Smith was a full-grown Jesuit. He lies directly and horribly about polygamy in Nauvoo, and then proceeds to instruct the elders to teach nothing but the "first principles" of the gospel, faith in Jesus Christ, baptism for the remission of sins, etc., all the sweet things called "milk for babies" from the pulpit, while polygamy, Danitism, treasonable endowments, blind obedience to the priesthood, etc., the "meat for strong men" are preached and practiced secretly for the benefit of the prophet and his next friends. All those things are holy *mysteries* to be taught when the fools are fixed and gathered to Zion. The same dodge has always been used on the outside and is used to-day by the missionaries everywhere. Here is Hyrum's letter, copied from page 474 of the *Times and Seasons :*
*

NAUVOO, March 15, 1844.

To the Brethren of the Church of Jesus Christ of Latter-day Saints, living on China Creek, Hancock Co., Greeting:—WHEREAS, Brother Richard Hewitt has called upon me to-day, to know my views concerning some doctrines that are preached in your place, and states to me that some of your elders say that a man *having a certain priesthood* may have as many wives as he pleases, and that doctrine is taught here: I say unto you that that man teaches FALSE DOCTRINE, for *there is no such doctrine taught here; neither is there any such thing practiced here.* And any man that is found teaching privately or publicly any such doctrine, is culpable, and will stand a chance to be brought before the High Council and lose his license and membership also: Therefore, he had better beware what he is about.

And again I say unto you, an elder has NO BUSINESS to undertake to PREACH MYSTERIES in any part of the world, for God has commanded us all to preach NOTHING BUT THE FIRST PRINCIPLES unto the world. Neither has any elder any authority to preach any mysterious thing to any branch of the church, unless he has a *direct commandment from God* to do so. Let the matter of the grand councils of heaven, and the making of Gods, worlds, and devils *entirely alone*: for you are *not called* to teach any such doctrine—*for neither you nor the people are capacitated to understand any such principles*—less so to teach them. For when God commands men to teach such principles the Saints will receive them. Therefore, beware what you teach! for the mysteries of God are not given to all men; and unto those to whom they are given they are placed under restrictions to impart only such as God will command them; and the residue *is to be kept in a faithful breast*, otherwise he will be brought under condemnation. By this God will prove his faithful servants who will be called and numbered *with the chosen.*

And as to the celestial glory, all will enter in and possess that Kingdom that obey the gospel, and continue in faith in the Lord unto the end of his days. Now, therefore, I say unto you, you must *cease preaching your miraculous things*, and let the mysteries alone until bye and bye. Preach faith in the Lord Jesus Christ; repentance and baptism for the remission of sins; the laying on of hands for the gift of the Holy Ghost; teaching the necessity of strict obedience unto these principles; reasoning out of the Scriptures; proving them unto the people. Cease your schisms and divisions and your contentions. Humble yourselves as in dust and ashes, lest God should make you an ensample of his wrath unto the surrounding world. Amen.

In the bonds of the everlasting covenant, I am,

Your obedient servant,

HYRUM SMITH.

I don't know, but this letter seems to me one of the most meaty little documents in the history of Mormondom. Talk of the *sincerity* of those sleek chaps! They seal and get sealed, right and left, that it seems a sort of regular exercise for them, as playing at skittles is for plethoric gentlemen—but there is not " ANY such thing practiced here ! '' The *mysteries* are for Joe, Hyrum, Kimball,

Brigham, policeman Lee and other "chosen" ones, policemen or not; they are the Lord's confidential employes
in the department for "the making of Gods, worlds and
devils"—for it seems they make devils too: I take this as
a delicate allusion to the swearing in of *Danites* and
Destroying Angels. "The making of Gods, worlds and
devils!" Am I not right in saying that they are a set of
infernal scoundrels, but at the same time immensely
funny?

When Aminadab writes this at once rascally and nonsensical piece of a Jesuitical denial, he is over head and
ears in polygamy himself. We have seen him on July
12, 1843, using all his influence with Joe to make him
write the revelation. At or about this time the saintly
Hyrum gets sealed to his own sister-in-law, a widow,
apparently a good, simple soul of the type of the old
spinster who gives fifteen hundred dollars to Joseph in
Kirtland. She is yet alive, poor soul, over eighty years
old and has only recently* published her little sealing
story in the church organ. This is so characteristic that
I cannot help inserting it here. It is directed to Joseph
Smith, son of the prophet, and president of the reorganized Mormon church, which denies Joseph's having been
a polygamist:

"After having asked my Father in heaven to aid me, I sit down to
write a few lines as dictated by the Holy Spirit. My beloved husband,
R. B. Thompson, your father's [the Prophet's] private secretary to the
end of his mortal life, died August 27, 1841. Nearly two years after
his death your father [the prophet] told me that my husband *had
appeared to him several times,* telling him that he did not wish me to
live such a lonely life and wished him to request your uncle Hyrum to
have me sealed to him *for time.* Hyrum communicated this to his
wife (my sister), who, by request, opened the subject to me, when
everything within me rose in opposition to such a step; but when your
father [the prophet] called and explained the subject to me, I dared
not refuse to obey the counsel, lest, peradventure, I should be found
fighting against God; and especially when he told me the last time my
husband appeared to him, he came *with such power,* that it made him
tremble."

A very pretty novel. Hyrum likes the widow, so

* Deseret News, February 6. 1886.

Joseph has to get a dream, and then not Hyrum, but Mrs.
Hyrum has to do the wooing. Mrs. Hyrum obeys counsel, but Mrs. Thompson hesitates, so Joseph has to labor
with her personally, and he does so, fortified by the
remembrance of that bleeding Spaniard. I see him sitting
with Mrs. Thompson and telling her, with what *power* the
spirit of poor Mr. Thompson came to him, so that he
made even a prophet tremble and shake; and I see poor
Mrs. Thompson listening with wide-open eyes. The fixing moment for the fools has arrived:

> " He [Joseph] then inquired of the Lord what he should do; the
> answer was, 'Go and do as my servant [the late lamented Mr. Thomp-
> son] has required.' Joseph then took an opportunity of communicat-
> ing this to your uncle Hyrum, who told me that the Holy Spirit rested
> upon him [Joseph] from the crown of his head to the soles of his
> feet."

This little passage proves clearer than anything that
the force of Mormonism lies in the superstition of simple
souls, the devotion of loving hearts, the best instincts and
purest virtues of womanhood. Mrs. Thompson cannot
resist the command of a man who is steeped in Holy Ghost
as Achilles was in Lethe water. So the sealing humbug gets
performed:

> " The time was appointed with the consent of all parties, and your
> father [the prophet] sealed me to your uncle [Hyrum] *for time*, in my
> sister's [Mrs. Hyrum's] room, *with a covenant to deliver me up in the
> morning of the resurrection to Robert Blaskel Thompson, with what-
> ever offspring should be the result of that union*, and I remained his
> wife, the same as my sister, to the day of his death.
>
> [Signed,]   ❦   MERCY R. THOMPSON.

Oh, you lucky dog of a Blaskel, won't you jump for
joy when Hyrum, the martyred patriarch, steps up in the
morning of the resurrection and hands the old woman
over to you, Blaskel, with a pair of kids! "I had her
for time, Blaskel," will he say, with a voice vibrating with
Pecksniff emotion: "I would have kept her longer and
the *offspring* would be more satisfactory as to number, if
the hellish mob hadn't shot me at Carthage. But never
mind, Blaskel, she is now yours for all eternity; take her.
By the way, let me introduce you to the Lord who sits
yonder chatting with David Patten, our first martyr."——

William Smith, who became an apostle of the church, was a horrible character. Drinking, fighting, and ruining virtuous females by the wholesale, were his saint-like occupations. He was the chief manager of the organized system of horse and cattle stealing constantly practiced on the "Gentile" neighborhood of the Mormon settlements, and in the distribution of counterfeit money. You might call him a professor of the art of "*milking the Gentiles.*" He is yet alive, if I am not mistaken; and more pious than ever. I have a very oily little pamphlet, written by him, about the origin of the Book of Mormon. * He shows in it that he can lie to perfection, just like old Mother Smith and Joe. The little book contains a pretty good likeness of Lucy Smith, the mother of so many holy men. She looks just like her book† on Joseph, the prophet.

PRESIDENT SIDNEY RIGDON.

Joseph a Magnet—Rigdon the real Inventor of Mormonism— Frightful Accident with the Keys of the Kingdom— Joseph the Wrestler and Rigdon the Craw-Fish—Nancy Rigdon—Criminal Masonry—A Hundred Thousand Dollars in Gold—Sidney Predicts Joseph in the Bible— Sad End of the First Mormon Fanatic.

It becomes now our duty to have a little chat about Joseph's friends. The prophet was a magnet of the greatest force for all kinds of adventurers, for "*Catilinarian existences,*" as Prince Bismarck would say. Already, when a boy in Palmyra and Manchester, he was captain of a

---

* Published in Lamoni, Iowa, 1883.

† By a bull from Pope Brigham this very edifying little volume was ordered to be destroyed. In Yankee slang, it unwittingly let too many cats out of the Mormon bag.

band of vagabonds, petty thieves and swindlers, and lived
with them on the credulity and cupidity of the neighborhood.   To live on the spoils of dupes became the principle of his life.   Men broken in business, others with half
education and spoiled reputations, reckless fortune-seekers
ready to embark in any scheme that would feed and clothe
them—all were welcome to join the new gospel, but under
condition *to obey counsel*, that is, to become slaves of
Joseph, and to be, heart and soul, professors of the great
fundamental imposture, the lie about the golden plates,
the apparitions of angels, etc.

Sidney Rigdon, a farmer's son, and tanner by trade,
later a Campbellite preacher, had three prominent qualities:
1. He was half illiterate ; no education is better than
half a one.   2. He was a fanatic : theocracy, community
of goods, spiritual wifery (marrying for eternity) were his
chief hobbies.   3. He was entirely unprincipled : any
means that would lead him to a position of ease and
importance, were welcome.   So constituted, having
obtained possession of Spaulding's "Manuscript Found," he
got Smith to publish it.   The Mormon leaders try to ridi-
cule the " Spaulding romance ;" but if anything is proved
in history, the story of the conversion of Spaulding's
"Manuscript Found" into the Book of Mormon is proved.
Sidney having very little education and Smith none at all,
the imposture turned out a very clumsy one.   But it is
clever enough for the kind of proselytes the Mormon missionaries angle for, foreign peasants and the poorest ele-
ments of manufacturing towns.   It is always to be remembered that the missionaries do not hold out the " Book of
Mormon," but bait their hooks with the "gospel of Christ,"
with "purity, love, brotherhood," etc.   The Book of
Mormon was originally the work of a dullard, and i
not and will never be anything but a stupid, tasteless,
ridiculous travesty of the Bible, the most somniferous of all
existing books.

Sidney was the most self-conceited crank of the century.   He was a coarse, ready, gabbling speaker, with
some slight, very slight pretensions as a writer, on Bible
themes ; but, as one who knew him well said of him, was

"wholly lacking in the moral make-up." His picture reminds me of some ancient, seedy, half-dazed Israelite, with a strong admixture of the Jesuit. But the only picture I have seen of him was taken in later life. Sidney used to say he had suffered ten times as much as Jesus Christ. But the great martyr liked fine clothes, gold watches, and good comfortable houses. He made his dupes provide him with all these luxuries; if they hesitated, he threatened that the "Keys" would be taken away from the church.

A day or two after the tarring and feathering of "my servants Sidney and Joseph" in Hiram, Ohio, March 25, 1832, the "Keys of the Kingdom" are taken in earnest from the church by my servant Sidney. Let me give a page here from old Lucy's inimitable chronicle:

"Immediately after Sidney's arrival, we met for the purpose of holding a prayer meeting, and, as Sidney had not been with us for some time, we hoped to hear from him upon this occasion. We waited a long time before he made his appearance; at last he came in, seemingly much agitated. He did not go to the stand, but began to pace back and forth through the house. My husband said: 'Brother Sidney, we would like to hear a discourse from you to-day.' Rigdon replied in a tone of excitement: '*The Keys of the Kingdom are rent from the church*, and there shall not be a prayer put up in this house to-day.' 'Oh! no,' said Mr. Smith, 'I hope not.' 'I tell you *they are*,' rejoined Elder Rigdon, 'and no man or woman shall put up a prayer in this place to-day.' This greatly disturbed the minds of many sisters and some brethren. The brethren stared and turned pale and the sisters cried; sister Howe, in particular, was very much terrified. 'Oh, dear me!' said she, 'what shall we do? What shall we do? *The Keys of the Kingdom are taken from us*, and what shall we do?' 'I tell you again,' said Sidney, with much feeling, 'the Keys of the Kingdom are taken from you, and you never will have them again *until you build me a new house.*'"

This is a delightful little scene. Mr. and Mrs. Micawber Smith are excited; Mrs. Gummidge Howe weeps over the lost Keys, and Sidney, (who is still smarting from the tar and feathers, and mad because his dupes have not provided him a suitable private residence in Kirtland) crushes all those weak creatures with the "firmness" of a Murdstone. A new house, or the Keys are gone! O those wonderful Keys in Mormonism!

The situation is critical. Brother Hyrum jumps on horseback to fetch the prophet from Hiram, where Rigdon and Joe have been translating and revelating. Joseph comes at once, and puts things in order. "I myself," says he, "hold the keys of this last dispensation, and will forever hold them, both in time and eternity; so set your hearts at rest upon that point; all is right." Sister Howe could breathe again, the Keys were not lost. Sidney was duly disciplined, and even permitted his license to be taken from him "for having lied in the name of the Lord." My servant Sidney had opened his foaming mouth too wide, and had incontinently put his foot in it! Nor was this all. "He had to suffer for his folly," says old Lucy, "for, *according to his own account,* he was dragged out of bed by the devil, three times in one night, by his heels."

Comedies of Errors in that kind were by no means rare between Joseph and his Mentor. Sidney, twelve years Joseph's senior, tried to play the first violin now and again, but Joseph always put him back among the common fiddlers of his gospel orchestra. John D. Lee tells a very lively and amusing story of "a tussle between the prophet and his mouthpiece," which happened in the "war" between Missourians and Mormons, in 1838.

"During the time that we were camping at Adam-ondi-Ahman the men were shivering over a few fire-brands, feeling out of sorts and quite cast down. The prophet came up while the brethren were moping around, and caught first one of them and then another and shook them up and said: 'Get out of here and wrestle, jump, run, do anything but mope around, warm yourselves up; this inactivity will not do for soldiers.' The words of the prophet put life and energy into the men. A ring was soon formed. The prophet stepped into the ring, ready for a tussle with any comer. Several went into the ring to try their strength, but each one was thrown by the prophet, until he had thrown several of the stoutest of the men present. Then he stepped out of the ring and took a man by the arm and led him to take his place, and so it continued, the men who were thrown retiring in favor of the successful one. While the sport was at its height, Sidney Rigdon, the mouthpiece of the prophet, rushed into the ring, *sword in hand*, and said that he would not suffer a lot of men to break the Sabbath day in that manner. For a moment all were silent, then one of the brethren, with more presence of mind than the others, said to the prophet: 'Brother Joseph, we want you to clear us from blame, for, we formed the ring by your request. You told us to wrestle, and now Brother Rigdon is bringing us to account for it.'

"The prophet walked into the ring and said, as he made a motion with his hand: 'Brother Sidney, you had better go out of here and let the boys alone; they are amusing themselves according to my orders. You are an old man. You go and get ready for meeting, and let the boys alone.' Just then, catching Rigdon off his guard, as quick as a flash he knocked the sword from Rigdon's hand, then caught him by the shoulder and said: 'Now, old man, you *must* go out, or I will throw you down.' Rigdon was as large a man as the prophet, but not so tall. The prospect of a tussle between the prophet and his mouthpiece was fun for all but Rigdon, who pulled back like a craw-fish; but the resistance was useless, the prophet dragged him from the ring, bareheaded, and tore his fine pulpit coat from the collar to the waist. Then he turned to the men and said: 'Go in, boys, and have your fun. You shall never have it to say that I got you into any trouble that I did not get you out of.' Rigdon complained about the loss of his hat and the tearing of his coat. Joseph said to him: 'You were out of your place. Always keep your place and you will not suffer. You have no one to blame but yourself.' After that Rigdon never countermanded the orders of the prophet —*he knew who was boss.*"

This is surely as good a portrait of the two impostors as was ever drawn. As to Rigdon's personal appearance, my witnesses tell me that he was rather good-looking and "gentlemanly" in his ways; of stoutish build. He had a pretty and charming wife. Nancy, his daughter, was an attractive, good girl, like her sisters; their mother had given them a good education. Joseph took a fancy to Nancy. He got her to that "often engaged" room, where he tried to make of Martha Brotherton, a handsome, high-strung English girl, one of the concubines of the inner circle of the priesthood. (See the most dramatic account of Martha in the Documents at the end of Part I.)

Nancy, that stubborn wretch, refused to be *sealed* to the man who tried to make prostitutes of *all* the wives and daughters of his friends. The story of his attempt upon her virtue made a great noise in Nauvoo: read the very graphic account of it in Bennett's book. Sidney, while in Nauvoo, had become a sedate man of about fifty years. He liked spiritual wifery, but in a discreet way, you see, and he felt that Joseph was doing things too boisterously and that it would lead them all to the demnition bow-wows, so to speak. And as to giving away his own daughter, he objected to that, of course, although he liked a little frolicking with other people's daughters well enough.

As a speaker Rigdon outdid Joseph by far. He spoke very rapidly, and used to get tremendously excited, so that he foamed at the mouth. Jedediah Grant became in Utah his successor in this beastly fury.

As a good specimen of Rigdon's chaste pulpit style, which I find emulated by Joe, Brigham, Heber C. Kimball, "Jeddy" Grant, John Taylor, and the lesser Mormon lights, take the following passage from Rigdon's Conference speech, April 6, 1844, as given in the *Times and Seasons*, p. 524: "I want devils to gratify themselves; and if howling, yelping, yelling will do you any good, do it till you are all damned. If calling us devils, etc., will do you any good, let us have the whole of it, and you can then go on your own way to hell without a grunt." And this set of piratical ruffians, not content with calling themselves a "church," want to be church and State in one. Says Rigdon in the same speech, "When God sets up a system of salvation, he sets up a *system of government*; when I speak of a government, I mean what I say, I mean a government that shall rule *over* TEMPORAL *and spiritual affairs.* Every man is a government of himself, and infringes on no government. A man is not an honorable man if he is not *above all law and above government.* THE LAWS OF GOD ARE FAR ABOVE THE LAWS OF THE LAND." Here you have Mormonism in a nutshell, statesmen and students of the Mormon problem, fresh from the lips of its real founder.

Rigdon was the heart and soul of Mormonism in the first time. It was with religion just as with the Kirtland bank —Rigdon was president and Joseph cashier. In Nauvoo there came a great change. Mormonism gave up the strictly Scriptural dodge and turned from the parody of Bible to a travesty of *Masonry*, which is the little understood key of Mormonism in its present state. "Mormonism is nothing but CRIMINAL MASONRY," said to me one of my most thoroughly informed witnesses. As long as this feature, represented in the secret endowments, is not understood, Mormonism will continue to be a riddle to the world.

Joseph outgrew Rigdon in Nauvoo and put him on the shelf. Rigdon was great with his tongue, but he lacked Joseph's verve and brigand daring. After Joseph's death Brigham, who was a born bandit, and wore, as he often preached in Salt Lake, a bosom pin in Nauvoo, meaning a big bowie knife—Brigham put Rigdon, the foaming pulpit hero, easily out of the field. He was kept quiet with a pension and threatened with Danite vengeance if he ever split. But he mumbled a little, anyhow, just enough to give away the whole thing. After leaving Nauvoo he told James Jeffries in St. Louis that he had taken Spaulding's manuscript and given it to Joseph Smith to publish. From that time — 1844 — up to his death, Mormon gold kept him quiet, just as it did in the cases of publisher Howe and "Dr." Hurlbut, who got the MS. of Spaulding's "Manuscript Found" from Spaulding's widow and sold out to the Mormon leaders.

Sidney died in Pennsylvania in 1876, aged 83, a nobody, and a confirmed infidel. He was wont to declare, when near his end, "If I had ten years more of vigorous life I would overthrow all religions."

One more anecdote of him. At the time when through the zeal of noble Judge McKean, the Utah kingdom seemed about to collapse, Sidney wrote to Brigham that he would save the church if Brigham would give him one hundred thousand dollars *in gold.* Brigham was sick when the letter came. When he got better it was read to him. Rolling over in his bed slowly he drawled out: " *I wonder if Sidney wouldn't take one hundred thousand dollars in greenbacks?*" I have this delightful little story from an ex-Mormon, who used to be at home at the " Lion House."

Let me conclude this Rigdon chapter with a little novel of mine. It was in June, 1830. Joe and Rigdon, his " Director," were sitting in some log cabin. The Book of Mormon was printed, the church founded. Joe felt good as new-established prophet. " That is all very well," said Sidney, " but all is not yet done. We must get the old Bible to *predict you,* Joe, your father and the Book of Mormon. Do you catch on, Joe?" The prophet opened his eyes wide. " Splendid idea, old fellow," says he, " But how can you manage this new trick?" Says Sidney: " Didn't I create a whole new Bible out of that stuff of old crank Spaulding? Just let me sit down for a while and I shall make blush all those old prophets, take my word for it, Joe, old boy."

And Sidney sat down in July, 1830, and the " inspired translation and correction " of the good old Bible was finished in July, 1833. " It was all in the hand-writing of Sidney Rigdon," said Mr. Blair, the careful editor of Sidney's Bible, to my friend Cobb ; and Cobb said gravely, " Oh, thank you, much obliged." Friend C. is always much obliged when interesting people give themselves away, you see. Are they not a set of funny knaves, Sidney, Joe and the rest of them? They *translate* everything. It would have been the easiest thing in the world for them to give us a new Homer, and prove that Achilles shot Hector with a cavalry pistol and that fair Helen was Paris's spiritual wife !

But look at Rigdon, the inspired translator and corrector of the Bible :

BIBLE (King James translation):

And Joseph said unto his brethren, I die: and God will surely visit you and bring you out of this land unto the land which He sware unto Abraham, Isaac and Jacob. (Genesis, L., 24.)

THE HOLY SCRIPTURES, TRANSLATED AND CORRECTED by the Spirit of Revelation, by Joseph Smith, Jr., the Seer:

" And Joseph saith unto his Brethren, I die and go unto my fathers; and I go down to my grave with joy .... and it shall come to pass that they (my people) shall be scattered again; and a branch shall be broken off, and shall be carried into a far country [America]; nevertheless they shall be remembered in the covenants of the Lord, when the Messiah cometh; for he shall be made manifest unto them in the LATTER DAYS .... A *seer* shall the Lord my God raise up, who shall be a choice seer unto the fruit of my loins ....., and that seer [Mr. Joseph Smith, Jr.,] will I bless, and they that seek to destroy him shall be confounded; *and his name shall be* CALLED JOSEPH, *and it shall be* AFTER THE NAME OF HIS FATHER [Mr. Joseph Smith, Sr.] .... The thing which the Lord shall bring forth by his [General Joseph Smith's] hand shall bring my people unto salvation."

They are all predicted, you see, old Micawber-Smith, and the Lieutenant-General, his son. It's a pity they didn't predict Eliza and the broomstick, the log by the river, and Charlie, the family horse. But this is not all. Joseph's or rather Sidney Rigdon's inspired " correction" of the Bible predicts also the Book of Mormon, and not only Joseph Senior and Joseph Junior. Look at the prophecies of Isaiah XXIX., and compare them with the new inspired additions:

"And it shall come to pass that *the Lord God* shall bring forth unto you the words of a BOOK .... and the book shall be a revelation from God, from the beginning of the world to the ending thereof .... The eyes of none shall behold it, save it be that THREE WITNESSES shall behold it by the power of God [Messrs. Martin Harris, Oliver Cowdery and David Whitmer]; and they shall certify to the truth of the book and the things therein. And woe be unto him that rejecteth the word of God ...."

I have given enough of this woeful stuff to show the monumental cheek of its concoctor, Sidney Rigdon, Esq. Laugh I must, but graver students who feel interested in this matter of sect-framing and lunacy-breeding may compare at their leisure the Bible with Rigdon's " inspired " rubbish, published by the "re-organized" Mormon church, 1867. It seems to me, however, that the prophet's son, (whose coming forth in the latter days is *not*, strange to say, predicted in Genesis along with the coming forth of his honored sire and grandsire,) who is the visible head of the "Reorganized Church," doesn't half understand the business of book-publishing. Why not call it "Lucy's family Bible" or, "the true Bible key," or, "the three-cornered family diamond?"

Since this was written, I have been credibly informed of the following facts: Rigdon, after having retired to Pittsburg, Pennsylvania, organized a little Mormon Eden, or more properly speaking, a little Mormon hell of his own, where community of goods, his favorite and life-long hobby, played an important part. He bought, after having obtained from a relative a loan of one thousand dollars, a tract of four hundred acres in the mountainous region of the State, intended as the *nucleus* of the true "Zion." This tract he laid out in lots, and his followers "gathered" to the place. But it was not all dry, serious religion what they practiced; there was some *fun*, "and that too most holy," to be sure. On the tract aforesaid was a big barn, and this barn was "ordained and set apart" for religious ceremonies, which were in substance the same kind of pastime indulged in by Joseph and his inner circle in Nauvoo, and in Southampton, England, by Elder Margetts. I cannot help thinking, in my Gentile corruption, what decent fellows those Turks are compared with the founders and upholders of the new and ever-lusting gospel.

DOCTOR JOHN C. BENNETT.

The Napoleon of Nauvoo—A Modern Sejanus—A Fine Blessing by Hyrum Smith—"My Servant Bennett"— Joab, General in Israel—Visits in the Historian's Office—Apostle Richards and other Interesting People—The Author Gets a Holy Bouncing—They Cannot Lie—Joab Leaves Nauvoo—Dies in Obscurity.

Dr. John C. Bennett, physician, quartermaster general, master in chancery, major general, mayor, chancellor of the Nauvoo University—this is another star, or rather, meteor in the history of Nauvoo. We know him already; Mrs. Sarah M. Pratt has given us a portrait of him, which shows conclusively that one can be a great man in the world while he would be a very little one in the penitentiary. But I like that fellow Bennett first-rate all the same, in an artistic way, of course, because he is such an excellent type of the "Catilinarian existences" above quoted.

Who was Dr. Bennett? In the opinion of Governor Ford * he was the greatest scamp in the West. In his own conceit he was, if second to anybody, so only to Napoleon the Great. He was a physician, had some military knowledge, picked up God knows where, a towering ambition and a very keen sense of female beauty, or, to speak like a Mormon elder, for the blessings of Abraham, Jacob, Solomon and David. He thought he could use Joseph as a ladder to greatness, but Joseph used him as a tool, and when he had learned all the tricks of Bennett, he threw him away, as he did his first master and mentor, "my servant Sidney," as he did "that old granny, Martin Harris." Bennett lived eighteen months in Nau-

---

* See "History of Illinois." The part of this book which treats of the Mormons is admirable in substance and spirit.

voo, organized the new Mormon empire, wrote the charters
of the city and procured their passage in the State legislature ; drilled the Nauvoo legion, practiced abortion for
the prophet, treated professionally the *maladies galantes*
of the high priesthood, helped Joseph to organize the
criminal masonry of the endowment, in which he assumed
the role of " Holy Ghost," was his accomplice in the attempted murder of Governor Boggs, and who knows in
how many other schemes of this kind, and enjoyed the blessings of Isaac and Jacob, etc.   But all of a sudden he fell
like *Sejanus*.   Yes, he fell, after having been mayor of
the city, chancellor of the Nauvoo " University," major-
general of the Nauvoo Legion, and, as my homespun
friend Webb says, " chief cook and bottle-washer " in
general.   And why did he fall?   *Look out for the woman !*
as the Frenchman has it.   He and Joseph wanted, it
seems, to shower the blessings of Abraham and Jacob on
the same beauties.   Dismissed from his high position, he
lectured in the States against Joseph and wrote a book
which in its theatrical pathos reminds me often of Fal-,
staff's excellent friend " Pistol ; " but this book * is, besides being a clever compilation of Howe's and other
anti-Mormon publications, *true* in all essential points ;
what Bennett tells is true.   I had his tale confirmed by all
my old witnesses.   The only thing to be said against the
book is the fact, that he does not tell the *whole* truth.
He avoids this partly because it would damn himself, and
then because the whole truth about Mormonism cannot be
printed—it is too filthy for type.

How big a light the doctor was in Nauvoo, in the beginning of his eighteen months career, is best seen by a
blessing pronounced on Bennett's head by Patriarch Hyrum
Smith.   I wonder whether the two augurs did not laugh
to each other while this " blessing "-comedy was going
on ?   Here are some tid-bits of the document :

" John C. Bennett— I lay my hands upon thy head in the name of
Jesus Christ, and inasmuch as *thou* art a son of Abraham, I bless *you*
with the holy priesthood, with all its graces and gifts and with wisdom

---

* The History of the Saints, or, an expose of Joe Smith and Mormonism.   Boston, 1842.

in all the mysteries of God. Thou shalt have knowledge given thee, and shalt understand the *keys* by which all mysteries shall be unlocked. Thou shalt have great power among the children of men and shalt have influence among the great and the noble, even to prevail on many and bring them to the knowledge of the truth. Thou shalt prevail over thy enemies. Many souls shall believe because of the *proclamation* which thou shalt make. The Holy Spirit shall rest upon thee, insomuch that thy voice shall make the foundation on which thou standest to shake—so great shall be the power of God."

This is a very fine metaphor. Hyrum has learned a good deal from Micawber–Smith, his father. But let him go on :

"God's favor shall rest upon thee in dreams and visions, which shall manifest the glory of God. Beloved Brother, if thou art faithful thou shalt have power to heal the sick ; cause the lame to leap like an hart, the deaf to hear, and the dumb to speak and their voice shall salute thine ears. Thou shalt be like unto Paul and shalt have the visions of heaven open, even as they were to him.

" Thy name shall be known in many nations, and thy voice shall be heard among many people. Yea, unto many of the remnants of Israel shalt thou be known, and thou shalt proclaim the gospel unto many tribes of the house of Israel.

" God is with thee and has wrought upon thy heart to come up to this place that thou mayest be satisfied that the servants of God dwell here [in Nauvoo]. God shall reward thee for thy kindness. Thou must travel and labor for Zion, for this is the mind and will of God. Be like Paul. Let God be thy shield and buckler, and he shall shield thee forever. Angels shall guide thee, and shall lift thee out of many dangers and difficulties.

" Thou shalt have power over many of thy friends and relations, and shalt prevail with them, and when thou shalt reason with them, it shall be like Paul reasoning with Felix, and they shall tremble when they hear thy words. Thou shalt be blessed with the blessings of Abraham, Isaac and Jacob [aha], and if thou art faithful, thou shalt be yet a Patriarch, and the blessings thou shalt pronounce shall be sealed in heaven. If thou continue faithful and steadfast in the everlasting *covenant*, thou shalt have power over the winds and the waves, and they shall obey thy voice when thou shalt speak in the name of Jesus Christ. Thou shalt be crowned with immortality in the celestial kingdom, when Christ shall descend. Even so, Amen."

Hyrum's blessing bears the date of September 21, 1840. The Lord seems to have been pretty well satisfied with the services of the Doctor, since He speaks of him four months later, in a revelation dated Jan. 19, 1841, in very flattering terms. If a subscriber to the *Times and Seasons*, the church organ, the Lord must have been highly pleased in seeing His words printed in No. 15, Vol. II. :

"Again, let my servant John C. Bennett help you [Joseph] in your labor in sending my word to the kings of the people of the earth, and stand by you, even you my servant Joseph Smith *in the hour of afflic- tion*, and his reward shall not fail *if he receive counsel*; and for his love he shall be great; for he shall be mine if he does this, *saith the Lord.* I have seen the work which he hath done, which I accept, if he con- tinue, and will crown him with blessings and great glory."

I see lots of interesting things in this little bit of a heavenly dispatch. That old " pard " of Joe's is a wicked wag. Don't you see his villainous allusions? " Hour of affliction"—what else does it mean but those eternal troubles with that obstinate " legal " wife of Joe's, the elect lady? And, besides, doesn't it mean those disagreable cases whenever "*one of Joseph's women was in trouble ?*" Well, Bennett did surely his best to get Joe out of his scrapes. He advises him to get a revelation that polyga- my is right, and as to the other " afflictions," he does all a skillful physician can do in such cases. The Lord " has seen the work he has done," and no doubt that crooked instrument, too, described by Mrs. Pratt, and He has " accepted it." I have never seen anything in all my life which comes near this in the way of a handy, comfortable religion. Have you?

General Bennett tries, besides, to send the prophet's word to the kings and people of the earth. He thunders in the *Nauvoo Wasp,* a little weekly edited by Joseph's brother William, the prototype of all criminal brutes in Mormondom. Here is one of his Pistol-letters :

The grievances of this people must be redressed and my hands shall help to do it—should they have to reach to the highest courts of heav- en, dig to the lowest bowels of hell, or encompass the broad expanse of the universe of God, to consummate so desirable a result.

JOAB,
General in Israel.

I hope the Lord has seen this "work" of his servant Joab Bennett and *accepted* it. Or did he like that other better? It is a little more poetical :

" *Missouri* has been to the Saints like the bohan upas to the weary pilgrim, and though my hands be bound, my feet fettered and my tongue palsied, yet will I defend this people by the great power of God, until they shall shine in righteousness among the nations of the earth like a glittering gem sparkling on a maiden's brow, and be envied only for their good works."

Fine, Doctor, very fine. That shows the poet and the scholar. But you didn't put those exquisite gems in your little book, you sly dog, eh? They would not do alongside with your demand for Joseph in the name of Missouri, eh?

Ah, it was a grand time, when the *Times and Seasons* could say, *editorially*: "The Nauvoo Legion appeared in its glory and presented a beautiful appearance. It will soon compare with the best military organization in the Union." When those high-sounding "GENERAL ORDERS" were given, signed by Joseph Smith, Lieutenant-General, and John C. Bennett, Major-General. Doesn't it read splendid:

"In forming the Legion, the adjutant will observe the rank of companies as follows, to-wit:

1st cohort—the flying artillery first, the lancers next and the riflemen next: visiting companies of dragoons next the lancers and cavalry next the dragoons."

And that great display on the occasion of laying the corner stones of the new temple! Hear it, ye nations and kings:

"At eight o'clock a. m. Major-General Bennett left his quarters to organize and prepare the Legion for the duties of the day, which consisted of about fourteen companies, besides several companies from Iowa and other parts of the country, which joined them on this occasion.

"At half-past nine Lieutenant-General Smith was informed that the legion was organized and ready for review, and immediately, *accompanied by his staff*, consisting of four aid-de-camps and twelve guards, nearly all in *splendid uniforms*, took his march to the parade ground. On their approach they were met by the band, *beautifully equipped*, who received them with a flourish of trumpets and a regular salute, and then struck up a lively air, marching in front to the stand of the lieutenant-general. On his approach to the parade ground the *artillery* was again fired, and the legion gave an appropriate salute while passing. This was indeed a glorious sight, such as we never saw, nor did we ever expect to see such a one in the West. *The rich and costly dresses of the officers* would have become a BONAPARTE or a WASHINGTON.

"After the arrival of Lieutenant-General Smith, the *ladies*, who had made a beautiful silk flag, drove up in a carriage to present it to the legion. Major-General Bennett very politely attended on them, and conducted them in front of Lieutenant-General Smith, who immediately alighted *from his charger* and walked up to the ladies, who presented the flag, making an appropriate address. Lieutenant-General Smith acknowledged the honor conferred upon the legion, and stated that as long as he had the command it should never be disgraced; and then, politely bowing to the ladies, gave it into the hands of Major-General Bennett, who placed it in possession of Cornet Robinson, and it was soon seen gracefully waving in front of the legion. During the time of presentation, the band struck up a lively air, and another salute was fired from the *artillery*. After the presentation of the flag, Lieutenant-General Smith, *accompanied by his suite*, reviewed the legion, the different officers saluting as he passed. Lieutenant-General Smith then took his former stand, and the whole legion, by companies, passed before him in review.

"Immediately after the review, General Bennett organized the procession to march to the foundations of the temple, in the following order, to-wit:

Lieutenant-General Smith,
Brigadier-Generals Law and Smith,
Aids-de-Camp and conspicuous strangers,
General Staff,
Band,
Second Cohort (foot troops),
Ladies, eight abreast,
Gentlemen, eight abreast.
First Cohort (horse troops).

"The procession then began to move forward in order, and on their arrival at the temple block, the generals, with their staffs and distinguished strangers present, took their position inside the foundation, the ladies formed on the outside immediately next the walls, the gentlemen and infantry behind, and the cavalry in the rear. The assembly sung an appropriate hymn. *President Rigdon* then ascended the platform and delivered a suitable oration, which was listened to with the most profound attention by the assembly."

Those were the glorious May-days of 1841. The Mormon "Lord" felt good. Having *accepted* Bennett's work (and crooked instrument,) He was now to get a fine temple. He was happy to see so many of *my servants* in fine uniforms, and he might have thought, with a truthful Mormon historian, "it is a singular fact, that after Washington, Joseph Smith was the first man in America who held the rank of lieutenant-general.''* Poor, dear old Jehovah! He had not had such a holiday since the great times of General Joshua; and this splendid morning of the Nauvoo kingdom was a proud one for Emma and the "ladies" in general. There was such a crowd of Bonapartes and Washingtons, thunder of artillery, soul-stirring martial music, polite bows, grand speeches, sweet smiles—it was the glorious summer of Zion, and they didn't dream that winter was so near. Bennett was the proudest of them all. Was it not all *his* work, his brains, science and experience? He felt himself Bonaparte and Washington in one. The clever little fellow! When at the height of his glory in Nauvoo, he was five feet five inches—just like Napoleon I., you know—and 142 pounds in weight. Joseph weighed 212 pounds, and was six feet—Lee says six feet two inches.

"All decent people in Nauvoo," says Mr. K.,"regarded Bennett as a perfect scoundrel." And he was the prophet's Pylades; was with him day and night! Mr. Webb says: "He was a very small, villainous-looking man. I hated him from sight. Ambition and women filled his soul." "He was full of low cunning and licentiousness," says Mrs. Pratt. Several well-informed witnesses tell me that he used to promise abortion to those females that objected to the "blessings of Abraham" on the ground of fear for the consequences. "I heard him preach against the Gentiles," said a lady of eighty-eight years to me. "He seemed raving mad. I said, 'The fellow is a devil,' but my friends warned me not to talk like that of the best friend of the prophet."

I saw the Nauvoo *Wasp* in the "historian's office." Fine, snug place for study, that office. But they wouldn't *let* me study there, you see. Let me tell you how this "came to pass." First, I was very well received there. Apostle Richards, the present manager,† is as nice a

---

* "And that Brigham Young was [to be] the next."—Tullidge, *Brigham Young*, p. 30.

† Apostle Woodruff, the real "historian," is "in obscurity," as Apostle Richards told me. The poor old gentlemen cannot bear the sight of a deputy marshal.

polygamic gentleman as I have met in Utah. He has a young clerk who tries, in a really touching manner, to outdo Uriah Heep in the pleasant and useful art of grinning. I saw other interesting people there; for instance, Elder Jaques, who is as grim as Minos. His last smile must have happened somewhere in 1850. And Musser I saw there, too, even A. M. Musser, a great diplomat, who has done many a noble deed, seen and *accepted* by Brigham. Musser had just been in the Pen for six months, for having "lived his religion" with some crisp and dashing young wives instead of with the tough and tedious old woman; and this sad experience of religious persecution gives him a sort of noble, martyrly bearing, an odor half church incense, half harem perfume. Well, everything went lovely for two or three visits, you know. They showed me the *Wasp*, and some other things; but the *kind* of books and papers which I wanted to see did not fail to arouse suspicion pretty soon. They began to catechise me in the approved teacher-style, and wanted to tell me "the facts" about the Mountain Meadows Massacre and other interesting topics. I was stupid enough to let them see my set of Gentile teeth too soon. I told them about a forgery committed by one of their great writers in printing a most important dispatch of Brigham Young. I gave them a bit of my mind about polygamy and theocracy. My die was cast, my doom was sealed. When I asked for the *Nauvoo Neighbor*, another very interesting weekly of 1843-4, they "had lent it to somebody." They are so sly. But I do not blame them. I never saw a cosier, cooler little place for a little practice in lying, for the holiest of purposes. And then, looking out on the splendid lawn before John Taylor's palace, could I help thinking: You CANNOT lie to Gentiles!

But let us return to the *Wasp*, whose columns were so often enriched by the fertile pen of Pistol-Joab-Bennett. Joseph's great friend in all kinds of affliction calls Joseph, on one of those yellowish leaves, a "great philanthropist and devout Christian!" The same *Wasp* calls Bennett, scarcely a month later, June 25, "an impostor and base adulterer." *Sic transit gloria mundi,* as the learned prophet would say, or " *O tempora, O mores!*" as quoted in the same number of Apostle William's little weekly. How did this come to pass? Had the Lord ceased to accept the Doctor's work, or had he become jealous of Joseph's new " pard?"

Bennett, after having exposed Prophet Joseph, joined Prophet Strang, who had set up a little Mormon inferno of his own on an island in Michigan lake. A stormy petrel was Dr. John C. Bennett. He had been everything in this world, even a Methodist, and a Campbellite preacher, and had left, in the spirit of a Mormon martyr, no doubt, wife and children, before coming to worship in Nauvoo. * Joab died in obscurity, in the State of Iowa.

Farewell, thou portentous meteor, great general, mighty mayor and judge, most handy doctor and most learned chancellor! Farewell, noble Paul! Farewell, earth-shaking Joab, wave-stilling Pistol! Thou, too, art a son of Abraham, and you shall pass by the angels and the gods to thine exaltation and glory, little " Forty-two-pounder!" †

---

* I wonder why Lee doesn't say: " We used to call such fellows *widowers.*"

† This was General Joab's pet name in Nauvoo.

THE NAUVOO CATASTROPHE.

———

*A New Kind of Friends — William and Wilson Law,
Dr. Galland, etc.—Postmaster Rigdon—The Great
Revelation of January 19, 1841—The Lord's " House
of Boarding," and " Stockholders" — My Servant
Isaac Galland—Blessings and Keys— The Messianic
Wave—The " Nauvoo Expositor" — The Nuisance
Abated—Affidavits of William and Jane Law—Hell
an Agreeable Place— The Nauvoo Trap— The Car-
thage Tragedy.*

———

Sidney Rigdon had used Joseph as a tool to bring
the big fraud before the world. Joseph learned two
things from Sidney: first, the theatrical make-up of a
prophet ; second, the art to use men as he himself had
been used by the ingenious Pittsburg tanner. Joe was
shrewd enough to find out what qualities in a man were
best adapted for the purposes of the Latter-day kingdom.
In Martin Harris and the Whitmers it was the phenom-
enal superstition and credulity ; in Oliver Cowdery, low
rascality and a certain general cleverness combined with
the occult sciences of reading and writing, so little known
among the founders of the new gospel. The brothers
Pratt were two quite different natures. Parley was bru-
tally sensual and perfectly unscrupulous ; Orson a
fanatic of the Rigdon type and of a burning ambition
badly matched with the scholarship of a dilettante. This
explains why Cowdery and Parley Pratt were on the inside of the imposture from the beginning, while Orson
Pratt was kept on the outside to be a great fisher of
men as a missionary and perhaps never given a look into
the strong box of the great fraud.

Oliver was the first type of willing criminal tool for
the schemes of Joseph and Rigdon, and he was the first

to fall, when he knew too much and when he shrank before certain logical consequences of the new system
adopted recklessly by the prophet in Missouri in 1838.
Cowdery's disgrace was a forerunner of the fate of Dr.
Avard and Dr. Bennett. In Dr. Sampson Avard, who
went heart and soul into the bold Mahomet-scheme of
Joseph, we get the first clear type of the adventurers,
then swarming in the virgin West, who saw in the prophet
a new star leading them to coveted greatness and enjoyment. He understood and fell in with Joseph's purposes,
and seems to have formed the plan, readily endorsed by
Rigdon and Joseph, to cement the motley, low adventurers of the "faithful" by the means of most terrible
oaths and secret signs. More of this in a special chapter
about the *Danites.*

The Mahomet scheme had been a great fizzle in
Missouri. Joseph and the *elite* of his tools went to prison,
after barely escaping to be shot by court-martial. The
prophet disclaimed, unblushingly, any connection with
the organization of the *Danite* band, and made good his
retreat to Nauvoo. It is well known that the good people
of Illinois, not being informed about the real causes of
the Missouri troubles, willingly accepted the Mormon lie
about "religious persecution," and did their best to
make the fugitives forget their sufferings. It did not take
them more than one or two years to find out that they
had warmed a big snake in the bosom of their great State.

Nauvoo was a fresh field, full of fresh men. Adventurers of all kinds offered their services to the man who,
howbeit he might be as great a rascal as there ever was,
had success on his side represented in thousands of
"followers," who were in reality a formidable army of
fanatic Mamelukes. ·Lots of settlers and men of enterprise were what the new West wanted: Joe was one of
the latter, and *possessed the former.* Dr. Isaac Galland
—they're all "doctors," those chaps—offered to Joseph
land enough to build a big city on. He had been a
horse-thief in earlier times, and had stolen the land; but
Joe's "Lord" *accepted* him and his offer all the same.
Then came Bennett, the useful man *par excellence,* who

knew and could do anything. He was as smooth and
ready in the drafting of political and military organiza-
tions as he was in the most delicate cases of personal
affliction — as we have seen. But not only rascals came
to Zion to rise with the rising prophet; not only penniless
adventurers, as Joe had been himself before his dupes
were commanded to feed, clothe and house him, and
before he could buy gold watches from the savings of
poor old maids. but honest and well-to-do business men
came too, looking out for the opportunities offered by a
new settlement in a good agricultural and commercial
situation. William and Wilson Law were men of this
calibre; commercially, their position in Nauvoo bears a
distant resemblance to that of the Walker brothers in Salt
Lake City, about 1870. All those men crowded around
the great prophet, hoping to gain influence and money
through him, and therefore willing to help on his schemes
as lieutenants and tools in general. They are received
with open arms, and honors of all kinds are showered
upon them. Before the people they are the lieutenant-
general's brilliant staff, and behind the coulisses they help
him to scheme and to conspire.

But where is President Rigdon, my servant Sidney,
always named first in the early revelations of the Lord?
Where is the Lord's Messenger and Mouthpiece, the inspired projector. architect and great Messianic feetwasher
of the Kirtland temple, the great interpreter of the
Nephite, and scores of other records and tongues? He is
nowhere, I am sorry to say. I don't see him in the
galaxy of Bonapartes and Washingtons. He is not even a
colonel, like our visionary astronomer, "Professor"
Orson Pratt; not even a "cornet." You see him in a
poor little office, a log shanty, probably, the Lord's *postmaster;* but only a postmaster after all. How are the
mighty fallen, and the most puissant become as a thing of
naught! "My Servant the Branch" is on the shelf, you
see, like the old rusty armor kept in Don Quixote's castle.
Good enough to preach an *oration* now and then, but he
was no Bonaparte or Washington, like great little Bennett.
I doubt whether he had any uniform at all, and as to his

pulpit coat and hat, he kept those costly treasures well out of the reach of the wrestling prophet since 1838. He was an excellent fellow for expounding the new gospel on Sundays, but he was no practical kingdom-builder, no business-man. Already with Bennett and Joe in Nauvoo, "the Mormon God is a business God," as that worthy leader, George Q. Cannon, so well and forcibly puts it. Religion is all very well for the people, but look at the Jesuits; they are men of the world, the friends and advisers of emperors and kings; that's what we want now —"mark it, Elder Rigdon."

Yes, Elder Rigdon, you prepare for meeting and let the boys have their fun. And don't they have it? The Bonapartes enjoy their uniforms, write on their waving banner, "The blessings of Abraham, Isaac and Jacob," and conquer Eliza's, Martha's and Phebe's in the absence of frowning castles and fortresses. The smart business men of the Law type make hay while the sun shines. High above the swarm of fortune-seekers Joseph holds the prophetic *rod*, and his friends hope devoutly that it will *work to the money* and make them rise, those *chests of money*, discerned with such scientific acumen by Mr. Joseph Smith, Senior, the "Abraham of this dispensation." * Those smart fellows don't believe any too much in the Seer and Revelator; they know that he is a "hell of a fellow with the women," but he is young, you know, and he will cool down bye and bye, and then doesn't he laugh about the Gold Bible humbug himself, when among his nearest friends? We want to make money, and we don't care how we make it. And so greed and ambition make them gulp it all down, get their endowments and swear even the Danite oaths. They see that the great mass of people really believe it all, that they work hard and pay willingly, that they "buy at our stores," build up the country and city rapidly—that's all we want. Let Joseph get his revelations and print them in the *Times and Seasons*—they are cranky enough, but we don't care as long as we make $50 a day by them. In five or six years, ten

---

* Tullidge, Joseph Smith, p. 299.

at the longest, we will be rich enough to make our own way without a prophet and endowment garments.

Joseph didn't care if they made game of his prophetic role now and then; he kept them with a strong hand in their place as tools, all the same, and made them *pay and obey*, never losing sight for a moment of his own interests and his far-reaching plans. This makes him a leader in in my eyes. His generals may scoff at the blindly fanatic herd, but Joseph, with the instinct of the French kings who relied on the people against the aspiring nobles, feels himself strong on the broad basis of the believing masses, and proclaims to the whole people the will of the Lord concerning his clever and wealthy friends, exerting in this manner a powerful pressure on those who would hesitate to work for his schemes and "doe over" the ready cash they possessed.

But let the "Lord" himself speak. January 19, 1841, He favours His servant with the longest revelation of all the lot. It must have been a busy time for the *Urim and Thummim* and that old white hat:

"Verily, thus saith the Lord, unto you my servant Joseph Smith, I am well pleased with your offerings and acknowledgments which you have made. I say unto you that you are now called immediately to make a solemn proclamation of my gospel. This proclamation shall be made to all the kings of the world, to the four corners thereof —*to the honorable President-elect, to the high-minded governors* of the nation in which you live and to all the nations of the earth scattered abroad. Awake! O kings of the earth! Come ye, O! come ye *with your gold and your silver* to the help of my people—to the house of the daughter of Zion."

Yes, don't come with empty hands. *Consecration* before all, and don't forget to bring your wives and daughters.

After having given this great outline of a financial programme, the Lord proceeds to occupy himself with Joseph's friends. The prophet's Richelieu, Dr. Bennett, is the first named; we have already heard the Lord's will concerning the proprietor of the crooked instrument. The Lord tackles next apostle Lyman Wight, Joe's Lieutenant in 1838, a crazy Danite, who had sworn to conquer St. Louis and all Missouri:

"And again I say unto you, that it is my will, that my servant Lyman Wight should continue in preaching for Zion, that when he shall finish his work I may receive him unto myself, even as I did my servant David Patten, who IS WITH ME AT THIS TIME, and also my servant Edward Partridge, and also my aged servant Joseph Smith, Sr., *who sitteth with Abraham*, at his right hand, and blessed and holy is he, for he is mine."

Here is fun for fifty generations. David Patten, President of the twelve, and leader of the *Danite* band, had been killed in a skirmish with the Missourians. "He is with me at this time," says the Lord. And so is Partridge, the first bishop of the church and father of the two poor, good girls, sealed and unsealed inside of a few hours, as we have seen. And so is our excellent friend Micawber-Smith, who *sitteth* with Abraham and is, no doubt, amusing the venerable patriarch by telling him those awfully funny stories about the "chests of money," with which he used aforetime to fix the fools for Joseph Smith, Jr. "He is mine," says the Lord, but it strikes me that Old Scratch would be the man to say it.

Let my servant George, and my servant Lyman, and my servant John Snider and others build a house unto my name, such a one as my servant Joseph shall show unto them, upon the place which he shall show unto them also. And it shall be for A HOUSE OF BOARDING, a house that strangers may come from afar to lodge therein—therefore, let it be a good house, worthy of all acceptation. This house shall be a healthy habitation; it shall be holy, *or the Lord your God will not dwell therein.*"

Joseph, Joseph, you are the master-wag of your epoch! How happily you give the vulgar, hash-smelling "boarding-house" a biblical smack by terming it the "house of boarding!" You want it on your own property, of course, and a good house and healthy, or you—beg pardon, the Lord your God—will not dwell therein. Frankly, I admire you, and would do so yet more, if you had *revealed* your hotel terms at the same time, say in a little card like this:

THE NAUVOO MANSION HOUSE
IS NOW
THE LEADING HOTEL IN ZION.

It is quiet and home-like. The rooms are large and elegantly furnished. The finest beds in the city. First-class Barber Shop, fine Billiard Saloon, first-class Dining Room, the tables loaded with the best the market affords. In place of $3 and $4 per day, charges only $2.

THE LORD & HIS SERVANT,
JOSEPH SMITH, JR., *Proprietors.*

Now comes the temple business. Joe opens a public subscription for the building. The leading idea is that it should not cost him a cent, but he hides it very happily with biblical language :

"And again, verily, verily I say unto you, let all my Saints come from afar; and send ye swift messengers, yea chosen messengers and say unto them, come ye all with your gold, and your silver, and with your precious stones and with all your *antiquities*; and with all who have knowledge of antiquities, and bring the box tree, the fir tree and the pine tree, together with all the precious trees of the earth, and with iron and with copper and with brass and with zinc, and with all your precious things of the earth, and build a house to my name, for the Most High to dwell therein."

All the antiquities except the old ladies, I suppose. But apropos the temple, the Mormon Lord gets all of a sudden a violent attack of Missouriphobia.

"The iniquity and transgression of my holy laws and commandments I will visit upon the heads of those who hindered my work, unto *the third and fourth generation,* so long as they respect not, and hate me, *saith the Lord God.* Therefore have I accepted the offerings of those men whom I commanded to build up a city and a house unto my name IN JACKSON COUNTY, MISSOURI, and were hindered by their enemies, saith the Lord your God, and I will answer judgment, wrath, indignation, wailing, anguish and gnashing of teeth, upon their heads, and I will save all those of your brethren who have been slain in the land of *Missouri,* saith the Lord."

The Lord has evidently had a chat with D. Patten, "who is with me," and Patten said, "Give it to them," meaning Boggs and the Missourians. But He cools off and proceeds again to business. He takes up his favorite project, the *house of boarding,* and wants Joseph and his posterity to be comfortable in it, without being bothered by bills and similar inventions of Satan. I have given this piece of revelation already on page 40. But another question arises. How get the funds for building? The Lord finds an *escape.* He has learned a good deal since the simple days of Abraham and Jacob. He suggests, in his mild Biblical language, a *stock company* to his servant Joseph. Who knows whether he has not had a like talk about the matter with our friend Micawber, interrupting him while lecturing to the other Abraham about the chests of money? The "Abraham of this dispensation" would be just the fellow to suggest such a plan to *work to the money* with. I say it is an excellent religion. In Missouri the Lord teaches them to steal as his agents, and in Illinois he finds ever so many new ways to raise the chests of money. It is a "business religion," by Jove, and no wonder that you see nothing of religion at all in the leaders, but only business, and sometimes crooked, too, like Bennett's instrument. But hear Joe's mentor again:

"Behold! Verily I say unto you, let my servant George Miller, and my servant Lyman Wight, and my servant John Snider, and my servant Peter Hawes, *organize themselves* and appoint one of them to to be a president over their quorum for the purpose of building that house."

"Organize themselves"—hem, that sounds like the new Abraham. Might he not have drafted the whole thing? I conclude this mainly from the following piece, which shows that there was a danger that the four fellows, after having *organized* themselves, would steal like hell, not as the Lord's agents, but on their own hook. Now it strikes me that the new Abraham knows those fellows best. Maybe they owe him yet three dollars apiece for blessings. So he goes on drafting for the Lord:

"And again, verily I say unto you, If my servant George Miller, and my servant Lyman Wight, and my servant John Snider, and my servant Peter Hawes receive *any stock* into their hands, in *moneys or in properties wherein they receive the real value of moneys,* they shall not appropriate any portion of that stock to any other purpose, and if they do, *without the consent of the stockholders*, and do not *repay four-fold*, they shall be accursed, and shall be removed out of their place, saith the Lord God, for I the Lord am God, and cannot be mocked in any of these things."

You see, there are good reasons to be afraid that my servants will steal. Well, never mind, if they repay four-fold they may do it. "Four-fold"—I have seen that word somewhere. Oh, yes, I remember now. Lucy Munchausen promises, "in the name of the spirit," to repay four-fold a little loan of four or five dollars (p. 18). You see, that strengthens my scientific theory that her husband, the new Abraham, did draft the whole revelation, perhaps (who knows) with the advice of the *old* Abraham. I like that "cannot be mocked." That shows the Lord's own hand again; he added this to the new Abraham's draft. You see that white-dog-story (p. 79) is not yet entirely forgotten, and it was disgraceful, to be sure, to cheat *such* a Lord. Why take a white sheep, instead of trying honestly to get a real dog, *coute que coute !*

"Let my servant, Isaac Galland [the horse thief] *put stock in that house*, for I the Lord loveth him for what he hath done, and will forgive all his sins, therefore let him be remembered for an *interest* in that house from generation to generation."

You will have to shell out, Doctor, there is no help for it. The little remark about "his sins" shows again Micawber's hand, or I am no critic at all. I feel sure the fellow got lots of "blessings" and never paid a red cent for them. The old blesser "cannot be mocked in any of these things."

"Let my servant William Law *pay stock* in that house for himself and his seed after him. Let him not take his family unto the eastern lands, even to Kirtland. Let my servant William go and proclaim mine everlasting gospel unto the inhabitants of Warsaw, of Carthage, of Burlington and Madison, and then wait patiently for further instructions at *my general conference*, saith the Lord. If he will do my will let him from henceforth hearken to the counsel of my servant Joseph and *publish the new translation of my holy word* unto the inhabitants of the earth."

There is a whole programme for the wealthy merchant. "Pay stock" in the prophet's hotel; not leave Nauvoo; go preaching and wait for orders to be received at *my* conference; obey and pay, especially for the printing of that beautiful *inspired* translation and correction of the Bible, done by Sidney Rigdon, now the postmaster of the Lord. Yes, General Law, do as Martin Harris did, who mortgaged his farm to pay three thousand dollars for the printing of five thousand copies of the Book of Mormon. You are sure to get the reward Martin got, the title of "old granny" in the church organ. But it is worth trying, to fix that fool, so the Lord makes him a counsellor of the prophet. Hyrum has to step aside; he becomes official blesser of the church.

"And again, verily I say unto you, let my servant William be appointed, ordained and *anointed* as a counselor unto my servant Joseph; that my servant Hyrum may take the office of patriarch, that from henceforth he shall hold the *keys* of the patriarchal blessings [at three dollars apiece; reasonable terms for families] upon the heads of all my people, that whoever he blesseth shall be blessed and whoever he curseth shall be cursed—that whatsoever he shall bind on earth shall be bound in heaven, and whatsoever he shall loose on earth shall be loosed in heaven; and from this time forth I appoint unto him that he may be a *prophet*, and a seer, and a revelator unto my church, as well as my servant Joseph, and that he shall receive counsel from my servant Joseph, who shall show unto him the *keys*, whereby he may be crowned with the same blessings. I crown upon his head the bishopric and blessing and glory and honour and gifts of the priesthood, that once were put upon him that was my servant Oliver Cowdery. Let my servant William Law also receive the *keys* ......"

My head begins to spin in this chaos of blessings, titles and *keys*. So brother Hyrum is to be another prophet. How will they manage about the old White Hat and the Urim and Thummim? An old hat can be bought cheap enough, but those three-cornered diamonds set in glass—will they use them alternately, or is Hyrum to get his own set? This seems very important and has been overlooked entirely by historians of the depth of Stenhouse and Tullidge. And poor Oliver Cowdery, he *was* my servant. All his blessings and gifts go to the dogs—no, to Hyrum.

Last and least, in this endless revelation, comes our friend Sidney Rigdon, like a lame mare behind a train.

" And again, verily I say•unto you, if my servant Sidney will serve me, and offer unto me an acceptable offering [Nancy] and remain with my people, he shall again be a spokesman before my face."

It's plain enough. He shall be a slave, and all he gets for it is the liberty to preach. Wouldn't it be better, Elder Rigdon, to be an honest little tanner in some village, than to be treated like that? What did you say in New York in the fall of 1844? "I guided the prophet's tottering steps till he could walk alone." It seems Joe walks alone now and *your* steps are tottering, old Go-to-grass.

In this manner the "Messianic wave swept onward"* A. D. 1841. Mormonism, the "grand universal scheme of salvation and stupendous structure of divine purposes and divine beneficence"† was doing its best to work to the money and raise those chests, abroad and at home. But—as it had been in Kirtland and in Missouri—Joseph's talents and instincts as a leader were overborne by his follies and crimes. He was too great, too hot a brute to be successful as a schemer. He could not wait. He could never defer a pleasure for a moment. If a Vanderbilt were to have given him a million, he would have cried: "Where is the rest of it?"

That was his motto as to all manner of enjoyment—money, power, women—where is the rest of it? Having seduced a goodly number of the wives and daughters of his immediate slaves, the apostles, he now wants, forsooth, my pretty Jane, my dearest Jane, William Law's wife, pretty and charming Jane Law; he wants spirited Nancy Rigdon, the daughter of the man to whom he and his father's house were indebted for all they had and were. But these men, weren't they, like Joseph himself, Freemasons, the honor of their wives and daughters sacred by the rules of this order? It is not to be expected, however, that Masonry can hold the prophet in any restraint. Had he not prostituted the ordinances and secrets of the order by mimicking and burlesquing them in his endow-

* Tullidge, p. 326.
† Idem, p. 133.

ments and proclaiming that he had found among the wondrous secrets of that old white hat, the crowning "key" lost by the Masons, for long ages; so that, like his religion, *his* masonry was the true and only original Jacobs?* His beastly desires and reckless impudence were even greater than his cunning.

All this was more than the Laws and their friends had bargained for. The means at their command and their abilities in business—which could be carried on anywhere—made them independent. They were not forced, like the half-illiterate tramps called apostles, to drag the prophet's triumphal chariot. They were not *forced* to make prostitutes of their wives and daughters to satisfy a passing caprice of Caligula. Like causes, like effects. First a frown, then a whisper, and then a plain talk between friends and the conspiracy is begotten. They resolved to kill the tyrant, whose ravings had become intolerable and who was sure to ruin not only their families, but also their whole future prospects, by bringing down the vengeance of all decent citizens of Illinois on himself and his city. But they didn't want to kill him with daggers—they chose a modern weapon, and decided to kill him an inch every week, by a weekly, the celebrated EXPOSITOR.

You know how Macbeth felt when he saw the woods marching against him. Well, Joe Smith must have felt much the same when he found out that a handful of intimate friends and accomplices of his were going to start a newspaper against him, in his own city, in June, 1844. The difference betwixt the old time and the new is here: then you marched against a tyrant with an army, now you *start a little paper* and it makes him tremble more than the hordes of Xerxes. A newspaper is a horrible thing: it sets your roof ablaze while you sit there, arms bound, and can do nothing.

Who were the men who started the *Expositor* and

---

* Brigham used to call the Utah endowments *Masonry after the order of Enoch*, and Kimball said often: "This is *true* Free Masonry and all you that have been Masons will find how much superior this is to common Free Masonry."

published the first number, June 7, 1844? The Laws
were decent, intelligent, well-to-do people; so they are
described by Mrs. Pratt. I think they were the cleverest
fellows in the whole *Expositor* outfit. Foster was a
sharper, Higbee is called a Mormon hoodlum by Mr.
Webb. Leave aside the Laws and you may say that the
whole explosion of June 7 was a case of "rogues falling
out." But the paper was decent enough. It exposed
Smith, but by no means in an indecent manner; to make
it short, I may truly say that the editors did not tell the
tenth part of what they knew. But let the reader judge
for himself by looking at my reprint of the most important parts of the *Expositor.*

But Joe was furious. A theocracy is always a *noli
me tangere* as to opposition and free press in general,
and Joseph had especially good reasons to hate the
electric light of the press in his skeleton-filled museum.
What, oppose and *expose* him? Him who had defied
everything and everybody, laws and courts, sheriffs and
militia, warrants and posses? No, that nuisance must be
abated. Great special meeting of the Nauvoo city council on June 8. Joseph, then mayor — since Bennett's
ungathering from Zion—thunders: "I WOULD RATHER
DIE TO-MORROW AND HAVE THAT THING SMASHED, THAN
LIVE AND HAVE IT GO ON!"

The city council, a nice little crowd of *valets de
chambre* of his prophetic highness, hastens to pass the
decree of doom on the nuisance. Says that invaluable little catechism already quoted repeatedly:

Q.—What was the nature of the contents of the *Expositor?*
A.—It contained *all manner of lies and abuse of Joseph* and the
Saints.

Q.—What did the city council do in regard to this paper?
A.—It declared it a nuisance and as such ordered it to be abated.

Q.—How was the order carried out?
A.—The city marshal and several policemen threw the printing
press, etc., into the street and destroyed them.

Q.—What was the result of this act?
A.—It caused great excitement among the *wicked*, and they sought
the life of Joseph and the destruction of Nauvoo.

This is the way theocracies always wrote and always will write their history.

The city council does the prophet's bidding and the police, with the marshal at its head, storms the fortress of modern progress—a printing office. I see, in my mind's eye, our pious, zealous churchman, John D. Lee, work like mad to destroy that wicked press: I see him break a crowbar or two, to please the Lord. Have things changed in our days?. No. The unterrified *Salt Lake Tribune* is as well hated by the Mormon leaders as the *Expositor* was hated by Joseph and his creatures, and the present city marshal and his Lees would be only too happy to be ordered to abate the nuisance. That the valiant paper has continued so long, " belching forth all manner of lies and abuse of the Saints," is due now solely to saintly forbearance and magnanimity? That is the way Mormon organs and leaders put it. John Taylor, who was then editor of the *Times and Seasons* and had a main hand in squelching the freedom of the press in Nauvoo, is most forbearing towards this infernal "Expositor" of our days. He is warned by his prophet's fate. The Nauvoo *Expositor* and the Nauvoo prophet were both destroyed in one month. A free press is, indeed, a most outrageous and horrible *nuisance*. It is the mirror of the public conscience, the little stone of the prophet's dream, you know, that shall fill the whole earth—awful, awful—breaking people up, playing smash with the biggest, and grinding to powder the most top-lofty reputations !

There is scarcely any history of Mormonism without the following statement : "*The first issue (June 7th, 1844) contained the statement of sixteen women, that Joseph Smith or other Mormon leaders had attempted to seduce them under the plea of heavenly permission to do so.*"*

Now, this statement is entirely erroneous. The celebrated and short-lived *Expositor* contained only three affidavits and only one of those three comes from a woman. Here are the three affidavits :

---

* See for instance Beadle, Polygamy, *p. 78.*

I.

I hereby certify that Hyrum Smith did (in his office) read to me a written document, which he said was a revelation from God. He said that he was with Joseph when it was received. He afterwards gave me the document to read, and I took it to my house and read it and showed it to my wife and returned it next day. The revelation (so called) authorized *certain men* to have more wives than one at a time, in this world and in the world to come. It said this was the law, and commanded Joseph to enter into the *law*. And, also, that he should administer to others. Several other items were in the revelation, supporting the above doctrines.

(Sworn to May 4, 1844.)   WM. LAW.

II.

I certify that I read the revelation referred to in the above affidavit of my husband. It sustained in strong terms the doctrine of more wives than one at a time, in this world and in the next. It authorized some to have to the number of *ten*, and set forth that those women who would not allow their husbands more wives than one should be under condemnation before God.

(Sworn to May 4, 1844.)   JANE LAW.

III.

To all whom it may concern :

Forasmuch as the public mind hath been much agitated by a course of procedure in the Church of J. C. of L. D. S., by a number of persons declaring against certain doctrines and practices therein (among whom I am one), it is but meet that I should give my reasons, at least in part, as a cause that hath led me to declare myself. In the latter part of the summer, *1843*, the patriarch, Hyrum Smith, did, in the High Council, of which I was a member, introduce what he said was a revelation given through the prophet; that the said Hyrum Smith did essay to read the said revelation in the said Council; that according to his reading there was contained the following doctrines: 1. The sealing up of persons to eternal life, against all sins, save that of shedding innocent blood, or consenting thereto; 2. the doctrine of a plurality of wives, or marrying virgins; that "David and Solomon had many wives, yet in this thing they sinned not, save in the matter of Uriah." This revelation, with other evidence that the aforesaid heresies were taught and practiced in the church, determined me to leave the office of first counselor to the president of the church at Nauvoo,* inasmuch as I dared not to teach or administer such laws.

(Sworn to May 4, 1844.)   AUSTIN COWLES.

Those three are all the affidavits contained in the

---

* This was Wm. Marks, who afterwards joined the Josephites.

celebrated "Expositor," in its first and last number, of June 7, 1844. But there are other pretty things in it. Look at this little anecdote:

> " Many of us have sought a reformation in the church, without a public exposition of the enormities and crimes practiced *by its leaders;* but our petitions were treated with contempt, and in many cases the petitioner spurned from their presence, and particularly by Joseph, who would state that if he had sinned, and was guilty of the charges we would charge him with, he would not make acknowledgment, but would rather be damned; for it would detract from his dignity, and would consequently ruin and prove the overthrow of the church; he often said that *we would all go to hell together*, and convert it into a heaven by casting the Devil out; and, says he, hell is by no means the place this world of fools supposed it to be, but on the contrary, it is *quite an agreeable place.*" . . .

Could Don Juan have bettered this? But there is another choice bit in that paper, describing Nauvoo as a very dangerous trap for innocent females:

> "It is a notorious fact that many females in foreign climes have been induced by the sound of the gospel to forsake friends and come over the water, as they supposed, to glorify God. . . . But what is taught them on their arrival at this place? They are visited by some of the strikers and are requested to hold on and be faithful, for there are great blessings awaiting the righteous; and that God has great mysteries in store for those who love the Lord and cling to Brother Joseph. They are also notified that Brother Joseph will see them soon and reveal the mysteries of heaven to their full understanding, which seldom fails to inspire them with new confidence in the prophet, as well as a great anxiety to know what God has laid up in store for them, in return for the great sacrifice of father and mother, gold and silver. . . . They are visited again. They are requested to meet Brother Joseph, or some of the Twelve, at some insulated point, or at some particularly described place on the bank of the Mississippi, or at some room which bears upon its front: *Positively No Admittance.* The unsuspecting creatures are so devoted to the prophet and the cause of Jesus Christ, that they do not dream of the deep-laid scheme. They meet him expecting a blessing and learn the will of the Lord concerning them, when instead they are told, after having been sworn to secrecy in the most solemn manner, with a penalty of death attached, that God Almighty has revealed it to him that she should be his (Joseph's) *spiritual wife*, for it was right anciently, and God will tolerate it again; but we must keep those pleasures and blessings from the world, for until there is a change in the government we will endanger ourselves by practicing it — if we do not expose ourselves to the law of the land. She is thunderstruck, faints, recovers and

refuses. The prophet damns her if she rejects. She thinks of the great sacrifice, and of the many thousand miles she has traveled over sea and land that she might save her soul from ruin, and replies: 'God's will be done, and not mine.' The next step, to avoid public exposition, from the common course of things, they are sent away for a time until all is well, after which they return, as from a long visit!"

Now you wouldn't expect the prophet to subscribe for such an infernal sheet, would you? And you wouldn't expect either that he would display it in his hotel, preserve it with care all the year through, and then have the file nicely bound for reference? Oh no, Joseph did with the *Expositor* what Taylor and Cannon would like to do with the *Tribune* every day of the year, if they dared. The Prophet promptly destroyed the young viper, putting the full weight of his heavy foot on it.

A few days afterwards he had to go to Carthage, where the county court was. He had very grave misgivings about that trip, this mayor-prophet and general. His temper was eminently sanguine and kept him generally on top, where others would have sunk, but this time he saw the coming tempest. He had moments now when he cursed his own folly. "Joseph repented of his connection with the spiritual wife doctrine and said that it was *of the devil* . . . he said that he was going to Carthage to die." So says Sheen, an old friend of the Prophet. Ah, pay-day had come round and Joseph felt it.

"There are sins which can only be atoned by the shedding of blood." Didn't you say so often, brother Brigham? Verily, there are!

THE LYNCHING OF JOSEPH SMITH.

The Scene in Carthage Jail—Death of Hyrum Smith— A Fighting Lamb — Execution of the Prophet — His Last Miracle — The "Expositor" Once More — The Dissenters' Prospectus of May 10, 1844—Stern Protest Against Theocracy — The Godbeites of 1844 — Protest Against Danitism and Endowments — A Nauvoo Trial—Lee Babbles Again—Review of Joseph's Career and Character—A Vision of Joseph's Monument—Calvary and Carthage.

Joseph Smith died in good western style, with his boots on. The circumstances of the prophet's "martyrdom" were of a highly dramatic character. Says an eye-witness:

"Elder John Taylor had been singing a hymn. From this pleasant communion they were aroused by curses, threats and the heavy and fierce rush of the mob up the stairs. Hyrum stood near the center of the room, in front of the door. The mob fired a ball through the panel of the door, which entered Hyrum's head, at the left side of his nose. He fell upon his back exclaiming: 'I am a dead man!' In all, four balls entered his body. One ball (it must have been fired through the window from the outside) passed through his body with such force—entering his back—that it completely broke to pieces a watch which he wore in his vest pocket.

"A shower of balls were poured through all parts of the room. A few hours previous to this a friend of General Joseph Smith put in his possession a revolving pistol with six chambers, usually called a 'pepper box.' With this in hand he took a position by the wall at the left of the door. Joseph reached his pistol through the door, which was pushed a little ajar, and fired three of the barrels, the rest missed fire. He wounded three of the assailants, two mortally."

That revolver in the hand of the "lamb that goes to the slaughter" is highly characteristic. That Joseph fired three shots, is true. As to wounding anybody, still less mortally, I have no proof. Mr. Webb says he never heard of it.

" Elder Taylor took a position beside the door with Elder Richards and parried off their muskets with walking sticks, as they were firing. Elder Taylor continued parrying their guns, until they had got them about half the length into the room, when he found resistance vain and attempted to jump out of the window. Just then a ball from within struck him on the left thigh. He fell on the window-sill and expected he would fall out, when a ball from without struck his watch and threw him back into the room. Elder Richards was still contending with the assailants at the door, when General Joseph Smith dropped his pistol upon the floor, saying : ' There, defend yourselves as well as you can.' He sprang into the window, but just as he was preparing to descend, he saw such an array of bayonets below that he caught by the window casing, where he hung by his hands and feet, his body swinging downwards. He hung in that position three or four minutes, during which time he exclaimed, two or three times, ' O Lord, my God !' and *fell to the ground.* While he was hanging in that position, Colonel Williams halloed : ' Shoot him ! God damn him ! shoot the damned rascal !' However, none fired at him."

While looking out of the window, or while hanging suspended by it, Joseph cried, " Is there no help *for the widow's son ?*" One of the prophet's spiritual wives, Zina Huntingdon (see about her, pp. 67, 70) gave this detail in a packed public meeting in Brigham's theatre, some years ago. Joseph's cry was an appeal to the Masons, whom he had betrayed and who were surely rather infuriated than calmed by this appeal.

" Joseph seemed to fall easily. He struck partly on his right shoulder and back, his neck and head reaching the ground a little before his feet. He rolled instantly on his face. From this position he was taken by a young man who sprang to him from the other side of the fence, who had a pewter fife in hand, was barefoot and bare-headed, having on no coat, with his pants rolled above his knees, and shirt-sleeves above his elbows. He set Smith against the south side of the well-curb that was situated a few feet from the jail. While doing this, he muttered aloud : ' This is old Jo ; I know him. I know you, old Jo ; damn you !' When Smith began to recover from the effects of the fall, Colonel Williams ordered four men to shoot him. Accordingly, four men took an eastern direction, about eight feet from the curb, and made ready to execute the order. The fire was simultaneous. A slight cringe of the body was all the indication of pain that he betrayed when the balls struck him. He fell upon his face. I was close by him, and I know that he was not hit with a ball until after he was seated by the well-curb. The murder took place at fifteen minutes past five o'clock p. m., June 27, 1844."

Now comes a little pious lie to show up the Messianic character of the peeper. The "Lord" had looked on quietly while His servant was hanging to the window-sill, and while the mob were shooting him, but now He finds it's time to work a little miracle:

"The ruffian who set him against the well-curb now secured a bowie knife for the purpose of severing his head from the body. He raised the knife, and was in the attitude of striking, when a light, sudden and powerful, burst from the heavens, passing its vivid chain between Joseph and his murderers; that they were struck with awe and filled with consternation. The arm of the ruffian who held the knife fell powerless; the muskets of the four who fired fell to the ground, and they all stood like marble statues, not having power to move a single limb of their bodies. By this time most of the men had fled in great disorder. I never saw so frightened a set of men before. Colonel Williams saw the light and was also badly frightened, but he did not entirely lose the use of his limbs or speech. Seeing the condition of these men, he halloed to some who had just commenced to retreat, for God's sake to come and *carry off these men*. They came back and carried them by main strength towards the baggage wagons. They seemed as helpless as if they were dead."

I need scarcely say that no Gentile witnessed this miracle; they are not made for the eyes of the wicked, those miracles, but are just like the apparitions of angels, golden plates, etc.; they belong to the *pearl*-order, so you had better move aside, you Gentile hogs. We will now compare this Mormon tale with the statement of the young "border ruffian" from Iowa, who set Joseph against the well-curb: *

"When I got to him [Joseph] he was trying to get up. He appeared stunned by the fall. I struck him in the face and said: 'Old Joe, damn you, where are you now?' I then set him up against the well-curb and went away from him."

The name of the youth is Wm. Web. He is apparently one of the *Sansculottes*, always springing up in times of popular excitement. I would not like to sleep in the same room with that fellow, neither would you, my gentle reader, I guess. The whole crowd that concocted and enacted the tragedy is not at all to my taste. Suppose we

---

* See both statements in full in "The Martyrs," by Lyman O. Littlefield, 1882.

had been in Rome at the time that Julius Cæsar was killed,
we would most probably not have felt like embracing his
murderers, though Brutus is surely one of the noblest figures in history.   There is always something revolting in a
man's taking the law in his own hands : streaming blood
is a terrible accuser.   Charles I. was a sinful, treacherous
king, but his bloody spectre will always stand near the
great figure of Cromwell.   But have we the right to be
sentimental and, because we detest deeds of violence and
brutality, close our eyes to the causes which, with stringent
need, produced them?   Are we justified in saying, with a
recent writer, that the killing of Joseph was one of the
most disgraceful murders ever committed?   It may well
be urged that lynching is disgraceful in itself—I have
nothing to do with that point, and wish to leave it aside.
The assassination of Joseph Smith was surely no common
murder, no act of private vengeance ; it was a violent
manifestation of the *vox populi*, the execution of a most
dangerous criminal by the people.   The men who did it
were entirely right *in their view of the character of their
man*.   This is the only side of the question I feel justified
in dealing with.

Let us first look at the nearest cause of the tragedy,
the destruction of the *Expositor* office.   Put yourself in
the place of the editors of that sheet, and would it surprise
you if they had prepared a bomb filled with scores of
scandalous anecdotes and the most scathing abuse?
They surely did not lack that kind of matter, and they
had a good example in the little book of Dr. John C.
Bennett. . He acted against Joe as my friend Henri
Rochefort acted against the little nephew of the great
Napoleon in his *Lanterne*.   Mormon writers. to palliate
Joseph's proceeding against the new-born weekly, describe
the *Expositor* as such a poisonous sheet.   We have already
heard the opinion of the little Catechism about it.   Mr.
Littlefield verdantly remarks in his pamphlet, "The Martyrs" : "They [the editors of the *Expositor*] knew that
establishing a libelous and venal newspaper *would not be
agreeable* to Joseph ; hence a paper of that class was
started.   Its columns teemed with *vituperative abuse* of

Joseph and his friends. The tone of the sheet was *vulgar, scurrilous and untruthful.* The *people* felt themselves outraged."

The reader has already convinced himself that the *Expositor* was nothing of the kind. It was rather a timid and gentle kind of opposition sheet, quite cautious and guarded and modest. On the 10th of May the editors had issued their prospectus. Among the things they proposed to advocate were:

"The unconditional repeal of the charter of Nauvoo, to restrain and correct the abuses of the UNIT POWER, to ward off the rod which is held over the devoted heads of the citizens of Nauvoo and the surrounding country, to advocate unmitigated DISOBEDIENCE TO POLITICAL REVELATION, to advocate and exercise the FREEDOM OF SPEECH in Nauvoo, independent of the ordinance abridging the same—to give toleration to every man's religious sentiments and sustain ALL in worshiping their God according to the monitions of their consciences, as guaranteed by the Constitution of our country, and to oppose with uncompromising hostility any UNION OF CHURCH AND STATE OR ANY PRELIMINARY STEPS TENDING TO THE SAME."

Is there a citizen's heart in this immense, free country, without an echo to such words? Could free citizens express better sentiments, and could it be done in more decent and dignified language? Is this not absolutely the same cry for justice, coming since so many years from the lips and pens of every true American citizen in the Territory of Utah, and resounding so nobly from the official acts of Governor Murray, and the writings of one of the most able and fearless editors of this country, Judge Goodwin?

The first and last number of the *Expositor*, dated June 7, 1844, was just as temperate and truthful as the prospectus, issued four weeks before. The editors of the paper, as will be seen, acted as Godbe and his friends did twenty-five years later, with the same danger to their lives and property. Their motto was not subversion, but purification of Mormonism and the desire to harmonize it with modern civilization, with individual freedom of thought and action. Says the *Expositor:*

" The editors believe that the religion of the Latter-day Saints, as originally taught by Joseph Smith, which is contained in the Old and New Testaments, Book of Covenants, and Book of Mormon, is VERILY TRUE. But with Joseph Smith, and many other official characters in the church, faith, hope, virtue and charity are words without meanings attached. We hope many items of doctrine, as now taught, some of which, however, are *taught secretly and denied openly*, and others publicly, considerate men will treat with contempt. We are earnestly seeking to explode the vicious principles of Joseph Smith and those who practice the same abominations and whoredoms. The sword of truth shall not depart from the thigh until we can enjoy those glorious privileges which nature's God and our country's laws have guaranteed to us — freedom of speech, the liberty of the press, and the right to worship God as seemeth us good. We are aware that *we are hazarding every earthly blessing*, particularly property, and probably *life itself. . . .* "

Is this libelous and venal? Is it vulgar, scurrilous and untruthful, or is it the essence of sobriety and dignity, compared with Joseph's piratical expressions, that he would rather be damned than confess his sins, and that they would all go to hell together, cast the Devil out, etc.? Is it not all most truthful in the light of facts published in this volume? and is it not extremely moderate, coming from men who knew ten times more of the abominations practiced in Nauvoo than I do? But hear the *Expositor* further:

" We protest against the doctrine of unconditional sealing up to eternal life against all crimes except that of shedding innocent blood. . . . We disapprobate every attempt to unite church and State, the effort being made by Joseph Smith for POLITICAL POWER and influence. . . . We protest against the hostile spirit and conduct manifested by Joseph Smith and many of his associates towards MISSOURI. . . . We hold that all church-members are alike amenable to the laws of the land. . . . We consider the religious influence exercised in financial concerns by Joseph Smith unjust. . . . We consider the *gathering* (to Zion) in haste and by sacrifice, to be contrary to the will of God ; it has been taught by Joseph Smith and others for the purpose of selling property at most exorbitant prices. . . . The wealth which is brought to this place is swallowed up by the one great throat. . . . The monies collected by missionaries sent abroad, for the temple and other purposes, are a humbug practiced by Joseph and others, as we do not believe that the monies and property so collected have been applied as the donors expected. . . . Joseph buying the lands near Nauvoo and selling them to the saints at *tenfold* advance. . . . We consider all SECRET SOCIETIES under PENAL OATHS and OBLIGATIONS to be anti-Christian. . . . That we will not acknowledge any man as KING or law-giver to the church, for Christ is King. . . . We protest against the SPOILING OF THE GENTILES."

The bare fact that Joseph could not stand more than one number of this little paper, shows how true its allegations were; and don't they put it home, Messrs. Brutus and Cassius Law? The complaint about Joseph's trafficking for political power, the incendiary attacks on Missouri, all the while belched forth in Mormon "sermons" and papers, the Danite and endowment oaths, the robberies practiced on non-Mormons—is it not all simple truth, and decently and manfully expressed? Was it not cheap, after all, at $2 per annum, and with a fine novel in the bargain, "Adelaine, or the Two Suitors"?

There is a little line in this first *Expositor* number that made the "ruler over many things" feel a good deal worse than his Lord had felt over the white sheep. It is this: "In our subsequent numbers *several affidavits* will be published to substantiate the facts alleged." It is bad enough to be killed once; but to be told that you will be beheaded once a week, fifty-two times in the year — that was a good deal worse than Emma's resistance against the *law of Sarah.* The high spirits of Mine Anointed were gone; nothing pleased him any more, not even the works of Abraham. That sacred log near the river must have felt deserted and melancholy. No more talk about all the women. I doubt if the prophet could have got sealed to more than half a dozen new wives between June 7 and 27; times were too squally.

One of the minor conspirators, Higbee, went to Carthage and made a complaint before the justice of the peace. The constable came to Nauvoo, and immediately the usual comedy was enacted. Joseph had built a sort of unconquerable castle of charters and ordinances. Whenever he or one of his friends was accused, the case was brought before the municipal court of Nauvoo, of which the prophet was president by virtue of his office as mayor. That court had power to grant writs of *habeas corpus*, and to decide as to the merits of any case. What else could such a proceeding be but a most contemptible farce? Judge the Pope by a court of twelve common monks! Says Mr. Littlefield :

> "It was decided by the Court that Joseph Smith had acted under proper authority in destroying the establishment of the Nauvoo *Expositor :* that his orders were executed in an *orderly and judicious manner, without noise or tumult :* that this was a malicious persecution on the part of F. M. Higbee, and that said Higbee pay costs of suit, and that Joseph Smith be *honorably* discharged from the accusation of the writ and go hence without delay. The other [seventeen] brethren were arrested the next day, and they also petitioned and obtained a writ of *habeas corpus* and were tried before the municipal court on that day: and, after witnesses had been examined as in the case of Joseph, they were *all honorably discharged* from the accusations and arrests. The court decided that Higbee pay the costs of the suits."

The "orderly and judicious manner, without noise or tumult," is intensely funny. Says Lee * the great admirer of the prophet :

> "The printing press and the grocery of Higbee & Foster were declared nuisances and ordered to be destroyed. The owners refused to comply with the decision of the city council, and the mayor [Joe] ordered the press and type destroyed, which was done. The owner of the grocery employed John Eagle, a regular bully, and others to defend it. As the police entered, or attempted to enter, Eagle stood in the door and knocked three of them down. As the third one fell the prophet struck Eagle under the ear and brought him sprawling to the ground. He then crossed Eagle's hands and ordered them to be tied, saying that he could not see his men knocked down while in the line of their duty, without protecting them."

What a truly formidable "lamb!" A lamb worth six policemen, at the very lowest. It would have been a match for Sullivan, that lamb. It was too weak for work, but as to knocking down a fellow and enjoying any amount of comfortable living and pleasure, there was no end of endurance in that lamb.

Let us return to the sad scene in the yard of Carthage jail. A twenty years' career of deception and crime has

---

* Confession, p. 153.

been concluded. The citizens of Illinois had found out the impostor, law-breaker and conspirator, just as the citizens of Ohio and Missouri had done. Twelve years before, he and Rigdon had been tarred and feathered by outraged citizens in Ohio; six years before, the same founders of the new gospel had to flee for their lives from Kirtland, hotly pursued by the victims of their swindles; a few months afterward the "commander-in-chief of the armies of Israel" barely escaped military execution in Missouri for armed rebellion and crimes of all kinds.

The criminal career of the impostor had been constantly widening, and his schemes, all calculated to be a profit to himself and an injury to all others, had constantly become deeper and more systematic. Originally bent on living without work, he concludes by trying to become a millionaire; originally seducing a poor girl, now and then, he finally wants *all* the women he sees; originally the ruler of a handful of fanatics, he finally dreams of an empire; originally intent on making a little speculation with the Gold Bible, he turns the small fraud into a gigantic one by pretending to be a prophet and inseparable friend and mouthpiece of the Almighty, and superior to the old prophets and apostles. Every success in crime makes him wish for more in the same line; the sight of a hundred dupes creates the desire to dupe thousands, and finally the whole world, with visions, revelations and translations.

The impostor aggravates his crimes by heartless sneers at those who have been useful to him and are so no more. His laugh at the damned fools he has fixed becomes speedily a threat of murder to those who refuse to join him in his criminal schemes. Not content to commit crimes himself, he educates large masses of a dangerously ignorant and fanatic kind systematically to become despisers and breakers of political and social laws. To his pernicious teachings he adds the most dangerous element of profound secrecy, terrible oaths and punishments. He tempts men by pandering to their basest instincts, and, worst of all, covers all his open and secret wrongs with the mantle of religion. He exasperates the peaceful inhabitants of Ohio, Missouri and Illinois by impudently "consecrating" their homes and property, and by depriving them of all legitimate political power, wherever he and his fanatics are in the majority. He makes them feel that he is capable of any deed of violence, any dark scheme, and that the only obstacles that separate him from his ends are not conscience, law and duty, but want of opportunity and fear of defeat. He makes them feel that, as a body, his followers are not only a dark cloud of ravenous locusts, but a band of desperadoes, knowing no law but the command of their brigand chiefs, and not hesitating to help each other in any emergency, be it with a club, knife or gun in a skirmish, be it with hard false swearing in court.

But is there no law, are there no judges, are there no juries? Sure enough, there are lots of those splendid institutions, but they don't always work as they should. You have read of old Scrooge, that bad weather did not know where to have him? Well, the law didn't know where to have the prophet. From the beginning of this "church," blind obedience has drowned ordinary conscience in its followers; blind obedience has always had this result and always will have. This unconditional serfdom always insured on Joseph's side any amount of exculpating witnesses, *alibi*'s, entire ignorance of facts, and, if need be, perjury. Add to this, that juries and judges can be intimidated in certain cases: many a good man doesn't want his cattle to be stolen and his house to be burned just for the satisfaction of having found guilty a petty thief. And when Joseph's political power was growing, he used it not only to steal into unheard-of city charters, he used it on all weak representatives of the law, among whom, just as to-day, were many demagogues looking out for office. Besides, Joseph was never sparing of the money of his dupes, where he could employ legal talent to save his prophetic hide. I have seen statements of very large sums spent in this way, and money went no doubt very often to bribe witnesses or spirit them off. In this manner the fact that he was tried and acquitted about forty times is easily explained.

Now, Judge Lynch is an eminently practical gentleman, with a very small amount of regard for technical niceties, and with a fell resolve to lose as little time as possible. This latter characteristic may be explained by the total absence of any fee-system observable in this branch of justice. Judge Lynch doesn't want any office; he measures neither a man's political influence, nor his pocket—he measures only his neck, so as to limit the expenses for rope, etc., with a high sense of economy, as far as compatible with decency and efficiency. In the case of "Generals" Joseph and Hyrum Smith some extra outlay for powder and balls was readily allowed, the military rank of the delinquents justifying fully such extravagance, not to speak of their yet higher rank as prophets, seers and revelators.

Good-bye, Joseph and Hyrum! Your bloody end fills me with something like awe, and with a certain sympathy for you. Your manner of death was not altogether unworthy of braver and better men than you were. I am not naturally given to hating people, and I might even feel a gentle stirring of something like sympathy for the most cunning of rascals and murderers, Brigham Young, had he finished on the end of a rope instead of dying comfortably by dysentery. You, Joe Smith, were an original, and will, as such, always claim the warm interest of artistic gentlemen like myself. Brigham was only your copy, Joe; he stole your church and kingdom ideas, and made a vast and cold system of robbery and murder out of them. Your passions made a splendid harlequin of you— he was too cold, too cunning, too avaricious to lose his head; for if there is an expensive thing it's a craze. You are intensely funny; Brigham never had the merit of being ridiculous. You were an irregular bandit, he was a methodical Shylock; you were amusing, he is tedious; you are interesting, he is only detestable.

Yes, Joe, you will live in the memory of mankind as a grand harlequin, when Brigham, the great scoundrel, will be long forgotten. You are the boss juggler and conjurer of the age. Your gold plates, your mysterious book, your peep-stone, your sword of Laban and breast-plate,

your uniform, your titles, your white dog and your bleeding Spaniard, your banking sand-boxes, your "Lord," your
house of boarding, your log on the river, your little room
for the celestial business, your oil-bottle—was there ever
a choice little outfit like this? Why, Joe, I assure you, I
felt tired at Barnum's in half an hour, but in the galleries
of your Vatican I feel good since many months. No,
don't blush, it is no compliment. I speak the truth.
You will stand out in history a grand figure with your face
in the hat and *the* stone in the hat. Sculptors will have
no difficulty in designing your monuments. I see a statue
of yours right before my mind's eye, your right foot on
the neck of a tax-collector, your right fist behind the ear
of bully John Eagle, your left holding the little oil bottle.
I see the shining gold letters of the pedestal : " Do ye the
works of Abraham," or, " It is your privilege to have all
the wives you want," or, " Where is the rest of it ? "
and the little bas reliefs on the pedestal of your monument—oh, I wish I could resurrect Benvenuto Cellini to
work them. I see the immaculate white dog and the
bleeding Spanish ghost ; I see you kneeling in the corn-
field and praying with all the fervor of a new-born Methodist ; I see you taking a handful of fifty-cent pieces and
covering carefully the sand in the boxes at Kirtland; I see
the new Abraham, your excellent father, holding a rod
and surrounded by innumerable chests of money ; I see
your little mother, holding in either hand a big, three-
cornered diamond ; I see cunning little Bennett, asking
for Orson Pratt's rifle, and then there he is again, with
something " hid up " in his left sleeve. I see all those
things worked admirably in lustrous bronze and set in
marble, just as the three-cornered diamonds were set in
glass. And far beyond all mundane effigies, I see thee a
god, Joe, in the celestial kingdom, your white hat shining and radiant like the morning sun ; and thou sittest
smiling betwixt the two Abrahams. The Lord steps up
to *ye*, arm in arm with David Patten, and thou hast, all
of you, a glorious chat about the good old Nauvoo times.

Mormonism produces not only great prophets, it gives
us great writers, too, and more especially poets and his-

torians. Let me recommend to you, before all, Edward Tullidge, Esq., for love of truth, just comparisons, and graphic power in general. Says this passionately veracious historian, of Joseph's death:

"Thus lived, and labored and loved and died the martyr prophet of the nineteenth century. Thus flashed athwart the *black midnight* of this age the light of the latter days. But the darkness comprehended it not; and even as one of old was he betrayed and sacrificed. Back to that scene on *Calvary* leaps the thought of man. Instinctively are associated the tragedy of that day and the tragedy of this. In the agony of death appears the self-same spirit," etc.

Calvary and Carthage—the comparison is just, after all. But leave out the cross in the centre, will you?

DANITES AND DESTROYING ANGELS.

John Taylor Hides Another Pearl—"Gath" and Phil Robinson—Origin of Danitism—Smith and Rigdon Preach "Oneness" or Death—The "Salt Sermon"—Fight at Gallatin—Death of the Danite Apostle—Brigham Young, the Treacherous Danite—Murderers as Preachers and Missionaries—Martyr Parley Pratt an Assassin—Affidavits of Apostles Marsh and Hyde—Joe Goes Back on Dr. Avard—Clinching Statement of David Whitmer—The Danites of 1868—Mrs. Pratt Settles the Question.

The Mormon leaders kept up their lying about polygamy for a period of more than ten years, calling, as accused criminals often do, God and the angels as witnesses that they were speaking the truth. Since 1852 their tactics have changed. They now confess polygamy, but not that they have been lying. Lying in this "church" is "hiding pearls from the swine;" stealing is taking as the Lord's agents; seducing other people's wives is exalting, and killing people is saving them.

A man who has ten wives living and declares solemnly that he never heard of polygamy, is naturally just the person to whom you would look when in search of a reliable statement. At that very same discussion in Boulogne, France, 1850, where John Taylor denied the existence of polygamy in the Mormon "church," Rev. James Robinson, one of his opponents, asked :

"Was there not a body of men amongst the Mormonites called "Danites," or "Destroying Angels." who were banded together to assassinate such as were supposed to be enemies of the body? And had not the existence of these men caused the hostility of the Americans to the Mormonite body?"

In reply John Taylor said :

"We are again very soberly told about "Danites" and "Destroying Angels." I never happened to be acquainted with any of those among the Latter-Day Saints."

John Taylor was advanced to the Mormon apostleship in 1838, and David Patten, who was then president of this quorum of twelve, being also a leading spirit among the Danites, I cannot doubt for a moment that Taylor had taken the Danite oaths himself in Missouri in 1838. But he was resolved to hide this other pearl, too. I saw once in Paris, in the *Hotel de Ventes*, a collection of pearls, belonging to Madame Blanc, exposed for sale. I thought then I had never seen so many, so big and so fine pearls. But I confess I was mistaken ; those pearls were a handful of dried peas compared with that splendid church collection, now guarded by old John Taylor. I wonder whether they don't employ Joe's bleeding Spaniard as a kind of night watchman for their church pearls. It would be just the kind of a job such a fellow would like.

Whenever a stranger who is thought of some consequence arrives in Salt Lake City, the church diplomats "make a business of it" to get hold of him and give him "the facts" about important points of church history. By accident Apostle Richards, the keeper of the historian's pearls, did so with me. No wonder that a man like Gath, the brilliant journalist, wrote in 1871, after having had chats with Brigham, George A. Smith, George Q. Cannon and other great men :

"Human life in Utah is safer than probably anywhere in civilization...... The industrious political vagabonds who write letters from Utah to the East, have created the band of ' Danites ' and other hobgoblins out of air and foolscap."

Gath had, of course, no idea that he was furthering the schemes of the most cunning rascals on earth while he wrote these lines. He could not conceive the idea that those smooth, smiling, clean-shaved gentlemen were liars. I guess that Gath, if invited by King Claudius, would write to the *Enquirer:* "I find the king to be the essence of chivalry and hospitality. Polonius is a great diplomat and scholar on the decline. Prince Hamlet is an intolerable crank, if not an outright madman." For doesn't Gath call Porter Rockwell, who is never remembered by decent people here without a shudder, "a fat, curly-haired, good-natured chap?" And he had a talk with him! Again, what does he say of the disgusting, dull, beastly fanatic, George A. Smith, Brigham's tool and courier in preparing the murder of the Arkansas emigrants in 1857:

"Smith is one of us literary folks; a man of the stamp of THACKERAY and WASHINGTON IRVING—not equal to them in degree, perhaps, but in nature *the same* .....a chaste, tender and religious husband, father, friend and gentleman."

How they must chuckle, those Mormon diplomats, when they read the books and articles of those most gloriously fixed fools! George A. Smith, a Thackeray or Washington Irving! Gath might have told us of Sappho R. Snow, Caius Sempronius Rockwell, Cornelius Tacitus Tullidge! If men of the talent and calibre of Gath are capable of such atrocities in open daylight, what would you expect from the "illustrious obscure" smaller fry of strolling scribblers — not to speak of wretched literary outcasts who sell themselves so much a page or line?*

* It is a notorious fact, known here to all persons interested in such matters, that PHIL ROBINSON, who came here some years ago, sent by the then tottering *New York World*, wrote "Saints and Sinners" in the pay of the Mormon leaders. He confessed this fact in Ogden just before leaving this profitable territory. But no confession is needed, the " book " shows the patent fact on every page.

Missouri. "the land of your enemies," was the cradle of the Danites, and fanatic Sidney Rigdon their inventor. I believe that Sidney, impostor and scoundrel as he was, was still a greater crank and fanatic. I feel sure that he came half to believe in the fraud fabricated by himself, and really imagined himself to be the man called by the Lord to restore the "House of Israel." John D. Lee gives a graphic description of the stormy times in Missouri immediately preceding the "Mormon war." He makes it plain that the eternal cry of PERSECUTION is nothing but a most impudent and outrageous lie. He proves that Sidney and Joseph transformed, in the summer of 1838, their followers into a band of desperadoes, ready to commit any horror. Hear him:

"On Monday, the 6th day of August, 1838, the greater portion of our people in the settlements near me went to Gallatin to attend the election. In justice to truth I must state that just before the general election in August 1838, a general notice was given for all the brethren of Daviess county to meet at Adam-Ondi-Ahman. Every man obeyed the call. At the meeting *all the males over eighteen years of age were organized into a* MILITARY BODY, according to the law of the priesthood and called "THE HOST OF ISRAEL." The first rank was a captain with ten men under him; next was a captain of fifty. That is, he had five companies of ten. The *entire membership* of the Mormon church was then organized in the same way. This, I was then informed, was the first organization of the military force of the church. It was so organized at that time by command of God as revealed through the Lord's prophet, Joseph Smith. God commanded Joseph Smith to place the Host of Israel in a situation for defense against the enemies of the church of Jesus Christ of Latter-Day Saints.

"At the same conference another organization was perfected, or then first formed, it was called the DANITES. The members of this order were placed under the most secret obligations that language could invent. They were sworn to stand by and sustain each other. *Sustain, protect, defend and obey the leaders of the church, under any and all circumstances unto death;* and to disobey the orders of the leaders of the church, or divulge the name of a Danite to an outsider, or to make public any of the secrets of the order of Danites, was to be punished with DEATH. And I can say of truth MANY HAVE PAID THE PENALTY for failing to keep their covenants. They had *signs and tokens* for use and protection. The token of recognition was such that it could be readily understood, and it served as a *token of distress* by which they could know each other from their enemies, although they were entire strangers to each other. When the sign was given it must be responded to and obeyed, even at the risk or certainty of death. The Danite that would refuse to respect the token and comply with all its requirements, was stamped with dishonor, infamy, shame, disgrace, and his fate for cowardice and treachery was DEATH."

Doesn't this "persecuted" people look just like a flock of innocent lambkins? This is the way they prepare themselves for an election! A blind man can see that those Missourians were awfully wicked people and Boggs was really much worse than Nero. Dr. John C. Bennett gives in his book the Constitution of the Danite Band. The document is really grotesque in its pomp; 'tis Sidney Rigdon all over. Here are some choice bits of it:

"WHEREAS, In all bodies laws are necessary for the permanency, safety and well-being of society, we, the members of the society of the Daughter of Zion,* do agree to regulate ourselves under such laws as, in righteousness, shall be deemed necessary for the preservation of *our holy religion*, and of our most sacred rights and of the rights of our wives and children. But, to be explicit on the subject, it is especially our object to support and defend the rights conferred on us by our venerable sires, who purchased them with the pledges of their lives, their fortunes and their sacred honors. And now, to prove ourselves worthy of the liberty conferred on us by them, in the providence of God, we do agree to be governed by such laws as shall perpetuate these high privileges, of which we know ourselves to be the rightful possessors, and of which privileges wicked and designing men have tried to deprive us by all manner of evil, and that *purely* in consequence of the tenacity we have manifested in the *discharge of our duty towards our God*, who has given us those rights and privileges, and a right in common with others to dwell on this land. But we, not having the privileges of others allowed to us, have determined, like unto our fathers, to resist tyranny, whether it be in kings or in the people. It is all alike unto us. Our rights we must have, and our rights we shall have, in the name of Israel's God.

"The executive power shall be vested in the PRESIDENT OF THE WHOLE CHURCH and his councilors.

"The legislative powers shall reside in the president and his councilors together, and with the generals and colonels of the society.

---

* The Danite band was instituted for the purpose of driving out from Missouri—Canaan—all apostates or dissenters from the Mormon faith. It was, therefore, first called the "BIG FAN," inasmuch as it fanned out the chaff from the wheat. "Brother of Gideon," "Daughter of Zion," and "Danites," are later names, all founded, as was Rigdon's manner, on biblical allusions.

" Punishment shall be administered to the guilty in accordance to the offense.

" All officers shall be subject to the commands of the *captain-general*, given through the *secretary of war.*"

There was never a more genuine document. It is composed of the same notes which form the daily-evening-music in the *Deseret News*, the present church organ. This is a persecuted people; they only ask for the rights guaranteed in the Constitution; "wicked and designing men," the Murrays, Zanes, Dicksons of yore, denied them their rights, and they do so to-day. Lorenzo Snow, the aged apostle, sings to-day the same tune which he, poor old fellow, sang in 1838. He was a Danite then, I have no doubt, and is one to-day.

John C. Bennett, Esq., favors us with a copy of the oath taken by the Danites in Missouri :

" In the name of Jesus Christ, the Son of God, I do solemnly obligate myself ever to conceal and never to reveal the secret purposes of this society, called the Daughter of Zion. Should I ever do the same, I hold my life as the forfeiture."

The oath was subsequently altered in Nauvoo. I have no doubt that " Joab, a general in Israel," was the author of this revised edition :

" In the name of Jesus Christ, the Son of God, I do solemnly obligate myself ever to regard the prophet and first presidency of the Church of Jesus Christ of Latter-day Saints as the supreme head of the church on earth, and to *obey them in all things the same as the supreme God;* that I will stand by my brethren in danger or difficulty, and will uphold the presidency, RIGHT OR WRONG, and that I will ever conceal and never reveal the secret purposes of this society, called the Daughter of Zion. Should I ever do the same, I hold my life as the forfeiture, in a caldron of boiling oil."

Boiling oil — that smells of the drug-store. I see the little doctor behind it. By the way, Doctor, didn't you compose it, too — that beautiful blessing which your prophet used to administer to the Danites in person, assisted by Patriarch Hyrum Smith and George Miller, the president of the high priests' quorum ? It reminds me very much of your " Joab " style:

" In the name of Jesus Christ, the Son of God, and by the

authority of the Holy Priesthood, we, the first president, patriarch and high priest of the Church of Jesus Christ of Latter day Saints, *representing* the first, second and third Gods in heaven — *the Father, the Son, and the Holy Ghost* — do now anoint you with holy, consecrated oil, and by the imposition of our hands do ordain, consecrate and set you apart for the holy calling whereunto you are called; that you may *consecrate the riches of the Gentiles to the House of Israel*, bring *swift destruction upon apostate sinners*, and execute the decrees of heaven, without fear of what man can do with you. So mote it be. Amen."

In Bennett's time the number of the Danites was over two thousand. From their "elite," to use the word of George Q. Cannon, twelve men were selected, called *Destructives*, or *Destroying Angel*, and sometimes *Flying Angel*. Their duty was to act as spies, and to report to the first presidency. Their oath was as follows:

" In the name of Jesus Christ, the Son of God, I do covenant and agree to support the first presidency of the Church of Jesus Christ of Latter-day Saints, in all things, RIGHT OR WRONG; I will faithfully guard them and report to them the acts of all men, as far as in my power lies; I will assist in executing all the decrees of the first president, patriarch or president of the twelve; and that I will cause *all who speak evil of the presidency*, or heads of the church, *to die the death of dissenters or apostates*, unless they speedily confess and repent, for *pestilence, persecution and death shall follow the enemies of Zion.* I will be a swift herald of salvation and messenger of peace to the saints, and I will never make known the secret purposes of this society, called the DESTROYING ANGEL, my life being the forfeiture in a fire of burning tar and brimstone. So help me God, and keep me steadfast."

Doctor, Doctor, I smell your little laboratory again. Burning tar and brimstone — that shows a good deal of practical chemistry.

But let us return to Lee. He is anxious to give us all the information he has acquired in his interesting career as Mormon policeman, Danite and life guard of his admired prophet.

" The *sign or token of distress* is made by placing the right hand on the right side of the face, with the points of the fingers upwards, shoving the hand upward until the ear is snug up between the thumb and fore-finger."

I wish the wise men of this nation would study the history of the *Mafia* in Sicily, which is such a thorn in the flesh of the young Italian kingdom. I have lived there for months and feel justified in saying that Mormonism is nothing but the RELIGIOUS MAFIA of the United States. Absolute secrecy, conspiracy against the laws, murder and perjury are the characteristics of both institutions. But I have yet to show Sidney Rigdon's part in this Danite business. It was on a Fourth of July, the great national memorial day of the Declaration of Independence, that the crazy restorer of the " House of Israel" unfurled the flag of treason and rebellion. Hear Danite Lee :

"That day (July 4, 1838, in Far West, a new Mormon settlement) Joseph Smith made known to the people the substance of a revelation he had before received from God. It was to the effect that all the saints throughout the land were required to sell their possessions, gather all their money together and send an agent to buy up all the land in the region round about Far West, and get a patent for the land from the government, then deed it over to the church ; then every man should come up there to the land of their promised inheritance and consecrate what they had to the Lord. Sidney Rigdon was then the mouth piece of Joseph Smith, as Aaron was of Moses in olden times. *Rigdon* told the saints that day that if they did not come up as true saints and consecrate their property to the Lord, by laying it down at the feet of the apostles, they would in a short time be compelled to consecrate and yield it up to the Gentiles. That if the saints would be united as one man in this consecration of their entire wealth to the God of Heaven, by giving it up to the control of the apostolic priesthood, then there would be no further danger to the saints ; they would no more be driven from their homes on account of their faith and holy work, for the Lord had revealed to Joseph Smith that He would then fight the battles of his children and save them from all their enemies. That the Mormon people would never be accepted as the children of God unless they were united as one man, *in temporal as well as spiritual affairs*, for Jesus had said, unless ye are one, ye are not mine ; that ONENESS must exist to make the saints the accepted children of God."

Give a quart of infernal whisky to each member of a tribe of Indians, or tell such stuff as this to a horde of beggarly, brutal fanatics, and it will come to the same. No wonder that Lee felt like "consecrating." He says :

"The words of the apostle and the promises of God, as then revealed to me, made a deep impression on my mind, as it did upon all who heard the same. We that had given up all else for the sake of the gospel, felt willing TO DO ANYTHING on earth that it was possible to do, to obtain the protection of God and have and receive His smile of approbation. Those who, like me, had full faith in the teachings of God, as revealed by Joseph Smith, his prophet, were willing to comply with *every* order and to obey *every* wish of the priesthood. A vote of the people was then had to determine the question whether they would consecrate their wealth to the church or not. The vote was *unanimous* for the consecration. The prophet and all his priesthood were jubilant and could hardly contain themselves; they were so happy to see the people such dutiful saints."*

Who is there among my readers who does not feel that all this infernal humbug is nothing but a conspiracy of scoundrels to dupe a horde of fanatics under religious pretences? To make them give up every cent they have, and make tools of them for all sorts of criminal purposes?

Sidney gave the fools, to fix them thoroughly, a big speech on the same Fourth of July. That speech has become celebrated in Mormon history as the "SALT SERMON." Sidney had found somewhere a Bible text: "If the salt have lost its savour, it is thenceforth good for nothing but to be cast out and trodden under the foot of men." You see it as clearly as I do, reader, that this means the apostates or, in a larger sense, all the wicked fellows who wouldn't consecrate; finally the Missourians and all Gentiles. Sidney was strong at the old Bible, and his interpretations were always just what Joseph's "kingdom" needed. He told the Mormons that the story of Ananias and Sapphira falling dead at the rebuke of Peter, was no work of the heavens, but that "the young men" who were with Peter literally trod them under their feet till their bowels gushed out! And Judas the traitor—he didn't die by his own hand, Sidney knew better. His fellow apostles killed him, and his bowels came out by the same religious proceeding. But hear the "Salt Sermon":

"We take God and all the holy angels to witness this day that we warn all men in the name of Jesus Christ, to come on us no more for

* "Laying all at the Apostles' feet" was a life-long dream and hobby with Rigdon. This takes the form of the so-called "Order of Enoch" in Mormonism, now figuring for the time as Z. C. M. I., the mercantile anaconda of Utah.

ever. The men or the set of men that attempts it does so at the expense of their lives. And the mob that comes on us to disturb us, it shall be between us and them a war of EXTERMINATION, for we will follow them *till the last drop of blood is spilled*, or else they will have to exterminate us; for we will carry the seat of war to their own houses and their own families, and one part or the other shall be utterly destroyed. Remember it then, all men! No man shall be at liberty to come in our streets, to threaten us with mobs, for if he does he shall atone for it before he leaves the place; neither shall he be at liberty to vilify or slander any of us, for suffer it we will not in this place. We therefore take all men to record this day, as did our fathers, and we pledge this day to one another our fortunes and our sacred honours to be delivered from the PERSECUTIONS which we have had to endure for the last nine years, or nearly that. Neither will we indulge any man or set of men in instituting vexatious LAW-SUITS against us, to cheat us out of our just rights; if they attempt it we say *woe* be unto them. WE THIS DAY, then, PROCLAIM OURSELVES FREE, with a purpose and a determination that can never be broken. No, never! No, never!! No, NEVER!!!"

This is a very fair specimen of Mormon political programme. Let me tell you, by the way, that this piece of frenzy, absurd as it seems, is just the stuff that fills to-day the brains of the invisible head of the church, President John Taylor. He is absolutely the same kind of foaming fanatic that Sidney was. He has preached "Salt Sermons" by the hundred, and he would do so to-day were it not for "scoundrels" like Zane, Dickson and Ireland. Scoundrels? It is one of the mildest terms used by him, when talking of the officers of the law.

But there had been in June a fore-runner to the "Salt Sermon," a wonderful little document, addressed to the Dissenters, wicked fellows, who would not become criminal conspirators and desperadoes. The little thing is full of the spirit of the "pure-in-heart;" it smells all over of the goodness and peace-of *Zion*. Curious enough, among the wicked are to be found the original witnesses of the Book of Mormon. All of the leaders of the Dissenters had been chosen servants and instruments of the Lord so long as they had been absolute tools but the very moment they dared to think for themselves, they became dangerous for the kingdom. Here is the anathema which was drawn up by Rigdon and signed by over eighty leading Mormons :

"Far West, June 1, 1838.

"To Oliver Cowdery, David Whitmer, John Whitmer, W. W. Phelps and Lyman E. Johnson, Greeting:

"Whereas, The [Mormon] citizens of Caldwell county have borne with the abuse received from you, at different times, and on different occasions, until it is no longer to be endured; neither will they endure it any longer, having exhausted all the patience they have, and conceive that to bear any longer is a vice instead of a virtue. We have borne long and suffered incredibly; but we will neither bear nor suffer any longer; and the decree has gone forth from our hearts, and shall not return to us void. Neither think, gentlemen, that in so saying we are trifling with either you or ourselves, for we are not. There are no threats from you—no fear of losing our lives by you, or by anything you can say or do, will restrain us; for *out of the country you shall go*, and no power shall save you. And you shall have three days after you receive this communication to you, including twenty-four hours in each day, for you to depart with your families, peaceably; which you may do, undisturbed by any person; but in that time, if you do not depart, we will use the means in our power to cause you to depart: for go you shall. We will have no more promises to reform, as you have already done, and in every instance violated your promise, and regarded not the covenant which you had made, but put both it and us at defiance. We have solemnly warned you, and that in the most determined manner, that if you did not cease that course of wanton abuse of the [Mormon] citizens of this county, that vengeance would overtake you sooner or later, and that when it did come it would be as furious as the mountain torrent, and as terrible as the beating tempest; but you have affected to despise our warnings, and pass them off with a sneer or grin, or a threat, and pursued your former course; *and vengeance sleepeth not*, neither does it slumber; and unless you heed us this time and attend to our request, it will overtake you at an hour when you do not expect, and at a day when you do not look for it; and for you there shall be no escape; for there is but one decree for you, which is: Depart, depart, or a more fatal calamity shall befall you."

Nero Boggs' order for the expulsion or extermination of the Saints appears mild enough contrasted with this hyena yell. The Mormon president issues his order of expulsion or extermination in June, 1838, and the Missouri governor issues *his* in October, 1838. The Christ-like Rigdon anathematizes and would kill peaceable, law-upholding victims of his own miserable fraud. Nero Boggs, in order to avoid a civil war, is for expelling or extermintaing armed law-breakers. Rigdon is the crazy fanatic, Boggs the zealous officer, and in the finale as usual

innocent dupes have to suffer with designing knaves.
Yet the Mormons were a horribly PERSECUTED body of
RELIGIOUS worshippers in the "land of Missouri," you
know.

But how things change in this fickle world! You had
seen the plates and dozens of angels, David Whitmer;
the angels had even worked for you in the fields, they
had treated you like an old playmate of theirs. And now
they give you three days to "get out" with your family.
There is a little consolation in the fact that each of these
three days "includes" twenty-four hours, but still it is
hard for a friend and confidant of angels to be treated
like this. And you, Oliver Cowdery, how must you feel
in reading that "no power shall save you," and "there
shall be no escape"! It makes my heart bleed to look
at that excellent little book, the Sunday-school Catechism,
No. 1, printed in 1882, p. 17:

Q. When were Joseph and Oliver baptized?
A. On the same day that the Aaronic priesthood was conferred
upon them.
Q. Who was baptized first?
A. Oliver Cowdery.
Q. Who baptized him?
A. Joseph Smith.
Q. Who was next baptized?
A. Joseph Smith.
Q. Who baptized him?
A. Oliver Cowdery.
Q. What took place next?
A. Joseph ordained Oliver to the Aaronic priesthood.
Q. And who ordained Joseph Smith?
A. Oliver Cowdery.
Q. What happened after this?
A. The Holy Ghost fell upon them and they prophesied.

Those were glorious times, Oliver. Then the day
included twenty-four happy hours. But more glories
were to be yours. Says our little Catechism, p. 19:

Q. By whom was the holy apostleship restored to the earth?
A. Christ's ancient apostles, Peter, James and John.
Q. Upon whom did they confer this power?
A. Joseph Smith and Oliver Cowdery.

But I am not yet through with your glories and special blessings, Oliver. Let me look at the little Catechism, p. 32:

Q. What glorious things were revealed on the next Sunday (April 3, 1836)?
A. The heavens were opened to Joseph Smith and Oliver Cowdery, and the glories thereof were shown to them.
Q. Who appeared to them on this occasion?
A. Our Lord and Savior Jesus Christ.
Q. What did He say of Himself?
A. "I am the first and the last, I am he who liveth, I am he who was slain, I am your advocate with the Father."
Q. After this vision was closed who next appeared?
A. Moses, the great law-giver of ancient Israel.
Q. What did he commit to *them?*
A. The keys of the gathering of Israel.
Q. Who *appeared next?*
A. Elias.
Q. Who appeared after Elias?
A. The prophet Elijah, who gave them the keys to turn the hearts of the fathers to the children and the children to the fathers.

To have a whole museum of *keys*, Oliver, and then be given three days to "git up an' git!" What else could you do, after all, than turn a Methodist, like as your prophet had done?* This seems the only way out of difficulties of this kind, especially when nobody will "appear next." But what did you do with all *them* keys, pray?

The effect of all this fanatical nonsense must have been disastrous on the confused brain of a fanatic like John D. Lee. Says this great friend and spiritual foster-son of Brigham Young, most faithful and most celebrated of all Danites, after having reported Sidney's salt sermon: "At the end of each sentence Rigdon was loudly cheered, and when he closed his oration, I believed *the Mormons could* SUCCESSFULLY RESIST THE WORLD."

It is well known that the first serious disturbance

---

*All three of the original witnesses of the Book of Mormon apostatized. Cowdery became a member of the Methodist Protestant Church in the winter of 1842-3, in Tiffin, Ohio, expressing at the time his deep shame and contrition for his connection with Mormonism and the Book of Mormon.

between Mormons and Missourians occurred in the little
town of Gallatin, August 6, 1838.   It was at the election
for which the Mormons had been prepared so nicely by
their leaders.   They came to Gallatin as the "Host of
Israel," and as Danites, bound by secret oaths and
tokens.   Lee may tell us what happened on this ominous
day :

"Gallatin was a new town, with about ten houses, three of which
were saloons.   The town was on the bank of Grand River, and heavy
timber came near the town, which stood in a little arm of the prairie.
Close to the polls there was a lot of oak timber, which had been
brought there to be riven into shakes or shingles, leaving the heart,
taken from each shingle-block, lying there on the ground.   These
hearts were three-square, four feet long, weighed about seven pounds,
and made a very dangerous yet handy weapon.   When Stewart fell
[a Mormon who had been beaten by a Missourian in a scuffle at the
polls], the Mormons sprang to the pile of oak hearts, and each man
taking one for use, rushed into the crowd.   The Mormons were
yelling, 'Save him!' and the settlers yelled, 'Kill him, damn him!'
The *sign of distress was given* by the *Danites*, and all rushed forward,
determined to save Stewart or die with him.   One of the *mob* stabbed
Stewart in the shoulder.   He rose and ran, trying to escape, but was
again surrounded and attacked by a large number of foes.   The
Danite sign of distress was again given by John L. Butler, one of the
captains of the *Host of Israel.*   Seeing the *sign*, I sprang to my feet
and armed myself with one of the oak sticks.   *I did this because I
was a Danite,* and my oaths that I had taken required immediate
action on my part, in support of the one giving the sign.   I ran into
the crowd.   I was an entire stranger to all who were engaged in the
affray, except Stewart, but I had seen the *sign*, and, like Samson
when leaning against the pillar, I felt the power of God nerve my arm
for the fray.   *It helps a man a great deal in a fight to know that God
is on his side.*"

Was n't he well fixed, that fool Lee? That is the kind
of oak hearts to build celestial kingdoms with.   And
Joseph's kingdom went up like magic just then—consecration was flourishing.   Says Lee :

"The prophet, Joseph Smith, said it was a civil war; that by the
rules of war each party was justified in *spoiling his enemy.*   This
opened the door to the evil-disposed, and men of former quiet became
PERFECT DEMONS in their efforts to spoil and waste away the enemies
of the church.   I saw soon that it was the natural inclination of men
to steal and convert to their own use that which others possessed.
What perplexed me most was to see that religion had not the power

to subdue that passion in man, but that at the first moment when the restrictions of the church were withdrawn, *the most devout men* in our community acted like they had served a lifetime in evil, and were NATURAL-BORN THIEVES."

Is that so, Elder Lee? Then those bitter apostates are right after all, when saying that your leaders have always acted and do always act like natural-born thieves? Lee fortifies his general statement by a very remarkable special case :

" A company went from Adam-Ondi-Ahman and burnt the house and buildings belonging to my friend, McBrier. Every article of moveable property was taken by the [Mormon] troops; he was utterly ruined. This man had been a friend to me and many others of the brethren; he was an honorable man, but his good character and former acts of kindness had no effect on those who were working, as they pretended, *to build up the kingdom of God.* The Mormons brought in every article that could be used. . . . *Men stole simply for the love of stealing.* Such inexcusable acts of lawlessness had the effect to arouse every Gentile in the three counties of Caldwell, Carroll and Davies, as well as to bring swarms of armed Gentiles from other localities."

Those are the acts of a pure, slandered and persecuted people, told by one of their leaders, who was tried and shot for having "lived his religion." This book of the great Danite* should be studied by every patriotic American. It has become a favorite of mine. I find in it many of the qualities of that wonderful autobiography of Benvenuto Cellini, the Florentine goldsmith. He and Lee had some common traits : sensuality, superstition, and a certain volcanic *ensemble* which never fails to make a writer powerful. What is *style* after all without natural vigor? It is training in a Rozinante. It is curious, but still a fact, that Lee and Hickman, the greatest murderers of this "church," are the only interesting writers among scores of saints who have tried the path of authorship. Eliza R. Snow, I am sorry to say, beats them all in the impossible *genre*.

Lee is full of interesting "portraits." Let him describe the death of a famous Danite, Captain David

---

* Mormonism Unveiled, including the remarkable life and confessions of John D. Lee. St. Louis, Moffat Publ. Co., 1881.

Patten, the president of the twelve apostles, whose sudden exit opened wide the gates of success for ambitious Brigham Young.   Patten died in a skirmish with the Missourians called " battle of Crooked River."

"Captain David Patten, called *Fearnot*, was sent out by the prophet with fifty men, to attack a body of Missourians, who were camping on the Crooked River.   Captain Patten's men were nearly all, if not every one of them, *Danites*.   The attack was made just before daylight in the morning. Captain Fearnot wore a white blanket overcoat and led the attacking party. He was a brave, impulsive man. He rushed into the thickest of the fight, regardless of danger, really seeking it to show his men that God would shield him from all harm. But he counted without just reason upon being invincible, for a ball soon entered his body, passing through his hips and cutting his bladder. The wound was fatal, but he kept on his feet and led his men some time before yielding to the effects of his wound.   The Gentiles said afterwards that Captain Patten told his men to charge in the name of Lazarus, ' CHARGE, DANITES, CHARGE !' and that as soon as he uttered the command, which distinguished him, they gave tne Danite captain a commission with powder and ball, and sent him on a mission to preach to the spirits that were in prison."

The martyrdom of the "great warrior apostle " was a fearful blow to Mormon superstition, originated and fed by the crazy harangues of " my servants Sidney and Joseph."   "I had considered," says Lee, "that I was *bullet-proof*, that no Gentile ball could ever harm me or any saint, and I had believed that a Danite could not be killed by Gentile hands.   I thought that one Danite would chase a thousand and two could put ten thousand to flight.   We had been promised and taught by the prophet that henceforth *God would fight our battles*, and that nothing but disobedience to the teachings of the priesthood could render a Mormon subject to injury from Gentile forces.   We, as members of the church, *had no right to question any act of our superiors;* to do so wounded the spirit of God and led to our own loss and confusion."

We see from Lee's expressions that the "Host of Israel" was pretty much demoralized by the death ot Capt. Patten.   But the famous son of Lucy-Munchhausen was the greatest virtuoso of his age in the art of fixing the fools. Lee was "thunderstruck" when the "Commander-in-chief of the armies of Israel " said at the funeral of Capt.

Patten that the Mormons were liable to be killed by Gentile balls just like other men. " Joseph also said that the Lord was angry with the people, for they had been unbelieving and faithless; they had denied the Lord the use of their earthly treasures, and placed their affections upon worldly things more than they had upon heavenly things; that to expect God's favor we must *blindly* trust him; that if the Mormons would wholly trust in God, the windows of heaven would be opened and a shower of blessings sent upon the people; that all the people could contain of blessings would be given as a reward for obedience to the will of God as made known to mankind through the prophet of the ever-living God; that the Mormons, if faithful, obedient and true followers of the advice of their leaders, would *soon enjoy all the wealth of the earth*; that God would consecrate the riches of the Gentiles to the saints." I believed all he said, for he supported it by quotations from scripture, and if I believed in the Bible,[*] as I did most implicitly, I could not help believing in Joseph Smith, the prophet of God in these last days. Joseph Smith declared that he was called of God and given power and authority from heaven to do God's will; that he had received the keys [O Lucy!] of the holy priesthood from the apostles Peter, James and John, and had been dedicated, set apart and anointed as the prophet, seer and revelator, sent to open the dispensation of the fullness of times, according to the words of the apostles; that he was charged with the *restoration of the House of Israel* and to gather the Saints from the four corners of the earth to the land of promise, Zion, the Holy Land (Jackson county), and setting up the kingdom of God preparatory to the second coming of Christ in the latter days. Every Mormon, if true to his faith, believed as fully in Joseph Smith and *his holy character* as they did that God existed."

Is the effect of the *Prophetic* idea not wonderful? It seems at least as powerful an agent as the revolutionary idea of liberty: it makes the pulse beat just like the

---

[*] "Our sickness is an overdose of Bible," said an old Mormon lady to me.

Marseillaise. Surrounded as he was by a thousand or more Lees, is it surprising that Joseph began to see himself a Mahomet ?

Lee died an admirer of Joseph Smith. While sitting on his coffin at the Mountain Meadows, on that chilly March morning in 1877, he cursed treacherous Brigham Young and hoped to be soon united with his beloved prophet. He gives a most enthusiastic and really interesting description of the modern Mahomet : "Joseph Smith was a most extraordinary man ; he was rather large in stature, some six feet two inches in height, well built, though a little stoop-shouldered, prominent and well-developed features, a Roman nose, light chestnut hair, upper lip full and rather protruding, chin broad and square, an eagle eye, and on the whole there was something in his manner and appearance that was bewitching and winning ; his countenance was that of a plain, honest man, full of benevolence and philanthropy and void of deceit or hypocrisy. He was resolute and firm of purpose, stronger than most men in physical power, and all who saw were forced to admire him, as he then looked and existed."

The portrait is no doubt a strongly flattered one. In the prison where his Confession was written, Joseph seemed to Lee, compared with the two-faced, ungrateful Brigham, the essence of honor and chivalry. Still, there is enough in Lee's sketch to show that Joseph had something of the popular leader in him. Mrs. Pratt, who surely had every reason in the world to hate and despise Joseph, said once to me : "As a leader I would always prefer Joseph to low cunning Brigham."

There is scarcely a doubt that the apostles of Joseph Smith were all Danites, since their president was a Danite captain. It is not doubtful to me that, for instance, Brigham Young had also taken the Danite oaths, and this is the reason why Lee kept on hoping to the last moment that his life would be spared : he could not believe that Brigham would prove untrue to his COVENANTS, which bind any Danite to help another, as we have seen. Those horrible COVENANTS are a generic and dominating feature of Mormonism all through; they are the secret cement of the whole structure, and Mormonism cannot be understood without this secret-oath business, bloody punishments, etc., being taken into due consideration. The witnesses of the Book of Mormon were bound by covenants to testify; Rigdon and Smith bound themselves by a most solemn covenant to keep the great fraud secret:* every Danite was fettered by covenants, and finally every "good" Mormon becomes a part of this dreadful machinery through his endowment oaths.

Among the Danite Apostles of the time of the Missouri troubles, Parley P. Pratt seems to be one of the Patten kind. He did not find his martyrdom in Missouri † and this is deeply to be regretted, since Providence permitted him to live up to 1857 and to do incalculable mischief in the way of proselyting, in brutalizing the Mormon people by his coarse, filthy and fanatic preaching, and by corrupting all the *women* he approached. He was one of the saintly brutes of the William Smith and Orson Hyde type, which latter, however, developed in his full glory later, in Utah, preaching that Christ had lived in polygamy, and enjoying whiskey and polygamy much more than even his bull constitution could stand. Yes, Mormonism is a very peculiar religion. It preaches murder as a religious duty, and treats the murderer as a distinguished member of the "church." I am not joking. Said a poor Mormon widow to me, whose husband was killed in the foulest manner imaginable by the police of this holy city: "They bless the bread and wine in the tabernacle — there is half a dozen of murderers among them; I could point them out any time."

Did not President Joseph F. Smith, of the so-called first presidency of the Mormon church, pronounce the funeral eulogium over the body of the saintly O. Porter Rockwell, Esq.? I have been told so. You don't want

* "Keep all the commandments *and covenants by which ye are bound*, and I will cause the heavens to shake for your good;" so says the Mormon Lord to Joseph and Sidney, December, 1830.

† He was killed in Arkansas, 1857, for running away with another man's wife and trying to abduct the man's children.

to believe such things, gentle reader. You say this is not possible. If you had lived in 1560 or so, and had met a man fresh from priest-ridden Spain who told you about an auto-da-fe, would you have answered him the same way? I have myself heard a sermon in the tabernacle delivered by a man who is known all over Utah as having killed his first wife in 1857 because she opposed his taking a number four. I shall tell the case with all details in Part II. of this work. It is a notorious fact that men who have committed horrible deeds for the "church" are generally, to get them out of the way of the Federal authorities, sent out on some "mission." It is the general belief in Utah that Isaac C. Haight, who took such an important part in the Mountain Meadows Massacre, is preaching the gospel in some foreign country under an assumed name. Think of such a bloody spectre playing the gospel-dove! It is another notorious fact that the Danites, Lee, Haight and Hickman, were for many years, and after the massacre of 1857, members of the Territorial Legislature. How can I explain all this? Simply through the well-founded supposition that a Danite murderer is a sort of veteran, a decorated officer of the Mormon church. He has shown courage and zeal in the service of "the Lord," he has helped to build up "the kingdom of God on earth," he has destroyed some of the enemies of "Zion." How can you explain otherwise the *most intimate* relation between Joseph and Rockwell, and the fact, told me by Mrs. Pratt, that Brigham used (after 1857!) to walk with Lee, his arm around the brother's shoulder and whispering in his ear? Mrs. Pratt has seen this kind of scene often and often, and she has seen Brigham embracing Elder Hickman the same way. Doesn't it remind you of the relations of Richard and Macbeth with the "first" and "second" murderer? It does me.

But I wanted you to hear from Lee a little anecdote about Parley P. Pratt. It shows this brutal apostle, who is to-day a celebrated and much lamented martyr of the "church," in his true light. Here it is:

"I knew a man by the name of Tarwater, on the Gentile side

[in the 'battle of Crooked River'], that was cut up fearfully. He was taken prisoner. The Danites routed the Gentiles, who fled in every direction. The Mormons started for Far West, taking Tarwater along as a prisoner. After traveling several miles, they halted in a grove of timber and released Tarwater, telling him he was free to go home. He started off, and when he was some forty yards from the Mormons, Parley P. Pratt, then one of the twelve apostles, stepped up to a tree, laid his gun up by the side of the tree, took deliberate aim and *shot* Tarwater. He fell and lay still. The Mormons, believing he was dead, went on and left him lying where he fell. Tarwater came to and reached home where he was taken care of and soon recovered from his wounds. He afterwards testified in court against the Mormons that he knew, and upon his evidence Parley P. Pratt was imprisoned in the Richmond jail in 1839."

I asked my friend Webb about this statement of Lee's, and he said : " I have heard this story very often, and I do not doubt it at all. Parley was just the man to do such a thing." It is a *church* and a *religion* with such " apostles " and " martyrs," isn't it ?

For those who want further evidence, I introduce now the affidavit of Thomas B. Marsh, who apostatized in the hour of danger. He was president of the Twelve before Patten ; his apostacy and Patten's death opening the way for Brigham. Here is Marsh's affidavit :

RICHMOND, Mo., Octbr. 24, 1838.

" They have among them a company consisting of all that are considered *true Mormons*, called the DANITES, who have taken an oath to support the heads of the church in all things that they say or do, *whether right or wrong*. Many, however, of this band are much dissatisfied with this oath as being against moral and religious principles. I am informed by the Mormons that they had a meeting at Far West, at which they appointed a company of *twelve*, by the name of the *Destruction Company*, for the purpose of burning and destroying, and that if the people at Buncombe came to do mischief upon the people of Caldwell, and committed depredations upon the Mormons, they were to burn Buncombe, and if the people of Clay and Ray made any movements againt them, this destroying company were to burn Liberty and Richmond. *This burning was to be done secretly, by going as incendiaries.* At the same meeting, I was informed, they passed a decree that no Mormon dissenter (apostate) should leave Caldwell county alive, and that such as attempted to do it should be *shot down* and sent so tell their tale in eternity. In a conversation between Dr. Avard and other Mormons said Avard proposed to start a pestilence among the Gentiles by poisoning their corn, fruit, etc., and saying it was the work of the Lord, and said Avard advocated *lying* for the support of their religion and said it was no harm to lie for the Lord. The plan of Smith the prophet is to take this State, and he professes to his people to intend taking the United States, and ultimately the whole world. *This is the belief of the church* and my own opinion of the prophet's plans and intentions. It is my opinion that neither the prophet nor any one of the principal men who is firm in the faith could be indicted for any offense in the county of Caldwell. The prophet inculcates the notion, and it is believed by every true Mormon, that *Smith's prophecies are superior to the law of the land.* I have heard the prophet say that he should yet tread down his enemies and walk over their dead bodies; that if he was not let alone he would be a *second Mahomet* to this generation, and that he would make it one gore of blood from the Rocky Mountains to the Atlantic Ocean; that like Mahomet, whose motto in treating for peace was, 'the Alcoran or the sword,' so should it be eventually with us: '*Joseph Smith or the sword.*'"

AFFIDAVIT OF APOSTLE ORSON HYDE.

The most of the statements in the foregoing disclosure of Thomas B. Marsh *I know to be true*; the remainder I *believe* to be true. (Same date.)

The remark has already been made that Sidney Rigdon was the originator of the Danite band. The proof for this assertion is furnished by the Mormon leaders themselves. After Joseph's death, when there was a life and death struggle for the church dictatorship between impractical, fanatic Rigdon, and unscrupulous, business-man Brigham Young, the former was expelled from the church by a mock trial. One of the charges preferred against him was his course in Missouri in 1838. Says Brigham Young at this trial (*Times and Seasons*, p. 667):

"Elder Rigdon was the PRIME CAUSE OF OUR TROUBLES IN MISSOURI, by his Fourth of July oration."

And Orson Hyde says at the same trial (*Times and Seasons*, p. 651):

"He [Rigdon] was the cause of our troubles in MISSOURI, and although Brother Joseph tried to restrain him, he would take his own course."

Sister Snow, in her great psalm, dated "City of Nauvoo, 1842," says of Missouri: "Thou art a stink in the nostrils of the Goddess of Liberty." But this horrible stench, and it was a brutish and bloody one, sure enough, all came, as we now see, from my servant Sidney taking his own course, against the protests of your sweet spouse, the prophet; but never mind, sister, you saints *must* be *persecuted*, are nothing if not persecuted. And so Missouri has "butchered the saints of the Most High, and hunted the prophets like Ahab of old." And, again, "Thou art already associated with Herod, Nero and the bloody Inquisition — thy name has become synonymous with oppression, cruelty, treachery and blood." Oh, Sappho-Eliza-Roxanna-Snow-Smith-Young! But I think I sniff General Joab in this transcendent psalm. "Thou didst pollute the holy sanctuary of female virtue, and barbarously trample upon the most sacred *gems* of domestic felicity," is Pistol-Bennett, sure.

I believe readily that Joseph tried, in the beginning, to restrain the crankiness of his Mentor, who spoke and acted like a fanatic Jew of the times of Moses and Joshua, carefully embalmed at the fall of Jericho and resurrected in Jackson County, Mo. Joseph was not a man of nonsensical hobbies; *his* fanaticism lay in another direction —in that of "all the women." His idol was a huge enjoyment of life in the sense of Caligula and Nero. Hating honest work more than bitter death, he was forced to use all the ways and means of charlatans to steal the prize which he could not conquer by true talent and honest exertion. So every scheme was welcome that would lead to enjoyment on the grand style. But he may have hesitated, at the outset of the "Mormon war," at the idea of becoming openly a rebel and leader of armed bands. This hesitation was evidently overcome by his love for appearing in great roles, by parading as "commander-in-chief of the armies of Israel," by his intoxication at the idea of becoming a second Mahomet. There were always some about him who made a business of it to work up his brains to the boiling point. There was Rigdon, proving from the old Bible that the House of Israel was invincible; there was Dr. Avard, an adventurer of exactly the Bennett kind, intensely ambitious and entirely unscrupulous, who saw in Joseph the coming man. Avard was, like Bennett and Joe, an infidel, and the role of right-hand man of the new Mahomet tickled him.

Joseph may have hesitated, as Charles IX. did when hearing the bloody plans of his mother against the Huguenots, but he gave way like Charles IX. Could not Sidney show how the old Jews had exterminated the peaceful inhabitants of a whole country?

"He left none remaining, but utterly destroyed all that breathed, as the Lord God of Israel commanded. . . And they utterly destroyed all that was in the city, *both men and women, young and old*, and ox, and sheep, and ass, with the edge of the sword. . . ."

Blood, streams of blood, shed at the command of the Almighty! And could not Avard, the worldly adviser, prove to the illiterate peeper that so many of the emperors and kings had risen by shedding blood like water? Joe listened and listened, and they convinced him finally — the resurrected Jew to the right, and the modern Machiavel to the left.

Armed with the enthusiastic approval of Sidney Rigdon and the (perhaps hesitating) consent of Joseph, Dr. Avard goes to work with the energy of a gold-digger whose imagination is filled with tremendous nuggets. Friend Webb heard Avard speak to the brethren, and he says it was the most blood-curdling kind of speech he ever heard in his life.

"My brethren, it is written: 'The riches of the Gentiles shall be consecrated to my people, the House of Israel;' and in this way we will build up the KINGDOM OF GOD, and roll forth the little stone that Daniel saw cut out of the mountain without hands, until it shall fill the whole earth. For this is the very way that GOD destines to build up his kingdom in the last days. If any of us should be recognized, who can harm us? For we will stand by each other and defend one another in all things. If our enemies swear against us, we can swear also. Why do you startle at this, brethren? As the Lord liveth, I would swear a lie to clear any of you; and if this could not do, I would put them or him under the sand, as Moses did the Egyptian, and in this way we will consecrate much to the Lord, and BUILD UP HIS KINGDOM; and who can stand against us? And if any of this Danite society reveals any of these things, I will put him where the dogs cannot bite him."

There came a day when Rigdon, Joseph and Avard

awoke from their ambitious dream to the cold reality of
things. The awful formalities of a court-martial, the
reading of a sentence, "You will be shot to-morrow
morning at eight o'clock," and the atmosphere of a
court-room where you are tried for high treason, murder,
arson, etc., exert a remarkably cooling influence on the
aspirations of modern Joshuas, Mahomets and Napoleons.

When in the clutches of the law, Joseph dropped
Avard, as Brigham did faithful Danite Lee some forty
years after. Even how to sacrifice a friend in the hour of
danger did you learn from Joseph, great plagiarist Young.
Hear the prophet:

"While the evil spirits were raging up and down in the state
[Missouri] to raise mobs against the Mormons, Satan himself was no
less busy in striving to stir up mischief in the camps of the Saints, and
among the most conspicuous of his willing devotees was one Dr.
Sampson Avard, who had been in the church but a short time and
who, although he had generally behaved with a tolerable degree of
external decorum, was secretly aspiring to be the greatest of the great,
and become the leader of the people by forming a secret combination
by which he might rise a mighty conqueror, at the expense of the overthrow of the church; and this he tried to accomplish by his smooth,
flattering and winning speeches which he frequently made to his associates, while his room was well guarded by some of his pupils, ready
to give him the wink on the approach of anyone who would not
approve of his measures. In this situation he stated that he had the
sanction of the heads of the church for what he was about to do, and
persuaded them to believe it and proceeded to administer to the few
under his control an oath, binding them to everlasting secrecy to everything which should be communicated to them by himself. Thus
Avard initiated members into his band, firmly binding them, by all
that was sacred, in the protecting of each other in all things THAT
WERE LAWFUL."

This last lie gives away all the rest of them. So Avard
had to be one of the most willing devotees of *Satan*, to
teach nothing but what was *lawful!* Joseph continues:

"Avard would often affirm to his company that the principal men
of the church had put him forward as a spokesman and a leader of
this band, which *he* named DANITES."

So there *was* a Danite band with secret oaths, but
Joseph and the church had nothing to do with it. This
looks just like the truth! Joseph is at the head of an

organization which from its very beginning was built on
blind obedience and where every member was a spy on his
comrades.   But no, Joseph knew nothing, and the Lord
didn't tell him about it, neither did " Urim and Thummim."   Joseph remained in perfect ignorance even then
when Dr. Avard " held meetings to organize his men into
companies of tens and fifties, appointing a captain over
each company."   There is a method in those Mormon
lies.   The Danites?   Dr. Avard organized them.   Spiritual wifery?   That scoundrel Bennett introduced it.   The
Mountain Meadows Massacre?   Oh, the Indians did that,
you know.

Fortunately, we have got a good witness or two to *seal*
this Danite business *for all eternity*.   DAVID WHITMER is
a good witness to fix a doubtful point in early Mormon
history, isn't he?   A third of the proof of the divinity of
the Book of Mormon rests on his shoulders: he is is one
of the three original witnesses of the American Bible.   It
is my conviction, besides—and I shall give my reasons for
it—that David Whitmer was an *honest and sincere* witness
while testifying that he had seen the golden plates.   He
was, no doubt, immensely superstitious; it was easy to
dupe him and he *was* duped, but he was not a man to put
his name to a lie wittingly.   We have seen the anathema
pronounced by Sidney Rigdon and eighty-three leading
Mormons against the " Dissenters."   Mr. J. L. Traughber, Jr., a gentleman living in Missouri and an old friend
of David Whitmer, states in regard to the "Dissenters:"

" Martin Harris, Oliver Cowdery, David, John and Jacob Whitmer
and Hiram Page withdrew from J. Smith at Kirtland in 1837.   The
next year Smith and Sidney Rigdon had to flee from Kirtland by
night to keep from being imprisoned for banking without a charter.
They went to Far West, Missouri, where David Whitmer was president of the stake, and soon formed their Danite band to kill ' Dissenters,' and fight the enemies of Zion.   David Whitmer and others
were ' Dissenters.'   David Patten [the Danite Captain] went to them,
and told them that it was determined that they must die.   They went
out one evening to hunt their cows and did not go back again.   In a
few days the Danites ordered *the families* of those men to leave Far
West, *with nothing but the clothing they wore*.   But when the ' mob '
had captured the place, David Whitmer and the others went and got
their goods and property."

These are the doings of the "persecuted people." They try to kill their own friends and drive their families into·the woods. They ask solemnly for their constitutional rights in the name of religion, but when a crank like Morris sets up a little revelation-shop of his own, they demolish it with cannon, killing women, children and unarmed men. But let me now give the direct testimony of David Whitmer himself in the Danite question. Says the old man : *

"SMITH AND RIGDON issued a decree organizing what was termed the 'DANITES' or 'DESTROYING ANGELS,' who were bound by the MOST FEARFUL OATHS to obey the commandments of the LEADERS OF THE CHURCH. The 'Danites' consisted ONLY OF THOSE SELECTED BY SMITH AND RIGDON."

That old man, over eighty, is yet alive. He believes to-day in the Book of Mormon, the golden plates, the last dispensation and the new and everlasting covenant. But he believes that Joseph was a FALLEN PROPHET when he organized a band of armed law-breakers. David came from a good family and had some property, which may explain why he did not fall in, hand and heart, with the desperate schemes of penniless adventurers.

But I have got a real *bonbon* of a testimony in this Danite business, and I have saved it, as the French say, *pour la bonne bouche*, to make the reader keep a good taste in his mouth. Our fraud-hating friend Mrs. Pratt —she has become the reader's friend as well as mine by this time, I hope—tells the following story :

"One day, in 1868, shortly before Apostle Heber C. Kimball had his fatal attack of sickness, he returned to his home from a secret meeting held in the Endowment House. I was on intimate terms with the Kimball family and was visiting Vilate, the apostle's first wife, when Heber came in. We were all in the parlor together. Heber in his usual confidential manner, said to me : 'Sister Pratt, WE HAVE JUST REORGANIZED THE DANITE BAND in

* Interview with a reporter of the "Kansas City Journal," June 1881.

the Endowment House. FIFTY BRETHREN HAVE JOINED AND BEEN SWORN IN!' Said I: 'Oh, brother Heber, you have no use for the Danites here, at this time.' 'YES, WE HAVE,' replied the apostle, 'we'll have PLENTY OF WORK for them to do PRETTY SOON.'"

It was the time when the Union Pacific was coming in, promising a large influx of Gentiles and *enemies* of the church. Zion, the home of the pure, the only refuge of peace and brotherhood in this wicked world, wanted to prepare a warm reception for them, worthy of the grand memories of 1838 and 1857. It had become impossible to *save* them *en masse*, as had been done with the Arkansas emigrants in 1857. Then the Kingdom of God on earth had full sway, and one hundred and forty men, women and children were *saved* on the Mountain Meadows at one fell swoop. But the saving could still be done on a limited scale, by shooting a fellow or two in an alley now and then. Didn't they try to save U. S. Attorney Dickson in 1886? "HE NEEDED KILLING" as the popular saying was in the glorious time of the Utah "Reformation," when the blood of Gentiles and apostates was cheaper than water.

But, all the same, it is *a religion*, you see. The leaders may be fanatics, but they are sincere, no doubt. The Mormons have been *persecuted* in Ohio, Missouri and Illinois. The killing of Joseph Smith was one of the most disgraceful *murders* ever committed in this country. The Endowment House is only a sort of cranky religious laboratory for the making of Gods, worlds and devils; nonsense to talk of Mormon treason. Don't re-hash *Mormon horrors*, please. Rockwell was a good-natured chap, and Geo. A. Smith the Thackeray of Mormonism. That fellow W. Wyl is one of the industrious vagabonds who have created the *Danites* out of air and foolscap. He should have written a harmless "philosophical" book instead of playing scavenger. I am sorry for him.

JOSEPH AS SEER AND TRANSLATOR.

Joseph Mastering Seven Languages—His Cautious Successors—The Book of Mormon—Reformed Egyptian—The Fixing of Fool Martin Harris—Sample of Reformed Egyptian Hieroglyphics—Professor Anthon Describes Martin's Visit—Joseph Does the Same—The Urim and Thummim and the Old Peepstone—A Secret of the Historian's Office—Poor Emma Again.

Conscience makes cowards of us, and so does knowledge. The more you know the more cautious you get in asserting. The man who knows next to nothing at all is the most fearless in proclaiming what he calls his opinions. This was the case with our prophet. A minimum of reading, and still less writing, were the limits of his education. This state of mind enabled him to walk, with the courage of a somnambulist, the path on which the most learned proceed with fear and trembling. And then, even if he stumbled, who cares? Do not the thousands who surround him *believe* in him? Do they not consider any attack on the Lord's friend the work of the devil? Joseph Smith is not the first leader who felt safe in the stronghold of ignorance and fanaticism, and he will not be the last.

The boundless impudence with which Joseph parades as seer and translator makes a superb charlatan of him, and gives him a charm, an interest, lacked entirely by his successor, Brigham Young, and still more by the tame criminals now leading the "church," *id est*, keeping up the original fraud and pocketing the proceeds thereof. Those fellows are not interesting at all. Some of them, like John Taylor and George Q. Cannon, have just enough of a second-hand education to see through the tremendous blunders committed by the first prophet.

Cunning Brigham, discerning any dangers to his kingdom with the eye of the trembling coward Tiberius, began to eliminate from the church literature certain too palpable humbugs, like Rigdon's "inspired and corrected" Bible, and Mother Lucy's "Life of the Prophet." The present leaders continue this policy. They avoid, like Brigham, the dangerous tricks of seership, translating by inspiration, discoveries of plates and papyrus—all the juggleries performed by the great Nauvoo Blondin on the prophetic tight-rope. The "Urim and Thummim" has been enjoying a good long rest since 1844, and the utterances of the present leaders confine their impudence to attacks on Federal officers, and their lying to the old legend of the "persecuted people," "persecution for conscience' sake," etc.

Oh, give me an hour of Blondin, high above thousands of "faithful" heads at Nauvoo, and I make you a present of all the speeches and writings of the present type of oily, polygamic tithing-eaters. Why, Blondin is an arrant bungler compared with rope-walker Joe. Says the prophet in a letter dated Nauvoo, Nov. 13, 1843:

> "Were I an Egyptian, I would exclaim, *Jah-oh-eh, Enish-go-on-dosh, Flo-ees, Flos-is-is* [O, the earth! the power of attraction and the moon passing between her and the sun]; a Hebrew, *Haueloheem yerau;* a Greek, *O theos phos esi;* a Roman, *Dominus regit me;* a German, *Gott gebe uns das licht;* a Portugee, *Senhor Jesu Christo libordade;* a Frenchman, *Dieu defend le droit;* but as I am, I give God the glory, etc. . . . ."

Is this not superb? How he handles them—seven languages in one little paragraph! Why, I feel like a whipped school-boy with my poor, dusty relics of Latin and Greek and a smattering of French and Italian.

> "Problem is derived from *probleme* (French) or probleme (Latin, Italian or Spanish), and in each language means a question or proposition, whether true or false."

Joe knows that *problem* is originally Greek, but then a little modesty adorns even a prophet. But modesty would be out of its place where Joe speaks in the sublime character of head of the church and possessor of the greatest collection of KEYS ever known.   Says he, in the same letter :

> " The fact is, that by the power of God I translated the Book of Mormon from hieroglyphics, the knowledge of which was lost to the world . . . I have witnessed the visions of eternity, and beheld the glories of the mansions of bliss and the regions and the misery of the damned . . . I have heard the voice of God and communed with angels, and spake, as moved by the Holy Spirit, for the renewal of the everlasting covenant and for the gathering of Israel in the last days . . . I, who hold the Keys of the last Kingdom."

Where are you, Cannon and Taylor, eh ? You hide in the bushes like our first parents after the fall.   And you are nowhere at all, when you hear this flourish :

> " I combat the errors of ages; I meet the violence of mobs; I cope with illegal proceedings from executive authority; I cut the Gordian knot of powers, and I solve mathematical problems of Universities WITH TRUTH, diamond truth, and GOD IS MY RIGHT-HAND MAN."

This was written, or rather signed, by Joe seven months before the lynchers in Carthage cut the Gordian knot of the most cheeky imposture ever perpetrated.   Let us now review the greatest features of this fraud.   But bear it in mind, reader, I do not want to treat this exquisite bit of fun *au serieux*, as the gay Parisian has it.   I want to enjoy the fun and want you to enjoy it with me.   Have you ever seen a poor, ranting squib of a fellow, born to be a village tailor and nothing else, play Macbeth or Othello ? That's the kind of a treat I invite you to.   Don't expect any " philosophy," any high-toned discussion from me about a most ridiculous and patent humbug.

Let's first take up the *Book of Mormon*.   Rigdon, the cunning tanner, gets crazy about the theological strifes of his time and wants to be the founder of a religion himself.   He makes a bible of the scribblings of a pedantic crank.   His instinct tells him that the contemplated fraud would fall flat with the educated classes, but would work like a charm with the superstitious ignorant.   His experience as a preacher tells him how to succeed with this latter class: Lots of miracles, first and foremost, and the more incredible the better.   A new system of theology, a new frame for the old moral code?—no, that wouldn't do. Not convince, but surprise, daze, over-whelm them. How many honest physicians do succeed? A few. How many charlatans? Nearly all. So let us have golden plates, buried and dug up by angels; open the heavens and let them come down and talk to us, the father and the son, the old prophets and apostles.

But how avoid discovery? There's the rub. Peeper Joseph translates by the power of God, but what? We must invent some unheard-of language. Egyptian hiero-glyphics—very good.* But those learned fellows begin to translate them; that wouldn't be safe. They would ask to see a sample of our hieroglyphics, and that would give away our whole game. But *reformed Egyptian*, how is that? Any unintelligible scrawl can be shown as *reformed* hieroglyphics. Nobody can read them, and isn't this just what is prophesied in the Scriptures?

"And the vision of all is become unto you as the words of a book that is *sealed*, which men deliver to one that is learned, saying, read this, I pray thee; and he saith, I cannot, for it is sealed." (Isaiah 29.)

So we want a miraculous book in a language unknown to the whole world; it must be *sealed*. Any of the "pro-fessors" of this world will say: "I can't read it." That's what we want. Eureka! This prevents discovery and fulfills Scripture; it makes us a riddle with the edu-cated and a success with the ignorant. The "reformed Egyptian" was adopted, after many a sleepless night, no doubt, by Rigdon. But how get the rhino for publica-tion? My servants Sidney and Joseph had not a dollar in the world and their credit was surely not far above that

---

* The Book of Mormon contains the records of descendants of the Jews, and is written by Jews. But still they write in Egyptian hiero-glyphics, notwithstanding the notorious fact that Jews have the utmost jealous veneration for their own language, and hate all that's Egyptian-like, as the French do anything connected with Germany and Bismarck. But what is all this to the "restorers of the House of Israel?" They wanted a language "the knowledge of which was lost to the world," *id est*, a fraud that could not be detected by the vulgar at first sight. The "reformed Egyptian" and the hieroglyphics "thereof" are in harmony with Sidney's education, the clumsiest hoax ever invented, but they were mysterious and miraculous enough for the average Mormon neophyte.

enjoyed by tramps in general in this great and free country. A substantial fool had to be fixed, it is clear. And in there steps upon the scene of Mormon history the greatest and best fixed of all the innumerable fools fixed by this "faith"—farmer MARTIN HARRIS.

Did you ever know a Martin Harris? I have known lots of them, in pants and in petticoats. They believe anything, and the more miraculous it is, the easier they swallow it. Joe's Martin saw the devil, and "he looked like a jackass, and had hair like a mouse." He wrote prophesies like this:

> "I do hereby assert and declare that in four years from the date hereof, every sectarian and religious denomination in the United States shall be broken down, and every Christian shall be gathered unto the Mormonites, and the rest of the human race shall perish. If these things do not take place, I will hereby consent to have my hand separated from my body."

Not much fixing was needed with such a fool. He mortgaged his farm, and paid the $3,000 to the printer, and so Mr. Tullidge's "Messianic wave" could sweep on. But before shelling out he had a doubt now and then. So Joseph had to arrange with some one who was in the secret for the last finishing touch of this fixing job. Harris expressed a wish to show some of the hieroglyphics to some learned men east. Joe feels a little embarrassed, but a way is found out of the difficulty. He is somewhat of a penman, that pal behind the curtain, and he sits down and makes hieroglyphics, not the old kind seen on Egyptian temples and obelisks, but "*reformed*" ones. "You will see, Martin," says Joe to the man who has seen the devil, "those learned professors cannot read this book; it can only be read by the gift and power of God. They'll of course tell you they cannot read it, just as predicted by Isaiah; and if you tell them about a sealed book, or that the book was given to me by angels, they will laugh, Martin. Those wise fools always laugh at the wisdom of God."

When I first got a glimpse of the "reformed" hieroglyphics in some Gentile publication, I thought that they must be a hoax, invented by some wag, and published by some too credulous writer. But, to my infinite astonishment, I found the original in two church publications, in the " Prophet " and the *Millennial Star.* This is an exact copy:

Do you know of any smart boy of say ten or twelve years who could not make better " reformed " hieroglyphics? Better and more complete? For " 21+4= " is not complete; it should read, even in reformed Egyptian, " 21+4=25." Still they were Egyptian enough for

Martin, and he went with them to Professor Anthon in New York. Mr. Anthon had a great fame for learning in ancient languages. Before going to Anthon, however, Martin paid a call on Dr. Mitchell. Dr. M. could not read the hieroglyphics; you might as well have asked him for the meaning of the natural design of a piece of wood. Prof. Anthon gives, in a letter dated Feb. 17, 1834, a very lively description of Martin's visit:

"The whole story about my having pronounced the Mormonite inscription to be 'REFORMED EGYPTIAN HIEROGLYPHICS' is PER-FECTLY FALSE. Some years ago a plain and apparently simple-hearted farmer called upon me with a note from Dr. Mitchell, of our city, now deceased, requesting me to decipher, if possible, a paper which the farmer would hand me, and which Dr. M. confessed he had been unable to understand. Upon examining the paper in question I soon came to the conclusion that it was all a trick, perhaps a *hoax*. When I asked the person who brought it how he obtained the writing, he gave me, as far as I can now recollect, the following account:

"A '*gold book*,' consisting of a number of plates of gold, fastened together in the shape of a book by wires of the same metal, had been dug up in the Northern part of the State of New York, and along with the book an enormous pair of 'GOLD SPECTACLES!' These spectacles were so large that if a person attempted to look through them, his two eyes would have to be turned towards *one* of the glasses merely, the spectacles in question being altogether too large for the breadth of the human face. Whoever examined the plates through the spectacles was enabled not only to *read* them, but fully to *understand* their meaning. All this knowledge, however, was confined at that time to a young man who had the trunk containing the book and spectacles in his sole possession. This young man was placed BE-HIND A CURTAIN, *in the garret of a farm house*, and being concealed from view, put on the spectacles occasionally, or rather looked through one of the glasses, deciphered the characters in the book and, *having committed some of them to paper*, handed copies from behind the curtain to those who stood on the outside. Not a word, however, was said about the plates having been deciphered 'by the gift of God.' Everything, in this way, was effected by the large pair of spectacles.

"The farmer added that he had been requested to contribute a sum of money towards the publication of the 'golden book,' the contents of which would, as he had been assured, produce an entire change in the world and save it from ruin. So urgent had been these solicitations that he intended selling his farm and handing over the amount received to those who wished to publish the plates. As a last precautionary step, however, he had resolved to come to New York, and obtain the opinion of the learned about the meaning of the paper which he had brought with him, and which had been given him as a part of the contents of the book, although NO TRANSLATION had been furnished at the time by the young man with the spectacles.

"On hearing this odd story, I changed my opinion about the paper and, instead of viewing it any longer as a hoax upon the learned, I began to regard it as part of a scheme to cheat the farmer of his money, and I communicated my suspicions to him, warning him to beware of rogues. He requested an opinion from me *in writing*, which of course *I declined giving*, and he then took his leave, carrying the paper with him.

"This paper was in fact a singular scrawl. It consisted of all kinds of crooked characters, disposed in columns, and had evidently been prepared by some person who had before him at the time a book containing various alphabets. Greek and Hebrew letters, crosses and flourishes, Roman letters, inverted or placed sideways, were placed in perpendicular columns, and the whole ended in a rude delineation of a circle divided into various compartments, decked with various strange marks, and evidently copied after the Mexican Calendar given by Humboldt, but copied in such a way as not to betray the source whence it was derived. I am thus particular as to the contents of the paper, inasmuch as I have frequently conversed with my friends on the subject, since the Mormonite excitement began, and well remember that the paper contained ANYTHING ELSE BUT 'EGYPTIAN HIERO-GLYPHICS.'

Some time after the farmer paid me a second visit. He brought with him the golden book in print, [the first edition of the Book of Mormon] and offered it to me for sale. I declined purchasing. He then asked permission to leave the book with me for examination. I declined receiving it, although his manner was strangely urgent. I adverted once more to the ROGUERY which had been, in my opinion, practiced upon him, and asked him what had become of the GOLD PLATES. He informed me that they were in a trunk with the large pair of spectacles. I advised him to go to a magistrate and have the trunk examined. He said 'the curse of God' would come upon him should he do this. On my pressing him, however, to pursue the course which I had recommended, he told me that he would open the trunk if I would take 'the curse of God' upon myself. I replied that I would do so with the greatest willingness, and would incur every risk of that nature, provided I could only rescue him *from the grasp of rogues*. He then left me."

How good-natured and polite that professor was! How fatherly his talk to the poor fool! But Martin is fixed beyond redemption. Any objection only serves to show to him that scripture is being literally fulfilled, wherever the wicked world comes in contact with the new gospel. He returns to Joe and shows the curious form which the

New York events have taken in his devil-digesting brain. We have no direct tale from Martin, but Joe gives (in his truthful way) his version of the whole occurrence. Says he :

"Martin got the characters which I had drawn off the plates and started with them to the city of New York. For what took place relative to him and the characters I refer to his own account of the circumstances, as he related them to me after his return, which was as follows: I went to the city of New York and presented the characters which had been translated, with the translation thereof, to Professor Anthon, a gentleman celebrated for his literary attainments. Professor Anthon stated THAT THE TRANSLATION WAS CORRECT, MORE SO THAN ANY HE HAD BEFORE SEEN TRANSLATED FROM THE EGYPTIAN. I then showed him those which were not yet translated, and he said that they were EGYPTIAN, CHALDAIC, ASSYRIAC and ARABIC, and he said that they were the TRUE CHARACTERS. *He gave me a* CERTIFICATE, certifying to the people of Palmyra that they were true characters, and that the translation of such of them as had been translated was also correct. I took the certificate and put it into my pocket, and was just leaving the house when Mr. Anthon called me back, and asked me how the young man found out that there was gold plates in the place where he found them. I answered that an angel of God had revealed it unto him. He then said to me, Let me see that certificate. I accordingly took it out of my pocket and gave it to him, when he took it and tore it to pieces, saying that there was no such thing now as ministering of angels, and that if I would bring the plates to him he would translate them. I informed him that part of the plates were SEALED, and that I was forbidden to bring them. He replied, '*I cannot read a sealed book.*' I left him and went to Dr. Mitchell, who SANCTIONED what Professor Anthon had said, respecting both the *characters and translation.*' "

I doubt whether there ever was, since the world exists, more lying done to the square inch than we see in this tale of the peeper. And how he contradicts himself. He says he gave the characters to Martin, and then Martin shows to Anthon, all of a sudden, the characters *and translation*. Anthon says there was *no* translation. Joseph says Anthon found the translation from the Egyptian correct, more correct than any he had ever seen. From the Egyptian! Does Egyptian consist of Chaldaic, Assyriac and Arabic? Is your reformed Egyptian not a language entirely unknown to the world? Didn't you write, Nov. 13, 1843:

" By the power of God I translated the Book of Mormon from hieroglyphics, the knowledge of which was lost to the world?"

Has Professor Anthon, like you, the power of God as a help when translating? Or, if any man learned in hieroglyphics can translate your signs, what use is there for your "Seer Stone" or Urim and Thummim, power of God and special inspiration? But what's the use of cross-examining you before a set of fellows who could never make a fat living and ride in fine buggies, if not keeping up the fraud? Says our excellent little Sunday-school Catechism of 1882:

Q. To what city did Joseph send a copy of some of the characters?
A. To New York.
Q. Who took this copy?
A. Martin Harris.
Q. To whom did he show it?
A. To Professor Charles Anthon.
Q. Who was Professor Anthon?
A. A very learned man.
Q. What did the Professor say about the characters?
A. That they were TRUE and that THE TRANSLATION WAS CORRECT.
Q. When Martin Harris informed him that part of the plates were sealed, what did he say?
A. That he could not read a sealed book.
Q. By what ancient prophet was this circumstance foretold?
A. By Isaiah, Chapter 29. verse 11—14.
Q. How long ago was it that this prophecy was uttered?
A. About twenty-six hundred years.
Q. When was it fulfilled?
A. In April, 1828.
Q. Did Martin Harris show the characters AND THE TRANSLATION to anyone else?
A. Yes, to Dr. Mitchell.
Q. Who was Dr. Mitchell?
A. A gentleman learned in ancient languages.
Q. What did he say?
A. The same as Professor Anthon had said, that the CHARACTERS were TRUE ones and that the TRANSLATION was CORRECT.

But enough of this kind of rot. Look at the hieroglyphics, or let your little Freddy look at them, that bright boy who writes so nice a hand. He will soon find out the trick how to make " reformed " Egyptian hieroglyphics.

The chief element of the whole fun lies in its palpable clumsiness. Is it a wonder that there never was a Mormon with something like an education who has remained in the " church ? "

Take that other most holy hoax about the " Urim and Thummim." Harris speaks to Anthon of huge "*gold* spectacles." Lucy's three-cornered diamonds are set in *silver.* Harris says later: "The prophet possessed a SEER STONE, by which he was enabled to translate, as well as from the Urim and Thummim, and for convenience he then used the seer stone." David Whitmer says: " The tablets or plates were translated by Smith, who used a small oval or kidney-shaped stone, *called* "Urim and Thummim." * Emma says on her death-bed to her son Joseph :

" In writing for your father I frequently wrote day after day, often sitting at the table close by him, he sitting with his face buried in his hat with THE stone in it."

And finally comes the solemn church organ, the *Deseret News*, and hands us one of the anointed cats out of *its* bag :

" The next error is that the seer stone WHICH JOSEPH USED IN THE TRANSLATION was called Urim and Thummim. The instrument thus denominated was composed of two crystal stones set in the two rims of a bow. The seer stone was separate and distinct from the Urim and Thummim. The latter was delivered to the angel as well as the plates after the translation was completed. † The former remained with the church and IS NOW IN THE POSSESSION OF THE PRESIDENT."

Out with it, ye Mormon Historians and Presidents, and let us have a look at the whole juggling apparatus!

---

* There is no mention of the Urim and Thummim in the revelations as originally published in 1833. It was a later concoction, and I cannot but admire the skill of the Mormon Lord in amending his revelations. Like all great writers he never seems satisfied with his work. There's always room for improvement.

† That is, in the summer of 1829. But Endowment-House-Devil Phelps is really the originator of the Urim and Thummim in Mormonism. This was while our devil was conducting the *Evening and Morning Star* in the land of Missouri, 1832-3. But his brilliant idea arrived too late to be got into the first edition of the Lord's " revelations."

You have the old peep-stone, stolen from the children of
Mr. Chase (see Appendix, Documents) and you have even
the PLATES, with which Joe and Cowdery duped Martin
Harris, the Whitmers and poor Emma. I know you have got
them : somebody saw them in the safe of the Historian's
office and told me. They are a bundle of brass plates,
with some scratches on them, that fools would take for
" hieroglyphics." Cowdery made them and Joe showed
them to the " witnesses" with a great ado and hocuspo-
cus. People who swallow the hieroglyphics and your tale
about Martin's visit to Prof. Anthon, would swallow
anything, even if you had a mind to assert that humming
birds in the other world look just like our elephants. You
had a little bundle of brass plates, Joe, with some scratches
on them, cost of the whole thing two or three dollars, and
they explain a certificate like this :

> Be it known unto all nations, kindreds, tongues and people unto
> whom this work shall come, that Joseph Smith, Jun., the translator of
> this work, has shewn unto us the plates of which hath been spoken,
> which have the *appearance of gold :* and as many of the leaves as the
> said Smith has translated we did handle with our hands; and we
> also saw the ENGRAVINGS thereon, all of which has the appearance of
> ancient work, and of curious workmanship. And this we bear record
> with words of soberness, that the said Smith has shewn unto us, for
> we have *seen* and HEFTED, and know of a surety that the said Smith
> *has got the plates* of which we have spoken. And we give our names
> unto the world, to witness unto the world that which we have seen ;
> and we lie not, God bearing witness of it.

CHRISTIAN WHITMER,	HIRAM PAGE,
JACOB WHITMER,	JOSEPH SMITH, Sen.,
PETER WHITMER, Jr.,	HYRUM SMITH,
JOHN WHITMER,	SAMUEL H. SMITH.

I am aware the said Smith avers in his history that he
handed the plates over to " the angel" after he, the said
Smith, had translated them. But that statement, like
most of the said Smith's, don't count. As they have been
seen and handled, " hefted," and the engravings thereon
seen in the Historian's office in this city, now why can't
we all have a " go " at them, I ask ?

And those made-up plates explain a statement like this
from the pale lips of poor dying Emma:

"The plates often lay on the table without any attempt at concealment, wrapped in a small linen table-cloth, which I had given him [Joseph] to fold them in. I once felt of the plates as they thus lay on the table, tracing their outline and shape. They seemed to be pliable, like thick paper, and would rustle with a metallic sound when the edges were moved by the thumb, as one does sometimes thumb the edges of a book."

No, you poor martyr, you did not lie about the plates on the brink of eternity. You were no fool, but you were fixed, all the same, by the tenderness and confidence you felt for the man of your love.

But you, gentle reader, don't you see him now clear before your eyes, the greatest fool-fixer of the age? Don't you see him with hat and peepstone, a bundle of false plates, and Rigdon's crazy, absurd, tedious, disgusting nonsense about Lehi and Nephi, Nephites and Lamanites, Mormon and Moroni? Do I need anything else than his own stupid lies and impossible languages and hieroglyphics to convict him? But you might like a tremendous clincher, all the same, and you shall have it, to your heart's content, in the next chapter.

THE KINDERHOOK PLATES.

*A Superlative Hoax—John Taylor Prematurely Happy—
Affidavit of Fugate as to his Hieroglyphics—The Dollar
Sign as Hieroglyphic—Joe Finds and Gives the Key—
The Royal Descendant of Ham—A King Nine Feet
High—Orson Pratt Knows the Fraud—The "Sincerity" of a Lot of Cheats.*

The day came when the seer and translator was caught in a trap. The true story of the celebrated plates "found" at Kinderhook, Illinois, April 23, 1843, and unearthed, for the second time, by my indefatigable friend Cobb, after long digging and delving, nails the *translator* down for all eternity. Let me introduce the documents. The first is an article in the Nauvoo church organ, the *Times and Seasons.* I reproduce it in toto from the original:

(TO THE EDITOR OF THE "TIMES AND SEASONS.")

On the 16th of April, 1843, a respectable merchant, by the name of Robert Wiley, commenced digging in a large mound near this place; he excavated to a depth of ten feet and came to rock. About that time the rain began to fall, and he abandoned the work. On the 23d, he and quite a number of the citizens, with myself, repaired to the mound, and after making ample opening, we found plenty of rock, the most of which appeared as though it had been strongly burned; and after removing full two feet of said rock, we found plenty of charcoal and ashes, also human bones that appeared as though they had been burned; and near the eciphalon a bundle was found that consisted of SIX PLATES OF BRASS, of a bell shape, each having a hole near the the small end, and a ring through them all, and clasped with two clasps. The ring and clasps appeared to be iron, very much oxidated: the plates first appeared to be copper, and had the appearance of being covered with characters. It was agreed by the company that I should cleanse the plates. Accordingly I took them to my house, washed them with soap and water and a woolen cloth; but finding them not yet cleansed, I treated them with dilute sulphuric acid, which made them perfectly clean, on which it appeared that they were completely covered with characters, that none, as yet, have been able to read. Wishing that the world might know the hidden things as fast as they come to light, I was induced to state the facts, hoping that you would give them an insertion in your excellent paper, for we all feel anxious to know the true meaning of the plates, and publishing the facts might lead to the true translation. They were found, I judge, more than twelve feet below the surface of the top of the mound.

I am most respectfully, a citizen of Kinderhook,

W. P. HARRIS, M. D.

The following Certificate was forwarded for publication at the same time:—

We, citizens of Kinderhook, whose names are annexed, do certify and declare, that on the 23d of April, 1843, while excavating a large mound in this vicinity, Mr. R. Wiley took from said mound *six brass plates,* of a bell shape, covered with ancient characters. Said plates were very much oxidated. The bands and rings on said plates mouldered into dust on a slight pressure.

ROBERT WILEY,	G. W. F. WARD,	FAYETTE GRUBB,
W. LONGNECKER,	IRA S. CURTIS,	W. P. HARRIS,
GEORGE DECKENSON,	J. R. SHARP,	W. FUGATE.

John Taylor, now become "the invisible head of the church," was then editor of the church organ. In an editorial about the Kinderhook "find" he says: "Circumstances are daily transpiring which give additional testimony to the authenticity of the Book of Mormon. . . The man who owns the plates has taken them away for a time, but has promised to return with them." So says Taylor, and he feels that this "find" will "go a good way to prove the authenticity of the Book of Mormon;" expressing finally his firm belief that "the seer, the seer, Joseph, the seer," * will prove himself equal to the task of solving this new mystery. "We have no doubt," says he, "but Mr. Smith will be able to translate them." And Taylor, as the sequel shows, was fully justified in his confidence; a confidence expressed a second time in the *Times and Seasons* in the following lively manner:

"Why does the circumstance of the plates recently found in a mound in Pike County, Illinois, by Mr. Wiley, together with etymology and a thousand other things, GO TO PROVE THE BOOK OF MORMON TRUE? Answer: 'Because it is true.'"—[*Times and Seasons*, p. 406, Dec. 1, 1843.

But let us look at the trap with the translator's leg in it. Here it is, in the shape of a letter from Mr. Wilbur Fugate to Mr. James T. Cobb, in Salt Lake City:

MOUND STATION, ILL., JUNE 30, 1879.

Mr. Cobb:—

I received your letter in regard to those *plates*, and will say in answer that they are a HUMBUG, gotten up by Robert Wiley, Bridge Whitton and myself. Whitton is dead. I do not know whether Wiley is or not. None of the nine persons who signed the certificate knew the secret, except Wiley and I. We read in Pratt's prophecy that "Truth is yet to spring up out of the earth." We concluded to prove the prophecy by way of a joke. We soon made our plans and executed them. Bridge Whitton cut them (the plates) out of some pieces of copper; Wiley and I made the hieroglyphics † by making impressions on beeswax and filling them with acid and putting it on the plates. When they were finished we put them together with rust

---

* The title of a popular Mormon hymn composed by John Taylor.

† Wiley's name stands first and Fugate's last of the nine signers of the "certificate" touching the excavation.

made of nitric acid, old iron and lead, and bound them with a piece
of hoop iron, covering them completely with the rust. Our plans
worked admirably. A certain Sunday was appointed for digging.
The night before, Wiley went to the Mound where he had previously
dug to the depth of about eight feet, there being a flat rock that
sounded hollow beneath, and put them under it. On the following
morning quite a number of citizens were there to assist in the search,
there being *two Mormon elders* present (Marsh and Sharp). The
rock was soon removed, but some time elapsed before the plates were
discovered. I finally picked them up and exclaimed, "A piece of
pot metal!" Fayette Grubb snatched them from me and struck them
against the rock and they fell to pieces. Dr. Harris examined them
and said they had *hieroglyphics* on them. He took acid and removed
the rust, and they were soon out on exhibition. Under this rock was
dome-like in appearance, about three feet in diameter. There were a
few bones in the last stage of decomposition, also a few pieces of pottery and charcoal. There was NO SKELETON found. Sharp, the
Mormon elder, leaped and shouted for joy and said, Satan had appeared to him and told him not to go (to the diggings), it was a hoax
of Fugate and Wiley's,—but at a later hour the Lord appeared and
told him to go, the treasure was there.

The Mormons wanted to take the plates to Joe Smith, but we
refused to let them go. Some time afterward a man assuming the
name of Savage, of Quincy, borrowed the plates of Wiley to show to
his literary friends there, and took them to Joe Smith. The same
identical plates were returned to Wiley, who gave them to Professor
McDowell, of St. Louis, for his Museum.

W. FUGATE.

STATE OF ILLINOIS, }
  BROWN COUNTY. } ss.

W. Fugate, being first duly sworn, deposes and says that the above
letter, containing an account of the plates found near Kinderhook, is
true and correct, to the best of his recollection.

W. FUGATE.

Subscribed and sworn to before me this 30th day of June, 1879.
JAY BROWN, J. P.

Since 1843 the Kinderhook plates have been relied
upon by the Mormon leaders as a strong argument in favor
of Joe's plates, from which he translated his new "bible,"
and, in fact, they are coin from the same mint almost,
id est, silly fabrications. You don't find deep mysteries
on any of them, like the dark formula, $21+4=$, but
their characters seem inspired by a mind very much oc-

cupied with worldly affairs. At least, I find the vulgar
DOLLAR SIGN more than two scores of times in these
"hieroglyphics," now very clear, and then as the original idea of a sign. In this way I can trace it about ten
times alone in this single plate of the "engravings," two or

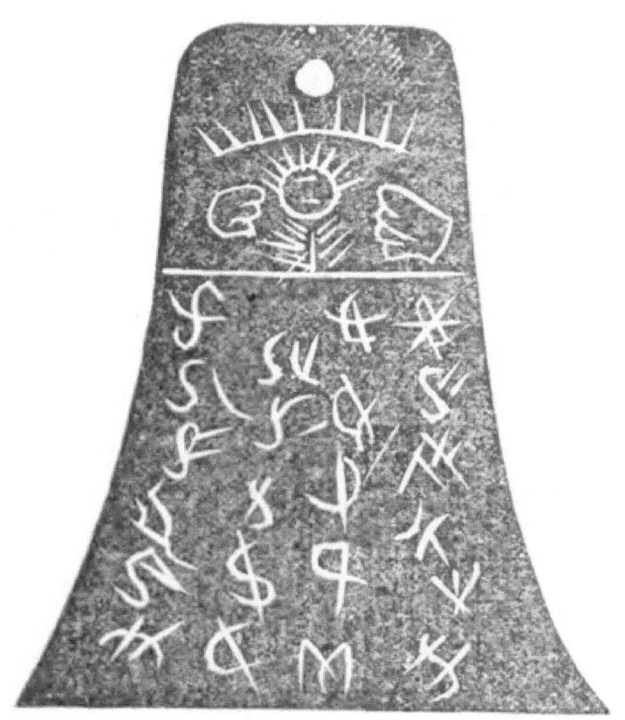

three of them very clearly. Notwithstanding the obvious
clumsiness of the fraud (Mr. Fugate calls it a *joke*) a
number of writers on Mormon history, among them the
best, including John Hyde and Captain Burton, have re-
produced a fac simile of the plates, and spoken seriously
of them, leaving the reader to guess what they might
mean, and apparently puzzled by them themselves.

I am able to solve the mystery. They *are* hieroglyphics, and Mr. Smith *could* translate them. The British
church organ, called the *Millennial Star*, printed in Liverpool, "gives us the key," as old Lucy would say. In

Vol. XXI., number of January 15, 1859, is an extract
from "Mr. Smith's" diary, dated Monday, May 1, 1843,
a week or so after the discovery of the plates was made.
Mr. Smith says: "I insert fac similes of the six brass
plates found near Kinderhook, in Pike County, Ill., on
April 23, 1843, by Mr. R. Wiley and others; while excavating a large mound, they found a *skeleton* about six
feet from the surface of the earth, *which must have stood
nine feet high.* The plates were found *on the breast of the
skeleton* and were covered on both sides with ancient
characters.

"I HAVE TRANSLATED A PORTION OF THEM AND FIND
THEY CONTAIN THE HISTORY OF THE PERSON WITH WHOM
THEY WERE FOUND. HE WAS A DESCENDANT OF HAM,
THROUGH THE LOINS OF PHARAOH, KING OF EGYPT, AND
THAT HE RECEIVED HIS KINGDOM FROM THE RULER OF
HEAVEN AND EARTH." (On pages 41, 43, *Millennial
Star*, Vol. XXI., is a *fac simile* of these plates.)

There you have him in his full glory, the son of old
Lucy-Munchhausen. He was not present at the excavating of the plates, but he finds a great many more things
than the buriers and excavators found themselves. The
discoverer and translator of the "Book of Abraham"
finds in that Illinois mound the skeleton of an antique
monarch. The peeper knows even the size of the fellow:
he was nine feet, the odd inches are not given. And then,
you see, the plates were found *on the breast* of the skeleton—
another touching and picturesque detail. And then comes
the crowning and glorious *translation !* That ruler came of
illustrious ancestors, but rather in a roundabout and laby-
rinthic sort of way. He descended (think of it and faint)
from Ham, through the loins of Pharaoh, king of Egypt.
Which Pharaoh? No doubt the father of that royal wench
whose bones were *diskivered* by old Lucy-Munchhausen.*
And then, who cares? Don't you see that this Dime Museum giant received his kingdom from our excellent friend,
Joe's "pard?" And a tremendous kingdom it must have

---

* See next chapter.

been, the kingdom of a chap nine feet high and perhaps two or three odd inches!

Don't you see it now in the trap, the *peeper's leg?* And still, gentle reader, you say: But surely the Mormon *leaders* do not know about such villainous frauds, 'twould make accomplices of all of them, and show that they are all deceivers, liars and hypocrites! Now just hear what was told me by a Mormon elder, an eye and ear witness: "A 'class of elders,' eleven or twelve, of whom I was one, was assembled in the Endowment House in 1858. Apostle Orson Pratt told us that he had been reading a work in which an account was given of the Kinderhook Plates. An archeological society had heard of the plates and they wanted to get a reliable account of them. They sent down to Kinderhook, Ill., two men to investigate the matter. These men had been there for two or three weeks without result. At last they learnt the names of the parties concerned, and that the plates were *made by a blacksmith;* they were told so by the artist himself. Pratt told the 'class' that he was well convinced that the plates were a fraud."

But let us return to the "Seer." The plates were taken to him and he made a rough estimate that their translation into English would make a volume of *some ten or twelve hundred pages!** Joseph, however, smartly refused to translate them until they were presented to some of the learned societies for translation. They *were* sent to one and returned with the word, *that they could not be translated.* And then Joseph went to work, aided by the "grace of God!"

Brigham Young and the other heads of the church knew the silly fraud of the "Book of Abraham" since the real translation of the papyrus by the French *savant.* They all know that the "*Spaulding myth*" is no myth, but the naked and damning truth. And still there is scarcely a book put forth on Mormonism that does not

---

* This detail is contained in another letter of Mr. Fugate to James T. Cobb; also the circumstance that Bridge Whitton, who cut out the plates, was *a blacksmith.*

ventilate gravely the question, whether Joseph, Brigham, Cannon, Taylor & Co., were sincere, or are so at this moment in their "faith!"

FIRST MORMON TEMPLE, KIRTLAND, OHIO.

THE BOOK OF ABRAHAM.

---

*Michael H. Chandler, the Village Barnum — Testimonial
Given by "a Gentleman" — The Writings of Abraham
and Joseph Discovered — Egyptian Grammar by Joe —
Astronomer Joe — W. W. Phelps — Lucy Discovering
and Lecturing — A Learned Polygamist — The Lord
Chatting with Old Abraham — Choice Extracts from
Abraham's Book — Prophet Joe's Translation Com-
pared with that of a Wicked Gentile — The Prince of
Pharaoh — Let us Laugh.*

It was in July, 1835, in Kirtland. The kingdom was
flourishing. The temple was going up rapidly. The
first "quorum" of the twelve apostles had been ordained;
classes of instruction and school of prophets commenced.
Joseph had just begun to "wrestle" with English
grammar—no wonder that he felt like reforming the
world on the scientific and educational side, after having
given it a new start as to religion and morals. The *Lord*
was with him in everything; and for the last four years He
had been giving him "special instructions" as to the
principle of celestial marriage, called "adultery" by the
wicked Gentiles, with that indecent vulgarity characteristic
of those who have no faith in bleeding Spaniards.

It was on July 3, 1835, just at the time when the first
idea of those glorious SAND BOXES might have struck the
imagination of our young prophet, when an event
occurred, not observed by the wicked and indifferent,
but notwithstanding of immense importance for the
salvation of mankind and the enrichment of science. The
chosen messenger who brought these "glad tidings" to
Kirtland was, as usual with Joe's *Lord,* a man whom the
initiated would have taken for anything else than an
instrument in the hands of the Almighty. It was no

peeper this time, however, but a sort of village Barnum, a "gentleman" who made a living by showing four Egyptian mummies to an enlightened public, probably at the modest rate of 25 cents for admission. Mummies — papyrus — Egyptian — reformed Egyptian — Joseph felt the seer's blood stir in his veins. Let himself relate the occurrence : *

> On the 3d of July, Michael H. Chandler came to Kirtland to exhibit some Egyptian mummies. There were four human figures, together with some two or more rolls of papyrus covered with hieroglyphic figures and devices. As Mr. Chandler had been told I could translate them, he brought me some of the characters, and *I gave him the interpretation*, and, LIKE A GENTLEMAN, he gave me the following certificate :
>
> KIRTLAND, July 6, 1835.
>
> This is to make known to all who may be desirous concerning the knowledge of Mr. Joseph Smith, Jun., in deciphering the ancient Egyptian hieroglyphic characters in my possession, which I have, in many eminent cities, showed to the most learned; and, from the information that I could ever learn, or meet with, I find that of Mr. Joseph Smith, Jun., to correspond in the most minute matters.
>
> MICHAEL H. CHANDLER,
Traveling with, and proprietor of, Egyptian mummies.

It may be that "traveling with and proprietor of" Mr. Chandler may have acted like a "gentleman" in many respects, for instance, in attesting the correctness of an interpretation of hieroglyphics of which he knew as much as Charlie, the family horse, or as Joe himself; but the syntax, etc., surely show rather the "colored gemman" than anything else. "Like a gentleman!" This is absolutely impayable. It shows as clear as sunlight that Joe knew that the certificate was straight lie, but lying for Joe, without hesitation, *cavalierement*, is acting like a gemman.

Joe takes a deep interest in the mummies, and the saints — accustomed to provide for him *whatsoever he needeth* — buy them for him from the "traveling with and proprietor of" *gentleman*. Joe tumbles at once to a tremendous discovery:

---

* *Millennial Star*, Vol. XV., p. 285.

" Some of the saints purchased the mummies and papyrus, and I, with W. W. Phelps and O. Cowdery as scribes, commenced the translation of some of the characters or hieroglyphics, and much to our joy found that one of the rolls contained the WRITINGS OF ABRAHAM, another the WRITINGS OF JOSEPH OF EGYPT, etc.—a more full account of which will appear in their place, as I proceed to examine or unfold them. Truly can we say : The Lord is beginning to reveal the abundance of peace and truth." *

It seems, however, that the *Urim and Thummim* did not work so well with the unreformed hieroglyphics as they did with the reformed ones. Says Joe :

" The remainder of this month [July, 1835] I was continually engaged in translating an alphabet to the Book of Abraham, and arranging a grammar of the Egyptian language as practiced by the ancients."

" Translating alphabets," arranging grammars—it is all as easy for Joe as eating a chop. Nothing that was " practiced by the ancients " is unknown to the peeper. He has the keys for all secrets. He is even an expert astronomer. Writes he, October 1, 1835, in his diary :

" This afternoon I labored in the Egyptian alphabet, in company with Brothers O. Cowdery and W. W. Phelps, and during the research the PRINCIPLES OF ASTRONOMY, as understood by FATHER ABRAHAM and the ancients, unfolded to our understandings."

Joe had studied (but not unfolded) the " LAW OF SARAH," the ingenuity of which proves, beyond doubt, that " Father Abraham" would be now-a-days a member of Congress at least. After having devoutly followed this law for four years or so, as opportunity presented, Joe takes up Abraham's astronomy. But he translates the great discoveries of Professor Abraham always in company with W. W. Phelps, you see. Mr. Editor Phelps was one of the cranky *dilettanti* under the banner of Mormonism. He had a literary smattering which turned to senseless mania of scientific *discoveries* under the influence of "revelation." Half an education is bad enough, but combined with fanaticism and pious lying it is one of the worst curses of humanity. Phelps played in those times a very important part in the fixing up and bringing forth of

---

*Millennial Star, Vol. XV., pp. 296–7.

Joe's revelations. He blabbed sometimes about it in the Utah Tabernacle, to Brigham's rage and despair. The old "Devil" was too proud of having been Joseph's revelational *sage femme* in olden times, and he *would* talk, notwithstanding Brigham's efforts to restrain him by jerking the Devil's coat tail. On one occasion, as known to all old Mormons, Phelps made a bow to Brigham, but *not* with his face turned toward Joe's successor. and said: "And Moses saw the Lord's hind part." I guess the Devil was right. All Mormon founders and leaders have ever seen of the Lord was nothing but the unspeakable part of a caricature of Old Scratch.

But let us return to our Egyptian scholar and Abrahamic astronomer. He felt great as seer and translator, but his joy was nothing compared with the rejoicings of that chaste guardian of truth, keys and three-cornered diamonds, Mrs. Lucy Smith-Munchausen. That dear creature was in raptures over the great *diskiveries* made by her darling Joe. She shows them to strangers and even lectures on them; admission fee very modest, to make science accessible to the most humble. * The excellent old lady had even made some learned investigations on her own hook, and the result was—what else could it be? —that one of the mummies was PHARAOH'S DAUGHTER, the same that had saved young Moses! The poor girl's mortal tenement, after having slept for four thousand years or so, had to perish in a Chicago dime museum, to the unspeakable sorrow of an admiring crowd of cowboys!

Don't weep, tender-hearted reader. The "Book of Abraham" is safe, all the same. Joe has *translated* it, and the private memoirs of Professor Abraham are a glorious heritage to civilization forever, together with a whole sys-

---

* "For a time," says Joseph, her grandson, "she derived a little income from the exhibition of some mummies and the papyrus records found with them, which had been left in her care by the church for this purpose. But after a time she parted with the mummies and records, how, the writer is not informed, though he afterwards saw two of the mummies and a part of the *records* in Wood's Museum in Chicago, where they were destroyed by the fire in 1871."

tem of Astronomy that puts Herschel, Copernicus, Kepler, Tycho and other ignorant Gentile savants, to use the picturesque expression of Danite Dr. Avard, "where the dogs cannot bite them." What is science compared to "revelation," after all? Is it not groping in the dark, is it not the mere groveling of swine amid husks, while the *chosen ones*—Joe, Lucy, Lee and other policemen—are wallowing in heaps of pearls?

I need not tell the reader, who has felt the full force of Mormon revelation so often in these pages, that the "Book of Abraham" is not only a fraud, but an unspeakably clumsy and silly one, too. It may be worth your while, all the same, to taste a little of the "beauty, grandeur and value of the truths made manifest by the Most High to his friend and servant Abraham." * The translation of Abraham's manuscript occupies ten pages in the *Pearl of Great Price*, a church publication, which contains among other *pearls*, "Visions" and "Writings of Moses," a "Key to the revelations of St. John," that Mormon Sevastopol "the Law of Sarah," etc., all revealed to Joseph the Seer. I miss among the pearls the "Writings of Joseph," which were likewise said to be among the treasures sold to Joe by the "traveling with and proprietor of *gentleman*." No doubt their "deciphering" did "correspond in the most minute matters," too, just as that of Father Abraham's astronomical note book. I bet they have them in the Historian's office. "hid up" somewhere, those "Writings of Joseph." I am sure they would, if translated properly, (*id est*, by inspiration,) rival Historian Tullidge's "stupendous *sweep* of the Prophet Joseph's theology," and "lay bare the infinite *sweep* of existence beyond the reach of the most poetic conception." Why not try *your* inspired hand at that job, brother Tullidge, and give your "Messianic wave" a good jerk?

What struck me first in Abraham's book was the familiar, "you're another" tone assumed in it by Je-

---

* Geo. Reynolds, the Book of Abraham, Salt Lake City, 1879. Elder Reynolds has been sent to the Pen for having fulfilled the "law of Sarah," but not yet to the lunatic asylum, from which place this eulogy on the "Book of Abraham" should have been dated.

hovah.   The book shows clearer than anything that
Abraham and the Lord were on splendid terms, just like
Joe and his *pard.*   " My name's Jehovah," says the Lord
to Abraham, "and I know the end from the beginning."
This sounds grand, but Jehovah's running talk, you will see,
is intensely fatherly, as your good old father-in-law would
talk to you about the necessity of putting a new roof on
the chicken-house.   Says Abraham:

> " And the Lord said unto me, the planet which is the lesser light,
> lesser than that which is to rule the day, even the night, is above or
> greater than that upon which thou standest, in point of reckoning, for
> it moveth in order more slow.   *This is in order,* because it standeth
> above the earth upon which thou standest; therefore the reckoning of
> its time is not so many as to its number of days, and of months and of
> years.   And the Lord said unto me: Now, ABRAHAM, THESE TWO
> FACTS EXIST ; behold, thine eyes see it . . . ."

I don't know how you feel while reading this stuff,
but I see the Lord in his dressing-gown and pipe, I can't
help it.   But let him go on, the " powerful visitor from
Canaan," who "was actually the instrument used of God to
instruct the Egyptians in the mysteries of the starry
worlds," and who, by the way, " superintended the erec-
tion of the great pyramid :"

> " Thus I, Abraham, talked with the Lord, face to face, as one man
> talketh with another; and He told me of the works which his hand
> had made ; and he said unto me, MY SON, MY SON, (and his hand
> was stretched out), behold, I will show you all these. And He put his
> hand upon mine eyes and I saw those things which His hand had
> made, which were many ; and He said unto me, This is Shinehah,
> which is the Sun.   And he said unto me, KOKOB, which is Star. And
> he said unto me, OLEA, which is the Moon.   And he said unto me,
> KOKAUBEAM, which signifies stars, or all the great lights which were
> in the firmament of heaven."

This is the way the Lord talked to Abraham on great
occasions, when he wanted to give away whole bucketfuls
of Astronomy.   For ordinary purposes Abraham, the
lucky patriarch, had the *Urim and Thummim,* just like
Joe.   Was he a peeper, too, in early times, before becoming so great a patriarch?

> " And I, Abraham, had the Urim and Thummim, which the Lord
> my God had given unto me, in Ur of the Chaldees; and I saw the

Stars, that they were very great, and that one of them was nearest unto the throne of God; and there were many great ones which were near unto it; and the Lord said unto me, These are the governing ones; and the name of the great one is KOLOB, because it is near unto me, for I am the Lord thy God: I have set this one to govern all those which belong to the same order of that upon which thou standest. And the Lord said unto me, by the Urim and Thummim, that Kolob was after the manner of the Lord . . . "

But hear the Lord again, when He talks to Abraham "face to face," without the peep-stone :

" And the Lord said unto me, Abraham, I show these things unto thee, before YE go into Egypt, that ye may declare all these words. IF TWO THINGS EXIST, and there be one above the other, there shall be greater things above them. Therefore, Kolob is THE GREATEST OF ALL THE KOKAUBEAM that thou hast seen, because it is nearest unto me.* Now, if there be two things, one above the other, and THE MOON BE ABOVE THE EARTH, that it may be that a planet or a star may exist above it; and there is nothing that the Lord thy God shall take in his heart to do but that he will do it. Howbeit that he made the greater star, as, also, if there be two spirits, and ONE SHALL BE MORE INTELLIGENT THAN THE OTHER, yet these two spirits, notwithstanding one is more intelligent than the other, have no beginning; they existed before, they shall have no end, they shall exist after, for they are GNOLAUM, or eternal."

Does not the *Lord* talk like a village schoolmaster, who gets crazy over some old books and a country weekly? But let us peer deeper into this abyss of stupidity :

" And the Lord said unto me, THESE TWO FACTS DO EXIST, that there are two spirits, one being more intelligent than the other; there shall be another more intelligent than they; I am the Lord thy God, I AM MORE INTELLIGENT THAN THEY ALL. The Lord thy God sent his angel to deliver thee from the hands of the priest Elkenah. I dwell in the midst of them all; I now, therefore, have come down unto thee to deliver unto thee the works which my hands have made, wherein MY WISDOM EXCELLETH THEM ALL, for I rule in the heavens above, and in the earth beneath, in all wisdom and prudence, OVER ALL THE INTELLIGENCES thine eyes have seen from the beginning; I came down in the beginning in the midst of ALL THE INTELLIGENCES thou hast seen."

This is religion, this is science, this is Utah's education of the rising generation in the nineteenth century! Is it

---

*As well as being " *after the manner of* the Lord."

not the eternal Mountain Meadows Massacre of the hopes and aspirations of this great region of country? I ask you, men and brethren, Mormon sisters and school-ma'ams, *shall* such a state of things be gnolaum, or eternal?

Abraham, after having given his interesting theories about the *Kokaubeam*, lectures on the creation:

"Now, the Lord had shewn unto me, Abraham, the INTELLI-GENCIES that were ORGANIZED before the world was; and among all these there were many of the noble and great ones; and God saw these souls that they were good, and he stood in the midst of them, and he said, These I will make my rulers; for he stood among those that were spirits, and he saw that they were good; and he said unto me, Abraham, thou art one of them, thou wast chosen before thou wast born. And there stood one among them that was like unto God, and he said unto those who were with him, We will GO DOWN, for there is space there, and we will take of these MATERIALS, and we will make an earth whereon these may dwell; and we will prove them herewith, to see if they will do all things whatsoever the Lord their God shall command them; and they who keep their first estate shall be added upon; and they who keep not their first estate shall not have glory in the same KINGDOM with those who keep their first estate; and they who keep their second estate shall have glory added upon their heads for ever and ever.

"And the Lord said, Who shall I send? And one answered like unto the Son of Man, Here am I, send me. And another answered and said, Here am I, send me. And the Lord said, I will send the first. And the second was angry, and kept not his first estate, and, at that day, many followed after him. And then the Lord said, Let us go down; and they went down at the beginning, and they ORGANIZED and formed (that is, THE GODS) the heavens and the earth. And the earth, after it was formed, was empty and desolate, because they had not formed anything but the earth; and darkness reigned upon the face of the deep, and the Spirit of the Gods was brooding upon the *faces* of the water."

In this twaddle we have not only the nucleus of Mormon theology as to the "making of gods, worlds and devils," but also a good deal of the recitations at the disgusting, though dangerous and treasonable, mummery called *Endowments*, of which more in Vol. II. of this work.

Let us close the quotations with another bit of "inspired and corrected" Genesis:

"And they (THE GODS) said, Let there be light, and there was ght, and they (THE GODS) comprehended the light, *for it was right;* and they divided the light, or caused it to be divided from le darkness; and THE GODS called the light day, and the darkness ley called night. And THE GODS also said, Let there be an expanse l the midst of the waters, and it shall divide the waters from the aters. And THE GODS ordered the expanse, so that it divided the aters which were under the expanse from the waters which were above le expanse; and it was so, even as they ordered. And THE GODS alled the expanse Heaven. And THE GODS ordered, saying, Let the aters under the heaven be gathered together unto one place, and let le earth come up dry; and it was so, as they ordered; and THE GODS ronounced the earth dry, and the gathering together of the waters, ronounced they, great waters; and THE GODS saw that they were beyed. And THE GODS said, Let us prepare the earth to bring forth rass; the herb yielding seed; the fruit tree yielding fruit, after his ind, whose seed in itself yieldeth its own likeness upon the earth; nd it was so, even as they ordered. And THE GODS ORGANIZED he earth to bring forth grass from its own seed, and the herb to bring orth herb from its own seed, yielding seed after his kind. And THE GODS ORGANIZED the lights in the expanse of the heaven, and caused hem to divide the day from the night; and ORGANIZED them to be for igns and for seasons, and for days and for years; and ORGANIZED hem to be for lights in the expanse of the heaven to give light upon he earth; and it was so. And THE GODS ORGANIZED the two great ights, the greater light to rule the day, and the lesser light to rule he night; with the lesser light they set the stars also. And THE GODS vatched those things which they had ordered until they obeyed."

Now, let us compare, just for fun and for the sake of another clincher, the interpretation of the pictures on Mr. Chandler's papyrus made by Joseph, the Seer, with one made by a competent French *savant,* Mr. T. Deveria:

THE RESURRECTION OF OSIRIS..

JOSEPH THE SEER.

FIG. 1. The Angel of the Lord.

2. Abraham fastened upon an altar.

3. The idolatrous priest of Elkenah attempting to offer up Abraham as a sacrifice.

4. The altar for sacrifice by the idolatrous priest standing before the gods of Elkenah, Libnah, Mahmackrah, Korash and Pharaoh.

MR. DEVERIA.

FIG. 1. The soul of Osiris under the form of a hawk.

2. Osiris coming to life on his funeral couch, which is in the shape of a lion.

3. The god Anubis effecting the resurrection of Osiris.

4. The funeral-bed of Osiris, under which are placed the four sepulchral vessels called *canopes,* each of them surmounted by the head of the four genii.

5. The idolatrous god of Elkenah.

6. The idolatrous god of Libnah.

7. The idolatrous god of Mahmackrah.

8. The idolatrous god of Korash.

9. The idolatrous god of Pharaoh.

10. Abraham in Egypt.

11. Design to represent the pillars of heaven as understood by the Egyptians.

5. Kebh-son-iw, with a hawk's head.

6. Tiomautew, with a jackal's head.

7. Hapi, with a dog's head.

8. Amset, with a human head.

9. The sacred crocodile, symbolic of the God Sebet.

10. Altar laden with offerings.

11. An ornament peculiar to Egyptian art.

12. Raukeegang, signifying expanse, or the firmament over our heads; but in this case, in relation to this subject, the Egyptians meant it to signify *Shauman*, to be high, or the heavens, answering to the Hebrew *Shaumahyeem*.

12. Customary representation of *ground* in Egyptian paintings. (The word Shauman is not Egyptian.)

Now to another picture described by the French *savant* as "initial painting of a funerary Manuscript of the Lower Epoch, which cannot be anterior to the beginning of the Roman dominion:"

FUNERARY MANUSCRIPT.

JOSEPH THE SEER.

MR. DEVERIA.

FIG. 1. Abraham sitting upon Pharaoh's throne, BY THE POLITE-NESS OF THE KING, with a crown upon his head, representing the Priesthood, as emblematical of THE GRAND PRESIDENCY IN HEAVEN; with the sceptre of justice and judgment in his hand.

FIG. 1. Osiris on his seat.

2. King Pharaoh, whose name is given in the characters above his head.

3. Signifies Abraham in Egypt; referring to Abraham as given in the first fac-simile.

2. The goddess Isis. The star she carries in her right hand is the sign of life.

3. Altar with the offering of the deceased, surrounded with lotus flowers, signifying the offering of the defunct.

4. PRINCE OF PHARAOH, King of Egypt, as written above the hand.

5. Shulem, one of the king's principal waiters, as represented by the characters above his hand.

4. The goddess Ma.

5. The deceased led by Ma into the presence of Osiris. His name is *Horus*, as may be seen in the prayer which is at the bottom of the picture, and which is addressed to the divinities of the four cardinal points.

6. Olimlah, a slave belonging to the prince.

Abraham is reasoning upon the principles of Astronomy, in the king's court.

6. An unknown divinity, probably Anubis; but his head, which ought to be that of a jackal, has been changed.

ABRAHAM AND PHARAOH.

Abraham *sitteth* upon Pharaoh's throne by the politeness of the king! The king acts "like a gentleman," you see. The politeness of the king! Well, this is Lucy

LUCY SMITH.

all over, and I hear her say it in her lectures, with such a winning smile and such a courtesy exactly imitating the *politeness* of Pharaoh! And there is a *grand presidency* in heaven, of which the one on earth, consisting of Peeper Joe, Hyrum, and Sidney Rigdon, is a most perfect copy! And there is, in Egypt, a *Prince of Pharaoh*, a sort of Prince of Wales, but being king all the same, and wearing, probably in Abraham's honor, female apparel! And Abraham is reasoning upon the principles of Astronomy! Are you sure, Joe, that he doesn't extol to the Prince of Pharaoh the beauties of the LAW OF SARAH?

Says Mr. Tullidge, ordained, set apart, and, let us hope, anointed as official Historian by the Salt Lake City Fathers: "The *Book of Abraham* is as closely identified with Joseph, AS ITS INSPIRED TRANSLATOR, as is the Book of Mormon." Yes; there can be no doubt, *these two facts exist*, that Joe was as divinely inspired to translate the one as the other.   I cannot say that "one is more intelligent than the other," but it seems to me, that among all the "organized intelligences" in Mormonism, there is one whom the Lord meant when he said, "one shall be more intelligent than the other," and it is none other than Historian Tullidge himself; his "wisdom excelleth them all."   He understands the prophet's "grand celestial view;" he feels that the "revelations of Joseph discover to us the economy of the heavens in one *everlasting sweep*."   Yes, by *Kokob, Kolob*, and the *Kokaubeam*, "what a lifting up of the race is this!"   *Now*, brother Tullidge, *these two facts exist*: Joseph is a prophet and you are Joseph's prophet!

Well, folks, do you want me to talk *philosophy* to you? want a *high-toned* refutation of the most impudent lies ever concocted by low, ignorant impostors and cheats? Or shall we, to favor our digestion impaired by eating our biscuits too hot, unite in the most tremendous peal of laughter that ever shook the walls of any peaceful habitation of man—laugh, laugh, till the celebrated laughter of the old Greek gods becomes like the low moaning of a new-born mouse?   Must not our laughter be GNOLAUM, *id est*, eternal?   Oh, ye eternal KOKAUBEAM, you shining stars, look down and laugh with us.   You can't help it, I am sure.   Laugh or burst!

SIDELIGHTS.

APPENDIX

OF

Documents and Facts Collected up to Fourth of July, 1886.

I.

THE AFFIDAVITS OF 1833 AND 1834.

Joseph Smith's Neighbors and Companions Testify About the Prophet's Character.

PETER INGERSOLL :--

"In the month of August, 1827, I was hired by Joseph Smith, Junior, to go to Pennsylvania to move his wife's household furniture up to Manchester, where his wife then was. When we arrived in Harmony, Pa., his father-in-law, Mr. ISAAC HALE, addressed Joseph, in a flood of tears: "You have stolen my daughter and married her. I had much rather followed her to the grave. You spend your time in digging for money, pretend to SEE IN A STONE and deceive the people." Joseph *wept* and acknowledged he could not see in a stone and *never could*, and that his former pretensions in that respect were all FALSE. He then promised to give up his old habits of digging for money and looking into stones. Mr. Hale told Joseph if he would move to Pennsylvania and work for a living, he would assist him in getting into business. Joseph acceded to this proposition. Joseph told me, on his return, that he intended to keep the promise which he had made to his father-in-law, "but," said he "it will be hard for me, for they will all oppose, as they want me to look in the stone for them to dig money," and, in fact, it was as he predicted. THEY URGED HIM, day after day, to resume his old practice of looking in the stone. One day he came and greeted me with a joyful countenance, and said: "As I was passing, yesterday, across the woods, I found, in a hollow, some beautiful white sand. I took off my frock, and tied up several quarts of it and then went home. On my entering the house I found the family at the table, eating dinner. They were all anxious to know the contents of my frock. At that moment I happened to think of what I had heard of a history found in Canada, called the GOLDEN BIBLE, so I very gravely told them it was the Golden Bible. To my surprise they were credulous enough to believe what I said. Accordingly I told them that I had received a commandment to let no one see it, for, says I, no man can see it with the naked eye and live. Now, said Joe, I HAVE GOT THE DAMNED FOOLS FIXED AND WILL CARRY OUT THE FUN."

WILLIAM STAFFORD:—

"The Smiths devoted much time to DIGGING FOR MONEY, especially in the night. They would say that in such a place, in such a hill, on a certain man's farm, there were deposited kegs, *barrels and hogsheads of coined silver and gold, bars of gold, golden images, brass kettles filled with gold and silver, gold candlesticks, swords*, etc. They would say also that nearly all the hills in this part of New York were thrown up by human hands and in them were large caves, which Joseph, Jr., could see by placing a STONE of singular appearance in his HAT in such a manner as to exclude all light; that he could see within those caves large gold bars and silver plates, that he could also discover the SPIRITS in whose charge those treasures were, clothed in *ancient dress*. New Moon and Good Friday were regarded as the most favorable times for obtaining these treasures. Joseph Smith, Sen., came to me one night and told me that Joseph, Jr., had been LOOKING IN HIS GLASS and had seen, near his house, two or three kegs of gold and silver some feet under the surface of the earth. Early in the evening we repaired to the place of deposit. Joseph, Sr., first made a circle 12 or 14 feet in diameter. This circle, he said, contained the treasure. He then stuck in the ground a row of witch-hazel sticks, around the said circle, to keep off the EVIL SPIRITS. Within this circle he made another, 8 or 10 feet in diameter. He walked around three times on the periphery of this last circle, muttering to himself something which I could not understand. He next stuck a steel rod in the centre of the circles and then enjoined profound silence upon us, lest we should arouse the evil spirits who had the charge of these treasures. After we had dug a trench about 5 feet in depth around the rod, the old man by signs and motions asked leave of absence and went to the house to inquire of young Joseph the cause of our disappointment. He soon returned and said that Joseph had remained all this time in the house LOOKING IN HIS STONE and watching the motions of the *evil spirit :* that he saw the spirit come up to the ring, and as soon as it beheld the cone which we had formed around the rod, *it caused the money to sink.* We then went to the house and the old man observed that we had made a mistake in the commencement of the operation ; if it had not had been for that, said he, we should have got the money. At another time they devised a scheme to satiate their hunger with the mutton of one of my SHEEP. They had seen in my flock a large, fat, black wether. Old Joseph and one of the boys came to me one day and said that young Joseph had discovered some great treasures which could only be procured in this way : that a black sheep should be taken on the ground where the treasures were concealed, that after cutting its throat it should be led around a circle while bleeding. This being done the *wrath of the evil spirit* would be appeased, the treasures could then be obtained and my share of it was to be FOUR-FOLD. To gratify my curiosity I let them have a large fat sheep. They afterwards informed me that the sheep was killed pursuant to commandment, but as there was some mistake in the process, it did not work. This, I believe, is the only time they ever made money-digging a profitable business. They had around them constantly a worthless gang.

WILLARD CHASE :—

"In 1820 the Smiths were engaged in the money-digging business, which they followed until the fall of 1827. In 1822 I was engaged in digging a well. I employed Alvin and Joseph Smith to assist me. After digging about twenty feet below the surface of the earth we discovered A SINGULARLY APPEARING STONE, which excited my curiosity. I brought it to the top of the well. Joseph put it into his HAT and then his face into the top of his hat. The next morning he came to me and wished to obtain the stone, alleging that he could SEE IN IT. I lent it to him. After obtaining it he began to publish abroad what WONDERS he could discover by looking into it. He had it in his possession about two years. Some time in 1825 Hyrum Smith came to me and wished to borrow the same stone. He pledged his word that he would return it, and I lent it to him. In the fall of 1826, when I asked Hyrum for the stone, he said : ' You cannot have it.' I repeated to him the promise he made me, upon which he said : ' I don't care who in the devil it belongs to, you shall not have it.'

"In the fall of 1826 Joseph wanted to go to Pennsylvania to be married, and having no money, set his wits to work. He went to Lawrence with the following story, as related to me by Lawrence himself : that he had discovered in Pennsylvania, on the banks of the Susquehannah, A VERY RICH MINE OF SILVER, and if he would go there with him, he might have a share in the profits ; that it was near high-water mark and that they could load it into boats and take it

down to Philadelphia to market.   Lawrence asked Joseph if he was
not deceiving him ; 'no,' said he, 'for I have been there and SEEN IT
WITH MY OWN EYES, and if you do not find it so when we get there,
I will bind myself to be your servant for three years.'   Lawrence
agreed to go with him, had to bear his expenses on the way, and
when he wished to see the silver mine, *they found nothing.*   After
his marriage Joseph, still out of money, set his wits at work how he
should get back to Manchester, his place of residence   He went to
an honest old Dutchman, called Stowel, and told him that he had
discovered on the bank of Black River a cave, in which he had found
A BAR OF GOLD, AS BIG AS HIS LEG and three or four feet long; that
he could not get it out alone, and if he would move him to Manchester, N. Y., they would go together, get a chisel and mallet and
get it and Stowel should share the prize with him.   Stowel moved
him.   After their arrival in Manchester Stowel reminded Joseph of
his promise, but he calmly replied that he would not go, because his
wife was now among strangers and would be very lonesome if he
went away.   Mr. Stowel was then obliged to return without any gold.

"In April, 1830, I again asked Hyrum for the stone; he told me I
should not have it, for Joseph MADE USE OF IT IN TRANSLATING HIS
BIBLE.   The Smiths were regarded by their neighbors as a PEST TO
SOCIETY.   I have always regarded Joseph Smith, Jr., as a man whose
word could not be depended upon.   Hyrum's character was but *very
little better.*   The whole family were WORTHLESS PEOPLE.   After
they became thorough Mormons their conduct was more disgraceful
than ever.   Their tongues were continually employed in spreading
scandal and abuse.   Although they left this part of the country without paying their just debts, *yet their creditors were glad to have them
do so, rather than have them stay.*"

I introduce now the statement of a living brother of
Willard Chase, Mr. Abel D. Chase, never published before.   It has a special interest in showing up Rigdon's
secret visits at the Smiths at the time when he and Joe
were engineering the Gold Bible fraud :

PALMYRA, Wayne Co., N. Y., May 2, 1879.

I, Abel D. Chase, now living in Palmyra, Wayne Co., N. Y., make
the following statement regarding my early acquaintance with Joseph
Smith and incidents about the production of the so-called Mormon
Bible.   I was well acquainted with the Smith family, frequently visit-
ing the Smith boys and they me.   I was a youth at the time from twelve
to thirteen years old, having been born Jan. 19, 1814, at Palmyra, N.
Y.   During some of my visits at the Smiths, I saw a STRANGER there
WHO THEY SAID WAS MR. RIGDON.   He was at Smith's several times,
and it was in the year of 1827 when I first saw him there, as near as
I can recollect.   Some time after that tales were circulated that young

Joe had found or dug from the earth a BOOK OF PLATES which the Smiths called the GOLDEN BIBLE. I don't think Smith had any such plates. He was mysterious in his actions. The PEEPSTONE, in which he was accustomed to look, he got of my elder brother Willard while at work for us digging a well. It was a singular looking stone and young Joe pretended he could discover hidden things in it.

My brother Willard Chase died at Palmyra, N. Y., March 10, 1871. His affidavit, published in Howe's "History of Mormonism," is genuine. Peter Ingersoll, whose affidavit was published in the same book, is also dead. He moved West years ago and died about two years ago. Ingersoll had the reputation of being a man of his word, and I have no doubt his sworn statement regarding the Smiths and the Mormon Bible is genuine. I was also well acquainted with Thomas P. Baldwin, a lawyer and Notary Public, and Frederick Smith, a lawyer and magistrate, before whom Chase's and Ingersoll's depositions were made, and who were residents of this village at the time and for several years after.

ABEL D. CHASE.

Abel D. Chase signed the above statement in our presence, and he is known to us and the entire community here as a man whose word is always the exact truth and above any possible suspicion.

PLINY T. SEXTON,
J. H. GILBERT. *

The statement of Abel D. Chase is corroborated by a letter from Mr. J. H. Gilbert, addressed to my friend Cobb, dated Palmyra, October 14, 1879. Mr. Gilbert says:

"Last evening I had about 15 minutes conversation with Mr. Lorenzo Saunders of Reading, Hillsdale Co., Mich. He has been gone about thirty years. He was born south of our village in 1811, and was a near neighbor of the Smith family—knew them all well; was in the habit of visiting the Smith boys; says he knows that RIGDON was hanging around Smith's for EIGHTEEN MONTHS PRIOR TO THE PUBLISHING OF THE MORMON BIBLE."

PURLEY CHASE, another brother of Willard, states:—

"The Smith family were lazy, intemperate and worthless men, very much addicted to lying. IN THIS THEY FREQUENTLY BOASTED THEIR SKILL."

DAVID STAFFORD:—

"Old Joseph Smith was a drunkard and a liar and much in the

---

* Mr. Sexton was at the time of this affidavit the village President of Palmyra and President of the first National bank there. Mr. Gilbert is the same who printed the first edition of the Book of Mormon.

habit of gambling. He and his boys were truly a lazy set of fellows
and more *particularly Joseph*, who very aptly followed his father's
example and in some respects was worse. When *intoxicated* he was
very quarrelsome. The general employment of the Smith family was
money-digging and FORTUNE-TELLING. They kept around them, constantly, a gang of worthless fellows who dug for money nights and
were idle in the daytime. It was a mystery to their neighbors how they
got their living."

BARTON STAFFORD :—

"Old Joseph Smith was a *noted drunkard* and most of the family
followed his example, *especially young Joseph*, who was very much
addicted to intemperance. No one of the family had the least claim
to respectability. One day, while at work in my father's field, Joseph
got quite drunk and fell to scuffling with one of the workmen who
tore his shirt nearly off from him. His wife threw her shawl over
his shoulders and escorted the prophet home."

ROSWELL NICHOLS :—

"For breach of contracts, for the non-payment of debts and borrowed money, and for duplicity with their neighbors, the Smith family were NOTORIOUS."

JOSHUA STAFFORD :—

"Joseph Jr., once showed me a piece of wood which he said he
took from a *box of money*, and the reason he gave for not obtaining
the box, was, that it *moved*. At another time Joseph called on me to
become security for a horse, and said he would reward me handsomely,
for he had found a *box of watches*, and they were *as large as his fist*,
and he put one of them to his ear and he could hear it 'tick forty
rods.' He said if he did not return with the horse I might take his
life. He was nearly *intoxicated* at the time of this conversation."

JOSEPH CAPRON :—

"Joseph, and indeed the whole family of Smiths, were *notorious for
indolence, foolery and falsehood*. Their great object appeared to be to
live without work. While they were digging for money they were
daily harassed by the demands of *creditors*, which they were *never*
able to pay. At length, Joseph pretended to find the *gold plates*.
This scheme, he believed, would relieve the family from all pecuniary
embarrassment. His father told me that when the book was published they would be enabled, from the profits of the work, to *carry
into successful operation the money-digging business*. He gave me *no*
intimation, at that time, that the book was to be of a religious character, or that it had anything to do with *revelation*. He declared it to
be a *speculation*, and said he : 'When it is completed, my family will
be placed ON A LEVEL ABOVE THE GENERALITY OF MANKIND.' "

G. W. Stoddard :—

"I have been acquainted with Martin Harris about thirty years. As a farmer he was industrious and enterprising; he possessed eight or ten thousand dollars, but his moral and religious character was such as not to entitle him to respect among his neighbors. He was fretful, peevish and quarrelsome, frequently abused his wife by whipping her, kicking her out of bed, turning her out of doors, etc. He was first an orthodox Quaker, then a Universalist, next a Restorationer, then a Baptist, next a Presbyterian, and then a Mormon. The *Smith family* never made any pretensions to respectability."

Testimony of Fifty-one Leading Citizens of Palmyra, December 4, 1833 :—

"We the undersigned, have been acquainted with the Smith family for a number of years while they resided near this place, and we have no hesitation in saying that we consider them destitute of that moral character which ought to entitle them to the confidence of any community. They were particularly famous for visionary projects; spent much time in digging for money. Joseph Smith, Senior, and his son Joseph were, in particular, considered *entirely destitute of moral character* and addicted to *vicious habits.* In reference to all with whom we were acquainted that have embraced Mormonism, from this neighborhood, we are compelled to say were most of them destitute of moral character."

Testimony of Eleven Leading Citizens of Manchester, Nov. 3, 1833 :—

"We, the undersigned, being personally acquainted with the family of Joseph Smith, Sen., state: That they were not only a lazy, indolent set of men, but also intemperate; and their word was not to be depended upon, and that we are truly glad to dispense with their society."

Isaac Hale, father-in-law of Joseph Smith :—

"I first became acquainted with young Smith in November, 1825. He was at that time in the employ of a set of men who were called 'money diggers;' and his occupation was that of seeing or pretending to see by means of a stone placed in his hat and his hat closed over his face. His appearance at this time was that of a careless young man, very saucy and insolent to his father. Smith and his father, with several other 'money-diggers,' boarded at my house while they were employed digging for a mine that they supposed had been opened and worked by the Spaniards, many years since. Young Smith gave the diggers great encouragement at first, but when they had arrived in digging to near the place where he had stated an immense treasure would be found, he said the enchantment was so powerful that he could not see. Then they became discouraged and soon after dispersed.

" Young Smith at length asked my consent to his marrying my daughter EMMA. This I refused, because he was a stranger and followed a business that I could not approve. Not long after this they were married without my consent. They came subsequently to the conclusion that they would reside upon a place near my residence. Smith stated to me that he had given up what he called 'GLASS-LOOK-ING,' and that he expected to work hard for a living. I was informed that they (Joseph and Emma) had brought a wonderful BOOK OF PLATES with them. The manner in which he pretended to read and interpret the plates was the same as when he looked for the money-diggers, WITH THE STONE IN HIS HAT AND HIS HAT OVER HIS FACE, while the Book of Plates was at the same time hid in the woods! I conscientiously believe, from the facts detailed and from many other circumstances, that the whole " Book of Mormon" is a SILLY FABRICA-TION OF FALSEHOOD and wickedness, got up for SPECULATION, in order that its fabricators may live upon the SPOILS of those who swallow the deception."

HEZEKIAH MCKUNE:—

" Joseph Smith said he was NEARLY EQUAL WITH JESUS CHRIST; that he was a prophet sent by God to bring in the Jews and that he was the GREATEST PROPHET that had ever arisen."

ALVA HALE, son of Isaac Hale:—

"Smith told me that this 'PEEPING' (in the stone) was all DAMNED NONSENSE, that he intended to quit the business (of peeping) and labor for his livelihood."

LEVI LEWIS:— *

" I heard Joseph Smith and Martin Harris both say that ADUL-TERY WAS NO CRIME.† I saw him three times INTOXICATED while he was composing the Book of Mormon and heard him use language of the GREATEST PROFANITY. He said, also, that he was AS GOOD AS JESUS CHRIST, that it was as bad to injure him as to injure Jesus Christ. With regard to the plates, he said GOD HAD DECEIVED HIM, which was the reason he did not show them."

---

* Clergyman, and uncle of Joseph's wife Emma. Joseph and Hiel Lewis were his sons. See their joint affidavit, pages 78—81.

† Anyone, except a Mormon leader, sees here the first glimpse of 'Celestial Marriage' and the rest.

II.

THE GOLD BIBLE COMPANY.

STATEMENT OF HENRY HARRIS :—

I became acquainted with the family of Joseph Smith, Sen., about the year 1820, in the town of Manchester, New York. They were a family that labored very little — the chief they did was to *dig for money*. Joseph Smith, Jr., used to pretend to TELL FORTUNES ; he had a stone which he used to put in his hat, by means of which he proposed to tell people's fortunes.

Joseph Smith, Jr., Martin Harris and others used to meet together in private, a while before the gold plates were found, and were familiarly known by the name of ' THE GOLD BIBLE COMPANY.' They were regarded by the community in which they lived as a lying and indolent set of men, and no confidence could be placed in them.

The character of Joseph Smith, Jr., for truth and veracity was such that I would NOT BELIEVE HIM UNDER OATH. I was once on a jury before a justice's court, and THE JURY COULD NOT AND DID NOT BELIEVE HIS TESTIMONY to be true. After he pretended to have found the gold plates I had a conversation with him and asked him where he found them and how he came to know where they were. He said he had a revelation from God that they were hid in a certain hill. and he looked in his stone and saw them in the place of deposit ; that an angel appeared and told him he could not get the plates until he was married. I asked him what letters were engraved on them : he said ITALIC LETTERS WRITTEN IN AN UNKNOWN LANGUAGE and that he had copied some of the words and sent them to Dr. Mitchell and Professor Anthon, of New York. By looking on the plates he said he could not understand the words, but it was made known to him that he was the person that must translate them, and on looking through the stone was enabled to translate.

After the book was published I frequently bantered him for a copy. He asked fourteen shillings a piece for them; I told him I would not give so much; he told me he had had a REVELATION that they must be sold at that price. Some time afterwards I talked with Martin Harris about buying one of the books, and he told me they had had a NEW REVELATION that they might be sold at ten shillings a piece.

STATEMENT OF ABIGAIL HARRIS:—

PALMYRA, N. Y., Nov. 28, 1833.

In the early part of the winter in 1828 I made a visit to Martin Harris's, and was joined in company by Joseph Smith, Sen., and his wife. The Gold Bible business, so called, was the topic of conversation, to which I paid particular attention that I might learn the truth of the whole matter. They told me that the report that young Joseph had found golden plates was true, and that he was in Harmony, Pennsylvania, translating them; that such plates were in existence, and that young Joseph was to obtain them, was revealed to him by the SPIRIT of one of the saints who was on this continent previous to its discovery by Columbus. Old Mrs. Smith observed that she thought he must be a QUAKER, AS HE WAS DRESSED VERY PLAIN. They said that the plates he then had in his possession were but an introduction to the Gold Bible—that all of them upon which the Bible was written were so heavy that it would TAKE FOUR STOUT MEN to load them into a cart — that Joseph had also discovered by looking through his stone the VESSEL in which the gold was melted from which the plates were made, and also the MACHINE with which they were rolled; he also discovered in the bottom of the vessel THREE BALLS OF GOLD, each as large as his FIST. The old lady said also that after the book was translated the plates were to be PUBLICLY EXHIBITED—admittance twenty-five cents. She calculated it would bring in annually an enormous sum of money— that money would then be very plenty and the book would also sell for a great price, as it was something entirely new—that they had been commanded to obtain all the money they could borrow for present necessity, and to repay with GOLD. The remainder was to be kept in store for their family and children. [Here follows the little anecdote related on p. 18].

In the second month following, Martin Harris and his wife were at my house. In conversation about Mormonites, she observed that she wished her husband would quit them, as she believed it was all false and a delusion. To which I heard Martin Harris reply: "What if it is a LIE? If you will let me alone, I WILL MAKE MONEY OUT OF IT!" I was both an eye and an ear witness of what has been stated above.

STATEMENT OF LUCY HARRIS:—

PALMYRA, Nov. 29, 1833.

Being called upon to give a statement to the world of what I know respecting the Gold Bible speculation and also of the conduct of Martin Harris, my husband, who is a leading character among the Mormons, I do it free from prejudice, realizing that I must give an account at the bar of God for what I say. Martin Harris was once industrious, attentive to his domestic concerns, and thought to be worth about $10,000. He is naturally quick in his temper and at times while I lived with him he has whipped, kicked and turned me out of the house. About a year previous to the report being raised that Smith had found gold plates, he became very intimate with the Smith family and said he believed Joseph could see in his stone anything he wished. After this he apparently became very sanguine in his belief.

Whether the Mormon religion be true or false, I leave the world to judge, for its effects upon Martin Harris have been to make him more cross, turbulent and abusive to me. HIS WHOLE OBJECT WAS TO MAKE MONEY BY IT. I will give one circumstance in proof of it. One day while at Peter Harris' house, I told him he had better leave the company of the Smiths, as their religion was false; to which he replied, "If you would let me alone, I could make money by it." It is in vain for the Mormons to deny these facts, for they are all well known to most of his former neighbors.   The man has now rather become an object of pity; he has spent most of his property.   He now spends his time in traveling through the country spreading the delusion of Mormonism and has no regard whatever for his family.

III.

SPAULDING'S "MANUSCRIPT FOUND."

STATEMENT OF JOHN SPAULDING :—

Solomon Spaulding [my brother] was born in Ashford, Conn., in 1761, and in early life contracted a taste for literary pursuits.   He entered Dartmouth College, where he obtained the degree of A. M. and was afterwards regularly ordained.   After preaching three or four years, he commenced the mercantile business.   In a few years he failed in business and in 1809 removed to Conneaut, Ohio. The year following I found him engaged in building a forge.   I made him a visit in about three years after and found that he had failed and was considerably involved in debt.   He then told me he had been writing a book, which he intended to have printed, the avails of which he thought would enable him to pay all his debts.   The book was entitled the *"Manuscript Found"* of which he read to me many pages.   It was an historical romance of the first settlers of America, endeavoring to show that the American Indians are the descendants of the Jews or the lost tribes.   It gave a detailed account of their journey from Jerusalem, by land and sea, till they arrived in America, under the command of *Nephi* and *Lehi*.   They afterwards had quarrels and contentions and separated into two distinct nations, one of which he denominated *Nephites* and the other *Lamanites*.   Cruel and bloody wars ensued, in which great multitudes were slain.   They buried their dead in large heaps, *which caused the mounds* so common in this country.   Their arts, sciences and civilization were brought into view in order to account for all the antiquities found in various parts of North and South America.   I have recently read the Book of Mormon and to my great surprise I find nearly *the same historical matter*, names, etc., as they were in my brother's writings.   I well remember that he wrote in the old style, and commenced about every sentence with "AND IT CAME TO PASS," or "Now it came to pass," the same as in the Book of Mormon, and according to the best of my recollection and belief *it is the same as my brother wrote*, with the exception of the religious matter.

STATEMENT OF HENRY LAKE :—

CONNEAUT, OHIO, September, 1833.

I left the State of New York late in the year 1810, and arrived at this place about the first of January following. Soon after my arrival I formed a co-partnership with Solomon Spaulding for the purpose of rebuilding a forge. He very frequently read to me from a manuscript which he was writing, which he entitled the "*Manuscript Found,*' and which he represented as being found in this town.   I spent many hours in hearing him read said writings and became well acquainted with its contents.   He wished me to assist him in getting his production printed, alleging that a book of that kind would meet with a rapid sale. This book represented the American Indians as the descendants of the lost tribes, gave an account of their leaving Jerusalem, their contentions and wars.   One time, when he was reading to me the tragic account of Laban, I pointed out to him what I considered an inconsistency, which he promised to correct ; but by referring to the Book of Mormon, I find, to my surprise, that it stands there just as he read it to me then.   Some months ago I borrowed the Golden Bible, put it into my pocket, carried it home and thought no more of it.   About a week after, my wife found the book in my coat pocket and commenced reading it aloud as I lay upon the bed.   She had not read twenty minutes till I was astonished to find the same passages in it that Spaulding had read to me more than twenty years before, from his "Manuscript

Found.'' Since that I have more fully examined the said Golden Bible and have no hesitation in saying that the historical part of it is principally, if not wholly, taken from the '' Manuscript Found.'' I recollect telling Mr. Spaulding that the so frequent use of the words, '' And it came to pass,'' '' *Now it came to pass*,'' rendered it ridiculous.

STATEMENT OF JOHN N. MILLER :—

SPRINGFIELD, Pa., Sept., 1833.

In the year 1811 I was in the employ of Henry Lake and Sol. Spaulding, at Conneaut, engaged in rebuilding a forge. While there I boarded and lodged in the family of said Spaulding for several months. I was soon introduced to the manuscripts of Spaulding and perused them as often as I had leisure. From the '' Manuscript Found '' he would frequently read some humorous passages to the company present. It purported to be the history of the first settlement of America, before discovered by Columbus. He said that he designed it as an historical novel, and that in after years it would be believed by many people as much as the history of England.

I have recently examined the Book of Mormon and find in it the writings of Solomon Spaulding, *from beginning to end*, but mixed up with Scripture and other religious matter, which I did not meet with in the '' Manuscript Found.'' Many of the passages in the Mormon book are *verbatim* from Spaulding, and others in part. The names of Nephi, Lehi, Moroni, and in fact *all the principal names* are brought fresh to my recollection by the Gold Bible.

STATEMENT OF AARON WRIGHT :—*

Spaulding showed me and read to me a history he was writing, of the lost tribes of Israel, purporting that they

---

* A Mr. Jackson, who was in a meeting at Conneaut when a Mormon preacher read from the Book of Mormon, says that '' Squire '' Wright shouted out : '' OLD-COME-TO-PASS HAS COME TO LIFE AGAIN ! '' '' And it came to pass,'' occurs in the book only about fourteen hundred times.

were the first settlers of America and that the Indians were their descendants. The historical part of the Book of Mormon I know to be *the same* as I read and heard read from the writings of Spaulding more than twenty years ago. The names, more especially, *are the same*, without any alteration. I once anticipated reading his writings in print, but little expected to see them in a new Bible.

STATEMENT OF OLIVER SMITH :—

All his [Spaulding's] leisure hours were occupied in writing a historical novel, founded upon the first settlers of this country ; he would give a satisfactory account of all the *old mounds*, so common to this country. Nephi and Lehi were by him represented as leading characters. But no religious matter was introduced. When I heard the historical part of the Book of Mormon related I at once said it was the writings of old Solomon Spaulding.

IV.

RIGDON AND SPAULDING'S MANUSCRIPT.

Rev. John Winter, who was intimate with Rigdon, states :

" In 1822 or 1823 Rigdon took out of his desk in his study a large manuscript, stating that it was a Bible romance written by a Presbyterian preacher whose health had failed and who had taken it to the printers to see if it would pay to publish it."

James Jeffries testified Jan. 20, 1884 :

" Forty years ago I was in business in St. Louis. The Mormons then had their temple in Nauvoo. I had business transactions with them. I knew Sidney Rigdon. He told me several times that there was in the printing office with which he was connected, in Ohio, a manuscript of the Rev. Spaulding, tracing the origin of the Indians from the lost tribes of Israel. This MS. was in the office several years. He was familiar with it. Spaulding wanted it published, but had not the means to pay for the printing. He [Rigdon] and Joe Smith used to look over the MS. and read it on Sundays. Rigdon said Smith took the MS. and said, ' I'll print it,' and went off to Palmyra, New York."

Adamson Bentley, Rigdon's brother-in-law, states :

" I know that Sidney Rigdon told me as much as two years before the Mormon Book made its appearance, or had been heard of by me, that there was a book coming out, the manuscript of which was engraved on GOLD PLATES."

Statement of Thomas J. Clapp, son-in-law of Adamson Bentley :

" Elder Adamson Bentley told me that as he was one day riding with Sidney Rigdon * and conversing upon the Bible, Mr. Rigdon told him that another book *of equal authority with the bible, as well au-thenticated and as ancient*, which would give an account of the *history of the Indian tribes* on this continent, with many other things of great importance to the world, would soon be published. This was before Mormonism was ever heard of in Ohio, and when it appeared, the avidity with which Rigdon received it convinced him that if Rigdon was not the author of it he was at least acquainted with the whole matter some time before it was published to the world."   [Letter from Mr. Clapp, dated Mentor, Ohio, April 9, 1879.]

Alexander Campbell was present at the conversation between Bentley and Rigdon, and says about it :

" Rigdon, at the same time, observed that on the plates dug up in New York there was an account not only of the aborigines of this con-tinent, but it was stated also that the Christian religion had been preached on this continent, during the first century, just as we were then preaching it on the Western Reserve."

Darwin Atwater, of Mantua, Ohio, testifies :

" That Rigdon knew beforehand of the coming of the Book of Mor-mon is to me certain from what he said during the first of his visits to my father, in 1826. He gave a wonderful description of the mounds and other antiquities found in some parts of America and said that they must have been made by the aborigines. He said there was a BOOK to be published containing an account of these things."

Zebulon Rudolph, Mrs. Garfield's father, states :

" During the winter previous to the appearance of the Book of Mormon, Rigdon was in the habit of spending *weeks away from home*, going no one knew whither. He often appeared preoccupied and

---

* Rigdon married a niece and adopted daughter of Bentley, living with and upon B. for quite a length of time.

would indulge in dreamy visionary talks, which puzzled those who listened. When the Book of Mormon appeared and Rigdon joined in the advocacy of the new religion, the suspicion was at once aroused that he was one of the framers of the new doctrine."

Mrs. A. Dunlap, of Warren, Ohio, a niece of Sidney Rigdon, visited her uncle, at Bainbridge, in 1826. She says:

"My uncle went into his bedroom and took from a trunk which he kept carefully locked, a manuscript and came back, seated himself by the fire and began to read. His wife came into the room and exclaimed: 'What, are you studying that thing again? I mean to burn that paper.' Rigdon replied: 'No, indeed you will not. THIS WILL BE A GREAT THING SOME DAY.' When he was reading this MS. he was so completely occupied that he seemed entirely unconscious of anything around him."

Rigdon was on terms of intimate association with one J. Harrison Lambdin, printer, Patterson's partner and active business manager, as well as with Silas Engles, the long-time foreman of Patterson's printing establishment in Pittsburg. This comes from Mrs. R. J. Eichbaum, who with her husband and father had the Pittsburg postoffice for over thirty years. Spaulding, while living in Pittsburg, had prepared a copy of his "Manuscript Found," for the printer, which he strongly suspected Rigdon of having appropriated. Mrs. Eichbaum has often heard foreman Engles say that Rigdon was forever hanging round the printing office. Lambdin died in 1825 and Engles in 1827. "Dead men tell no tales."

V.

THE ARMY OF ZION.

In obedience to direct revelation, Joseph had located *Zion* in Jackson County, Missouri. August 3, 1831, he located the Temple of Zion, three hundred yards west of the Court House, in Independence, Missouri. But the "House of Israel" did not behave in Missouri in a popular and acceptable way. The Mormons had to leave the new Zion, and October 30, 1833, there had even been a fight between the Mormons and "mine enemies." The Mormons killed two Missourians and shed the first blood in the war.

The Commander-in-chief of the armies of Israel could not remain a quiet, remote observer of so much wrong. Zion had to be *redeemed*. The "Lord" says through his mouthpiece:

"Therefore get ye straightway unto MY LAND; break down the walls of mine enemies; throw down their tower and scatter their watchmen; and inasmuch as they gather together against you, AVENGE ME OF MINE ENEMIES, that by and by I may come with the residue of my house and POSSESS THE LAND."

The preparations for "mine" war consisted mainly in gathering all the cash Joe could lay his hands on: "Let all the churches gather together all their monies." The expedition to Missouri will live in history as a parallel to the immortal enterprise of the ingenious "Hidalgo de La Mancha." Joe started on his fool's crusade early in 1834. One of his "sharp-shooters" may give us the history of the expedition:

"Old muskets, rifles, pistols, rusty swords and butcher knives were soon put in a state of repair, and scoured up. Some were borrowed, and some were bought, on a credit, if possible, and others were manufactured by their own mechanics. The first of May following being finally fixed upon as the time of setting out on the crusade, 'my warriors,' which were scattered in most of the eastern and northern states previous to that time, began to assemble at the quarters of the prophet in Kirtland preparatory to marching. Several places further west were also selected for rendezvous to those living in that direction. All the faithful pressed forward; but the services of some were refused by the prophet, in consequence of their not being able, from their own resources, to furnish some instrument of death, and FIVE DOLLARS IN CASH.

"On the second day of their march they arrived at New Portage, about forty miles distant, where about one hundred more fell into their ranks. Here the whole were organized in bands of fourteen men, each band having a captain, baggage wagon, tents, etc. Just before leaving this place, Smith proposed to his army that they should appoint a TREASURER to take possession of the funds of each individual, for the purpose of paying it out as he should think their necessities required. The measure was carried without a dissenting voice. The prophet was nominated and voted in as treasurer, no one, of course, doubting his right. After pocketing the cash of his dupes, the line of march was resumed, and a white flag was raised, bearing upon it the inscription of "PEACE," written in red.

"Somewhere on their route a large black snake was discovered near the road, over five feet in length. This offered a fair opportunity for some of the company to try their skill at miracles, and MARTIN HARRIS took off his shoes and stockings, to 'take up serpents' without being harmed. He presented his toes to the head of the snake, which made no attempt to bite, upon which Martin proclaimed a victory over serpents; but passing on a few rods further another of much larger dimensions was discovered, and on presenting his bare foot to this one also, he received a bite in the ankle which drew blood. This was imputed to his want of faith, and produced much merriment in the company.

"A large mound was one day discovered, upon which General Smith ordered an excavation to be made into it, and about one foot from the top of the ground the bones of a human skeleton were found, which were carefully laid out upon a board, when Smith made a speech, prophecying or declaring that they were the remains of a celebrated general among the NEPHITES, mentioning his name and the battle in which he was slain, some fifteen hundred years ago. This was undoubtedly done to encourage the troops to deeds of daring, when they should meet the Missourians in battle array."

Joe relates this most wonderful event in his usual simple and truthful way. The relation is in his journal of June, 1834, when he and his army are at the Illinois river:

"The contemplation of the scenery," writes Joseph, "produced peculiar sensations in our bosoms. The brethren procured a shovel and a hoe, and removing the earth of one of the mounds, to the depth of about a foot, discovered the skeleton of a man almost entire, and between his ribs was a LAMANITISH ARROW, which evidently procured his death. Elder Brigham Young retained the arrow. . . . And the visions of the past being opened to my understanding, by the Spirit of the Almighty, I DISCOVERED that *the person, whose skeleton was before us*, was a WHITE Lamanite, a large thick-set man, and a man of God. [John D. Lee was not very large, though thick-set and a man of God.] He was a warrior and chieftain under the great prophet Omandagus, who was known from the hill Cumorah, or Eastern Sea, to the Rocky Mountains. His name was ZELPH. The curse was taken from him, or, at least, in part. One of his thigh bones was broken by a stone flung from a sling while in battle years before his death. He was killed in battle by the arrow found in his ribs, during the last great struggle of the Lamanites and Nephites." *

But let our sharp-shooter go on with his tale :

"On arriving at Salt Creek, Illinois, they were joined by Lyman Wight and Hyrum Smith with a reinforcement of twenty men, which they had picked up on the way. Here the grand army, being fully completed, encamped for the space of three days. The whole number was now estimated at two hundred and twenty, *rank and file*. During their stay here the troops were kept under a constant drill of manual exercise with guns and swords, and their arms put in a state of repair. The prophet became very expert with a sword and felt himself equal to his prototype, Coriantumr."

If there is any better historic parallel to Don Quixote, I wish I could see it, but I think there is none half so good.

"Joseph had the best sword in the army, an elegant brace of pistols, which were purchased on a credit of six months, a rifle, and four horses. Wight was appointed second in command, or *fighting general*, who, together with the prophet, had an ARMOR-BEARER appointed, selected from among the most expert tacticians, whose duty it was to be in constant attendance upon their masters with their arms."

---

* Which came off (I must remind thee, Joseph) not in Illinois, but around the sacred hill "Cumorah," way back in New York.

Joe's armor-bearer was Geo. A. Smith, then a bud of a beastly fanatic, destined to become the Thackeray of Mormonism and Brigham's destroying angel in 1857.

"The generals then appointed a new captain to each band, organized two companies of rangers, or *sharp-shooters*, to act as scouts or flankers when they should arrive upon the field of carnage. After this they dubbed themselves the "ARMY OF ZION," and Hyrum Smith was chosen to carry the flag, which he kept unfurled during the remainder of the march.

"The march of the grand army was then resumed for two or three days, when it was agreed to spend half a day in a sham fight. For this purpose four divisions were formed and took position and went to work, agreeably to the most approved forms of Bonaparte, Black Hawk, Coriantumr or Shiz. After coming to close quarters, however, all discipline was lost sight of and each one adopted a mode agreeable to his taste. Some preferred the real British push with the bayonet, some the old Kentucky dodging from tree to tree, while others preferred the Lamanite mode of tomahawking, scalping, and ripping open the bowels. The final result was that several guns and swords were broken, some of the combatants wounded, and each one well pleased with his own exploits.

"After crossing the Mississippi, spies on horseback were kept constantly on the lookout, several miles in front and rear. The prophet went IN DISGUISE, changing his dress frequently, riding on the different baggage wagons, and, to all appearance, *expecting every moment to be his last.* Near the close of one day they approached a prairie, which was thirty miles in extent, without inhabitants. Here an altercation took place between the two generals, which almost amounted to a mutiny. The prophet declared it was not safe to stay there over night, as the enemy would probably be upon them. General Wight totally refused to enter the prairie, as they would not be able to find water, or to build a fire to cook their provisions. besides the great fatigue it would cause the troops. *Smith said he would show them how to eat raw pork.* Hyrum said he knew, *by the Spirit*, that it was dangerous to stay there. The prophet finally exclaimed: ' *Thus saith the Lord God, march on !* ' This settled the matter, and they all moved on about fifteen miles, and thinking themselves out of danger, they encamped beside a muddy pool. Here the controversy was again renewed between the two generals. Smith said ' he knew exactly when to pray, when to sing, when to talk, and when to laugh, *by the spirit of God*; that God never commanded anyone to pray for his enemies.' The whole camp seemed much dissatisfied and came nigh breaking out into open mutiny."

What a pity that Offenbach is dead ! Was there ever a better *libretto* just made for his ever-ready, bubbling melodies! Would he not have been happy to swap his " General Bum " for the three generals, Joe, Hyrum and Wight ?

" The prophet had, besides his other weapons, a large bull-dog, which was exceedingly cross during the nights and frequently attempted to bite persons stirring about. One of the captains, a high priest, one evening declared to the prophet that he would shoot the dog, if he ever attempted to bite him. Smith replied, ' that if he continued in the same spirit, and did not repent. the dog would yet eat the flesh off his bones, and he would not have the power to resist.' This was the commencement of a controversy between the prophet and his high priest, which was not settled till some time after their return to Kirtland, when the former [Joseph] underwent a trial on divers serious charges before his high priests, honorably acquitted, and the latter made to acknowledge that he had been possessed of SEVERAL DEVILS for many weeks. The dog, however, a few nights after the controversy commenced, was shot through the leg by a sentinel, near the prophet's tent, and died instantly.

" When within twelve miles of Liberty, Clay County, Missouri, the army of Zion was met by two gentlemen who had been deputed by the citizens of another county for the purpose of inquiring into the motive and object of such a hostile and warlike appearance upon their borders.

These gentlemen openly warned the military band and their prophet to desist from their intended operations and leave the settlement of their difficulties with the people of Jackson County, in other hands; advised them to be very careful what they did and said, as the citizens not only of Jackson but some of the adjacent counties were very much enraged and excited and were fully determined to resist the first attempt upon them by an armed force from other States. A FEW HOURS after this the prophet brought out a REVELATION for the use of his troops, which said, in substance, that they had been TRIED, even as Abraham had been tried, and the offering was accepted by the Lord; and when Abraham received his reward they would receive theirs. Upon this the war was declared to be at an end. A call for volunteers, however, was made, to take up their abode in Clay County, when about one hundred and fifty turned out. The next day they marched to Liberty and each man received an *honorable discharge* under the signature of General Wight. The army then scattered in different directions, some making their way back from whence they came the best way they could, begging their expenses from the inhabitants. The prophet and his chief men, however, had PLENTY OF MONEY and traveled as GENTLEMEN."

VI.

AFFIDAVITS OF FANNY BREWER AND OTHERS.

The following documents help to illustrate the characters of Joe, Hyrum and William Smith, Brigham Young, and other leading Saints:

FANNY BREWER states (Boston, Sept. 13, 1842):—

"In the spring of 1837 I left Boston for Kirtland to assemble with the Saints and worship God more perfectly. On my arrival I found brother going to law with brother, DRUNKENNESS prevailing to a great extent and every species of wickedness. The prophet of God was under arrest for employing two of the elders *to* KILL *a man* of the name of *Grandison Newell,* but was acquitted, as the most material witness did not appear! I am personally acquainted with one of the employees, Davis by name, and he frankly acknowleged to me that he was prepared to do the deed *under the direction of the prophet,* and was only prevented from so doing by the entreaties of his wife. There was much excitement against the prophet on another account, an unlawful intercourse between himself and a *young orphan girl* residing in his family, and under his protection! Martin Harris told me that the prophet was most notorious for *lying and licentiousness.* In the fall of 1837 the Smith family all left Kirtland; the prophet left between two days. I carried from this place (Boston) to Kirtland goods to the amount of 1,400 dollars, as I was told I could make ready sales to the Saints, but I was disappointed. I accordingly sent them to Missouri to be sold by H. Redfield. There they were stored in a private room. Smith, the prophet, hearing that they were there, took out a warrant, under pretence of searching for stolen goods, and got them into his possession. They were then, by a sham court, which he held, adjudged to him and the boxes were opened. As the goods were taken out, piece by piece, HYRUM SMITH, who stood by, said, in the most positive manner, that he could swear to every piece and tell where they had been bought, although a Mr. Robbins, who was present, told them that he knew the boxes and that the goods were mine, for I had charged him to take care of them. Dr. Williams, likewise, told them that they were my goods, and that Hyrum never saw a piece of them. They, however, refused to give them up, but kept them for their own profit."

G. B. FROST (Boston, Sept. 19, 1842):—

"In July, 1837, WILLIAM SMITH, brother of the prophet and one of the Twelve Apostles, arrived at Kirtland from Chicago, drunk, with his face pretty well bunged up; he had black eyes and a bunged nose, and told John Johnson that he had been MILKING THE GENTILES to his satisfaction for that time.* In October William told Joseph that if he did not give him some money, *he would tell where the Book of Mormon came from,* and Joseph gave him what he wanted.

"About the last of August, 1837, Joseph Smith, *Brigham Young* and others were DRUNK at Joseph Smith the prophet's house, all together; Bishop Vinson Knight supplied them with rum, brandy, gin and port wine from the (Mormon) cash store. Joseph told Knight in my hearing not to sell any of those liquors, for he wanted them for his own use. *They were drunk and drinking for* MORE THAN A WEEK.

"Joseph Smith said that the BANK was got up on his having a revelation from God, and said it was to go into circulation to MILK THE GENTILES. I asked Joseph about the money. He he said could not

———————————————————————

* Most probably by circulating counterfeit money.

redeem it; he was paid for signing the bills, as any other man would be paid for it—and they must do the best they could about it. The prophet and others went to Canada in September. Said he, Joseph, he had as good a right to go out and get money as any of the brethren. He took nine hundred dollars in Canada from a certain Lawrence and promised him a farm in Kirtland; but when he arrived there, Joseph was among the missing, and no farm for him."

D. W. AND EDWARD KILBOURN:—

"Joseph said once the world owed him a good living, and if he could not get it without, he would STEAL it—"and CATCH ME AT IT," said he, "if you can."

VII.

POLYGAMY IN KIRTLAND.

In the article on marriage in the Book of Doctrine and Covenants adopted by the conference in Kirtland April, 1834, we read: "Inasmuch as this Church of Christ has been *charged with fornication and polygamy.*" We have already seen it stated that young Joseph declared that adultery was no sin. Martin Harris told J. M. Atwater and Mr. Clapp and many others, that POLYGAMY WAS TAUGHT AND PRACTICED by Smith in Kirtland under the name of "spiritual wifery." W. W. Phelps stated that Smith while "translating" the *Book of Abraham* declared that polygamy would yet be a practice of the faith. Martin Harris told J. M. Atwater that the doctrine of spiritual wifery was first positively announced as a *revelation* by RIGDON, before a meeting of the officials of the church, in an old building that used to stand southwest of the Kirtland Temple. W. S. Smith and others testify that the practice of *sealing* women to men was so much talked of in Kirtland, that it became a by-word on the street; and that common report said that a bitter quarrel between Rigdon and Smith shortly before they left Kirtland was because Smith wanted to have Nancy Rigdon, then a girl of sixteen, sealed to him. Smith confesses himself that all classes of persons asked him daily and hourly, while he was journeying between Kirtland and Far West, "Do Mormons believe in having more wives than one?" All this accords perfectly with the statement of Apostle Orson Pratt that the *principle* was made known to the Prophet as early as 1831.

VIII.

DR. ISAAC GALLAND.

"I the Lord *loveth* him for the works he has done," says the revelation of January 19, 1841, of the horse-stealing doctor. Messrs. D. W. and Edward Kilbourn give an interesting sketch of the doctor's doings in the *Hawk-Eye and Patriot* of October 7, 1841. After having described the confused state of things on the tract of land reserved in 1824 by treaty for the use of the "Half Breeds of the Sac and Fox Nation of Indians," they continue:

"The ingenuity of Dr. Galland, however, found in this state of things a fine field for the exercise of his peculiar talents, and in the year 1839 he matured the plan of a stupendous fraud. He wrote to Joe Smith, then in prison on charges of high treason, arson, etc.,—inviting him to purchase his land at Commerce [Nauvoo], forty-seven acres. Smith after making his escape complied, and brought on his half-starved followers. Doctor G. then commenced selling Half-Breed lands, giving therefor warranty deeds, which, of course, could convey no title while the lands remained undivided. He at first asserted that he was the owner of seven-tenths of the tract [119,000 acres] and finally claimed to be the *sole proprietor*. That he might the more successfully carry out the scheme of swindling thus commenced, he attached himself to the Mormon church, became a confidant of Joe Smith, and in order to dupe persons daily arriving among them, he deeded to Mormon bishops and prophets thousands and tens of thousands of acres of the reservation alluded to, and they are daily deeding by warranty deeds the lands thus acquired and receiving therefor a valuable consideration. By a recent judicial decision it is ascertained that the interest to which this man Galland is entitled is but a small, undefined, undivided portion of the reservation.

With a full knowledge of all the facts stated, he is sent out with a 'Proclamation to the Saints abroad,' signed by Joseph Smith, Sidney Rigdon and Hyrum Smith, in which it is said that 'he (Galland) is the honored instrument the Lord used to prepare a home for us when we were driven from our inheritance, *having given him control of vast bodies of land* and prepared his heart to make the use of it the Lord intended he should.'

"Many instances might be mentioned of individuals in the east, who have exchanged with the 'agents of the church' their valuable possessions for these worthless land titles, and there are cases of suffering, of families reduced to beggary, by these villains. When it is known that one of the prophets acts in the absence of Galland as his agent for the sale of these lands, what further evidence, we ask, is wanted of the baseness and rascality of himself and his confederates?"

Galland died, a pauper, in Iowa.

IX.

SETTING UP THE KINGDOM.

On the little town-site of Montrose, Iowa, Joe Smith, "agent of Doctor Galland," resolved to erect his City of Zarahemla. Messrs. Kilbourn give a lively account of this bit of prophetic sharp practice:

"Early one morning in March, 1841, the quiet citizens of Montrose were surprised by a visit from some of Joe Smith's scullions from Nauvoo, headed by Alanson Ripley, a Mormon bishop, who says *that as to the technical niceties of the law of the land he does not intend to regard them; that the kingdom spoken of by the prophet Daniel has been set up and that it is necessary every kingdom should be governed by its own laws.* With compass and chain they strided through gates and over fences to the very doors of the Gentiles and drove the stakes for the lots of a city which, in extent at least — four miles square,— should vie with some of the largest cities of the world. They heeded not enclosures; why should they? Is not the earth the Lord's and the fulness thereof? And shall not his 'Saints' inherit and possess it forever? The kingdom spoken of by the prophet Daniel having een set up, its 'laws' authorized this Mormon bishop to threaten personal violence to one of the undersigned for removing a stake which had been driven within the bounds of his enclosure. A few days subsequently it was ascertained that the exterior line of this

' four mile ' town had been run by order of Joe Smith and a plot of
it made and *recorded*, to which he gave the name of Zarahemla.
Having sold to his dupes a large portion of the Half Breed tract, a
happy thought strikes him that they can yet be bled; he ordered
them by *revelation* to leave their fine farms and move into the ' city,'
sells them lots and conveys them by deeds.

   "On the 6th of April, at a conference held in Nauvoo, a Mormon
leader publicly read a *revelation** that the City of Zarahemla should
be laid out and built by the Latter Day Saints. Joe Smith then
stated that ' in accordance with this revelation ' a city had been surveyed and the Saints desirous of purchasing lots could now do so.
' The people over there,' said he, ' are very much opposed to it, but
they must know — if they know anything — that it would be for their
interest to have 5,000 inhabitants come in with back-loads of money.
Why, I sometimes think they *don't know beans when the bag is open;*
they needn't be scared; we don't want their improvements without
paying for them; we expect to pay them a good price for their possessions, and if that don't satisfy them, *we'll have them anyhow.*"

* * *

X.

ROCKWELL AND GOVERNOR BOGGS.

The reader remembers the statement of Mrs. Pratt,
which proves conclusively that Joseph, with the complic-
ity of Dr. John C. Bennett, gave orders for the assassination of Governor Boggs. He sent Danite O. Porter
Rockwell "to fulfill prophecy," and the prophecy came
very near being fulfilled on May 6, 1842. Boggs received
a terrible wound in the head, and I am informed that,
though cured for the time, he died a number of years
after from the effects of the very same wound.

On June 23 I had an interview with the only man
Brigham Young seems to have ever really feared, General

---

   * " Verily, thus saith the Lord, let [all My Saints] gather themselves together unto the places which I shall appoint unto them by
my prophet Joseph and build up cities unto my name. Let them
build up a city unto my name upon the land opposite to the city of
Nauvoo and let the name of Zarahemla be named upon it.—[*Doctrine and Covenants*, 1886, p. 447.]

Connor. To name the old soldier is to name honesty and kindness, as everybody knows. By a remarkable turn of affairs he became the patron of Brigham's professional murderers, Bill Hickman and O. P. Rockwell. All things considered, the church hyenas found it safer to serve an honest man in doing his useful and harmless business, and getting well paid for it, instead of robbing and murdering for the prophet of the Lord at their own danger and expense. "Bill Hickman," says General Connor," "told me half an hour after it occurred, that Brigham had promised him a thousand dollars if he would send a ball through my brain and lay the murder to the Indians. I don't believe that those men were butchers by nature: they were fanatics in their belief that they could not be saved if they would not obey any order of the prophet, right or wrong. As to Rockwell, he considered me his only friend in the last years of his life, and wrote to me, while I was in California, that I should come and help him in a law-suit. I employed him during one winter to guard my stock. He discharged this task with scrupulous honesty. He used, like Hickman, to tell me many of the horrible deeds he had committed for the church. Among other things he told me once that HE HAD SHOT BOGGS. '*I shot through the window,*' said he, '*and thought I had killed him*, but I had only wounded him ; *I was damned sorry that I had not killed the son of a b— !*' "

XI.

MARTHA BROTHERTON'S AFFIDAVIT.

This is *my* pearl. It shows the *works of Abraham* in all their glory. It proves absolutely the statements made by Bennett, the *Expositor*, and my witnesses. It shows the reprobateness of the lackeys, Brigham and Kimball, who never did anything afterward in Utah but put in

practice what they had learnt in the school of Mine Anointed. That little room, with "POSITIVELY NO ADMIT-
TANCE" is a pearl of peculiar lustre in Mormon history.
An old lady told me, only a few days ago, that a plural
wife of William Clayton, whom she used to visit often, said
to her that Joseph was wont to spend a great deal of his valuable time in this skeleton-closet of his amours. The Claytons kept a sharp lookout for Emma, the dreaded legal
wife, who used to hunt " Brother Joseph " all over town.
Whenever she approached the " brick store " the Claytons
warned the prophet by a certain signal. He would then
hurry down stairs, fix up before the mirror, and be discovered in animated conversation with some member of
the Clayton family when Emma entered.

John Taylor was one of the many who entered the little
sealing office for the holiest of purposes. Said a perfectly
reliable witness, a lady, to me : "A Mrs. Ann Dawson
went to Nauvoo from Preston, Lancashire, England; she
came with her whole family; one of her daughters, Mary,
got an invitation for " a special meeting. " They brought
her to that little sealing office; Joseph was there and told
her that it was the Lord's will concerning her that she
should be sealed to Brother John Taylor without delay as
his celestial wife; she refused. They (Joseph and Taylor) bolted the door, and wanted to force things, but she
managed to get away from them. This event caused the
whole Dawson family to apostatize and to leave Nauvoo. "
Mrs. Dawson had seven children when she came to Nauvoo.
The story was told my witness by Mrs. Elizabeth Cottom,
the sister of the intended celestial victim. But no, there
is not *any* such thing practiced here, Mr. Taylor, eh?
Now let us hear the brave English girl, Martha Brotherton :

ST. LOUIS, MO., July 13, 1842.

"I had been in Nauvoo near three weeks, during which
time my father's family received frequent visits from
Apostles BRIGHAM YOUNG and HEBER C. KIMBALL, when,
early one morning, they both came to my brother-in-law's,
where I was on a visit, and particularly requested me to go
and spend a few days with them. I told them I could

not at that time; however they urged me to go the next day and spend one day with them. The day being fine I· accordingly went. When I arrived at the foot of the hill, Young and Kimball were standing conversing together. They both came to me and after several flattering compliments, Kimball wished me to go to his house first. I went. Brigham went away on some errand and Kimball now turned to me and said: "Martha, I want you to say to my wife, when you go to my house, that you want to buy some things at Joseph's store, and I will say I am going with you, to show you the way. You know you want to see the prophet and you will then have an opportunity." I made no reply. I remained at Kimball's near an hour, when Kimball, seeing that I would not tell the lies he wished me to, told them to his wife himself. So Kimball and I went to the store together. As we were going along he said: "Sister Martha, are you willing to do ALL. that the prophet requires you to do?" I said I believed I was, thinking of course *he* would require nothing wrong. "Then," said he, "are you ready to take counsel?" I answered yes, thinking of the great and glorious blessings that had been pronounced upon my head, if I adhered to the counsel of those placed over me in the Lord. "Well," said he, "there are many things revealed in these last days that the world would laugh and scoff at, but unto us is given to know the MYSTERIES OF THE KINGDOM." He further observed: "Martha, you must learn to HOLD YOUR TONGUE and it will be well with you." When we reached the building he led me up some stairs to a small room, the door of which was locked and on it the inscription, "Positively no admittance." He observed: "Ah, brother Joseph must be sick, for, strange to say, he is not here. Come down into the tithing office, Martha." He then left me in the tithing office. Brigham Young came in and seated himself before me and asked where Kimball was. Soon after Joseph came in and then went up stairs, followed by Young. Now Kimball came in. "Martha," said he, "the prophet has come, come up stairs." I went and we found Brigham and the prophet alone. I was introduced to the prophet by Brig-

ham. Joseph offered me his seat and, to my astonishment, the moment I was seated Joseph and Kimball
walked out of the room and left me with Brigham, who
arose, *locked the door, closed the window, and drew the
curtains.* He then sat before me and said: "This is
OUR PRIVATE ROOM, Martha." "Indeed, sir," said

BRIGHAM YOUNG.

I, "I must be highly honored to be permitted to
enter it." He smiled and then proceeded: "Sister
Martha, I want to ask you a few questions—will you answer them?" "Yes, sir," said I. "And will you
promise *not to mention them to anyone?*" "If it is your
desire, sir," said I, "I will not." "And you will not
think any the worse of me for it, will you, Martha?"
said he. "No," I replied. "Well," said he, "*what are
your feelings towards me?*" I replied: "My feelings are
just the same towards you that they ever were, sir."
"But to come to the point more closely," said he, "have
you not an affection for me, that, were it lawful and right,
you could accept of me for your HUSBAND and compan-

ion ?'' My feelings at that moment were indescribable. What, thought I, are these men that I thought almost perfection itself, deceivers? I considered it best to ask for time to think and pray about it. I therefore said : '' If it was lawful and right perhaps I might, but you know, sir, it is not.'' '' Well, but,'' said he, '' Brother Joseph has had a REVELATION from God that it is lawful and right for a man to have TWO WIVES; for as it was in the days of Abraham, so it shall be in these last days, and whoever is the first that is willing to take up the CROSS will receive the greatest blessings ; and if you will accept of me, *I will take you straight to the celestial kingdom*, and if you will have me in this world, I will have you in that which is to come, and brother Joseph will *marry us here to-day*, or you can go home this evening and *your parents will not know anything about it.''* '' Sir,'' said I, '' I should not like to do anything of the kind without the permission of my parents.'' '' Well, but,'' said he, ''you are of age, are you not?'' ''No, sir,'' said I, '' I shall not be until the 24th of May.'' ''Well,'' said he, ''that does not make any difference. You will be of age *before they know* and you need not fear. If you will take my *counsel* it will be well with you, and if there is any sin in it, *I will answer for it.* But Brother Joseph will explain things — will you hear him?'' '' I do not mind,'' said I. '' Well, but I want you to say something,'' said he.· '' I want time to think about it,'' said I. '' Well,'' said he, '' *I will have a kiss anyhow.''* He rose and said he would bring Joseph. He then unlocked the door and took the key and locked me up alone. He was absent about ten minutes and then returned with Joseph. '' Well,'' said Brigham, '' Sister Martha would be willing if she knew that it was lawful and right before God.'' '' Well, Martha,'' said Joseph, it IS lawful and right before God — I KNOW it is. Look here, Sis ; DON'T YOU BELEIVE IN ME?'' I did not answer. ''Well, Martha,'' said Joseph, ''just go ahead and do as Brigham wants you to — he is the best man in the world, except me.'' '' Well,'' said Brigham, '' we believe Joseph to be a drophet. I have known him for eight years, and always found him the same." "Yes," said Joseph, "I know that this is lawful and right before God, and if there is any sin in it, I WILL ANSWER FOR IT BEFORE GOD; and I have the *keys of the kingdom* and whatever I bind on earth is bound in Heaven and whatever I loose on earth is loosed in Heaven; and if you will accept of Brigham, you shall be blessed; God shall bless you and my blessing shall rest upon you; and if you will be led by him, you will do well: for I know Brigham will take care of you, and if he don't do his duty to you, come to me and I will make him: and if you do not like it in a month or two, come to me and *I will make you free again*, and if he turns you off, I WILL TAKE YOU ON." "Sir," said I, rather warmly, " it will be too late to think in a month or two after. I want time to think first." "Well, but," said he, " the old proverb is: 'nothing ventured, nothing gained'—and it would be the *greatest blessing* ever bestowed on you. What are you afraid of, Sis.? *Come,* LET ME DO THE BUSINESS FOR YOU." "Well," said I, "the best way I know of, is to go home and think and pray about it." Brigham said: "I shall leave it with Brother Joseph, whether it would be best for you to have time or not." Joseph: "I see no harm in her having time to think, if she will not *fall into temptation*." "Oh, sir," said I, "there is no fear of my falling into temptation." "Well, but," said Brigham, "you must promise me you will *never mention it to anyone*." I promised. Joseph said: "You must promise me the same." I did. "Upon your honor," said he, "you will not tell?" "No, sir," said I, "I will lose my life first." "Well, that will do," said he, "*that is the principle we go upon*. I think I can trust you, Martha." I then rose to go, when Joseph commenced to beg of me again. He said it was the best opportunity they might have for months, for THE ROOM WAS OFTEN ENGAGED. I, however, had determined what to do. The next day I sat down and wrote the conversation. We went to meeting. Brigham administered the sacrament. After it was over, Young followed me out and whispered: "Have you made up your mind, Martha?" "Not exactly, sir," said I, and we parted."

XII.

SUBSTANCE OF THE EVIDENCE

*In the Trial of Joseph Smith and Others for High Trea-
son Against the State; Murder, Burglary, Arson, Robbery and Larceny.* (November, 1838.)

SAMPSON AVARD:—

"The officers of the Danite band were brought before Joseph
Smith, together with Hyrum Smith and Sidney Rigdon. Joseph blessed
thm and prophesied over them, declaring that they should be the means
in the hands of God, of bringing forth the millennial kingdom. *Joseph
said* that those who revealed the secrets of the Society should be PUT
TO DEATH. They declared, holding up their right hands: "In the
name of Jesus Christ, I do solemnly obligate myself ever to conceal and
never to reveal the secret purposes of this society. Should I ever do
the same, I hold my life as the forfeiture." The prophet and his
councilors, Hyrum and Sidney, were considered as the supreme head
of the church, and the Danite band felt themselves as much bound to
obey them as to obey the *Supreme God.* Instruction was given *by
Joseph,* that if any of them should get into a difficulty, the rest should
help him out and that they should stand by each other, RIGHT OR
WRONG. This instruction was given in a public address."

W. W. PHELPS:—

"Rigdon said in a public meeting that they meant to *resist the law*
and if a sheriff came after them with writs. they would kill him, and if
anybody opposed them they would take off their heads. SMITH AP-
PROVED of those remarks. On another occasion Rigdon administered
for forty or fifty Mormons, the covenanters taking their obligations with
uplifted hands. The first was, that if any man attempted to move out
of the country, or pack his things for that purpose, any of the covenanters seeing it should *kill him and haul him aside into the brush;*
and all the burial he should have should be in a turkey buzzard's guts,
so that nothing should be left of him but his bones. The next covenant was, that if any person from the surrounding country came into
their town, walking about—no odds who he might be—any one of
those covenanters should kill him and throw him aside into the brush.
The third covenant was, "Conceal all these things." *

---

* Bravo, old Phelps! And after this statement you went back to
the church and played for many years the picturesque part of Old
Scratch in the Endowment House!

G. M. HINKLE :—

" I have heard Joseph say that he believed MAHOMET was a good man ; that the Koran was not a true thing, but the world believed Mahomet, as they had believed him and that Mahomet was a true prophet. Joseph made a speech to the troops in which he said that the troops which were gathering through the country were a *damned mob.* That he had tried to keep the law long enough. That the whole State was a mob set and that if they came to fight him, he would play *hell with their apple carts!* "

JOHN CORRILL :—

" Joseph said if the people would let us alone, we would preach the gospel in peace ; but if they come on us to molest us, we would establish our religion by the sword and that he would become to this generation a SECOND MAHOMET. He spoke in his discourse of persons taking, at some times, what, at other times, it would be wrong to take ; and gave, as an example, the case of David eating the shewbread and also of the Savior and His Apostles plucking the ears of corn and eating, as they passed through the corn field."

JAMES C. OWENS :—

" I heard Joseph, in a speech to the Mormon troops say that he did not care any thing about the coming of the troops nor about THE LAWS and that he did not intend to try to keep the laws, or please them any longer ; that they were a *damned set,* and God should damn them, so help him Jesus Christ, and he meant to go his own course and KILL AND DESTROY and told the men to fight like angels, that heretofore he told them to fight like devils, but now he told them to fight like angels, that angels could whip devils. He said that they might think he was swearing, but that God Almighty would not take notice of him in cursing such a *damned set* as they were."

REED PECK :—

" I heard Joseph say in a speech in reference to STEALING that in a general way he did not approve of it, but that on one occasion our Savior and His deciples *stole* corn in going through the corn field, for the reason that they could not otherwise procure anything to eat. He told an anecdote of a Dutchman's potatoes and said that a colonel was quartered near a Dutchman from whom he wished to purchase some potatoes, who refused to sell them. The officer then charged his men *not to be caught* stealing the Dutchman's potatoes, *but next morning he found his potatoes all dug.* I heard Joseph in a public address say that he had a reverence for the Constitution of the U. S. and of this state (Missouri); but, as for the *laws* of this State he did not intend to regard them, as they were made by lawyers and black-legs."

ALLEN RATHBUN :—

" Mr. Carn remarked, that there would be in, that night, a considerable number of *sheep* and *cattle;* and further remarked, that it looked to him sometimes that it was not right to take plunder, but that it was ACCORDING TO THE DIRECTIONS OF JOSEPH SMITH and that was the reason why he did it."

BURR RIGGS:—

"While in Diahmon, I saw a great deal of plunder brought in, consisting of bed and bed-clothes; I also saw one clock, and I saw thirty-six head of cattle drove in. All the above property was called CONSECRATED property. I heard Joseph Smith say that the sword was now unsheathed and should not again be sheathed until he could go through those United States and live in any county he pleased, peaceably. I heard this from him on several occasions."

XIII.

JOSEPH'S REAL CHARACTER.

After having told so many "infernal lies" about Joe Smith, his family and his friends, I feel the necessity of telling the "truth" for once. So let me publish "the facts" about Joe in the words of the present church organ, printed Dec. 22, 1880 :—

THE MAN OF THE CENTURY.

"Seventy-five years ago to-day one of the most remarkable characters of the age was born at Sharon, Windsor County, Vermont. He was a child of destiny. Raised up by Divine Providence for a needful work, he came into the world shortly after the opening of this wonderful nineteenth century. Descended from the ancient Seers, he bore in his *body* and possessed in his spirit the qualities needful for the great work required of him. Pre-ordained to be a prophet to the latter-day dispensation, he was the man for the times, the central figure around which were grouped other strong souls born to be laborers in the vineyard at the eleventh hour, the star whose rays were shed forth in the midst of the spiritual darkness that prevailed for centuries, and whose light was to herald the speedy coming of the glorious Sun of Righteousness.

"Joseph Smith, son of Joseph, and of the lineage of that ancient Joseph who was sold into Egypt but became the ruler of the land, was one of the greatest revelators who ever dwelt on this fallen planet. He communed with angels; he translated sacred records written in forgotten languages; he was *susceptible to the* SEER-STONE and could read by Urim and Thummim; he restored lost divine things of the past; he perceived and declared important events of the future; he gazed into the glories of the eternal worlds; he *held converse with the Father and the Son*; he received the keys of the last dispensation and to him came those who stood at the head of all former dispensations, back to Michael, or Adam, the first of all and chief of all, who conferred upon him the spirit and power of their several callings; he laid the foundation of the *mightiest kingdom* that this world has ever seen; he established the sacred order of the everlasting priesthood and defined its powers and limits, its prerogatives and duties, its offices and callings, in all their detail and beauty and harmony; he grappled with the powers of darkness; he opened the gospel to the living and the way of redemption for the dead; he was spoken of for good or evil in all the nations on the globe; he sealed his testimony with his blood, and his name is recorded in the list of the martyrs, for whom shines the kingly crown in the midst of the majesty on high.

"We honor and revere his memory; but we do not worship him, as some people declare. *He was but a man* with human failings and human affections. But he was one of the mighty, and he has left an impress on the century that will not perish while time shall last. The spirit of his personality remains on this side of the vail, although he ministers beyond, and wherever the restored gospel is found among the tribes and tongues of men, he will be proclaimed as the *instrument in God's hand* of linking together the heavens and the earth, and of bringing to the sons and daughters of men the blessings of the plan of salvation.

"Thousands upon thousands have received in their souls a divine witness of his prophetic mission. And the people gathered from the ends of the earth who now inherit these fruitful valleys, and whose union, and force, and peculiarities and faith have attracted the attention of all nations, have been brought here by the power and influence of the religion which he taught and the spirit that he administered. And when the great work which he founded is finished, and the fulness of the Gentiles is come in, and Israel and Judah, restored to their former dominion, possess the lands bestowed upon them by patriarchal blessings, and the power of the wicked is broken, and Satan and his hosts are banished and bound, and the kingdoms of this world are the kingdom of God and His Christ, among the mighty ones who stand next the throne and join in the government of the regenerated earth will be Joseph Smith, once the Green Mountain boy and the derided of the proud, the scoffer and the worldly-wise, but now *the heaven-crowned ruler over many things*, and the honored associate of the immortal and Eternal Rulers of a universe redeemed."

While writing this cleverly arranged medley of impudent lies, editor C. W. Penrose had no idea that only a few years later he would have to skip Zion in woman's clothes, the anointed head buried in a big sun bonnet, for having fulfilled the *Law of Sarah*. He is now in old England, playing a *duo* on the flute of melancholy with bloody old sinner Daniel H. Wells. Penrose, being a man of talent, should use his leisure time in writing the memoirs of Wells, who can give him lots of curious details about church murders, engineered by him and Brother Brigham, especially the blood-atoning of Dr. J. King Robinson.

Brother Brigham, it would seem, knew his prophet better, and I think, if he was alive, he could not take exceptions to my views of Joseph's life and character, if I may judge from the following expressions in one of his speeches before thousands of his hearers :

"The doctrine the prophet Joseph teaches is all I care about. Bring anything against that if you can. As for anything else, I don't care if the prophet Joseph acted LIKE THE DEVIL. He brought forth a doctrine that will save us if we will abide by it. He may have got DRUNK every day of his life, SLEPT WITH HIS NEIGHBOR'S WIFE EVERY NIGHT, run horses and gambled EVERY DAY : I care nothing about that, for I never embrace any man in my faith. The doctrine the prophet Joseph produced will save you and me and the whole world. If you can find any fault with his doctrine, find it."

As a rule the leaders in Mormonism knew and know each other well. Apostle Heber C. Kimball, for example, read Brother Brigham's low cunning soul as clearly as if he had Joe's peepstone, though, in public, declaring him to be God's representative, ay, even God Himself. Kimball could not help seeing that Brother Brigham had a special weakness for dashing Gentile actresses. On one occasion Kimball had assembled his "family" for the usual evening prayer, but when beginning to pray for Brigham, he sprang to his feet excitedly, and exclaimed : "I can't pray for him, but he needs it badly enough, for the greater the strumpet, the more Brother Brigham is after her." I have this anecdote from a perfectly responsible source.

XIV.

PATRIARCHAL BLESSINGS.

Just as Joseph's old peepstone became the *Urim and Thummim* of " our holy religion, " so was the gibberish of the fortune-telling Smith family transformed into "patriarchal blessings. " We have already seen, in Dr. Bennett's history, a brilliant specimen of this kind of productions, which were a pious pastime for certain members of the " Church,"at once pleasant and profitable. I am not able to give one of the blessings pronounced by the *new Abraham*, Mr. Joseph Smith, Sr., but I was able to copy two pronounced by " Uncle John, " a brother of the new Abraham, who lived to a very advanced age in Utah. Both blessings bear the date of November 10, 1852. The good people who received them told me that " Uncle John " looked carefully into their eyes before pronouncing them, to ascertain to *what tribe of Israel* the blessing-candidates belonged. Considering the abundance of fine things promised in these valuable documents, they were really cheap, if not given away altogether. Ready money was scarce at that time, so the price, $2 50 apiece, had to be paid in wheat, "a bushel and a peck per head. " Seven persons were blessed on that same day, and the result was $17 50, or eight bushels and three pecks of wheat for the venerable Patriarch, who was, by the way, the father of the Thackeray of Mormonism, Apostle George A. Smith. Here is the first of the two blessings:

" Brother ———, I place my hands upon your head as a patriarch, and seal upon you a father's blessing, even all the blessings of Abraham, Isaac and Jacob, and all the priesthood that was placed upon the children of Jacob from everlasting. You are of the blood of Joseph that was sold into Egypt, and a lawful heir to all the blessings that was sealed upon the children of Joseph; you shall have faith in the priesthood to rebuke the waves of the sea, to turn rivers out of their courses, cause streams to break forth in the parched ground, and to gather the remnant of Jacob from among the Gentiles and lead them to Zion in spite of all opposition ; no power shall stay your hand; you shall cause many of the great and noble of the earth to *consecrate* their gain for the building up of Zion; you shall return to Zion with a great multitude of people when thou hast finished thy mission; you shall see thy Redeemer stand upon the earth in all his beauty and glory with all his twelve apostles at his right hand clothed with pillars of fire; shall share in all the blessings of His kingdom, with all your father's house. Amen."

After this "son of Joseph" comes his wife, a daughter of Abraham, through the loins of Joseph, of course.

"Sister ———, beloved of the Lord, in the name of Jesus of Nazareth, I place my hands upon thy head. As thou art a daughter of Abraham, through the loins of Joseph, I seal upon you the blessings of the new and everlasting covenant. You shall be blessed in your basket and store, in your house and about your habitation, be blessed with power in the priesthood to heal the sick and do miracles in the name of the Lord, have flocks and herds, horses and chariots, man and maid servants that will delight to obey thy voice. All these things shall be at thy disposal in the absence of thy companion. You shall be a 'mother in Israel.' Your sons and daughters shall be mighty men and women in the house of Jacob. Your name shall be had in honorable remembrance through your posterity from generation to generation. Your days shall be according to the desire of your heart, and you shall see all things fulfilled which the prophets have spoken concerning Zion, and inherit all the blessings and glories of the kingdom of Christ with all your father's household. Even so, Amen."

Permit me the closing remark, that this daughter of Abraham, who was to be a mother in Israel, had never a child.

XV.

HISTORY OF THE ENDOWMENTS.

Only a few days ago, passing near the gates of the Temple block, I asked a working man standing there:

" What kind of a temple is this? "

" A *Masonic* temple, sir," said the man, apparently belonging to the gang working on the building, which looks like a huge prison.

" For what is it intended? For what you call the endowments? "

" Yes, sir, for the endooments and other ordinances, baptisms, etc."

Mr. Webb has given me some very interesting details about the history of Mormon endowments. Joseph Smith, Brigham Young and John Taylor, were " Master Masons " when they came to Nauvoo.   Joseph drove the Elders into the order.   He received a charter from the Chief Lodge and had a fine Masonic Hall erected.   Through Joseph's

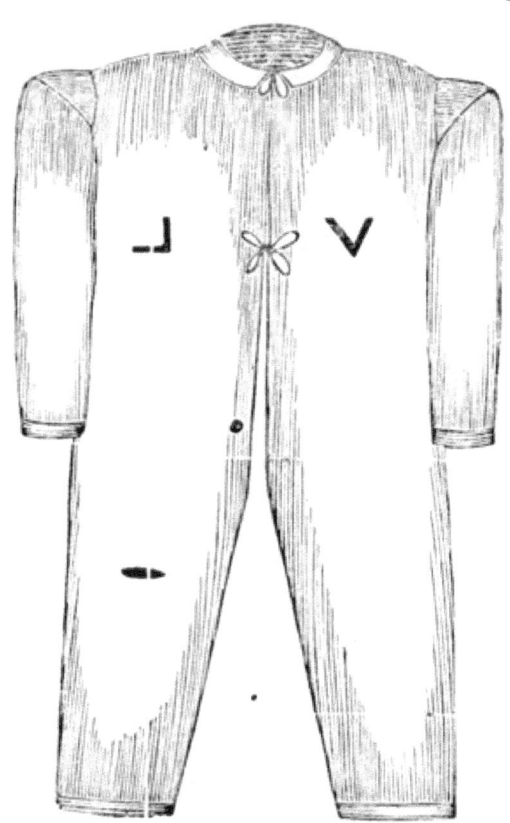

ADAM'S ENDOWMENT GARMENT.

influence nearly all male Mormons became Masons in a very short time.   Having succeeded in this, the prophet undertook to " restore the ancient order of things. "   A " revelation " put him in possession of a great secret, lost at the death of the architect of the temple of King Solomon. The organization of the Endowments was the result of this restoration of the ancient order.

The Nauvoo Endowments consisted of a long series of ceremonies, with oaths and grips, and covenants and signs in the manner of the Utah Endowments. Hence, Mormonism in Utah is to-day nothing but *Joseph's revised or restored Masonry.* Joseph made great changes in the Masonic rites, so that there remained but little of the original. But there was a change as from day to night between the Endowments in Kirtland and those in Nauvoo. In Kirtland they consisted in feet washing and anointings, taking of bread and wine, blessing, prophesying, and appari-

REVEALED FIG LEAF APRON.

tions of angels. The ceremonies lost most of the religious character and changed to Masonry. The anointings were about the only resemblance remaining. *

A third change in the Endowments was introduced by Brigham Young, after the death of Joseph and Hyrum Smith. He prescribed the terrible oaths binding the

---

* Joseph introduced in Nauvoo the ENDOWMENT GARMENTS, "worn by Adam in Paradise" and used by every "good" Utah Mormon day and night. Desdemona Fullmer, one of Joseph's spiritual wives—she died here last winter, poor and neglected—made for many years a scant living by making Endowment Garments after the pattern *revealed to Brother Joseph by the Lord.* Her "fig leaf aprons" were highly valued by Mormon *connoiseurs.* Poor Desdemona died, fixed in the faith, in the VI. ward. Wm. Clayton names her in his Leporello-Register, see p. 96.

brethren to avenge the blood of the prophets *on this nation* and to teach this to their children as a sacred duty. I shall deal with this treasonable feature of the Mormon Endowment in Vol. II. of this work.   Suffice here the remark, that it is not only denied by all "good" Mormons, but even by "apostates" who consider themselves bound by those quasi-Masonic oaths and do not wish to hurt the feelings or injure the social or legal position of the "brethren" or themselves.   Statements of this kind, some of them made in public speeches, have done yeoman service in deceiving the world as to the true character of this "church," which in its real essence is nothing but a secret criminal conspiracy for the purpose of defying the laws and keeping up a system radically inimical to republican institutions.

MAN'S ENDOWMENT CAP.

Thousands and thousands have "got their Endowments" in the Salt Lake "House," the well-known two-story adobe building in the Temple block.   This sinister little breeding-place for treason and polygamy is now deserted, but the three temples in the Territory, especially the one is Logan, are at full blast with the "work of God."   The Endowments and sealings given there bind many and many dupes every week to blind obedience towards the priesthood, to hatred against the United States, and to shame and misery in the form of "celestial marriage;" for it is a notorious fact that polygamous marriages, though more secret than ever, are still performed, and even more numerously than ever.   I am informed from a most reliable source that John Taylor, George Q. Cannon and Joseph F. Smith, the latest representatives of "Father, Son and Holy Ghost," have fine accommodations in the Logan temple with the best of furniture and carpets to be got for tithing-money, and rare plants in abundance. About thirty women "work" in the temple, most of them young, of course. They get baptized for any amount of "the dead," at 15 cents a soul. They go for you through the Endowments as "proxies," for "four bits." And Eliza R. Snow is there, washing, anointing and blessing the sisters, whispering *celestial names* in their ears and promising them eternal glory as the price of polygamy. People go there to have their children sealed to them; otherwise, they would not have them in "all eternity;" and then the whole fam-

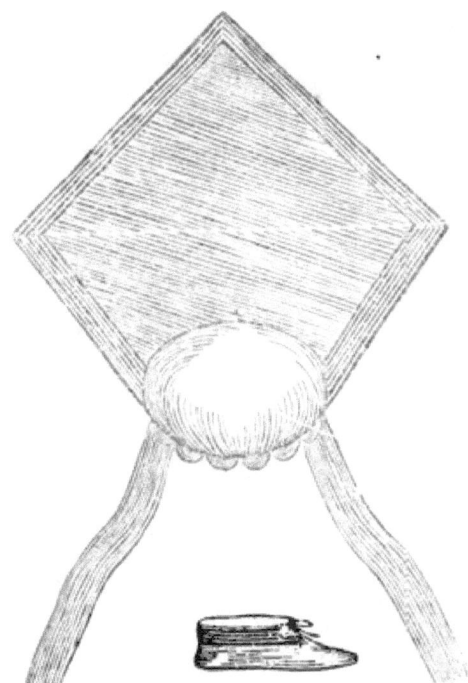

WOMAN'S CAP AND SLIPPER.

ilies get sealed to "Brother Taylor," to make sure of enjoying all the advantages of *his* "exceeding weight of glory." The temple makes lots of money. Even the brethren have to pay from two to five dollars for the simple going through as visitors. You cannot go through in your ordinary shoes, and a pair of immaculate linen slippers, as prescribed by revelation, costs $2 50.

Yes, they are turned into veritable "Templars" now: brother Taylor is there, blessing and sealing, and so is brother Cannon and brother Joseph F. Smith, son of prophet Hyrum, and a brute of the William Smith, Orson Hyde and Parley Pratt type. The whole nest of conspirators could be taken hold of at one grasp, but President Cleveland and Congress have other fish to fry, you see. Hence the wonderful amount of "no confidence at all in the serious intentions of this government" with all true friends of this territory, especially since the informal ousting of the "best governor Utah ever had," Eli H. Murray. That's what straight loyal and sensible people call Murray and will always call him.

XVI.

THE MORMON PROPHETESS.

I have given, now and then, a sample of the scientific discoveries of Mr. Tullidge, the special Mormon "historian." Not satisfied with having made a new Abraham of old Micawber Smith and a new Savior of Joe, he discovers Milton in petticoats in "our beloved sister, Eliza R. Snow, Zion's poetess." Says the Mormon Columbus of a new world of discoveries:

"Her influence in the Church of the Saints, through the medium of her holy sentiments and elevated thoughts, has been like a pure stream from a heavenly fountain. Her life has been of the divine cast in all its phases, and her sublime devotion to her God, coupled with that saintly meekness which has ever characterized her, is like her poetic genius, *Hebraic* in tone and quality. But she is something more than a mere poetess. She is also of the prophetess and priestess type. There are only two of the Latter-day Church who pre-eminently possess this triple quality, and they are Parley P. Pratt, who may be termed the Mormon Isaiah, and Eliza R. Snow."

And may not brother Tullidge be "termed" the

Mormon Homer? He feels keenly that Eliza is superior to all Gentile poetasters:

"We have Shakespeare, Byron, Shelley, Burns; but they are both Gentile and modern in their variety and tone."

Yes, "we have them," but they are all wretched "damned Gentiles," after all, not a drop of Abraham's blood in the whole lot. How sad it makes one, though, to see bitter apostates and ungodly Gentiles unite in slandering such a personification of talent and virtue! All decent and clear-headed people I have met in this territory consider "the divine cast in all its phases" as nothing but the fanaticism of the worst of *female roosters* that has roped into polygamy innumerable victims, men and women, and been, since the early times of the "church," altogether one of the most pernicious and re- pulsive figures of the imposture and its history, dreaded and despised by Emma Smith and all true wives and mothers in Mormondom up to this day.

Let me quote now some of the emanations of our "He- braic" genius, or *genus*, to use one of the happiest ex- pressions of Joseph Smith, Senior :

"Vermont, a land much fam'd for hills and snows
And blooming cheeks, may boast the honor *of*
The prophet's birth-place.

"Ere ten summers' suns
Had bound their wreath upon his youthful brow,
His father with his family remov'd;
And in New York, Ontario County, since
Called Wayne, selected them a residence;
First in Palmyra, then in Manchester."

I see lots of "genus" in this, Hebraic and other- wise. Prophetess Eliza is the affinity of Prophet Joseph, no doubt. Genus will always thrill responsive to *genus*. But here is more of it, in a poem on the New Year, 1852 :

"Its introduction bears the impress *of*
The Past, and casts its bold reflection *on*
The Future. Time's broad bosom heaves—on, on
Fast moves the billowy tide of change, that *in*
Its destination will o'erwhelm the mass
Of the degen'rate governments on earth,
And introduce Messiah's peaceful reign."

The year 1853 gets likewise a grand Hebraic welcome. from which I quote:

> " And verily
> The present, past and future are entwin'd
> So closely in their bonds of fellowship·—
> So firmly wedded each to other, *that*
> The mind must penetrate and circumscribe
> The deep, connecting intimacy *of*
> Those strange, mysterious occurrences
> Which sometimes most abruptly introduce
> Themselves into life's moving sceneries,
> And like a mighty engine, acting *in*
> The centre of the grand machinery
> Of earth's events, produce those features *which*
> Will form the data for all future time."

But one thing surprises me painfully. Can it be that
Eliza, the venerable Eve of the temple, indulges in the
vicious habit of *smoking?* She sings:

> " We'd better live in tents *and smoke*
> Than wear the cursed Gentile yoke,
> We'd better from our country fly
> Than by mobocracy to die."

I am myself an awful smoker, so I can appreciate re-
sults of the habit like this:

> " Though we fly from vile aggression,
> We'll maintain our pure profession,
> Seek a peaceable possession,
> Far from Gentiles and oppression."

Now isn't this just like Milton? It is even finer and
older than Hebrew; it looks exactly like *reformed Egyptian* poetry, translated by peepstone or Urim and Thummim, "of which the knowledge has been lost." Read
it over again, brother Tullidge, and tell me whether I
am wrong, after all.

XVII.

OLD JOE AND OLD LUCY.

Mrs. Dr. Horace Eaton, who has resided for thirty-two years in Palmyra, New York, makes the following highly interesting remarks about Lucy Smith:

"As far as Mormonism was connected with its reputed founder, Joseph Smith, always called 'Joe Smith,' it had its origin in the brain and heart of an ignorant, deceitful mother. Joe Smith's mother moved in the lowest walks of life, but she had a kind of mental power, which her son shared. With them both the imagination was the commanding faculty. It was vain, but vivid. To it were subsidized reason, conscience, truth. Both mother and son were noted for a habit of extravagant assertion. They would look a listener full in the eye, and, without confusion or blanching, would fluently improvise startling statements and exciting stories, the warp and woof of which were alike sheer falsehood. Was an inconsistency alluded to, nothing daunted, a subterfuge was always at hand. As one old man, who said to me, 'You can't face them down. They'd lie and stick to it.' Many of the noblest specimens of humanity have arisen from a condition of honest poverty; but few of these from one of dishonest poverty. Mrs. Smith used to go to the houses of the village and do family washings. But if the articles were left to dry upon the lines, and not secured by their owners before midnight, the washer was often the winner—and in these nocturnal depredations she was assisted by her boys, who favored in like manner poultry yards and grain bins. Her son Joe never worked save at 'chopping bees' and 'raisings,' and then whiskey was the impetus and the reward. The mother of the high-priest of Mormonism was *superstitious* to the last degree. The very air she breathed was inhabited by 'familiar spirits that peeped and wizards that muttered.' She turned many a penny by tracing in the lines of the open palm the fortunes of the inquirer. All ominous signs were heeded. No work was commenced on Friday. The moon over the left shoulder portended calamity; the breaking of a mirror, death. Even in the old Green Mountain State, before the family emigrated to the Genesee country (the then West), Mrs. Smith's mind was made up that one of her sons should be a prophet. The weak father agreed with her that Joseph was the "genus" of their nine children. So it was established that Joseph should be the prophet. To such an extent did the mother impress this idea upon the boy, that all the instincts of childhood were restrained. He rarely smiled or laughed. 'His looks and thoughts were always downward bent.' He never indulged in the demonstrations of fun, since they would not be in keeping with the profound dignity of his allotted vocation. His mother inspired and aided him in every scheme of duplicity and cunning. All acquainted with the facts agree in saying that the evil spirit of Mormonism dwelt first in Joe Smith's mother.

" Bad books had much to do with the origin of Mormonism. Joe Smith could read. He could not write. His two standard volumes were 'The Life of Stephen Burroughs,' the clerical scoundrel, and the autobiography of Capt. Kidd, the pirate. This latter work was eagerly and often perused. There was a fascination to him in the charmed lines :

> " My name was Robert Kidd,
>   As I sailed, as I sailed,
> And most wickedly I did,
> And God's laws I did forbid,
>   As I sailed, as I sailed."

Dr. McIntyre, who was, according to old Lucy, " the family physician " of the Smiths, testifies that Joseph Smith, Senior, was a drunkard, a liar * and a thief, and his house a perfect brothel. The new Abraham ran a little beer shop (with peanuts) in Palmyra, for a year or two, and then "squatted" on a piece of land belonging to some minor heirs. The Smiths did but little in the way of clearing, fencing and tilling. Their farming was done in a slovenly, half-way, profitless manner. They made a living by selling cord-wood, black ash baskets, birch brooms, maple sugar and cakes and root beer on public days. Most of the time of the boys was spent in trapping musk rats, fishing, hunting, digging out wood-chucks and loafing around stores and shops in the village. It was observed by all that Joseph was always the leader in enterprises of this kind, but never did any of the real work himself. As money-digger he observed the same comfortable rule.

---

* Purley Chase, brother of Willard, of Palmyra, New York, in a letter dated Rollin, Mich., April 3d, 1879, says : " When Smith first told of getting the book of plates he said it would tell him how to get hidden treasures in the earth ; and his father, soon after they got the plates, came in to my mother's one morning, just after breakfast, and told that Joe had a book and *that it would tell him how to get money that was buried in the ground*, and that he also found a pair of EYE-GLASSES on the book by which he could interpret it, and that the glasses were as big *as a breakfast plate ;* and he said that if the angel Gabriel should come down and tell him he could not get this hidden treasure, HE WOULD TELL HIM HE WAS A LIAR."

XVIII.

NAUVOO CITY ORDINANCES.

The following very liberal-sounding ordinance is the one alluded to in the *Expositor* (See p. 157). It may not look at first sight as a means of abridging the *freedom of speech*, but its vague expressions make it only too easy to use it as such, and a city council like the one we have seen in operation would surely not hesitate to punish, according to it, all offenders who dared to *speak evil* of the prophet or any member of the priesthood. Here is the ordinance :

" Be it ordained by the city council of the City of Nauvoo, that the Catholics, Presbyterians, Methodists, Baptists, Latter-Day Saints, Quakers, Episcopalians, Universalists, Unitarians, *Mohammedans*, and all other religious sects and denominations whatever, shall have toleration and equal privileges in this city; and should any person be guilty of RIDICULING, ABUSING OR OTHERWISE DEPRECIATING another, in consequence of his religion, or of disturbing or interrupting any religious meeting within the limits of this city, he shall, on conviction thereof before the Mayor, or Municipal Court, be considered a disturber of the public peace and fined in any sum not exceeding five hundred dollars, or imprisonment not exceeding six months, *or both*, at the discretion of said Mayor or Court. Passed March 1, 1841.

JOHN C. BENNETT, *Mayor.*

JAMES SLOAN, *Recorder.*

I quote now from "an act to incorporate the city of Nauvoo," drafted by Dr. Bennett. He was sent as delegate to Springfield, to urge the passage of the act through the legislature, and he succeeded easily by promising Mormon support to the leaders of both political parties :

Sec. 11. The City Council shall have power and authority to make, ordain, establish and execute all such ordinances, NOT REPUGNANT TO THE CONSTITUTION OF THE UNITED STATES, OR OF THIS STATE, as they may deem necessary for the peace, benefit, good order, regulation, convenience and cleanliness of said city . . . "

It is well known how the Mormon casuists interpreted this section. The city could, according to them, pass no ordinances repugnant to the *Constitution* of the United

States or the State of Illinois, but it could ordain things repugnant to the LAWS of both!

Sec. 16. The Mayor and Aldermen shall be conservators of the peace within the limits of said city, and shall have all the powers of Justices of the Peace therein, both in civil and criminal cases arising under the LAWS OF THE STATE.

Sec. 17. The Mayor shall have exclusive jurisdiction in all cases arising under the ordinances of the corporation; appeals may be had from any decision or judgment of said Mayor or Aldermen, arising under the ordinances of the corporation; appeals may be had from any decision or judgment of said Mayor or Aldermen, arising under the city ordinances, to the MUNICIPAL COURT, which shall be composed of the Mayor as Chief Justice and the Aldermen as Associate Justices. . . The Municipal Court shall have power to grant WRITS OF HABEAS CORPUS under the ordinances of the City Council.

If the prophet has wronged you as mayor, he will set you all right as " chief justice " of the Municipal Court, no doubt. Now comes the Nauvoo " University :"

Sec. 24. The City Council may establish and organize an institution of learning within the limits of the city, for the teaching of the arts, sciences and learned professions, to be called the "*University of the City of Nauvoo*," which institution shall be under the control and management of a board of trustees, consisting of a Chancellor, Registrar and twenty-three Regents, etc.

After the sciences and arts of peace, the frowning of Mars :

Sec. 25. The City Council may *organize the inhabitants* of said city, subject to military duty, into a body of INDEPENDENT military men to be called the NAUVOO LEGION, the Court Martial of which shall be composed of the commissioned officers of said Legion and constitute the *law-making department*, with full powers and authority to make, ordain, establish and execute all such laws and ordinances as may be considered necessary for the benefit, government and regulation of said Legion ; Provided, said Court Martial shall pass no law or act repugnant to or inconsistent with the Constitution of the United States or of this State. . . Said Legion shall perform the same amount of military duty as is now or may be hereafter required of the regular militia of the State, and shall be at the disposal of the MAYOR in executing the laws and ordinances of the city corporation and the laws of the State, and at the disposal of the Governor for the public defense, and the execution of the laws of the State or of the United States, and shall be entitled to their proportion of the PUBLIC ARMS : and Provided, also, that said Legion shall be EXEMPT FROM ALL OTHER MILITARY DUTY.

It is very interesting to see how Joseph *interpreted* this section of the city charter. Says he, in a "general order," dated May 4, 1841 :

"The officers and privates belonging to the Legion are exempt from all military duty not required by the legally constituted authorities thereof. They are, therefore, *expressly inhibited* from performing any military services not ordered by the general officers or directed by the court martial."

Joseph based this impudent interpretation on the opinion of Senator S. A. Douglas, the "able and profound jurist, politician and statesman," from which I quote the following, to show how the demagogues of the time tried to help the new Mahomet in his schemes :

> "I have examined so much of the Nauvoo city charter and legislative acts as relate to the Nauvoo Legion, and am clearly of opinion that any citizen of Hancock County who may attach himself to the Nauvoo Legion has all the privileges which appertain to that INDE-PENDENT military body, and is *exempt from all other military duty*, and cannot, therefore, be fined by any military or civil court for neglecting or refusing to parade with any other military body, or under the command of any officers who are not attached to the Legion."

You see that a city charter like this is a grand shield in the hands of unscrupulous men. But it was found to be too weak a protection for Joseph and his friends. It had been approved by Governor Carlin, December, 16, 1840. About eighteen months later the prophet's city council passed the following

ORDINANCE
Regulating the mode of proceeding in cases of habeas corpus, before the Municipal Court :

Sec. 1. Be it ordained by the City Council of the city of Nauvoo, that in all cases where any person or persons shall at any time hereafter be arrested or under arrest, in this city, under ANY WRIT OR PROCESS ; and shall be brought before the Municipal Court of this city, by virtue of a writ of habeas corpus, the Court shall in EVERY such case have power and authority and are hereby required to examine into the ORIGIN, VALIDITY and LEGALITY of the writ or process under which such arrest was made, and if it shall appear to the Court, upon sufficient testimony, that said writ or process was ILLEGALLY OR NOT LEGALLY issued, or did not proceed from proper authority, then the Court shall DISCHARGE the prisoner from under said arrest; but if it shall appear to the Court that said writ or process had issued from proper authority, and was a legal process, the Court shall then PROCEED AND FULLY HEAR THE MERITS OF THE CASE upon which such arrest was made, upon such evidence as may be produced and sworn before said Court, and shall have power to adjourn the hearing from time to time in their DISCRETION . . ."

Sec. 2. And be it further ordained, that if upon investigation it shall be proven before the Municipal Court, that the writ or process has been issued either through private pique, malicious intent, religious or other persecution, falsehood or misrepresentation, contrary to the Constitution of the State, or of the U. S., the said writ or process shall be quashed and considered of no force or effect, and the prisoner or prisoners shall be released and discharged therefrom.

Sec. 3. And be it also further ordained, that in the absence, sickness, debility or other circumstances disqualifying or preventing the Mayor from officiating in his office as Chief Justice of the Municipal Court, the aldermen present shall appoint one from amongst them to act as Chief Justice pro tempore.

Sec. 4. This ordinance to take effect, and be in force, from and after its passage.

HYRUM SMITH,
Vice Mayor and President pro tempore.

JAMES SLOAN,
    Recorder.
Passed, August 8, 1842.

This is as comfortable in the line of justice as Mormonism is in the line of religion. If Brigham or Kimball get arrested they are brought before His Honor Joe, and if Joe is arrested, they bring him before Hyrum, Brigham or Kimball, and those learned justices look into the *merits* of the case and discharge the prisoner. They seal, ordain, anoint, bless, consecrate, marry, divorce and discharge each other. The wicked Gentiles of Illinois had smelt a rat for a good while, but now the smell became rather too distinct. Said the *Sangamo Journal* of Sept. 2, 1842:

"We copy the above ordinance in order to show our readers the barefaced effrontery with which the holy brotherhood at Nauvoo set at defiance the civil authorities of the State. No man having claims to even an ordinary share of common sense can ever believe that there is the least shadow of authority in the City Council of Nauvoo to pass such an ordinance as the above; indeed *the Legislature* of this State *has not the power to do it.* The City Charter gives to the Municipal Court power to issue writs of *Habeas Corpus.* Evidently this power 'is only granted in reference to cases of arrest under the *municipal laws* and, by the most latitudinarian construction, cannot be made to extend to cases of an arrest under the LAWS OF THE STATE, but this Mormon ordinance not only extends to ALL cases of arrest, but sets the LAWS OF THE UNITED STATES at defiance, by giving authority to the Municipal Court to enquire into the CAUSES of the arrest — a power which even the Legislature of the State cannot confer.

" By the Constitution and the laws of the U. S., the governor of this State is bound to deliver up fugitives from justice on the requisition of the governor of any other State; and the judiciary of this State have no right to enquire, under any circumstances, into anything further than the sufficiency of the writ on which the arrest is made. If this is in due form and properly served, there is no power for any tribunal in this State to make any further inquiry. The guilt or innocence of the accused must be determined by the courts of the State from whence the requisition issued, and any court of law which institutes any inquiry of this nature oversteps the boundaries of its jurisdiction and openly sets at defiance the laws of the land.

" If these things are suffered to pass unheeded by the authorities of the State, who is safe whether in person or property? A Mormon cut-throat may take the life of one of our citizens and, returning to the City of the Saints, set at defiance the laws of the land. We believe that the Mormon Church is just such a body as can be shelter to every blackleg, cut-throat or horse-thief, who chooses to take refuge amongst them. While under the protection of Joe, who can harm them? What means has an officer of either discovering or arresting a man held by a band who regard *the law of the land as secondary to the commands of their prophet?*"

All this abuse comes from not understanding the value of Mormon *pearls.* Was this ordinance not given, like all other revelations, for the holiest of purposes? Who cares for the *technical niceties* of the law of Illinois or the United States, when the Kingdom of God has to be established? The above article was written by an " infernal scoundrel" of the Goodwin or Nelson type, just to please the *wicked,* who, at that very moment, were charging the prophet and brother Rockwell with an attempt on the life of Governor Boggs. Only the wicked can believe that the above ordinance, passed three months after the attempt of assassination, was just the thing to shield my servant Joseph and Elder Rockwell from the " corrupt officers" of Missouri. Yes, only the ungodly could believe such hell-devised slanders. Was not Joseph the man " who inspired the whole with an archangel's genius,"* his hotel, his

---

*Tullidge, Joseph, p. 108.

store, his bank, his harem, the Municipal Court, the Danites, and all the rest of it?

* * *

XIX.

NAUVOO CITY OFFICERS.

Mayor : John C. Bennett; *Recorder :* James Sloan; *Attorney :* Sidney Rigdon ; *Notary Public :* E. Robinson ; *Marshal :* H. G. Sherwood ; *Marshal ad interim :* D. B. Huntington ; *Treasurer :* John S. Fulmer ; *Surveyor :* A. Ripley ; *Assessor and Collector :* Lewis Robison ; *Supervisor of Streets :* James Allred ; *Weigher and Sealer :* Theodore Turley ; *Market Master :* Stephen Markham ; *Sexton :* W. D. Huntington.

FIRST WARD.

Aldermen: Samuel H. Smith, Hiram Kimball ; *Councilors :* John P. Green, Vinson Knight, Orson Pratt, Willard Richards ; *High Constable :* D. B. Huntington.

SECOND WARD.

Aldermen : N. K. Whitney, Orson Spencer ; *Councilors :* Hyrum Smith, Lyman Wight, Wilford Woodruff, John Taylor ; *High Constable :* George Morey.

THIRD WARD.

Aldermen : Daniel H. Wells, Gustavus Hills ; *Councilors :* John T. Barnett, C. C. Rich, Hugh McFall, H. C. Kimball ; *High Constable :* Lewis Robison.

FOURTH WARD.

Aldermen : William Marks, George W. Harris ; *Councilors :* Joseph Smith, Wilson Law, Brigham Young, William Law ; *High Constable :* W. D. Huntington.

The City Council consists of the Mayor, Aldermen

and Councilors, and sits on the first and third Saturday of every month, commencing at 6 o'clock, p. m.

MUNICIPAL COURT.

Chief Justice : John C. Bennett ; *Associate Justices :* Samuel H. Smith, Hiram Kimball, N. K. Whitney, Orson Spencer, Daniel H. Wells, Gustavus Hills, William Marks, George W. Harris ; *Clerk :* James Sloan.

The Municipal Court sits on the first Monday in every month, commencing at 10 o'clock, a. m.

MAYOR'S COURT.

This is the Criminal Court of the city, and sits at such times as the business of the city requires, the Mayor presiding.

(*Times and Seasons*, Vol. III., p. 638.)

XX.

THE NAUVOO UNIVERSITY.

BOARD OF REGENTS.

Chancellor : Gen. John C. Bennett, M. D. ; *Registrar :* Gen. William Law ; *Regents :* Gen. Joseph Smith, Sidney Rigdon, Esq., Attorney-at-law, Gen. Hyrum Smith, Rev. William Marks, Rev. Samuel H. Smith, Daniel H. Wells, Esq., Bishop N. K. Whitney, Gen. Charles C. Rich, Capt. John T. Barnett, Gen. Wilson Law, Rev. John P. Greene, Bishop Vinson Knight, Isaac Galland, M. D., Judge Elias Higbee, Rev. Robert D. Foster, M. D., Judge James Adams, Rev. Samuel Bennett, M. D., Ebenezer Robinson, Esq., Rev. John Snider, Rt. Rev. George Miller, Zenos M. Knight, M. D., Rev. John Taylor and Rev. Heber C. Kimball.

FACULTY.

James Kelly, A. M., *President;* Orson Pratt, A. M., *Professor of Mathematics and English Literature;* Orson Spencer, A. M., *Professor of Languages;* Sidney Rigdon, D. D., *Professor of Church History.*

PROFESSOR ORSON PRATT.

SCHOOL WARDENS FOR COMMON SCHOOLS.

Wardens of First Ward: John P. Greene, N. K. Whitney, A. Morrison.

Wardens of Second Ward: C. C. Rich, Wilson Law, Elias Higbee.

Wardens of Third Ward: Daniel H. Wells, R. D. Foster, S. Winchester.

Wardens of Fourth Ward: Vinson Knight, William Law, E. Robinson.

So they are A. M., D. D., Professors, Chancellors,

Presidents, Reverends and Right Reverends, a whole collection of "self-made" titles. Let me give a decree of mighty Chancellor Bennett, dated August 10, 1841:

"The Regents of the University of the City of Nauvoo will convene at the office of General Joseph Smith on Saturday, Sept. 4, at half past ten o'clock, A. M., for the transaction of important business. Punctual attendance is requested.

"The Department of English Literature is now in successful operation under the supervision of Professor Orson Pratt — a gentleman of varied knowledge and extensive acquirements, who is admirably qualified for the full execution of the high trust reposed in him, as an able and accomplished teacher. In this department a general course of mathematics, including Arithmetic, Algebra, Geometry, Conic Sections, Plane Trigonometry, Mensuration, Surveying, Navigation, Analytical, Plane and Spherical Trigonometry, Analytical Geometry and the Differential and Integral Calculus :— Philosophy ;— Astronomy ;— Chemistry ;— etc. etc., will be extensively taught.

"*Tuition:*— Five Dollars per quarter, payable semi-quarterly, in advance."

JOHN C. BENNETT,
Chancellor.

WILLIAM LAW,
Registrar.

XXI.

THE NAUVOO LEGION.

In Napoleon Bennett's time the Nauvoo Legion comprised "between two and three thousand well-disciplined troops." It was divided in two cohorts or brigades, and these cohorts subdivided into regiments, battalions and companies. The organization was intended to represent a *Roman Legion*. Bennett gives the following names " of a few of the most accomplished, brave and efficient of the corps : "

GENERALS : George W. Robinson, Charles C. Rich, Davison Hibard, Hiram Kimball, W. P. Lyon, A. P. Rockwood. To this list add Generals Joseph and Hyrum, William and Wilson Law and Gen. Bennett, and you have the truly imposing array of *eleven* generals. Reverend, Doctor Sidney Rigdon, attorney-at-law and post-master, I think might have been permitted to make the full dozen. He had always blood in his eye. John D. Lee was Major in the Legion.

MAJOR JOHN D. LEE.

COLONELS: John F. Weld, Orson Pratt, Francis M. Higbee, Carlos Gove, Chauncey L. Higbee, James Sloan, George Schindle, Amasa Lyman, D. B. Smith, George Coulson, Alexander McRae, Jacob B. Backenstos, L. Woodworth — thirteen colonels.

CAPTAINS: C. M. Kreymyer, Darwin Chase, John F. Olney, Justus Morse, William M. Allred, L. N. Scovil, Charles Allen, Marcellus Bates, Samuel Hicks — nine captains.

But those are only a *few* of the bravest, you see. Bennett doesn't name General Robert D. Foster, who is a pet aversion of his, so the real number of generals is an exact dozen. I extract now from "Ordinance No. 1" of the Court Martial of said Legion the following interesting sections:

Sec. 2. That from and after the 15th day of April next, it shall be the DUTY of every white male inhabitant of the city of Nauvoo, between eighteen and forty-five years of age, to enroll himself in some company of the Legion, by reporting himself to the captain thereof, within fifteen days; and every person neglecting or refusing to do so shall, on conviction thereof before a regular court martial, forfeit and pay the sum of one dollar for every subsequent fifteen days' neglect.

Sec. 4. That *no person whatever*, residing within the limits of the city of Nauvoo, of fifteen days' residence, between the ages of eighteen and forty-five years, excepting such as are exempted by the United States, shall be exempt from military duty, unless exempted by a special act of the Court Martial of the Legion, or a certificate of inability, under oath, signed by the Lieutenant-General, countersigned by the Surgeon-General, and recorded by the Major-General's WAR SECRETARY.

Sec 7. The staff of the Lieutenant-General shall consist of an Inspector-General with the rank of Major-General, a Drill officer, a Judge Advocate, and four Aids-de-camp, and a Herald and Armor-Bearer, with the rank of Captain.

Sec. 8. The staff of the Major-General shall consist of an Adjutant-General, a Surgeon-General, a Cornet, a Quarter-Master-General, a Commissary-General, a Pay-Master-General, a Chaplain, two Assistant Inspectors General, four Aids de-camp, and a War Secretary, with the rank of Colonel; a Quarter-Master, Sergeant, Sergeant-Major, a Chief Musician, with the rank of Major; and four Musicians, and a Herald and Armor-Bearer, with the rank of Captain.

Sec. 9. The staff of each Brigadier-General shall consist of two Aids-de camp, an Assistant Quarter-Master-General, an Assistant Commissary-General, and a Surgeon, with the rank of Lieutenant-Colonel; six Assistant Captains, with the rank of Major; and a Herald and Armor-Bearer, with the rank of Captain.

Sec. 10. The staff of each Colonel shall consist of an Adjutant, and a Quarter-Master-Sergeant and a Sergeant-Major, with the rank of Captain.

Sec. 11. Each Regiment shall be officered with a Colonel, a Lieutenant-Colonel, a Major and a company officer.

Sec. 12. Each company shall be officered with a Captain, three Lieutenants, five Sergeants, one Pioneer and four Corporals.

Sec. 13. The Lieutenant-General and the Major-General may, by their joint act, grant brevet commissions to such persons as may merit appointment and promotion at their hands.

Passed March 12, 1842.

JOSEPH SMITH,
Lieutenant-General and President of the Court Martial.

JOHN C. BENNETT,
Major-General and Secretary of the Court Martial.

XXII.

MISS NANCY RIGDON.

Dr. Bennett tells of Joe's attempt upon Nancy in his usual "Pistol" style. The facts themselves will not be doubted by the reader, after all he has heard of the Nauvoo Don Juan; they are, besides, warranted to be true by the testimony of Mrs. Pratt, who knew Nancy intimately and says that she was a very good, virtuous girl, and that Bennett's tale is true in all essential points. The main facts are as follows:

It was in the summer of 1841. Joe and Bennett were out riding over the lawn. Says the prophet to his bosom friend: "If you will assist me in procuring Nancy as one of my spiritual wives, I will give you five hundred dollars, or the best lot on Main street." Bennett, who was on very intimate terms with Rigdon and his family, refused. "But," said Joe, "the Lord has given her to me to wife. I have the blessings of Jacob, and there is no wickedness in it. It would be wickedness to approach her unless I had permission of the Lord; but as it is, it is as correct as to have a *legal* wife in a *moral* point of view." Joseph persisted in his plans, aided in their execution by two reliable friends, a Mrs. Hyde and Apostle Willard Richards. Dr. Bennett tried in vain to make Joe consider his obligations as a Master Mason: "Joseph, you are a Master Mason and Nancy is a Master Mason's daughter (like Mrs. Pratt); so stay your hand, or you will get into trouble."

Still Joe persisted, but Bennett warned the daughter of his friend. So Nancy was prepared when Joseph took her to the little celestial business office. The prophet locked the door, swore her to secrecy, and told her that she had long been the idol of his affections and that he had asked the Lord for her, but that if she had any scruples on the subject, he would *marry* her immediately; that *this would not prevent her from marrying any other per-*

son, and that all was lawful and right before God.* He
then attempted to kiss her and desired her to kiss him.
Nancy flew in a rage. She told the prophet she would
alarm the neighborhood if he did not open the door and
let her out immediately. In a day or two afterwards
apostle Richards handed Nancy a letter from the prophet,
written by Richards from Joe's dictation, and requested
her to burn it after reading. This letter is a perfect gem
in the line of oily rascal sophistry:

"Happiness is the object and design of our existence and will be
the end thereof, if we pursue the path that leads to it; and this path is
virtue, uprightness, faithfulness, holiness, and keeping all the commandments of God; but we cannot keep all the commandments without first knowing them, and we cannot expect to know all unless we
comply with or keep those we have already received. That which is
wrong under one circumstance may be and often is right under another. God said, Thou shalt not kill; at another time He said, Thou
shalt utterly destroy. This is the principle on which the Government
of Heaven is conducted, by revelation adapted to the circumstances
in which the children of the Kingdom are placed. Whatever God
requires is right, no matter what it is, although we may not see the
reason thereof till long after the events transpire. If we seek first the
Kingdom of God, all good things will be added. So with Solomon:
first he asked *wisdom*, and God gave it him, and with it every desire
of his heart, even things which might be considered abominable to all
who understand the order of Heaven *only in part*, but which in reality were right, because God gave and sanctioned them by SPECIAL REVE-
LATION. A parent may whip a child, and justly too, because he stole
an apple, whereas, if the child had asked for the apple and the parent
had given it, the child would have eaten it with a better appetite;
there would have been no stripes; all the pleasures of the apple would
have been secured, all the misery of stealing lost. This principle will
justly apply to all of God's dealings with His children. EVERYTHING
THAT GOD GIVES US IS LAWFUL AND RIGHT, and it is proper that we
shall ENJOY His gifts and blessings, whenever and wherever He is
disposed to bestow, but if we should seize upon those same blessings
and enjoyments without law, without revelation, without commandment, those blessings and enjoyments would prove cursings and vexa-
tions in the end and we should have to lie down in sorrow and wail-
ings of everlasting regret. But in *obedience* there is joy and peace
unspotted, unalloyed; and as God has designed our happiness He
never has, He never will institute an ordinance or give a command-

* "After the death of Joseph, Brigham Young told me that Joseph's
time on earth was short, and that the Lord allowed him privileges
that we could not have."—[Lee, Confession, p. 147.]

ment to His people that is not calculated in its nature to promote the happiness which He has designed and which will not end in the greatest amount of good and glory to those who become the recipients of His laws and ordinances. Blessings offered, but rejected, are no longer blessings, but become like the talent hid in the earth by the wicked and slothful servant. Our Heavenly Father is *more liberal in His views* and boundless in His mercies and blessings, than we are ready to believe or receive; He will be inquired of by His children; He says, ask ye and ye shall receive, seek ye and ye shall find; but if you will take that which is not your own, or which I have not given you, you shall be rewarded according to your deeds; but *no good thing* will I withhold from them who walk uprightly before Me and do My will in all things, who will listen to My voice and *to the voice of My servant*, whom I have sent; for I delight in those who seek diligently to know My precepts and abide in the LAW OF MY KINGDOM; for all things shall be made known unto them in Mine own due time and in the end they shall have joy."

I don't want anybody's testimony that this letter * is genuine; I feel it in every line, comparing it with Hyrum's jesuitical letter about the *mysteries* of the kingdom, the revelation on celestial marriage, the affidavits of Wm. Clayton, and other products of this holy-oil-refinery. Joe, Brigham and Kimball crawl up just in the same slimy path to the proud virtue of Martha Brotherton. It is the most disgusting Tartuffe business ever witnessed and Moliere would have made the greatest of his comedies out of it, had he lived in the Illinois Sodom.

The sequel of the story is well told in a letter from George W. Robinson, who was a very decent man according to Mrs. Pratt. Says he:

"Nancy repulsed him and left him with disgust. She came home and told her father [Sidney Rigdon] of the transaction, upon which Smith was sent for. He came. She told her tale in the presence of all her family and to Smith's face. *I was present.* Smith attempted to deny it at first and face her down with the lie; but she told the facts

---

* I am informed that on receiving Joe's letter from post boy, Apostle Richards, Nancy requested him to wait, while she retired to peruse it in secret. The patient doctor having waited an hour Nancy came back to him, letter in hand. She pretended to give it back, but with a sudden movement tore it to pieces and flung it into the stove. But she had in her retirement carefully *copied* it, and the next that was heard of it was in the columns of the Warsaw "*Signal,*" to the utter dismay of the prophet.

with so much earnestness, and the fact of a letter being present, which he had caused to be written to her and which he had fondly hoped was *destroyed*—all came with such force that he could not withstand the testimony; and he then and there acknowledged that *every word* of Miss Rigdon's testimony was *true*. Now for his excuse which he made for such a base attempt, and for using the name of the Lord in vain on that occasion : *He wished to ascertain whether she was virtuous or not*, and took that course to learn the facts ! "

This memorable visit of Joe's in Rigdon's house took place in June, 1841. High Priest George Miller, who was present when Nancy called the Lord's prophet a "cursed liar," screamed at the top of his voice : " *You must not harm the Lord's anointed ; the Lord will not suffer his anointed to fall !* " Could Moliere better this?

Captain Olney, another decent man who left the church because of Joe's abominations, declared in the *Sangamo Journal*, Sept. 14, 1842 :

" I wish to make a public withdrawal from the church of Latter Day Saints, as I cannot longer consent to remain a member of said church while polygamy, lasciviousness and adultery are practiced by some of its leaders. That *crimes of the deepest dye* are tolerated and practiced by them cannot be doubted. I have heard the circumstances of Smith's attack upon Miss Rigdon, from the family as well as from herself; and knowing her to be a young lady who sustains a good moral character, and also of undoubted veracity, I must place implicit confidence in her statement. The facts of Smith's wishing to marry her as a spiritual wife, of his attack upon her virtue, his teachings of his having the blessings of Jacob, etc., are TRUE. The letter published, purporting to be from Smith to Miss Rigdon, was not in Smith's handwriting, but in that of Dr. Willard Richards,* who officiated not only as scribe but *post boy* for the prophet, and who *did* say that he wrote the letter as dictated by Joseph Smith. George W. Robinson was formerly Joseph's secretary and general Church clerk and recorder, and I have heard Smith say that Robinson was *the*

---

* " Apostle Richards died in Salt Lake, many years afterwards. The quantities of whiskey he could stand were a caution to many a staunch expert in that line. He kept up here relations with *married* women to whom he had been sealed in Nauvoo. A choice lot of wives, left by him among his other moveable property, were " married " by a relative of his *en bloc*. Such a transfer of human cattle is called " proxy-marriage " by Mormon theologians. " Human cattle " is an ugly phrase, but it is Mormon enough, being an echo of Kimball's " cows."

bravest man in the Mormon Band and that he (Robinson) had not a drop of cowardly blood in his veins."

This Nancy story is typical from beginning to end; but what interests me most in it is that apostolic *post boy*, Dr. Richards. How eagerly he goes through all the phases of the wretched, holy-lackey-business! Can you doubt now, reader, that those apostolic slaves felt proud in the shame of their wives and daughters—can you fail to see that sin, vice and abomination were never, in all history, so closely united with abject slavery and negation of all that is manly and dignified as in Joe's holy city of Nauvoo?

XXIII.

THE LORD CORRECTS HIMSELF.

The Bible says God created man after his own image, but it seems rather man creates God after *his* image. Joseph Smith's and Brigham Young's "Lord" is a striking example of it. He has all the low passions of his prophets and even their abominable grammar. But he is "smart" at the same time, just like his prophets. He observes times bad and circumstances and adapts his *revelations* to them. You have seen the Lord's opinion about marriage in the earlier editions of the Book of *Doctrine and Covenants*, enjoining monogamy in the strongest terms. You can't find this article in the latest editions of this part of the *everlasting* gospel. The revelation on celestial marriage, given to Joseph July 12th, 1843, has taken its place.

Joseph was Brigham's original in this as in any other holy trick. Let me give a few examples of the manipulations of my servant Joseph:

Book of Commandments for the Government of the Church of Christ, Zion, Jackson County, Missouri, 1833.*

"If thou lovest me, thou shalt serve me and keep all my commandments; and behold, thou shalt *consecrate* ALL thy properties, that which thou hast unto me, with a covenant and a deed which cannot be broken ; and they shall be laid before the bishop of my church and two of the elders, such as he shall appoint and set apart for that purpose."

"And it shall come to pass, that he that sinneth and repenteth not shall be cast out, and SHALL NOT RECEIVE AGAIN that which he has CONSECRATED unto me : For it shall come to pass, that which I spake by the mouths of my prophets shall be fulfilled; for I will CONSECRATE THE RICHES OF THE GENTILES UNTO MY PEOPLE, which are of the house of Israel."

"And thou [Emma] needest not fear, for thy husband shall support thee FROM the church."

" O ! remember [Oliver Cowdery] these words and keep my commandments. Remember this is your gift. Now this is not all, for you have another gift, which is the gift of WORKING WITH THE ROD ; behold it has told you things ; behold there is no other power save God that can cause this ROD OF NATURE TO WORK IN YOUR HANDS, for it is the work of God ; and

Book of Doctrine and Covenants of the Church of Jesus Christ of Latter-day Saints, First Edition, 1835.

" If thou lovest me, thou shalt serve me and keep all my commandments. And behold, thou *wilt* REMEMBER THE POOR, and consecrate of thy properties for their support that which thou hast to impart unto them with a covenant and a deed which cannot be broken ; and inasmuch as ye impart of your substance unto the poor, ye will do it unto me, etc."

" He that sinneth and repenteth not shall be cast out of the church and shall not receive again that which he has CONSECRATED UNTO THE POOR AND NEEDY of my church, or in other words [!] unto me ; for as much as ye do it unto the least of these ye do it unto me ; for I will consecrate of the riches of THOSE WHO EMBRACE MY GOSPEL AMONG THE GENTILES unto the poor of my people who are of the house of Israel."

" And thou needest not fear, for thy husband shall support thee IN the church."

" O ! remember these words, and keep my commandments. Remember this is your gift. Now this is not all thy gift; for you have another gift, which is the GIFT OF AARON : behold, it has told you MANY things ; behold, there is no other power, save the power of God, that can cause THIS GIFT OF AARON TO BE WITH YOU ; therefore doubt not, for it is the

---

* Reprinted by the Salt Lake *Tribune* in 1884. A most valuable little volume.

therefore, whatsoever you shall ask me to tell you by that means, that will I grant unto you, that you shall know."

gift of God, and you shall hold it in your hands and do marvelous works; and no power shall be able to take it away out of your hands, for it is the work of God."

You see how the *Lord* avoids speaking of the *rod* in his revised edition, the *rod of nature* that *works* in Oliver's hand. That "rod" gives away too much of the hazel-witch, fortune-telling, and peeping business of the new Abraham and his family.

XXIV.

BROTHER BRIGHAM DAMNS SISTER EMMA.

"President Young" said in the Tabernacle, in the summer of 1874:

"Brother George A. Smith has been reading a little out of the revelation concerning celestial marriage, and I want to say to my sisters that if they lift their heels against this revelation *   * you will go to hell just as sure as you are living women. *Emma* took that revelation, supposing she had all there was: but Joseph had wisdom enough to take care of it, and he had handed the revelation to Bishop Whitney, and he wrote it all off. After Joseph had been to Bishop Whitney's he went home, and Emma began teasing for the revelation. Said she: 'Joseph, you promised me that revelation, and if you are a man of your word, you will give it to me.' Joseph took it from his pocket and said, 'take it.' She went to the fireplace and put it in, and put the candle under it and burnt it, and she thought that was the end of it. and SHE WILL BE DAMNED as sure as she is a living woman. Joseph used to say he would have her hereafter, *if he had to go to hell for her*, and he will have to go to hell for her s sure as he ever gets her."

XXV.

D. WHITMER ORDAINED JOSEPH'S SUCCESSOR.

In view of the independent stand taken by David Whitmer against the Danite craze in 1838 (see p. 191), the following hitherto unpublished fact is very interesting :

"On the 6th of July, 1834, in Clay County, Mo., Joseph Smith and Frederick G. Williams ordained David Whitmer President of the Stake of Zion, [Missouri]. Then Joe said the time had come when he must point out and ordain his successor. Said he : 'Some have supposed that Oliver Cowdery would be the man, but the Lord has made known to me that David Whitmer is the man.' Joe and Williams then stepped out and ordained David to be 'Prophet, Seer, Revelator and Translator and President of the whole Church' to be Joe's successor."

This statement comes from Dr. W. E. McLellin, one of the first twelve Mormon Apostles, who says he was present and saw it done. Joe had taken the cholera and thought he was going to die.

XXVI.

THE NAUVOO SERAGLIO.

After having been the Prophet's *alter ego* for eighteen months, John C. Bennett exposed him in a book and in public lectures. The book is "a holy terror," but my studies have convinced me that its disclosures are essentially true and reliable, and I have no good reason to doubt that part of them where the Doctor treats of the *secret regulations* introduced by Joe *for directing the relations of the sexes*. I introduce Bennett's own words :

"'The Mormon Seraglio is very strictly and systematically organized. It forms a GRAND LODGE, as it were, and is divided into three distinct orders or degrees.

"1.   THE CYPRIAN SAINTS.

"The members of the Female Relief Society have the power, when they know or even suspect that any Mormon female has, however slightly, lapsed from the straight path of virtue, of bringing her at once before the *Inquisition.* This body is solemnly organized in secret and select council, and by its members the poor terrified female is questioned and threatened until she confesses the crime she has committed. She is immediately, by the council, pronounced a *Cyprian,* and is excluded from any further connection with the Relief Society."

Bennett says that these women, branded as they are by the Relief Society, are at the service of the *trustworthy* members of the church.

"2.   THE CHAMBERED SISTERS OF CHARITY.

"This order comprises that class of females who indulge their propensities, whether *married or single,* by the express permission of the prophet. Whenever one of the Saints of the male sex becomes enamored of a female and she responds to the feeling, the loving brother goes to Holy Joe and states the case. It makes, by the by, no difference whatever *if one or both* parties are already provided with conjugal help-mates. The prophet gravely buries his face in his hat, in which lies his peep-stone, and inquires of the Lord what is His will and pleasure in the matter. Sometimes, when Joe wants the woman himself, an unfavorable answer is given ; but generally the reply permits the parties to follow the bent of their inclinations, which they do without further ceremony, though with a strict observance of *secrecy, on account of the Gentiles.* The result of this system is that not infrequently men having wives of their own are living with other women, and not infrequently with other men's wives. Families are estranged and separated and children neglected."

Bennett says that these "Sisters of Charity" were much more numerous than the *Cyprian Saints.*

"3. THE CONSECRATEES OF THE CLOISTER.

" This degree, also called *Cloistered Saints*, is composed of females, whether *married or unmarried*, who, by an express grant and gift of God, through his prophet, are *set apart and consecrated* for the benefit of particular individuals, as SECRET SPIRITUAL WIVES. They are accounted the special favorites of Heaven, and the most honorable among the daughters of Jacob. Their spiritual husbands are altogether from among the most eminent members of the Mormon church. This is the highest degree in the Harem and is held as the very acme of perfection. Its ranks are filled up in the following manner: When an apostle, high priest or elder conceives an affection for a female and he has satisfactorily ascertained that she experiences a mutual flame, he communicates confidentially to the prophet his *affaire de coeur*, and requests him to " inquire of the Lord whether or not it would be proper for him to take unto himself the said woman for his *spiritual wife*." Again, it is no obstacle whatever to this spiritual marriage *if one or both parties* should happen to have a husband or wife already united to them according to the laws of the land. * The prophet puts this queer question to the Lord, and if he receives an answer in the affirmative (which is always the case where the parties are in favor with Joe) the prophet, either in person or by a duly authorized administrator, proceeds to *consecrate* the sister in the following solemn manner:

"The parties assemble in the lodge room and place themselves kneeling before the altar. The administrator commences the ceremony by saying,—

"' You, separately and jointly, in the name of Jesus Christ the Son of God, do solemnly *covenant* and agree that you will not disclose any matter relating to the sacred act now in progress of consummation, whereby any *Gentile* shall come to the knowledge of the secret purposes of this order, or whereby the Saints may suffer *persecution;* your lives being the forfeit.'

" After the bow of assent is given by each of the pair, the administrator then proceeds—

---

* It is a chief tenet of Mormon theology that *no marriages except those performed by the Mormon priesthood are valid.*

"' In the name of Jesus Christ, and by the authority of the holy priesthood, I now *consecrate* you and set you apart by the imposition of my hands, as husband and wife, according to the laws of Zion and the will of God our Heavenly Father; for which especial favor you now agree to serve Him with a perfect heart and a willing mind, *and to obey His Prophet in all things* according to his divine will.'

"Again the nod of assent is given by the man and woman, and the administrator continues in a solemn and impressive manner—

"' I now *anoint* you with holy, consecrated oil, in the name of Jesus Christ and by the authority of the holy priesthood, that you may be fully and unreservedly consecrated to each other and to the service of God, and that with affection and fidelity you may nourish and cherish each other, so long as you shall continue faithful and true in the fellowship of the Saints; and I now pronounce upon you the blessings of Jacob, whom God honored and protected in the enjoyment of like special favors; and may the peace of Heaven, which passeth all understanding, rest upon you in time and in eternity!'

"The parties then rise and embrace each other, and the robe of investiture is placed upon and around them by the administrator, who says,—

"' According to the prototype, I now pronounce you ONE FLESH, in the name of the Father, and of the Son, and of the Holy Ghost. Amen.'

"The robe is then removed, and the parties leave the cloister, with generally a firm belief, at least on the part of the female, in the sacredness and validity of the ceremonial, and thereafter consider themselves as united in SPIRITUAL MARRIAGE, *the duties and privileges of which are in no particular different from those of any other marriage covenant.*"

I believe that Bennett helped Joe to organize this female order, and that the bustling little doctor, like Brigham Young, Heber C. Kimball, John Taylor and other members of the inner circle, freely availed himself of the blessings of Abraham and Jacob. Until fairly disproved I must believe *every word* of the *formulæ*, oaths, etc., given by Joe's accomplice and mentor, Bennett, as above. I find them to be in perfect harmony with the facts, documents and deductions presented in this volume.

The reader feels surely interested in the manner in which Joe and his friends treat that contemptible farce, the *Gentile* marriage. Joe's *liaisons*, were, as a rule, contracted with MARRIED women. I have given several examples, see pp. 55, 56. 66, 69. Some of the husbands found out very late that their wives had been exalted to the top round of the celestial ladder by the great annointer; I quote "Apostles" Orson Hyde and Erastus Snow, the latter of whom is said to have made this refreshing discovery only recently, but who was deep in other people's celestial secrets in Nauvoo, having kept there a house of refuge for celestial brides "in trouble." It has been a principle of this "church," and it is yet for all I know, that it is no good Saint's business to inquire into any doings of a man who has a *higher degree of priesthood* than himself. He may discover that the priest of high degree is on the most intimate terms with his (the lower priest's) wife—never mind; he has to say to himself: "It is none of my business; I was not able to *exalt* my wife; brother *X* assures her of a higher degree of glory: the Lord's name be praised !" I shall give more cases and names pertaining to this matter in Vol. II. of this work, and clinch this little chapter with a few choice remarks on marriage by Brother Brigham, "preached" in 1874:

"I have said a number of times, and I will say again to you ladies who want to get a bill of divorce from your husbands, because they do not treat you right, or because you do not exactly like their ways, there is a principle upon which a woman can leave a man, but if the man *honors his priesthood* it will be pretty hard work for you to get away from him. If he is just and right, serves God and is full of justice, love, mercy and truth, he will have the power that is sealed upon him, and will do what he pleases with you. When you want to get a bill of divorce you had better wait and find out whether the Lord is willing to give you one or not, and not come to me. I tell the brethren and sisters, when they come to me and want a bill of divorce, that I am ready to seal people and administer in the ordinances, and they are welcome to my services; but when they undertake to break the commandments and tear to pieces the doings of the Lord, I make them give me something. I tell a man he has to give me $10 if he wants a divorce. For what? My services? No, for his foolishness. If you want a divorce, *give me $10*, so that I can put it down in the book that such a man and such a woman have dissolved partnership. Do you think you have done so when you have obtained a bill of divorce? No, nor ever can if you are faithful to the *covenants* you have made. It takes a higher power than a bill of divorce to take a woman from a man who is a good man and honors his priesthood—IT MUST BE A MAN WHO POSSESSES A HIGHER POWER IN THE PRIESTHOOD, or else the woman is bound to her husband, and will be, forever and ever."

You see the chap *anointed with the higher priesthood* can "take a woman from a man"—and save and exalt her, but nobody else. This opens a grand field, truly, for prophetic and apostolic enterprise. It is a *religion*, you know, and, as never-lying George Q. Cannon has said and printed so often, "*we are the purest people.*" But to us unregenerated Gentiles and outsiders the whole thing, as from the first *secretly* taught and practiced by the leaders, will always seem the most consummate and devilish *system* of prostitution ever masked with the name and pretense of religion, in any epoch, any country!

XXVII.

A LOVE LETTER BY JOSEPH.

We have heard of Mrs. Emeline White, the tender-hearted lady, who could not stand the sight of a melancholy steamboat captain (see p. 60). She was the daughter of "General" Davison Hibard, and her sisters were like unto her, exceeding good-hearted. The Hibards lived at Commerce before the saints settled there and re-named the place *Nauvoo.* They were not vulgar Messalinas, these Hibard girls, but rather natural-born sisters of charity. They remind one of Jean Jacques Rousseau's generous friend, Mrs. Warren. Emeline was one of Joseph's pets. While yet trying to conquer her, he sent her a *billet doux*, which shows at once the ardor of his passion and his willingness to repay his Dulcinea's affection with the gifts and blessings of the Tithing Store. I would not miss this rich little bit of a document in my collection for anything :

"MY SWEET EMELINE.

"You know that my love for you, as David said to Jonathan, is 'wonderful, passing the love of women.' And how can that be? You know it is only *figurative.* I mean you have my most supreme affections [Poor Emma!] O that I had yours as truly! May I not hope that it will be so? At all events, be my friend, my best friend. If you want anything while I am gone, call upon either of the BISH-OPS — Vinson Knight or Alanson Ripley — and show them the signa-ture of 'Old White Hat,' and they will provide for you. Do not be afraid to receive anything from me, and these men are *confidential.* You need not fear to write me; and I do assure you that a few lines would be very consoling on a journey. Sign it 'Rosanna.' "

"Your humble servant,

"OLD WHITE HAT."

Now this is as charming as can be. The lion plays mouse. How condescending in a great Prophet thus to trifle with the divine source of revelation, the *Old White Hat.* It is Pythia joking about her tripod. I wonder to what high priest, apostle or secretary the *billet* was dic-tated; probably to Richards or Clayton, though may be to friend Bennett himself. Joe was then absent from Nauvoo, in Springfield, Ill., but there was surely some confidential "scribe" with him, such as were always on hand to take down the word of the *Lord.* "Joseph Smith," said Emma on her death-bed "could neither write nor dictate a coherent and well-worded letter." Bennett is evidently well posted in this matter, as he speaks of other love-letters addressed by the Prophet to "my sweet Em-eline."

Well, I am just "foolish" or "corrupt" enough to believe that the letter given above is entirely genuine. I see the prophetic earmarks, especially in the reference to Joe's faithful *bishops.* Vinson Knight was the wretch who dared to offer Mrs. Pratt his miserable Tithing House truck if she would hearken to the prophet's infamous prop-ositions. It is evident that it was one of Joe's *celestial* business rules, to offer to his intended victims either pro-visions from the "Lord's storehouse" or free board and lodging in the Lord's "house of boarding." Thus did this great fisher of *women* bait his gospel hook ! To illustrate the prophet's methods further, I quote from an affidavit of one Mrs. Melissa Schindle,* which I will not needlessly shock my readers by reproducing in full, the following characteristic passage :

> "And Joseph told her, that if she would consent she could make his house her home as long as she wished to do so, and that she would never want for anything it was in his power to assist her to. He then told her that she must never tell of his propositions to her, for he had *all* influence in that place [Nauvoo], and if she told he would ruin her character and she would be under the necessity of leaving."

This makes the whole infernal system clearer than ever. Same offers and same threats as used with Mrs. Pratt and so many other intended victims. And apostles, bishops, "lady" friends—they are all employees of the grand celestial institution which combines the features of harem and slave market ; while Brigham Young, H. C. Kimball, Willard Richards and a whole group of "ladies," do any service compatible with the character called *proxenetes* by the old Greeks. Does it not seem conceived by an "archangel's genius," the whole system, but an archangel with a mighty pair of arch-horns?

I see, now, where you have graduated, Brother Brigham : it was at the *Nauvoo University* of crime and deceit, of secret whisperings, of heartless selfishness and absolute unscrupulousness. Like Joe, you are fully steeped in these things and nobody is your friend, can be your friend, but such as would abet you in selfish, cunning, serpentine schemes. Joe and you, Brigham, were the two great salvation-merchants, and the price for "exaltation" was always the honour, the conscience, the virtue and purity, the money and property of your customers—the honor of man, the happiness of woman !

You learned to *rule* in secret Nauvoo, Brigham Young ; and you to *obey* secret orders, "martyr" John D. Lee ! Secrecy—it is the faith-word of Satan. Ah, the bloodstained ages rise before me burthened with it. "Had we not done in secret what we did," says Rigdon in 1844,

---

* Bennett, p. 253.

just before his first tools, the Smith brothers, were slaught-
ered, "the church would not have been where it is to-day."
To which I add, that *but for secret oaths and devil-covenants**
there would never have been a Mountain Meadows Massacre. Nice, is it not, O ye liberty-loving people of Utah,
squandering millions, wasting away life's glorious ener-
gies, fostering social and domestic hates and divisions,
murdering the intelligence and poisoning the patriotism
of rising generations with lying *catechisms*—still to perpetuate these silly *secret* mummeries of new revelation !

XXVIII.

"TWO MINUTES IN GOAL."

I insert here the well-known account of the death of
Joseph and Hyrum Smith, written on the very day by
Apostle Willard Richards, the only one of the four
attacked who received no wound. From this report it
would seem that Joseph fell from the window *dead*. It is
quite possible that the story of his being set up against
the well-curb has been manufactured later in order to make
the lynching a perfect cold-blooded Gentile murder. Certain it is, the *Times and Seasons* of 1844 makes no mention of the well-curb story, though W. Richards could
scarcely have helped witnessing the scene at the well-curb,
miraculous stroke of lightning and all, since he was at the
window. Moreover, but *three* gun-shot wounds are found
in the body of Joseph when it is washed and dressed for
burial.† There should have been seven (or at least four)

---

* Brigham Young preached in Provo after Lee's execution :
" Brother Lee went to hell — not because of the Mountain Meadows
Massacre, but for breaking his covenants and betraying the brethren."

† " Joseph was shot in the right breast, also under the heart in the
lower part of his bowels on the right side, and on the big wrinkle on
the back part of the right hip. One ball had come out at the right
shoulder blade."—*Deseret News*, Nov. 25, 1857.

wounds had the shooting at the well-curb been a fact. But hear the narrative of Apostle Richards:

"CARTHAGE, June 27th, 1844.

"A shower of musket-balls were thrown up the stairway against the door of the prison in the second story, followed by many rapid footsteps. While Generals Joseph and Hyrum Smith, Mr. Taylor and myself, who were in the front chamber, closed the door of our room against the entry at the head of the stairs, and placed ourselves against it, there being no lock on the door, and no ketch that was useable; the door is a common panel—and as soon as we heard the feet at the stairs' head, a ball was sent through the door, which passed between us, and showed that our enemies were desperadoes, and we must change our position. General Joseph Smith, Mr. Taylor and myself sprang back to the front part of the room, and General Hyrum Smith retreated two-thirds across the chamber, and directly in front of and facing the door.* A ball was sent through the door, which hit Hyrum on the side of the nose, when he fell backwards, extended at length, without moving his feet. From the holes in his vest (the day was warm and no one had a coat on but myself), pantaloons, drawers and shirt, it appears evident that a ball must have been thrown from without, through the window, which entered his back on the right side, and passing through, lodged against his watch, which was in his right vest pocket, completely pulverizing the crystal and face, tearing off the hands and mashing the whole body of the watch, at the same instant the ball from the door entered his nose. As he struck the floor he exclaimed, emphatically, '*I'm a dead man.*' Joseph looked twards him and responded, '*O dear! Brother Hyrum!*' and opening the door two or three inches with his left hand, discharged one barrel of a six-shooter (pistol) at random in the entry from whence a ball grazed Hyrum's breast, and entering his throat passed into his head, while other muskets were aimed at him and some balls hit him. Joseph continued snapping his revolver round the casing of the door into the space as before, three barrels of which missed fire, while Mr. Taylor, with a walking-stick, stood by his side and knocked down the bayonets and muskets which were constantly discharging through the doorway, while I stood by him, ready to lend any assistance, with another stick, but could not come within striking distance without going directly before the muzzles of the guns. When the revolver failed we had no more fire-arms, and expecting an immediate rush of the mob, and the doorway full of muskets—half-way in the room and no hope but instant death from within—Mr. Taylor

---

* "Joseph, Hyrum and Taylor had their coats off; Joseph sprang to his coat for his six shooter, Hyrum *for his single barrel*, Taylor for Markham's large hickory cane and Dr. Richards for Taylor's cane. . . . Hyrum was retreating back in front of the door and *snapped his pistol*, when a ball struck him in the left side of his nose, etc." *Deseret News*, Nov. 25, 1857.

rushed into the window, which is some fifteen or twenty feet from the ground. When his body was nearly on a balance, a ball from the door within entered his leg, and a ball from without struck his watch, a patent lever, in his vest pocket, near the left breast, and smashed it in 'pi,' leaving the hands standing at 5 o'clock, 16 minutes and 26 seconds— the force of which ball threw him back on the floor, and he rolled under the bed which stood by his side, where he lay motionless, the mob from the door continuing to fire upon him, cutting away a piece of flesh from his left hip as large as a man's hand, and were hindered only by my knocking down their muzzles with a stick; while they continued to reach their guns into the room, probably left-handed, and aimed their discharge so far around as almost to reach us in the corner of the room to where we retreated and dodged, and then I recommenced the attack with my stick again. Joseph attempted, as the last resort, to leap the same window from whence Mr. Taylor fell, when two balls pierced him from the door, and one entered his right breast from without, and he fell outward, exclaiming, *'O Lord my God!'* As his feet went out of the window my head went in, the balls whistling all around. He fell on his left side a DEAD man. At this instant the cry was raised, *'He's leaped the window,'* and the mob on the stairs and in the entry ran out. I withdrew from the window, thinking it of no use to leap out on a hundred bayonets, then around General Smith's body. Not satisfied with this, I again reached my head out of the window, and watched some seconds, to see if there were any signs of life, regardless of my own, determined to see the end of him I loved. Being *fully satisfied* that he was dead, with a hundred men near the body, and more coming round the corner of the goal, and expecting a return to our room, I rushed towards the prison-door, at the head of the stairs, and through the entry from whence the firing had proceeded, to learn if the door into the prison were open. When near the entry, Mr. Taylor called out, *'Take me.'* I pressed my way until I found all doors unbarred; returning instantly, caught Mr. Taylor under my arm and rushed by the stairs into the dungeon, or inner prison, stretched him on the floor, and covered him with a bed, in such a manner as not likely to be perceived, expecting an immediate return of the mob. I said to Mr. Taylor, ' This is a hard case, to lay you on the floor; but if your wounds are not fatal I want you to live to tell the story.' I expected to be shot the next moment and stood before the door awaiting the onset.

"WILLARD RICHARDS."

XXIX.

ORIGIN OF THE WORD "MORMON."

We have seen Joe playing the learned oracle of the
age.   After pretending inspiration he feigned science.   It
was the same vanity that had made him appear as "author
and proprietor" in the first edition of the "Book of
Mormon."   Author of a book written by ancient prophets and translated by a divine prompter!   The following
letter, printed in the *Times and Seasons*, is a rich specimen of the "oracles" given by the Peeper, and of course
devoutly accepted by the long-eared herd then composing
the great mass of the "faithful."   Having seen no "indignant protest" against it from the pen of Professor
Orson Pratt, or any other Mormon professor or educator,
I conclude that it still "stands independent" of learning.

The Greek word "Mormon" had been chosen by
scholarly infected Solomon Spaulding in the same kind of
a whim as he chose others from the Latin, such as *"Alma,"*
and the like.   "Mormon" means in Greek a hobgoblin,
and poor old crank Solomon was surely happy with a
Greek feather in his dreamy nightcap.   Joe saw his
chance for a tremendous bluff at the learned world.   So
he takes a good handful of "diamond truth" and (no
doubt with W. W. Phelps as scribe) sits down to "com-
bat" another "error of the age."   Writes he:

" SIR,—Through the medium of your paper, I wish to correct an
error among men that profess to be learned, liberal and wise; and I
do it the more cheerfully, because I hope sober-thinking and sound-
reasoning people will sooner listen to the voice of truth, than be led
astray by the vain pretensions of the self-wise. [That's too good,
Joseph.]   The error I speak of is the definition of the word 'Mormon.'   It has been stated that this word was derived from the Greek
word *mormo*. This is not the case.   There was no Greek or Latin
upon the plates from which I, through the grace of God, translated
the Book of Mormon.   Let the language of that book speak for itself.
On the 523rd page of the fourth edition, it reads:—'And now behold we have written the record according to our knowledge in the
characters which are called among us the REFORMED EGYPTIAN, be-

ing handed down and altered by us according to our manner of speech; and if our plates were sufficiently large, we should have written in Hebrew. Behold ye would have had no imperfections in our record, but the Lord knoweth the things which we have written, and also, that NONE OTHER PEOPLE KNOWETH OUR LANGUAGE; *therefore he hath prepared means for the interpretation thereof.'*

"Here, then, the subject is put to silence, for 'none other people knoweth our language;' therefore the Lord, and not man, hath to interpret, after the people were all dead. And, as Paul said, 'the world by wisdom know not God,' and the world by speculation are destitute of revelation; and as God, in His superior wisdom, has always given His saints, wherever He has had any on earth, the same spirit, and that spirit (as John says) is the true spirit of prophesy, which is the testimony of Jesus, I may safely say that the word Mormon *stands independent of the learning and wisdom of this generation.* Before I give a definition, however, to the word, let me say that the Bible, in its widest sense, means good; for the Savior says, according to the Gospel of St. John, 'I am the good shepherd;' and it will not be beyond the common use of terms to say, that good is amongst the most important in use, and though known by various names in different languages, still its meaning is the same, and is ever in opposition to bad. We say from the Saxon, *good;* the Dane, *god;* the Goth, *Goda;* the German, *Gut;* the Dutch, *Goed;* the Latin, *bonus;* the Greek, *kalos;* the Hebrew, *tob;* and the Egyptian, *mon.* Hence, with the addition of 'more,' or the contraction *mor,* we have the word Mormon, which means, literally, *more good.* Yours,

JOSEPH SMITH."

Here's solid chunks of wisdom! But compare the foregoing with Joseph's tale about Martin's visit to Prof. Anthon, and you see the Peeper again in one of those providential traps reserved for the sure punishment of impostors. "*None other people knoweth our language,*" the Reformed Egyptian; "*Therefore the Lord, and not man hath to interpret.*" But Prof. Anthon and Dr. Mitchell understand the hieroglyphics, all the same: the characters are *true* and the translation is *correct.* Oh, Kolob, Kokob and Kokaubeam! And then the heart-rending revelation which makes the Bible mean "good;" that little slip in giving *kalos* as the Greek word for good, instead of *agathos*; and finally, to speak with Tullidge, the *wondrous* announcement that Reformed Egyptian consists, at least in this special case, not of rotten Chaldaic, Assyriac and Arabic, but of the fresh, living *Saxon* of our days and embalmed *Egyptian: more* and *mon,* united in one word, like the Siamese twins, while one was dead and the other yet alive !

But you must not laugh. If you do, you're lost. Joseph Smith, Jr., held converse with holy angels, with the Father and Son — and he wrote (set his name to) this letter ! !

XXX.

APOSTOLIC SPREES.

Let us give one last glance at the high times in Kirtland, Ohio. Everything was flourishing then, revelation, consecration, translation, and even sealing, as we have seen. It was the time when Joe and his brothers and their next friends got money in their hands for the first time in their lives. They founded mills, stores, a bank, a city and a temple. How solid those enterprises were is well known. Honest David Whitmer told Joe one day, alluding to the famous bank, *that there were more lies than dollars passed over his counter.* *

The "Endowments" in the Kirtland temple were nothing but a big spree, so big, that the "apparitions of angels," etc., were not miraculous at all. I quote from a letter by Dr. McLellin, one of the first quorum of Mormon apostles :

"About five hundred ministers entered that great temple about sunrise and remained fasting until next morning sunrise, except a little bread and wine in the evening. The Twelve were required to take large servers and set glasses of wine and lumps of bread, and go through the house and serve the brethren. I did my part of the serving. During the night a purse was made up and a wagon sent to Painesville and a barrel of wine procured, and *then it was a time.* All the latter part of the night I took care of Samuel H. Smith [brother of the prophet], perfectly unable to help himself. And I

---

* "David Whitmer I believe to be an honest and truthful man. I think what he states may be relied on." So says Emma Smith on her death-bed.

had others removed from the house because they were *unfit to be in decent company.*"

Money came in from the dupes; town lots sold at high figures, and the eastern merchants sent goods on credit. The new prophets and apostles felt good. I quote from another letter of the same ex-apostle :

"Soon *fine dressing and fine parties* were the go, and soon a fine ride was determined upon. Some fifteen couples hired fine carriages, with fine harness and horses and, when all was in readiness, they set out for Cleveland, some nineteen miles away. They drove round and round through the streets. People gazed and inquired, 'Who is all this?' 'Oh, it's Joe Smith, the Mormon prophet, and his company.' They put up at a first-class tavern, called for a room, refreshments and something to *drink*. Some of them became intoxicated, and they broke up about twenty dollars' worth of dishes and furniture. Next morning they paid their bill and set out for home. They stopped at Euclid—half way—and took dinner and again *drank freely;* and after they set out for home they commenced running horses, and turned over a buggy and broke it up, so they had to haul it home on a wagon. But all went swimmingly. 'We are great merchantmen, money plenty.' But no confessions were ever required or made in the church for this wild-goose chase. They still continued their practices and their *drinking* to excess, until I sickened and, with a heavy heart, left the place and church and wended my way to Illinois, with my companion and two little children. *

Wiliam Smith, Joe's younger brother, and one of the Twelve, was the *enfant terrible* of that holy family. When drunk he was capable of anything, even giving away the *key* of the whole fraud. He used to beat Joseph and throw him down. He once struck Joe on the forehead and cut a watch-pocket over his eye, so that the prophet had to stay away from church a week or two. One afternoon a number of persons were playing town ball in the flat on the bank of the creek in Kirtland. There was whiskey on the ground, and "Bill" Smith got so drunk that he had to sit down between the roots of a stump and lean back against the stump to sit up. Some of the brethren reminded him that he was announced to preach

---

* David Whitmer told Mr. Traughber that Oliver Cowdery was on the ride to Cleveland, and that he said about it, "it would be a disgrace to *worldlings.*" David said he heard it was Hyrum Smith who broke up the dishes *with his cane.*

XXXII.

THE TREASURES OF SALEM.

In the year 1836, Joseph, about to become a big bank-er, visits the ancient and wealthy town of Salem' Mass. And here he receives a *revelation*, perhaps the most unique of them all. Why, it reads—not to speak profanely—it reads just as you might expect a prophet's revelation to read who had been on a big spree! It seems that Joe had heard there was money buried in the cellar of a vacant house in Salem. He rents the house, takes a house-keeper along, (one of the nice, accommodating sisters from the neighbor city of Boston) and proceeds to dig in the cellar for the buried gold and silver. I copy now the "revelation" from the latest edition of the Book of Doctrine and Covenants, p. 406:

Revelation given through Joseph the Seer, August 6th, 1836:

I, the Lord, your God, am not displeased with your coming this journey, notwithstanding your follies.

I have much treasure in this city for the benefit of Zion, and many people in this city whom I will gather out in due time for the benefit of Zion, through your instrumentality!

Therefore it is expedient that you should form acquaintance with men in this city, as you shall be led and as it shall be given you.

And it shall come to pass in due time that *I will give this city into your hands*, that you shall have power over it, insomuch that *they shall not discover your secret parts;* and its wealth pertaining to gold and silver shall be yours.

Concern not yourselves about *your debts*, for I will give you power to pay them. This place you may obtain by hire, etc. * And inquire diligently concerning the more ancient inhabitants and founders of this city. For there are *more treasures* than one for you in this city; therefore be ye as wise as serpents and yet without sin, and I will order all things for your good, as fast as ye are able to receive them. Amen.

I have nothing to say. I give the floor to the in-ventor of the "archangel's genius."

---

* This " etc." in the Lord's mouth is of special richness.

XXIII.

DESTRUCTION OF THE "EXPOSITOR."

I have asserted (see p. 249) that John Taylor "had a main hand in squelching the freedom of the press in Nauvoo." This appears, among many other valuable details, by the following extract from the minutes of the proceedings of the Nauvoo city council relative to the destruction of the press and fixtures of the *Expositor*. I quote from the *Deseret News*, Sept. 23, 1857, pp. 225–6:

"CITY COUNCIL, Sessions of June 8 and 10, 1844.

"Mayor [Joe] suggested that the Council pass an ordinance to prevent misinterpretation and libelous publications and conspiracies against the peace of the city. Mayor said the conduct of such men and such papers are calculated to destroy the peace of the city; and *it is not safe that such things should exist*, on account of the mob spirit which they tend to produce.

"Councilor Hyrum Smith spoke of the importance of *suppressing* that spirit which has driven us from Missouri, etc.; that he would go in for an *effective ordinance*.

"Mayor [Joe] said if he had a city council who felt as he did, the establishment [of the *Expositor*] would be declared a nuisance before night. Here is a paper that is exciting our enemies abroad, *They* [the editors of the *Expositor*] *make it a criminality for a man to have a wife on earth while he has one in heaven*, according to the keys of the priesthood; and he then read a statement of Wm. Law's from the *Expositor*, where the truth of God was transferred into a lie concerning this thing [!!] What the opposition party want is to raise a mob on us and take the spoil from us as they did in Missouri; *said he would rather die to-morrow and have the thing smashed, than live and have it go on*, for it was exciting the spirit of mobocracy among the people and bringing death and destruction upon us. Mayor said he had never preached the revelation [on polygamy] in private, but he had in public, had not taught it to the anointed in the church in private, which statement many present confirmed. * Mayor said the Constitution did not authorize the press to publish libels, and proposed that the Council *make some provision for putting down the* "*Nauvoo Expositor*."

"Councilor Hyrum Smith was in favor of declaring the *Expositor* a nuisance.

---

* What did Apostle Snow tell the author about the scene on the log, and what does Wm. Clayton say in his affidavit? Who lies?

"Councilor J. TAYLOR said no city on earth would bear such slander, and he would not bear it, and was decidedly in favor of *active measures.* He then read from the Constitution of the United States on the freedom of the press, and said: 'We are willing they should publish the truth; but it is unlawful to publish libels; the *Expositor* is a nuisance and *stinks in the nose of every honest man.*'

"Mayor [Joe] read from Illinois Constitution, touching the responsibility of the press for its constitutional liberty.

"Councilor Hyrum Smith *believed the best way was to smash the press and 'pie' the type.*

"Mayor [Joe] remarked he was sorry to have one dissenting voice in declaring the *Expositor* a nuisance.

"Councilor Warrington did not mean to be understood to go against the proposition; but would not be in haste in declaring it a nuisance.

"Councilor Phelps had investigated the Constitution, charter and laws; the power to declare that office a nuisance is granted to us in the Springfield CHARTER, *and a resolution declaring it a nuisance is all that is required.*"

The result of the session was, that the following resolution was read and passed *unanimously*, with the exception of Councilor Warrington:

"*Resolved*, By the City Council of the city of Nauvoo, that the printing office from whence issues the 'Nauvoo Expositor' is a public nuisance and also all of said Nauvoo *Expositors*, which may be or exist in said establishment, and the Mayor is instructed to cause said printing establishment and papers to be removed without delay in such manner as he shall direct.

GEO. W. HARRIS,

"Passed June 10, 1844.   *President pro tem.*"

The following order was immediately issued by the Mayor:

"STATE OF ILLINOIS, }
    City of Nauvoo. }

" *To the Marshal of said City, Greeting :*

"You are hereby commanded to destroy the printing press from whence issues the Nauvoo *Expositor* and pie the type of said printing establishment IN THE STREET, and BURN the *Expositors* and libelous handbills found in said establishment, and if resistance be offered to your execution of this order by the owners or others, DEMOLISH THE HOUSE: and if anyone threatens you, or the Mayor, or the officers of the city, ARREST those who threaten you, and fail not to execute this order without delay, and make due return hereon.

"By order of the City Council.

JOSEPH SMITH, *Mayor.*"

Marshal's return:. The within named press and type is destroyed and pied according to order, on this 10th day of June, 1844, at about 8 o'clock p. m.

J. P. GREENE, *C. M.*

So much for Mayor Joseph Smith. But the Lieut.-General of the Legion cannot be mocked, either, in such "libelous" affairs. So he decrees as follows:

"HEADQUARTERS NAUVOO LEGION, }
June 10, 1844. }

"To Jonathan Dunham, Acting Major-General of the Nauvoo Legion:

"You are hereby commanded to hold the Nauvoo Legion in readiness forthwith to execute the city ordinances, and especially to remove the establishment of the Nauvoo *Expositor*, and this you are required to do at sight, under the penalty of the laws; provided the Marshal shall require it and need your services.

JOSEPH SMITH.
Lieut.-General Nauvoo Legion."

According to these orders, *two companies* of the Nauvoo Legion assisted in destroying the *Expositor!*

I insert the following extracts from the "History of Joseph Smith," contained in the *Deseret News* of 1857:

"SUNDAY, JUNE 9, 1844. At home. My health not very good in consequence of my lungs being impaired by so much public speaking. My brother Hyrum preached at the stand. At 2 p. m. several passengers of the steamer 'Osprey' from St. Louis and Quincy arrived and put up at the Mansion. I helped to carry in their trunks and chatted with them in the bar room.

"MONDAY, JUNE 10. I was in the City Council from 10 a. m. to 1:20 p. m. and from 2:20 to 6:30 p. m., investigating the merits of the Nauvoo *Expositor* and also the conduct of the Laws. Higbees, Foster and others, who have formed a conspiracy for the purpose of destroying my life and scattering the Saints, or driving them from the State. About 8 p. m. the Marshal returned and reported that he had removed the press, type, printed paper and fixtures into the street and destroyed them. The posse, accompanied by some hundreds of citizens, returned with the Marshal to the front of the Mansion, when I gave them a short address and told them that they HAD DONE RIGHT; and that not a hair of their heads should be hurt for it; that they had executed the orders which were given me by the City Council; that I would *never submit to have another libelous publication established* in the city; that I did not care how many papers were printed in the city if they would print the truth, *but would submit to no libels or slanders from them.* I then blessed them in the name of the Lord. This speech was loudly greeted by the assembly with three times three cheers."

On the same day, June 10, the City Council had passed an "Ordinance concerning libels and for other purposes." Compare its language with that of the *Expositor* and you will find where the "libel" is. The ordinance says of the publishers of the *Expositor*:

"They have turned traitors in the church and combined and leagued with the most corrupt scoundrels and villains that disgrace the earth unhung, for the heaven-daring and damnable purpose of revenge on account of disappointed lust, disappointed prospects of speculation, fraud and unlawful designs to rob and plunder mankind with impunity; and whereas such wicked and corrupt men have greatly facilitated their unlawful designs, horrid intentions and murderous plans, by polluting, degrading and converting the blessings of the utility of the press to the sin-smoking and blood-stained ruin of innocent communities, by publishing lies, false statements, slandering men, women, children [!], societies and countries, by polishing the characters of blacklegs, high-waymen and murderers as virtuous . . . "

The plans of the "degraded" publishers are "horrid, bloody, secret;" they want to "destroy Mormonism, men, women and children, as *Missouri* did." Therefore,

" Be it ordained by the City Council of the city of Nauvoo, that if any person or persons shall write or publish in said city ANY FALSE STATEMENT or libel any of the citizens, for the purpose of exciting the public mind against the chartered privileges, peace and good order of said city, or shall SLANDER any portion of the inhabitants of said city, or bribe any portion of the citizens of said city for malicious purposes, *or in any manner or form excite the prejudice of the community* against any portion of the citizens of said city, *for evil purposes*, he, she or they shall be deemed disturbers of the peace and upon conviction before the Mayor, OR Municipal Court, shall be fined in any sum not exceeding $500 or imprisoned six months, *or both*, at the discretion of said Mayor or court."

The ordinance adds, evidently by way of a joke, that "nothing in this ordinance shall be so construed as to interfere with the freedom of speech, or the liberty of the press, according to the *most liberal* meaning of the Constitution, the dignity of freemen, the voice of truth and the rules of virtue!"

At a mass meeting of the citizens of Hancock County, convened at Carthage June 13, it was stated that

" Hyrum Smith did, in the presence of the City Council and the citizens of Nauvoo, offer a reward for the destruction of the printing press and materials of the *Warsaw Signal.* Hyrum Smith has within the last week publicly threatened the life of Thos. C. Sharp, the editor of the *Signal.*"

The destruction of the *Expositor* is declared a lawful act by Joseph Smith in a letter to Governor Ford dated June 14, in consideration of the following section of the Nauvoo City charter:

"SEC. 7. To make regulations to secure *the general health* of the inhabitants, TO DECLARE WHAT SHALL BE A NUISANCE AND TO PREVENT AND REMOVE the same."

Isn't this interpretation the acme of impudence?

Let us close with a look at the widow of the prophet:

"Dimick B. Huntington, with the assistance of Wm. Marks and W. D. Huntington, washed the bodies from head to foot . . . he put cotton soaked in camphor in each wound and laid the bodies out with fine, plain drawers and shirts, white neckerchiefs, white cotton stockings and white shrouds. After this was done, EMMA (who was at this time pregnant) was permitted to view the bodies. On first seeing the corpse of her husband she screamed and fell, but was supported by D. B. Huntington. She then fell upon his face and kissed him, calling him by name and begged of him to speak to her once."

XXXIV.

"TALLERED RAGS."

Apostle Heber C. Kimball had been a potter in his early days. Full of the spirit of the *Kingdom*, he used to preach blind obedience to the holy priesthood. He had two standard images showing how far this obedience should go. One was that the faithful should be in the hands of the authorities like clay in the hands of the potter; the other was not taken from pottery, still it was very fine in its kind: good Saints should be like " *tallered rags.* " He was a master spirit, Kimball was. Like Brigham, he had learned his little lesson in Nauvoo. Joe Smith used to treat his apostles like tallowed rags, indeed. A perfect illustration is furnished by a passage in the prophet's autobiography, written in April, 1843, and contained in the *Mill. Star*, Vol. XXI., Number 2 :

"At three p. m. I met with Brigham Young, William Smith, P. P. Pratt, O. Pratt, W. Woodruff, J. Taylor, Geo. A. Smith and Willard Richards, of the quorum of the Twelve, in my office, and told them to go in the name of the Lord God of Israel, and tell Lucien Woodworth to put the hands on to the Nauvoo House and begin the work and be patient till means can be provided.

"Call on the inhabitants of Nauvoo, and *get them to bring in their means;* then go to La Harpe and serve them the same. Out of the stock that is handed to me you shall have as you have need; for the labourer is worthy of his hire.

"*I hereby command* the hands to go to work on the house, trusting in the Lord. Tell Woodworth to put them on and he shall be backed up with it. *You must get cash, property, lands, horses, cattle, flour, corn, wheat, etc.* The grain can be ground in this place. If you can get hands on the Nauvoo House, it will give such an impetus to the work, *it will take all the devils out of hell* to stop it.

"Brigham Young asked if any of the Twelve should go to England.

"I replied : '*No! I don't want the Twelve to go to England this year.* I have sent them to England and they have broke the ice; and now I want to send some of the elders and try *them.*

"You can never make anything out of Benjamin Winchester, if you take him out of the channel he wants to be in. Send Samuel James to England, thus saith the Lord! also Reuben Hedlock. Send these two now ; and when you think of some others, send them.

"John Taylor, I believe you can do more good in the editorial department than preaching. You can write for thousands to read, while you can preach to but a few at a time. We have no one else we can trust the paper with, *and hardly with you;* for you suffer the paper to come out with so many mistakes.

"Brother Geo. A. Smith, I don't know how I can help him to a living, but to go and preach, *put on a long face, and make them doe over to him.** The Lord will give him a good pair of lungs yet.

"Woodruff can be spared from the printing office. If you both stay you will disagree. I want Orson Pratt should go.

"Brother Brigham asked if he should go. ' YES, GO.' "

---

* Rather hard on Thackeray, isn't it ?

TABLE OF CONTENTS.

SIDELIGHTS—(Appendix.)

ILLUSTRATIONS.

www.ingramcontent.com/pod-product-compliance
Lightning Source LLC
Chambersburg PA
CBHW060526030726
47498CB00004B/1093